TREACHERY IN DEATH

TREACHERY IN DEATH

J. D. ROBB

**Doubleday Large Print
Home Library Edition**

G. P. Putnam's Sons

New York

This Large Print Edition, prepared especially for Doubleday Large Print Home Library, contains the complete, unabridged text of the original Publisher's Edition.

PUTNAM

G. P. PUTNAM'S SONS
Publishers Since 1838
Published by the Penguin Group
Penguin Group (USA) Inc. 375 Hudson Street, New York, New York 10014, USA • Penguin Group (Canada), 90 Eglinton Avenue East, Suite 700, Toronto, Ontario M4P 2Y3, Canada (a division of Pearson Penguin Canada Inc.) • Penguin Books Ltd, 80 Strand, London WC2R 0RL, England • Penguin Ireland, 25 St Stephen's Green, Dublin 2, Ireland (a division of Penguin Books Ltd) • Penguin Group (Australia), 250 Camberwell Road, Camberwell, Victoria 3124, Australia (a division of Pearson Australia Group Pty Ltd) • Penguin Books India Pvt Ltd, 11 Community Centre, Panchsheel Park, New Delhi–110 017, India • Penguin Group (NZ), 67 Apollo Drive, Rosedale, North Shore 0632, New Zealand (a division of Pearson New Zealand Ltd) • Penguin Books (South Africa) (Pty) Ltd, 24 Sturdee Avenue, Rosebank, Johannesburg 2196, South Africa

Penguin Books Ltd, Registered Offices: 80 Strand, London WC2R 0RL, England

Published simultaneously in Canada

ISBN 978-1-61129-213-8

Printed in the United States of America

**This Large Print Book carries the
Seal of Approval of N.A.V.H.**

There is no such thing in man's nature as a settled
and full resolve, either for good or evil,
except at the very moment of execution.

—NATHANIEL HAWTHORNE

Nursing her wrath to keep it warm.

—ROBERT BURNS

The old man lay dead on a scattered pile of candy bars and bubble gum. Cracked tubes of soft drinks, power drinks, sports drinks spilled out of the smashed glass of their cooler in colorful rivers. Tattered bags of soy chips spread over the floor of the little market, crushed to pulp.

On the wall behind the counter hung a framed photo featuring a much younger version of the dead man and a woman Eve assumed was his widow standing arm-in-arm in front of the market. Their faces shone with pride and humor, and all the possibilities of the future.

That young, happy man's future had ended today, she thought, in a puddle of blood and snack foods.

In the middle of death and destruction, Lieutenant Eve Dallas stood studying the body while the first officer on scene filled her in.

"He's Charlie Ochi. He and his wife ran this market for damn near fifty years."

The muscle jumping in his jaw told Eve he'd known the victim.

"Mrs. Ochi's in the back, got the MTs with her." The muscle jumped again. "They smacked her around some on top of it."

"They?"

"Three, she said. Three males, early twenties. She said one's white, one's black, and one's Asian. They've come in before, got run off for shoplifting. They had some kind of homemade device, the best she can say. Jammed the security cam with it."

He jerked his chin toward the camera. "Stoned senseless, she thinks, laughing like hyenas, stuffing candy bars in their pockets. Smacked her with some kind of sap when she tried to stop them. Then the old guy came out, they smacked him but he kept at them. One of them shoved the device into his chest. Mrs. Ochi said he dropped like a stone. They grabbed a bunch of shit—candy, chips, like that— laughing all the while, smashed the place up some and ran out."

"She gave you a description?"

"Pretty good one, too. Better yet, we've got a wit saw them run out who recognized one of them. Bruster Lowe—goes by Skid. Said they took off south, on foot. Wit's Yuri Drew. We've got him outside. He called it in."

"Okay, stand by, Officer." Eve turned to her partner. "How do you want to work it?" When Peabody blinked her dark eyes, Eve told her, "You take primary on this one. How do you want to work it?"

"Okay." Peabody's detective shield wasn't spanking, but it was still pretty shiny. Eve let her take a moment, align her thoughts.

"Let's run Lowe, get an address, a sheet if he's got one. We might get known companions. We need to get the descriptions out now, add the names when and if. I want these assholes picked up quick and fast."

Eve watched her former aide, and current partner, gain confidence as she went.

"We need the sweepers here. These dickheads probably left prints and trace everywhere. We'll see what we've got on security before they jammed it, leave the rest to EDD."

Peabody, dark hair pulled back from her square face in a short, bouncy tail, looked down at the body. "Better do the numbers, confirm his ID."

"On that," Eve said and Peabody blinked again.

"Really?"

"You're primary." Long legs braced, Eve read off the screen of her PPC. "Lowe, Bruster, aka Skid, Caucasian, age twenty-three. No current address. Last known on Avenue B—his mother's place. Got a sheet, and an unsealed juvie record. Illegals possession, malicious mischief, shoplifting, destruction of private property, vehicle boosting, blah blah."

"Cross-reference for—"

"Done. You're not the only one who can work one of these things," Eve reminded her. "Cross-referencing arrests nets us Leon Slatter, aka Slash, mixed-race male, age twenty-two, and Jimmy K Rogan, aka Smash, black male, age twenty-three, as known companions most probable to be involved."

"That's really good. Addresses?"

"Slatter's got one, on West Fourth."

"Excellent. Officer, take the data from the lieutenant. I want these three individuals picked up. My partner and I will aid in the search when we're done here, but let's get this going."

"You got it."

"I'll take the wit," Peabody told Eve. "You take the wife. Okay?"

"You're—"

"Primary. Got it. Thanks, Dallas."

It was a hell of a thing to be thanked for passing on a dead body, Eve thought as she crouched to confirm the ID with her pad. But they were murder cops, after all.

She spent another few minutes examining the body—the bruising on the temple, the arms. She had no doubt the ME would confirm none of them had been fatal. But the homemade electronic jammer pushed into the chest had most likely given Ochi a jolt that had stopped his eighty-three-year-old heart.

She stood, took another look around at the useless destruction. They'd run a nice place from what she could see. The floors, the window, the counter sparkled clean under the spilled drinks, the spatter of blood. The stock that hadn't been dumped or smashed sat tidily shelved.

Fifty years, the first on scene had said, she thought, running a business, providing a service, living a life, until a trio of fuckheads decide to destroy it for a bunch of candy bars and soy chips.

After a dozen years as a cop, nothing human beings did to other human beings surprised her. But the waste and carelessness of it still pissed her off.

She walked into the back, into the small combination office and storeroom. The medical tech was packing up his gear.

"You really should let us take you in, Mrs. Ochi."

The woman shook her head. "My children, my grandchildren are coming. I'm waiting for my children."

"After they get here, you need to go into the health center, get looked over." His tone, kind and soft, matched the hand he laid gently on her arm. "Okay? I'm real sorry, ma'am."

"Thank you." She shifted her eyes, a blazing green in a face lined with time, marred by bruises, and met Eve's. "They killed Charlie," she said simply.

"Yes, ma'am. I'm sorry for your loss."

"Everyone is. The three who killed him, they'll be sorry, too. If I could, I'd make them sorry with my own hands."

"We'll take care of that for you. I'm Lieutenant Dallas. I need to ask you some questions."

"I know you." Mrs. Ochi lifted a hand, tapped a finger in the air. "I saw you on screen, on *Now*. I saw you with Nadine Furst. Charlie and I like to watch her show. We were going to read that book she wrote about you."

"It's really not about me." But Eve let it go as there were more important things to talk about—and because it embarrassed her a little. "Why don't you tell me what happened, Mrs. Ochi?"

"I told the other cop, and I'll tell you. I was at the counter and Charlie was back here when they came in. We told them not to come in any more because they steal, they break things, they insult us and our customers. They're trouble, these three.

Punks. The white boy, he points the thing he had at the camera, and the monitor on the counter goes to static."

Her voice chipped the words like a hammer on stone, and those eyes remained fierce and dry. No tears, Eve thought, not yet. Just the cold blaze of anger only a survivor really knew.

"They're laughing," Mrs. Ochi continued, "slapping each other's backs, bumping fists, and the black one, he says, 'What're you going to do now, old bitch,' and grabs a bunch of candy. I yelled at them to get out of my place, and the other one—Asian mix—he hits me with something. I saw stars, and I tried to get in the back, to Charlie, but he hit me again, and I fell down. They kept laughing. Stoned," she said. "I know what stoned looks like. Charlie came out. The mix, he's going to hit me again I think when I'm on the floor, but Charlie hits him, knocks him back. I tried to get up, to help, but . . ."

Her voice broke now, and some of the fierceness died in guilt.

"You were hurt, Mrs. Ochi."

"The black one, he hit Charlie like the mix hit me, but Charlie didn't fall. He's not big, Charlie, not young like those *killers*, but he's strong. He was always strong."

She took a long breath, steadied herself a little. "He hit back. I tried to get up, and I tried to find something to hit them with. Then the white one, he said, 'Fuck you, you old fuck,' and he shoved the thing— the jammer or stunner, or whatever it was—into Charlie . . . here."

She laid a hand on her heart.

"It made a sound, an electrical sound— like the static, if you know what I mean. And it went snapping, and when it did, Charlie fell down. He pressed a hand to his heart, he said 'Kata,' he said my name." Her lips trembled, but she firmed them again. "He said, 'Kata,' then he fell. I crawled toward him. They kept laughing and yelling, breaking things, stomping on things. One of them, I don't know which, kicked me in the side, and they ran out."

Mrs. Ochi closed her eyes for a moment. "They ran out, and then, soon—a minute? Maybe less, Yuri ran in. He tried to help Charlie, tried to start his heart. He's a good boy, Yuri—his daddy worked for us long ago—but he couldn't help Charlie. He called for the police and an ambulance, and he got ice from the freezer for my head. He sat with me, with me and Charlie until the police came."

She leaned forward now. "They're not important people. We're not important either, not the kind of important people you talk about on *Now* with Nadine Furst. But you won't let them get away with this?"

"You're important to the NYPSD, Mrs. Ochi. You and Mr. Ochi are important to me, to my partner, to every cop working this."

"I believe you when you say it, because you believe it."

"I know it. We're already looking for them, and we'll find them. It would help if I could have your surveillance disc. If they didn't jam it before they came in, we'll have them on record. And we have you, we have Yuri. They won't get away with it."

"There's cash in the box under the counter. Not much—we don't keep much, but they didn't want money. Candy, soft drinks, chips. They didn't really want those either. They just wanted to break and hurt and rip and tear. What turns boys into animals? Do you know?"

"No," Eve said. "I don't know."

* * *

Eve watched Mrs. Ochi's family load her in a car to take her to her doctor—and watched Mr. Ochi's body loaded up for transport to the morgue.

The summer of 2060 had been a scorcher, and that didn't appear to be changing any time soon. She stood in the heat, shoved a hand through her short crop of brown hair, wishing for a breeze. She had to check the impulse, a couple of times, to move Peabody along, to direct, to order.

Thorough was good, she reminded herself, and photos of the suspects were already making the rounds, cops were already knocking on doors.

Belatedly, she remembered her sunshades and was mildly surprised to find them actually in her pocket. She slid them on, cut the glare that had beamed into her whiskey-colored eyes, and continued to stand, long and lean in a tan jacket and dark pants, scuffed boots until Peabody crossed to her.

"Nobody home at either of the addresses we have, and Bruster's mother says she hasn't seen her son in weeks—and good riddance. But one of Slatter's neighbors states he saw all three of them head out this morning. He says they're all flopping there, have been for the past couple weeks."

"They're assholes," Eve concluded. "They'll go back to their hole."

"I've got eyes on it—two men for now. The wit—Yuri Drew—was just crossing the street when he saw them run out. Recognized Bruster because they'd had a couple run-ins during pickup basketball games at some hoops not far from here—and he'd been in the store once when our vic ran them off. Recognized all three of them, but only knew Bruster by name. Guy broke down, twice, giving me his statement," Peabody added. "His father used to—"

"Work for them," Eve finished. "I got that."

"He looked at pictures. I brought a sample up on my PPC, and he picked all three of them, no hesitation, out of the mix. He'll not only testify against them, he's eager to. Did you hand me this because it's a slam dunk?"

"The minute you think slam dunk is the minute you bounce the ball off the rim."

Now Peabody put on shades, and Eve found herself staring at her own reflection in the mirrored, rainbow-hued lenses. "How the hell do you see out of those? Does everything look like a freaking fairy tale?"

"You don't look through a rainbow— everybody else looks into one. Totally mag."

Completely uncoplike, in Eve's opinion, but she only shrugged. "What do you want to do now?"

"We should probably go talk to the mother, to neighbors, see if we can dig out any other known associates. But I thought we could do that by way of a ride-around. They were high, got the munchies, hit the store. Now they're riding on how hysterically funny it was to bash the place up and knock an old couple around. Maybe they know Ochi's dead, maybe they don't."

At least the shades didn't turn her brain into a rainbow, Eve decided. Peabody thought like a cop. "I'm betting don't, and that they're stupid enough to hang out, maybe try to score some more junk."

"I've got a handful of usual hangouts from the wit, from the mother. Plenty of cops looking for them, but—"

"So what's two more? Who's driving?"

"Seriously?" Now Peabody's mouth dropped open.

"You're primary."

"Okay, yay. I'm driving." Thrilled, Peabody plopped behind the wheel. "I've been wanting to do this ever since Roarke gave it to you. It looks like crap, but oh, baby, she is loaded squared."

She was, Eve agreed. Her husband never missed a trick, plus he just loved giving her presents. One of his first, a tear-shaped diamond twice the size of her thumb, rode under her shirt.

It was beautiful, exquisite, and probably worth more than the gross national product of a small country. But if she'd had to choose between it and the crap-looking vehicle, the crap would win, hands down.

"I've got a sex bar, a game parlor, pizza joint, and the public ball court," Peabody began. "I could plot a route into the navi that would take us by all of them in the most efficient time frame."

"Sounds like a plan."

"But? Come on. I give you input when you're primary."

"They ran out loaded with junk food, so why go to a pizza joint to hang out, especially when they're juiced? Sex club, maybe, if they're after a bang."

"But?" Peabody repeated.

"They just knocked a couple of old people around. It's unlikely they know they killed one of them. It's all fun and games. They didn't take any money, didn't snatch the Ochis' wedding rings, their wrist units, the DB's wallet."

"And a sex club costs," Peabody concluded. "The bang costs more."

"They scored junk food and proved how frosty they are. When you're stoned, think you're frosty, and having such a fucking good time, you want to brag, maybe smack a few more heads."

"Game parlor or basketball. I get it. We'll try those first. If we don't hit, we'll swing by the others."

Eve nodded approval. "Better plan."

Peabody keyed in the locations. "You really think they don't know Ochi's dead?"

"They're stoned, they're stupid, they're major assholes. But none of them has a murder under his belt. They ran out laughing, high-fiving. Odds are if they'd known they'd done murder, they'd have finished

the wife off, had a conversation, acknowledged the kill. They didn't."

They hit the game parlor first, found
it packed. Cooler than outside, Eve
thought, but the cacophony of bells, whis-
tles, screams, roars, blasts, and the spinning, blinking, flashing lights made her
wonder why anyone would want to spend
a summer afternoon glued to a machine.

The pudgy, pasty-faced attendant near
the entrance took a gander at the ID shots.

"Yeah, true. They game regular. Slash
banged high score on Assassins couple
days ago. Still standing. Gonna take it down
personal when I got space 'cause he's an
asswipe."

"Have they been in today?" Peabody
asked him.

"Untrue. Night gamers mostly. Stone
heads when they can get it." He shrugged.
"What do?"

"We need to talk to them." Peabody
pulled out a card. "If they come in, contact
me. What's riding top on Bust It?"

His attention focused. "You game?"

"Solid true G-bitch. Slayed the ace on
Bust It." She held up three fingers. "Triple."

"Major ups," he said with respect. "You wanna whirl?"

"On the move, but maybe back around."

"Take you on," he said with a grin.

"Set. Taking it out," she added. "If they whirl, tag me."

He swiped a finger over his heart and pocketed her card.

"What," Eve demanded, "was that?"

"Maybe he'd tag us, but odds are against because he didn't really give a shit, and I thought he might just toss the card. So I got his attention, his respect. Gamer-bop. It's kind of stupid, but it worked."

"True," Eve said and made Peabody laugh.

They wound their way through traffic, past graffiti-laced prefabs tossed up after the Urban Wars where men with nothing better to do sat on crumbling stoops sucking brew and rotgut out of bottles wrapped in brown paper.

Street toughs stood in small packs, most of them in snug tanks to show off a range of tattoos and sweaty muscles.

Rusted fencing surrounded the cracked and faded blacktop court. Somebody had gone to the trouble to push or sweep the piles of litter to the fence line where broken glass glittered like lost diamonds.

A group of men—late teens to early twenties—were playing shirts and skins. And some of the skins were scraped and bruised. Onlookers leaned or sat against the fence, and except for the teenage couple currently attempting to reach each other's navels from the inside with their tongues, they shouted at, insulted, and harangued the players.

Peabody pulled in behind the husk of a stripped-down compact.

Someone had painted FUK U on the dented trunk.

"What does it say about the literacy rate when you can't even spell *fuck*. It's sad," Eve decided.

"Bruster," Peabody said, lifting her chin toward the court.

"Yeah, I saw him, and his asshole companions."

"I'll call for backup."

"Uh-huh."

Eve watched a moment. They'd come in as shirts, and those shirts were glued to their torsos with sweat. Jimmy K had rolled his baggy pants above his knobby knees, and from his rhythm, his moves, Eve judged he had a little game in him. Maybe he'd have more if he wasn't currently coming down from a high and sweating like a pig in the heat.

Bruster's face was lobster red and dripping, and from the fury on it, she expected the skins were kicking ass. Leon panted like a dog as he ran cross-court. Even with the distance she could see his chest heave in and out.

"They're cooked," Eve said. "Bottoming out, winded. They couldn't outrun a one-legged toddler."

"Backup, four minutes." When Eve only nodded, Peabody shifted in her seat. "Okay, let's take these assholes."

"Looking forward to it."

Eve stepped out of the car. A few of the fence sitters made them as cops halfway across the street. Some sneered, some looked nervous, others tried the blank look she assumed meant an attempt to be invisible.

On court Bruster stole the ball by ramming his elbow into his opponent's gut. The short, vicious war that broke out gave

Eve and Peabody time to cross the street, ease through the gate of the fence.

Eve kicked the navel ticklers lightly with her foot. "Beat it." She tapped the weapon under her jacket to add incentive. They scrambled up and out, and clear, she thought, of any potential harm.

She ignored the others who suddenly decided they had better places to be and sidled out of the gate. She focused on Bruster, but took the opportunity to plant her boot on Slatter's chest where he lay wheezing and bleeding on the ground.

"Stay down. Get up, try to run, I'll stun you enough to drop you, enough so you piss your pants." To emphasize the point, she drew her weapon and watched Peabody try to avoid jabbing elbows and flying fists from the combatants still on the ground and reach through to grab Bruster.

Jimmy K sat on the ground nursing a busted lip. "We ain't done nothing. Little white bastard in there punched me."

"Yeah?" He'd forgotten, she concluded, all about the Ochis, the market. The lives he'd broken into jagged bits. "Sit, stay," she told him.

But Bruster hadn't forgotten. She saw his

eyes fire when Peabody hauled him off the kid he was currently pounding. She dodged the swing, avoided the kick, all while trying to identify herself as a police officer.

Slatter tried to roll out from under her boot. Eve merely increased the pressure. "I can crack a couple ribs," she told him, "and say it happened during the game. Think about it."

Instead of drawing her weapon, Peabody blocked a punch. Some of it got through, glanced off her shoulder, and the follow-up connected, fairly solidly in Eve's judgment, with her ear.

The rainbow shades slid, cocked crookedly on her face.

Peabody managed a half-assed jab that had Eve shaking her head.

Heavy on her feet, she noted, telegraphing her moves.

When Bruster grabbed the jammer out of his pocket, Eve lifted her weapon, prepared to fire. And Peabody said, "Oh, fuck this!" and kicked him in the balls.

The jammer spurted out of his hand as he dropped, retching. Eve gave Peabody reflex points for managing to catch it on the fly.

"You are so completely under arrest." Peabody dropped down, rolled Bruster over, and slapped on restraints. "You want some of that?" she shouted as Jimmy K started crab-walking backward.

He froze. "Uh-uh. Come on, man. Just a b-ball game. No deal."

"Bet your ass no deal." She pulled herself up, glanced over as Eve cuffed Slatter. "On your face," she ordered, and finished the job with Jimmy K as their backup screamed in.

"Call for a bus," Peabody ordered the first officer to reach them. "A couple of these guys need medical attention. Get names," she added. "We'll add assault on these bleeders to the mix. And get a wagon for these three."

"Yes, sir."

Peabody glanced at Eve, grinned. She mouthed, "He called me 'sir.'" Then cleared her throat. "Lieutenant, will you inform these jerkwads of the charges and read them their rights?"

"Absolutely. Bruster Lowe, Leon Slatter, Jimmy K Rogan, you're under arrest for murder—"

"We done no murder!" Jimmy K nearly screamed it as a couple of uniforms hauled him up. "You got the wrong dudes, man. We playing b-ball."

"Additional charges include attempted murder, assault, destruction of property, theft, and in Bruster's case resisting arrest and assault on a police officer. We may be able to bump that one up, just for fun, to attempted murder of a police officer."

When it was done, and the three men were loaded in the wagon, Peabody swiped her hands over her face. "That was good, good work. But *ow!*" She patted her hand on her ear.

"You're heavy on your feet."

"Hey, no fat comments while I'm primary."

"Not your weight, Peabody—except you keep too much of it on your feet. And you hesitate. Good reflexes, but your moves are slow. You need to polish up your hand-to-hand."

"Since my ear's still ringing I can't argue. I'll work on it."

"But you took him down, so yeah, that's good work." Eve swung around at the high-pitched scream of her vehicle alarm.

She watched the hopeful booster land on his ass in the street as the warning charge engaged. His lock popper rolled into the gutter.

"It works. Good to know."

She strolled back, letting the booster limp off—considering it a valuable lesson learned.

"I'm thirsty. I want a fizzy." Peabody slid a glance at Eve. "I'm stopping on the way to Central for a fizzy. I want to give them a little time to sweat anyhow. I told the uniforms to keep them separate, and to book the interview rooms. Jimmy K's the weak link, right? I thought we'd take him first."

"Works for me."

"I want to be bad cop."

Eve shifted to look at her partner—the cop with rainbows in her eyes. "I worry about you, Peabody."

"I never get to be bad cop. I want to be the über-bitch, and you be the sympathetic one. He was blubbering when they loaded him. I don't even have to be that bad. Besides," she muttered, "I'm primary."

"Fine." Eve settled back. "You pay for the drinks."

Jimmy K was still blubbering when they walked into Interview. Peabody scowled at him. "Peabody, Detective Delia, and Dallas, Lieutenant Eve, in Interview with Rogan, Jimmy K, on the matter of the murder of Ochi, Charlie, and connected charges."

"I didn't kill nobody!" Jimmy K wailed it.

"Oh, shut the fuck up." Peabody slapped the file on the table, took out the still of the dead, slapped that down on top. "See that, Rogan? That's what you and your friends did."

"Did not. Did not."

"And this." She laid out the photos of Mrs. Ochi, the close-ups of her bleeding head, her black eye, swollen jaw. "I guess you like beating up on grandmothers, you asswit punk."

"I didn't."

Peabody started to lunge out of her chair.

"Hold on, hold on." Playing her part, Eve laid a hand on her partner's shoulder. "Give him a chance, okay? He looks pretty shaky. I brought you a cold drink, Jimmy K. You want a tube of Coke?"

"Yeah man, yeah." He took it from her, gulped it down. "I didn't kill nobody, no way."

"We got witnesses, you fuckhead."

"Uh-uh." Jimmy K shook his head at

Peabody. "Nobody was in there when we went in, and Skid, he zapped the cam. So you don't."

God, Eve thought, what a moron. "You were in Ochi's Market today?" she asked him. "With Bruster Lowe—Skid, and Leon Slatter—Slash?"

"Okay, yeah. We wanted some munch, you know? So we go in to get some."

"You always zap the cam when you go for some munch?" Peabody demanded.

"We're just playing around, see?"

"Playing?" Peabody roared it, shoved Ochi's photo in Jimmy K's face. "Is this playing around?"

"No, man, no, sir. I never did that."

"Relax, Jimmy K," Eve told him and made sure he saw her shoot Peabody a disapproving look. "You know jammers are illegal—even homemade ones."

"Yeah." He sighed it out. "But see, I was just experimenting, like. Sometimes I pick up some scratch working in an e-store, and you learn shit. Educational shit. I told the dudes I could make up a jammer from some of the shit we got around, and they're all, 'Bullshit you can, motherfucker,' like that. So I showed them. I worked on it for, like, hours, man. We got a buzz going. You know how it be when you're hanging."

"Yeah." Eve nodded. "Sure."

"We tried it out, and it fucked Slash's comp good. That's some funny shit, man. Skid and I busted gut. Slash was a little pissed, and so he starts to grab it from me, and I try to hold it, and I, like, hit the control. Zapped him. Jesus, shoulda seen him jump. Laughed our asses to the *ground*. We just fooled around, zapped each other a few times, did more Ups. And you know, we got hungry, and we decided, hell, we'd go hit Ochi's, get our munch, play with the zipzap. That's what we called it. Zipzap. I made it myself."

He said that with no little pride, and Eve could see Peabody felt sorry for him.

"That's a real talent, Jimmy K," Eve said, and gave Peabody a kick under the table.

"You asshole." Peabody toughened her face. "You went to Ochi's Market to steal from them, to bust their place up, to bust them up carrying an illegal device that jammed security and emitted an electronic charge? Carrying saps?"

"Okay, listen, okay, just listen." He patted the air down with his hands. "We were buzzing, had the munch on. Ochi has good munch, and that old man, he's always running us off, even had the cops go to Skid's old lady's place once just because we knocked a few things over. We just wanted the munch, and to show them not to keep messing with us. Just spook them up, get me?"

"So it was just going to be a robbery," Eve said, picking up the rhythm. "The three of you took your zipzap, the saps, and went in intending to steal, to intimidate, maybe, if they gave you grief, rough them up a little, break a few things."

"Yeah, that's it. We were buzzing, man. We had a really good buzz going. Skid had the zipzap. It was his turn, and hey, the old guy called the cops on him and all that. Zapped the cam good, too. The old lady, she got all, you know, so Slash clipped her some."

"Leon Slatter—Slash—hit her with the sap," Eve encouraged, "because she was yelling at you to stop."

"That's it. She was yelling and bossing, so Slash sapped her a little to shut her up. Me, I got some candy and chips and shit, and the old man comes out half crazy.

He's, like, attacking me, so I just defended myself and gave him a knock. And he's going after Skid, and he's screaming, like, *insane* shit, so Skid, he gave him a zap. We were buzzing and all so we broke the place up, then we left. See? We didn't kill nobody."

Peabody pulled a paper out of the file. "This is the autopsy report on Ochi. Do you know what an autopsy is, you asshole?"

He licked his lips. "It's like when they cut up dead people. Sucks, man."

"And when they cut up this dead person, it turns out he died of coronary arrest. His heart stopped."

"See, like I said, we didn't kill him."

"It stopped due to an electric shock, which also left electrical burns on his chest. Your fucking zipzap's the murder weapon."

Jimmy K's eyes bulged. "No. Shit, no."

"Shit, yes."

"It was an accident, man. An accident, right?" he said, pleading, to Eve.

She was tired of good cop. "You went into Ochi's Market, intending to rob, to destroy property, to cause intimidation and physical harm to the Ochis and whoever else might have been present. You went in carrying an illegal device you knew caused physical harm, and weighted bags fashioned into saps. You indeed did rob, did destroy property, and did cause physical harm by your own admission. Here's what happens when a death incurs as a result of a crime or during the course of committing a crime. It bumps it up to murder."

"Can't be."

"Oh," Eve assured him, "it be."

2 Eve let peabody set the pace. It took a bit longer than it might have, but she couldn't say the interviews weren't thorough. At the end of the long process, three dangerous idiots were in cages, where she didn't doubt they'd spend many decades of their idiot lives.

In her office, she gestured to her AutoChef. "I don't have coffee," she said, as if slightly puzzled. "When you correct that situation, you can get one for yourself."

Peabody programmed two cups, handed one off.

"Good work," Eve told her, tapped mugs.

"It was pretty much a slam dunk."

"If it was it's because you slammed it. You got details and information from a wit, combined that with the information I got from the vic's wife, with what we observed and compiled from the scene."

Eve sat, plopped her booted feet on her desk. "From there, you followed instinct and located the suspects, even though you could have left that part of it to the officers already on the lookout."

Peabody lowered to the spindly visitor's chair. "You'd have kicked my ass if I'd done that. Our case, our vic, our suspects."

"You're not wrong. You, correctly in my opinion, identified the weak sister and played him first, played him well, intimidating him into babbling out a confession, and relating specific details. Who did what, when, how. You got intent, and that was key. You understood to amp up the pressure and the heat on Slatter because he's tougher than Rogan."

"Mashed potatoes are tougher than Rogan, but don't stop now. Please continue to tell me I'm a mag investigator."

"You didn't screw up," Eve said, and

made Peabody grin over her coffee regular. "You cooked Slatter because he was pissed enough at Rogan rolling—and knew Rogan had because you laid out the details—to try to roll harder on his pals. He figured since Rogan made the murder weapon, and Lowe had the bright idea to go to the market, Lowe used it on Ochi, he'd be something of an innocent bystander. You let him think it."

"Yeah. You led him there with the helpful good cop. A mag investigator has to utilize teamwork."

"You've got a few more minutes to milk it," Eve decided.

"Yay. We worked Lowe like a draft horse."

"If you say so. It was smart to go with the sneering, it's already in the bag, asshole, angle. Sarcasm and ugly amusement instead of threats and intimidation. He has almost half a brain and may have lawyered up if you'd gone with the heat. The cold worked on him."

"I think, on some level, he knew Ochi was dead when he ran out of the market, and on some level he pressed that device to the old guy's heart because he knew it would do serious damage."

Not only instinct, not only teamwork, Eve thought, but insight was an important tool of the mag investigator.

And so was practicality.

"I don't disagree, but we were never going to get them on Murder One. You got what we could get, and adding the assault on police officers—the attempt on you by Lowe, they're sewed, Peabody. They'll be in a cage longer than they've been alive. Mrs. Ochi won't get her husband back, but when you contact her she'll know the people responsible for it are already starting to pay."

"I think you should tell her. You talked to her—she knows you—and it would probably mean more if you told her we've got them."

"Okay."

"I'll contact the wit." Peabody blew out a breath. "I liked being bad cop—a lot actually. But . . . it kind of gave me a headache."

"Because it's not natural for you. Your natural technique is to finesse, to relate and use that to cause the suspect to relate to you. It's a good trait, Peabody. You can pull out the whoop-ass when you need to, but you're better with the grease. Now write it up."

"I'm primary. Don't I get to tell you to write it up?"

"I outrank you—and milking time has passed. I'll put my notes together, send them to you. Contact your wit, write the report, then go home."

Peabody nodded, got up from Eve's crappy visitor's chair. "It was a good day. Not for the Ochis," she said with a little wince, "but . . . you know. I'm feeling pumped. Maybe when I get home I'll play bad cop with McNab."

Eve pressed fingers to the corner of her eye when it twitched. "Why do you think I want to know about your perverted sex games with McNab?"

"Actually, I was thinking about practicing investigative techniques, but now that you mention it—"

"Out."

"Outting. Thanks, Dallas."

Alone, Eve sat another minute with her coffee, feet up. She'd write up her notes, and she'd write a strong evaluation of Peabody's work on the case for her file.

Then she'd go home, which did indeed make it a good day.

She glanced at her wrist unit, swore a

little. She was already seriously late. According to the marriage rules, she needed to contact Roarke, give him her ETA.

Even as she turned to her desk 'link, it signaled.

"Homicide. Dallas."

"Lieutenant." Mrs. Ochi came on-screen. "I'm sorry to interrupt your evening, but I wanted to know if you've . . . if you have any news for me."

"It's all right, Mrs. Ochi. I was just about to contact you. We have all three of them. We have confessions. We have them behind bars now, and the prosecuting attorney is confident he'll get a conviction that will keep them there for a very long time."

"You caught them."

"Yes, ma'am."

Those fierce green eyes filled with tears before Mrs. Ochi put her hands over her face. "Thank you." She began to sob, to rock. "Thank you."

Eve let her weep, and when the woman's son and daughter came on-screen, flanking her, holding her, Eve answered their questions.

By the time she was done, her mind was

focused on completing the work—and not on the marriage rules. When she'd wrapped it up, she walked out, through the bullpen where Peabody hunched, intent over the work.

"See you tomorrow."

"Yeah, cha," Peabody muttered.

McNab would have to play bad cop by himself for a while, Eve thought as she started out—then wished to God she hadn't had the thought. On the heel of it, she remembered she hadn't called home.

"Shit." She reached for her pocket 'link.

"LT!" Detective Carmichael hustled after her. "Santiago and I are working a floater. I wanted to run a couple of the angles by you."

"Walk and talk, I'm heading out."

She listened, questioned, considered, taking the glides down rather than the elevator to give her detective more time. They paused on a level, with Carmichael tugging her ear.

"Are we cleared for the overtime, to move on this tonight?"

"I'll clear it. Push it."

"Thanks, Lieutenant."

"How's it working out with you and the new guy?"

"Santiago's okay. Got a good nose. We're getting a rhythm on."

"Good to know. Good hunting, Carmichael."

Eve took the elevator the rest of the way to the garage, thinking of Carmichael's floater, the angles, authorizing the OT.

She crawled through traffic awhile, played a little game of outwit the other drivers by changing routes a couple times. By the time she remembered the marriage rules again, she was nearly home.

No point now, she decided. She'd just . . . make it up to Roarke. He'd have worked while waiting for her, she thought, so now they could have a nice dinner together. She'd even program it herself—one of those fussy, fancy deals he liked—open a bottle of wine.

Relax, hang. Maybe she'd suggest they watch one of those old vids he liked. A very married evening at home, she thought, followed by some very married sex.

No murder, no mayhem, no work, no pressure. Just the two of them. Hell, she might even dig out one of those sexy, seduce-your-partner getups, just to top it off.

She could program some music—go full-out romance.

Pleased with the plan, she zipped through the gates of home. Her mood throttled up another notch or two as she watched the lights shine in the multitude of windows in the gorgeous stone house. They could eat outside, she decided, on one of the terraces. She looked up as she drove, considering the towers and turrets. Maybe the rooftop terrace with its little pool and sweeping view of the city.

Pretty damn perfect.

She left her vehicle out front, and telling herself she was in too good a mood to be bothered by Summerset lurking in the foyer ready to sneer at her for being late, she jogged inside.

The foyer was empty, hitching her stride a moment.

No Summerset?

"Don't question your luck," she told herself, and continued her jog upstairs.

She swung into Roarke's office first,

surprised not to find him there, wheeling some deal, calculating some complicated equation.

Frowning, she turned to the house monitor. "Where is Roarke?" she demanded.

Darling Eve, Roarke is on the terrace, main level, rear, section two.

"We have sections? Which is—"

Location highlighted.

"Okay." She pursed her lips, studied the house map and the blinking light. "Got it."

She headed down. What was he doing out there? she wondered. Maybe having a drink with Summerset—which would answer the other question. Talking about old times, jobs pulled, booty stolen, burglaries accomplished.

The sort of thing it wasn't . . . polite to reminisce about with a cop present.

Time to break up the nostalgia and—

She pulled up short when she stepped out. Roarke was indeed with Summerset, but they weren't having a drink—or not only—and they weren't alone.

Two people she'd never seen before in her life sat with them at a white-draped table, with candles flickering prettily against the late-summer evening, apparently enjoying a very fussy, fancy dinner.

The strangers, a couple she judged in their middle sixties, included a woman with gold-coin hair forming a short, straight frame for a face dominated by big, round eyes, and a man sporting a trim goatee that set off his angular, somewhat scholarly face.

Everyone laughed uproariously.

She felt her shoulders tighten even as Roarke lifted his wineglass. He looked relaxed, happy, those strongly sculpted lips curved as he listened to something the complete stranger, female, said to the group at large in a tony Brit accent.

His sweep of midnight hair gleamed in the candlelight nearly to the shoulders of his suit jacket. She heard him respond— the richness and warmth of Ireland like wisps of smoke in his voice.

Then his eyes, wickedly blue, met hers.

"Ah, here's Eve now." He pushed back his chair, stood long and lanky, and held a hand out to her. "Darling, come meet Judith and Oliver."

She didn't want to meet Judith and Oliver. She didn't want to talk to strangers with tony Brit accents, or have all attention focused on her coming home late, probably sweaty and with blacktop grime on the knees of her trousers from her altercation with three assholes.

But she could hardly just stand there.

"Hi. Sorry to interrupt."

Before she could think to stick it in her pocket, Roarke had her hand and pulled her another foot toward the table. "Judith and Oliver Waterstone, my wife, Eve Dallas."

"We were so hoping to meet you." Judith sent her a smile, sunny and bright as her hair. "We've heard so much about you."

"Judith and Oliver are old friends of Summerset's. They're in New York for a couple of days before they travel back to England."

"You work murder cases here in New York," Oliver began. "It must be fascinating and difficult work."

"It can be both."

"I'll get another setting." Summerset started to rise, but Eve shook her head.

"No, don't worry about it. I've got a few things to deal with." They were, as far as she could tell, nearly finished with the meal, so what was the point of squeezing her into the party? "I just wanted to let you know I was back. So . . . it was nice to meet you. Enjoy your dinner."

She'd managed to retreat inside before Roarke caught up with her. "Eve." He snagged her hand again, and this time tugged her in for a welcome-home kiss. "If you've caught something hot, I can make my excuses and come up."

"No." The fact that he would made her feel smaller, and crankier. "It's nothing hot. Just—"

"Well then, come out and have some food, some wine. You'll like these people."

She didn't *want* to like these people. She already had more people in her life than she could keep up with.

"Look, it's been a long day, and I'm dirty and sweaty on top of it. I said I had things to deal with, so go back to your little dinner party and let me deal with them."

She strode away, annoyance vibrating from every step. Roarke watched her. "Well then," he murmured, and went back to his guests.

*   *   *

At Central, Peabody finished and filed her report, completed the murder book—and gave it a little pat.

Case closed, she thought. She'd already tagged McNab, told him she'd be late, so she took a few minutes to organize her work station as she liked to when she had the time.

As she tidied her space, she went over the stages of the investigation in her head, well satisfied, and a little bit smug. Until she remembered the punches Lowe had landed—and Eve's critique of her hand-to-hand.

"She's right, too," Peabody admitted, gently rubbing her sore ear. "Definitely need to sharpen up in that area." She considered switching bad cop with McNab to hand-to-hand practice.

But they'd just end up hot and sweaty, and having sex. Which would be good—really good—but not if she was serious about sharpening up.

She'd take an hour in the workout area, right there at Central. Set a program that would home in on her weak spots, help her improve them. Then she could grab a shower, change clothes, and be all fresh and shiny when she got home.

For some really good sex.

She headed down to her locker and, after pushing her change of clothes and workout gear into a hand duffle, made a note to remind herself to bring in a new change to replace what she took.

New deal, she told herself. An hour in the gym every day—okay that would never happen. Three times a week.

She could do three times a week. And keep it to herself, or herself and McNab. Then in maybe a month, dazzle Dallas with her light feet and lightning reflexes.

She walked to the gym that served her sector of Central, but with one foot in the door spotted half a dozen cops—buff cops—pumping, running, sparring.

She thought of her workout gear, the baggy shorts, the ugly sports bra she'd bought because it had been cheap. She thought of the size of her ass. And backed out again.

She just couldn't go in there, especially not with cops she knew, and strip down that way, pant and sweat with all those toned, ripped, light-footed bodies.

And look fat and stupid.

Which is why, she reminded herself,

she never used the sparkly, shiny gym at Central—or joined a fitness club. Which was why her ass was too big, she decided, and why, following the laws of gravity, she carried too much weight in her feet.

She ordered herself to suck it up, started to swipe her card and go in, then remembered the old, far from sparkly or shiny gym two levels down.

Nobody used it, she thought as she hurried off. Or hardly anybody. Because the equipment was old, the lockers stingy, and the shower barely offered a trickle.

But it would suit her and her new deal just fine.

She found the security pad deactivated and strolled into the empty room. The lights flickered on as she went in, dimmed, flickered again, then held. There were rumors about rehabbing the area, but she sort of hoped they'd leave it be. It might be ratty, but it could serve as her personal gym.

At least until she got ripped, light on her feet, and whittled her ass down.

She peeked into the locker area, listened. Smiled. Yep, her personal gym, she thought, and choosing a locker at random changed into her ugly—and soon to be replaced—gear. She managed to stuff everything else in the breadbox-sized locker, and feeling righteous, went out to set her program.

It was the first day in the life of the new lean and mean Peabody.

An hour later, she lay on the grubby floor wheezing like the dying. Her quads and hamstrings burned, her glutes wept, and her arms couldn't stop screaming for mama.

"Never doing this again," she announced. "Yes, you are," she corrected. "Can't. Dying. Can. Will. Help me, I think I broke my ass. Wimp, pussy. Shut up."

She wheezed a little more, then rolled over, made it to her hands and knees.

"Should've started out slower, on a lower level. I *knew* that. Cocky bitch." She gritted her teeth, determined not to crawl to the locker room and the showers.

But she did limp.

She peeled and tugged and fought the sticky sports bra off her sticky body, dropped it on the floor. Then rolling her eyes because her mother's voice came clear in her ear—*Respect what you own, Dee*—she bent and picked it up again.

She stuffed the sweaty bra, shorts, shoes in a second locker, grabbed one of the thin, placemat-size towels because she was afraid she'd be electrocuted if she risked the ancient drying tube—and stepped into one of the skinny shower stalls.

She stepped out again when she found the soap dispenser empty and worked her way down the line until she found one with about half a teaspoon of green goo still in the dispenser.

Maybe the water was cold, and more like a drip from a leaky faucet than an actual spray, but she wasn't going to complain. Instead, she turned right, left, back, front until she'd managed to wash away most of the sweat.

By the time she'd lathered and rinsed, she felt closer to human again, and began to consider splurging and picking up some ice cream on the way home. Not the real deal—that sort of thing was out of her splurge zone. But there was that place not far from the apartment that had a nondairy frozen dessert that was pretty damn good.

And she'd earned it, she thought, turning off the taps. Man, she'd earned it. She grabbed the towel, scrubbed it over her hair.

She patted at her face, her shoulders, and started to step out where she had some room to dry off when she heard the raised voices. And the locker room door slammed.

"Don't fucking tell me you didn't screw up, Garnet, when you damn well did!" The female voice, hot and pissed, bounced off the old tiles.

Peabody opened her mouth to warn whoever was out there they had company when she heard the response, and the male voice—equally hot and pissed.

"Don't blame me when you let this get out of control."

Peabody looked down at her naked body, the excuse for a towel, and just squeezed into the back corner of the shower.

"I let it get out of control? Well, maybe I did by trusting you to handle it, to deal with Keener. Instead, he slipped your leash and cost us ten K."

"You're the one who said he wouldn't be a problem, Renee, who pushed him to deliver the product when you knew he could rabbit."

"And I told you to work him. I should've done it myself."

"No argument."

"Goddamn it."

Somebody—probably the woman—punched a shower door. Peabody heard it slap against its side wall. And just stopped breathing.

"I've been running this operation for six years. You'd better remember that, Garnet, you'd better remember what can happen if you push me."

"Don't threaten me."

"I'm warning you. I'm in charge, and with me in charge you've raked in plenty the past few years. Think of your nice house in the islands, all the toys you like to play with, the women you like to buy, and remember you wouldn't have any of them on a cop's salary. You wouldn't have any of them without me running this show."

"I don't forget, and don't forget you get a bigger cut of every pie."

"I earn it. I brought you in, and I made you a rich man. You want to stay in, think twice before you yank me into some moldy locker room to point fingers."

"Nobody comes in here." Another shower door, closer now, slammed open, and Peabody felt fresh sweat pearl on her forehead.

Naked, weapon in the locker. No defense except her fists. So she curled them by her side.

If McNab tagged her, if her 'link signaled, she was screwed. If either of the people just inches outside the door slammed it open in temper, sensed her, heard her, smelled her, she'd be trapped, back to the wall. No escape.

Bad cops. Seriously bad cops. *Renee, Garnet. Don't forget, don't forget. Keener. Remember all the details, just in case you live through it.* She glanced up, saw with horror the drip of water sliding out of the fist-sized showerhead.

Throat slamming shut, she eased out a hand, palm up, and caught the tiny drop. Wondered if the sound of it meeting her palm was actually as loud as a hammer strike.

But they kept arguing until the woman— *Renee, Renee*—sighed. "This isn't getting us anywhere. We're a team, Garnet, but a team has a leader. That's me. Maybe that's a problem for you, maybe it's because we used to sleep together."

"You're the one who called that off."

"Because now it's business. We keep it business, we keep getting rich. And when I make captain, well, we're going to expand. Meanwhile, there's no point in arguing about Keener. I've taken care of it."

"Goddamn it, Oberman. Why the fuck didn't you say so?"

Oberman, Peabody thought. *Renee Oberman. Has rank, pushing toward captain.*

"Because you annoyed me. I put our boy on it, and it's done."

"You're sure?"

"You know how good he is, and I said it's done. When they find him it'll look like an OD. Just another chemi-head who pumped in too much junk. Nobody's going to care enough to dig into it. You're just lucky Keener hadn't gotten far, and he still had the ten K."

"You're fucking kidding me."

The laugh was bright, and sharp as steel. "I don't kid about money. I'm taking ten percent of your share as a bonus for our boy."

"The hell you—"

"Be grateful you're getting any of it." The words slapped hard and warned of worse. "Keener was a valuable tool when worked right. Now we have to replace him. In the meantime . . ."

Peabody heard the light pat on the stall door, watched it ease open a crack. The sweat dried to ice on her skin, and she balled her fists again.

Through the crack she saw part of an arm, a glimmer of red high heels, and a flash of blond hair.

"No more locker room meets," Renee said, tone cool now, crisp. Commanding. "You keep your head, Garnet, and you'll keep enjoying those island breezes. Now, I've got a hot date, and you've made me late. Walk me out like a good boy."

"You're a piece of work, Renee."

"I am. I am one fine piece of work." Her laugh trailed back, echoed, faded.

And Peabody closed her eyes, stayed where she was, forced herself to count slowly to a hundred. In her mind she reconstructed the locker room, gauged the distance to the locker where she'd stowed her weapon.

She eased the door open, scanned, sucked in her breath, and made the dash to the locker. She didn't release her breath until her weapon was in her hand.

Still naked, she crossed to the door connecting to the gym, eased it open an inch.

Dark, she noted. The lights would go off when the room was empty over a minute. Still she searched, made herself be sure before she backtracked.

She kept the weapon in her hand as she pulled out her 'link.

"Hey, She-Body!" McNab grinned at her, then gave her a green-eyed leer. "Hey, you're naked, and so, so very built."

"Shut up." The shakes started; she couldn't hold them off. "I need you to come, meet me at Central. Outside the south entrance. Come in a cab, McNab, and keep it. Make it fast."

He didn't grin, didn't leer. His eyes went from lover to cop. "What's wrong?"

"Tell you then. I gotta get out of here. Make it fast."

"Baby, I'm practically there."

3 Roarke gave Eve time to stew, since that was obviously what she was in the mood for. He enjoyed the rest of his dinner, and the company, the conversation.

He liked, very much, hearing stories of Summerset's past, hearing the angles and details of them from old friends of the man who'd become a father to him. And it pleased him to watch Summerset engage with them, laugh with them. Remember with them.

As long as they'd known each other, as much as they'd shared since Summerset had taken in a battered, beaten, half-starved boy, there was, Roarke discovered, a great deal yet to be learned.

He indulged in coffee and brandy, a bit of dessert before he said his good-nights.

The house monitor told him he'd find her in the bedroom.

She'd changed into the cotton pants and tank she favored during her down-time. He could smell her shower on her as he bent down to kiss her head. She sat brooding over a slice of pizza.

"You missed a lovely dinner," he told her, and peeled off his suit jacket. "And truly delightful company."

"I had things."

"Mmm-hmm." He loosened his tie, removed it. "So you said in your thirty-second appearance."

"Look, it was a long day, and I didn't expect to come home to a dinner party. Nobody told me about it."

"It was spur of the moment. I'm sorry," he continued, brutally pleasant, "am I supposed to check with you before I join Summerset and a couple of his old friends for dinner?"

"I didn't say that." She took a sulky bite of pizza. "I said I didn't know about it."

"Well then, perhaps if you'd contacted me, let me know you'd be very late coming home I'd have informed you."

"I got busy. We caught a case."

"Earth-shattering news."

"What are you so pissy about?" she demanded. "I'm the one who came home and found a party going on."

He sat to remove his shoes. "It must've been quite a shock—the brass band, the drunken revelers. But then, that kind of madness happens when adults leave the children on their own."

"You want to be pissed at me, fine. Be pissed." She shoved the pizza away. "I wasn't in the mood to socialize with a couple of strangers."

"You made that abundantly clear."

"I don't *know* them." She pushed to her feet, tossed up her hands. "I'd just spent the bulk of the day dealing with three assholes who killed some old guy for a bunch of goddamn candy bars. Damned if I want to come home and sit around having dinner with Summerset and his old pals and listening to them talk about the old days when they scammed marks and picked fat pockets. I spend all day with criminals, and

I don't want to spend the evening asking them to pass the fucking salt."

He said nothing for a moment. "I'm waiting for the corollary, where you remind me you married a criminal. But we can consider that unsaid."

She started to speak, but the icy resentment in his voice, in those brilliant blue eyes, slammed between them.

"Judith is a neurosurgeon—chief of surgery, in fact, at a top London hospital. Oliver is a historian and author. If you'd bothered to spend five of your precious minutes with them, you'd have learned that they met and worked with Summerset as medics during the end of the Urbans, when they were only teenagers."

She jammed her hands in her pockets. "You want me to feel like shit, well, I'm not going to." But of course she did, which only throttled her resentment to fire against his ice.

"I didn't know what was going on because nobody told me. You could've tagged me, then I'd have known I'd be walking in on you guys halfway through a fancy meal when I'm grubby from work."

"When you don't bother to let anyone

know when you'll come home I have to assume you're tied up with something. And
I'm damned, Eve, if I'm going to start tagging you asking what you're doing, when
you're coming home like some nagging
spouse."

"I meant to contact you. I started to—
twice—but both times I got interrupted. By
the end of the interruption, I forgot. I just
forgot, okay? Get a rope. You're the one
who married a cop, so you're the one who
has to deal with it."

He rose, walked toward her as she continued to rant.

"Locking up the bad guys is just a little
bit more important than being home on
time to have dinner with a couple of people I don't know anyway."

Eyes on hers, he flicked her shoulder.
Her mouth fell open.

She started stomping the floor.

"What in God's name are you doing?"
he demanded.

"Trying to kill the giant tarantula, because the only reason I can figure you just
fucking *flicked* me is because there was a
big, fat spider on my shoulder."

"Actually, I was knocking the chip away

that was balanced there. It looked awfully heavy."

She strode away from him before she did something violent. She eyed the AutoChef. "How do you program this thing for a steaming cup of *fuck you*?"

"Children," Summerset said from the doorway.

They both whirled on him, both snarled, "*What?*"

"I'm sorry to interrupt your playtime— and might suggest the next time you want to behave like a pair of morons you shut the door as I could hear your clever banter halfway down the hall. However, Detectives Peabody and McNab are downstairs. She seems very upset, and informs me she needs to speak with you. Urgently."

"Crap." Eve hurried to her closet for shoes as she ran through the investigation they'd just completed. Had they missed something?

"They're waiting in the parlor. By the way, Judith and Oliver said to tell you good-bye, and they hope to see you again when you have more time."

She caught the chilly glance before he melted away, and decided she probably would feel like two jumbo scoops of shit. But later.

"You don't have to go down," she said stiffly to Roarke. "I can handle this."

"I'll do more than flick you in a minute." He walked out ahead of her.

They maintained a fuming silence all the way down and into the parlor with its rich colors and gleaming antiques. Amid the stunning art, the glint of crystal, Peabody sat, sheet-pale, with McNab's arm tight around her.

"Dallas." Peabody got to her feet.

"What the hell, Peabody? Did those three idiots execute a jailbreak?"

Instead of smiling, Peabody shuddered. "I wish it was that easy."

When Peabody sank down again, Eve crossed over. She sat on the table so they were face-to-face, eye-to-eye. "Are you in trouble?"

"Not now. I was. I had to come, to tell you. I'm not sure what to do."

"About what?"

"Tell it from the beginning," McNab suggested. "You won't jump around so much. Just start at the top."

"Yeah, okay. I—ah—Okay. After I finished

the paperwork, I decided I'd do an hour in the gym, work on my hand-to-hand. You said it was a weak spot. I went down to the second-level facilities."

"Jesus, why? It's a pit."

"Yeah." As she'd hoped, the comment had Peabody taking a breath. "It really is, so nobody much uses it, and my gear's old and ugly, and I just didn't want to sweat and stuff with the hard bodies in the new space. I put in an hour, overdid it."

Peabody raked a hand through the hair she hadn't bothered to brush. "I was toasted, you know. Went in for a shower. I had my things stuffed in a couple of the lockers. I'd just finished, started drying off in the stall when the locker room door bangs open, and two people come in, arguing."

"Here." Roarke pushed a glass of wine in her hand. "Sip a bit."

"Oh boy, thanks," she said as he offered McNab the e-man's favored beer. Peabody sipped, breathed. "Female, seriously pissed. I started to call out so they'd know I was in there, so they'd take the fight elsewhere, then the other one goes off. Male. I'm in the damn stall with nothing but a towel that wouldn't cover a teacup poodle, so I sort of squeeze back into the corner, and hope they go away. But they didn't, and I hear them talking about the operation she runs, how he fucked up and cost them ten K. God."

"Slow down a little, Dee." McNab murmured it while he rubbed a hand on her thigh.

"Okay. Yeah. So they keep at each other, and I realize they're not talking about a police op, but a side one. A long-running one, Dallas. I've got a couple of dirty cops right outside the shower door, talking about product and profit, about houses in the islands. And murder.

"I'm naked, and trapped, and my weapon's in the locker. So's my 'link, and they're slamming the shower doors open—one I'd've been in if there'd been any damn soap in there."

Roarke stood behind her and, reaching down, laid his hands on her shoulders and began to rub. Taking another breath, she leaned back.

"I've been scared before. You've got to be scared going into some situations or you're just stupid. But this . . . When the fight burns out, and they're back in control, she, like, pats my shower door, and, Jesus, it opens a little. I can see her arm, her dress, her shoes. All she has to do is shift an inch, and I'm made—back in the corner of the stall with nothing."

Beside her, McNab continued to rub her thigh, but his pretty, narrow face hardened like stone.

"I can't breathe, can't move, can't risk it because I know if they see me, I'm dead. No way around it. But they leave, they never saw me. I got out, got McNab to get a cab and meet me so I could come here. So I could tell you."

"Names?" Eve demanded, and Peabody shuddered out another breath.

"Garnet—she called the male Garnet. He called her Renee. Oberman. Renee Oberman. She was in charge."

"Renee Oberman and Garnet. Description?"

"I didn't get any sort of look at him, but she's blond, between five-four and five-five, I think. She was wearing heels, but that's about right. Caucasian. Strong voice—at least when she's pissed."

"Did they ever use their ranks?"

"No, but she said when she made captain, they were going to expand the business. She referred to it as a business several times. And they used to be lovers."

"Did you run the names?" she asked McNab.

"Not yet. Peabody was pretty shaken."

"She had somebody named Keener killed—said she had their boy take care of it, and that it would look like an OD. Keener's a chemi-head, and one of their tools, contacts. He tried to rabbit on them, with this ten K. Garnet was supposed to have him on a leash, but he slipped. That's what they were fighting about. They got the ten K, too—she let Garnet know that after she'd raked him down. And she was taking ten percent of his cut as a bonus for the boy, the killer. It was a business meeting."

"Did you get the impression they used that space often for meetings?"

"No. No, the opposite. She was really peeved he'd yanked her in there, let him know there'd be no more meets there. Six years," Peabody remembered. "She said she'd been running the business for six years. And the way she talked about 'the boy,' it was clear this Keener wasn't the first kill she'd put him on."

"Did anyone see you enter or leave that facility?"

"No." Peabody paused, thought it through. "No, I really don't think so. It's like a tomb down there."

"Okay."

"Crappy report," Peabody added. "Sorry. I'm jumbled."

"You got names, a partial description, details of cops running a sideshow—sounds like illegals—and ordering hits. McNab, peel yourself off Peabody and run those names. Try the Illegals Division out of Central first. You're going to find Oberman, Lieutenant Renee, there—I know who she is, but pin it. And pin this Garnet."

"You know her?" Peabody demanded.

"I know who she is, and I know her father's Oberman, Commander Marcus. Retired."

"Jesus, Jesus, Saint Oberman? He ran Central before Whitney." Every last remaining ounce of color drained out of Peabody's cheeks. "Oh God, what did I step in?"

"Whatever it is, it's a big, messy pile, so we take this slow and easy, and by the numbers."

"Garnet, Detective William." McNab glanced up from his PPC. "Second-grade, assigned the last four years to Illegals, out of Central, under Oberman, Lieutenant Renee."

"Okay, let's take this upstairs. McNab, you're going to get me ID shots and any data on these two you can get without sending up a flag. Peabody, you're going to give me a full, cohesive, and detailed report, on record. This Keener likely started out as a weasel for either Garnet or Oberman. We find him."

"What do we do with this?" Peabody asked her.

Eve looked her dead in the eye, her own flat and cool. "We put it together in a very tidy package, and we take it to Whitney and to IAB. Other than that, nobody outside of this room hears a whisper of this until we're otherwise directed."

"Commander Oberman. He's like a legend. Like a god."

"I don't care if he's the second coming of

Jesus. The daughter's dirty. She's a wrong cop, Peabody, and the blue line breaks for wrong cops. Let's get started."

"You haven't eaten," Roarke interrupted, smoothing a hand over Peabody's hair.

"No, guess not."

"She'll do better with some food in her," he said to Eve.

"You're right." She buried impatience as she'd buried the raging fury during Peabody's report. "We'll get some fuel, then we'll lay it all out."

"I got the shakes," Peabody confessed. "After. They keep wanting to come back, but it's better. I have to tag my mom, thank her."

"For what?"

"I dropped my sweaty crap on the locker room floor, and I would've left it there if I hadn't heard her voice in my head telling me to respect what belongs to me. If I'd left that ugly sports bra on the floor, they'd have seen it. They'd have found me. And I wouldn't be here telling you Saint Oberman's daughter's a wrong cop."

"Thank her in the morning," Eve ordered. "Let's get to work."

Now Roarke draped his arm over Peabody's shoulders when she rose. "How about a steak?"

"Really?"

He kissed the top of her head, made her flush. "Leave the menu to me. You're a brave soul, Peabody."

"My soul was scared shitless."

He kissed her again. "You don't want to argue with a man who's about to fix you a steak."

In her home office Eve set up a case board while Peabody and McNab ate. Roarke had been right about the food, the wine, the shoulder rub—all of it. He was usually on target about those things.

And it was better to give Peabody a little breathing room before opening the door to what would be an ugly and difficult process.

"She's attractive," Roarke commented, studying the ID shot of Oberman on the board.

"Yeah, and she has a rep for using it— and using her father's rep. Just whispers— nothing said too loud. I . . . ."

Eve shook her head, then stepped out of the room.

"What?" Roarke asked when he followed her.

She kept her voice down. "If they'd found her, they'd have killed her. No way around it. She was right about that."

"It must have been brutal, being trapped as she was."

"We had this scuffle with these three assholes today, and one of them gives her a couple pretty good knocks. I told her she had heavy feet, needed to work on her technique, so what does she do? She goes down to that empty shithole of a gym. If it had tipped the other way, that's where they'd have found her body. She takes a punch in the ear, and I can't just say everybody takes a knock? I've got to tell her to work on it, to do better."

"Because the next time she might take a knife in the ear. You're not just her partner, Eve, you're still training her. And you've done a damn brilliant job of it so far, in my opinion. She went down because she wants to improve, and yes, because she wants to meet your standards. It didn't tip the other way," he reminded her. "And if it had, though it makes me just as sick as you to think that, it would be on the heads of those bollocks excuse for cops. You know that."

She sucked in a breath. "You're still mad at me."

"I am, and you're still mad at me. But we both understand there are more important things just at the moment."

They could count on each other for that, she thought. Count on each other to hold the line when it needed to be held. "So, truce."

"Agreed. She's precious to me, too."

Because her eyes stung, Eve pressed her fingers to them. "Don't pet me," she said, anticipating him. "I need to hold it together." Eve dropped her hands. "She's counting on me to hold it together."

"So you will." He petted her anyway, just sleeking a hand down her hair. Then he gripped one of the short strands, gave it a hard tug.

"Hey. Truce."

"See, you're a little pissed again. You'll work better." He strolled back into the office.

She held it together, and in short order it took no effort. She simply fell into the rhythm of the work.

"We can't look at their financials, even first-level, without sending up a flag. Much less go digging around for buried accounts and real estate."

She caught Roarke's glance, knew he was considering his illegal and unregistered equipment. No flags there. But she sent him a subtle shake of the head. She had to toe every inch of the line on this.

"If we go to IAB with this," Peabody began, "with what we have, which when I look at it all laid out, isn't really that much, it could bust open. It could give Renee— I can't call her Oberman because it makes me think of her father. It could give her and the others time to rabbit, or cover, or ditch. They must have contingency plans, escape routes."

"I can work that. I'm going to reach out to Webster." Again she caught Roarke's glance, the cock of his eyebrow. She supposed it was impossible for Webster's name to come up in this particular room without both of them seeing Roarke beat the hell out of him.

"I'll feed this to him, but with conditions," she continued. "I can work that, especially if Whitney adds his weight. We want to keep this narrow for as long as we can."

"Keener!" McNab punched a fist in the air, did a little spin in Eve's chair that had his long, blond ponytail flying. Then he pointed the index fingers of both hands at her computer. "Found him. I did some crosses on some of her closed cases, mixed in others from here and there for cover, skimming wit lists and suspects like a standard search for—"

"Just give me Keener, McNab."

"Keener, Rickie. Street name Juicy. I can't dig to see if he's listed as a weasel without the flag, but he's got a long sheet. Possession, possession with intent to distribute, other petty shit, and he got busted for selling a primo case of variety packs to a couple of undercovers. One of them, listed as the arresting officer, is our girl Renee."

"Put the data on-screen," Eve ordered, and scanned it. "Look there, he gets probation, community service, mandatory counseling. That's a deal happening there, that's her turning him weasel as a get-out-of-jail card. With his priors, he should've done at least three solid. But he gets time served? Six years ago."

"That's how long she said she'd been running the business," Peabody put in.

"So, this Keener could've been her springboard. Her way in."

She paced in front of the screen. "He knows something. He has more, offers it. Hey, I can give you this and that, but you gotta get me out of this. Alternately, she's already looking, already getting it off the ground and sees him as an asset. Either way, this is the turn."

"He's dead. She was really clear about that," Peabody added.

"So, we find the body. If 'her boy' found him alive, we can find him dead."

She paced a bit more. "Not in his flop. He was fixing to rabbit, with the money. He had another hole he thought was safe, secret. Take the locations of his busts, his flop, locations of his varied and bullshit employment. According to Peabody's statement Renee said he hadn't gotten far. Let's map out his territory, run some probabilities on most likely locations for his hole."

"We want to find the body," Peabody began, "because you think the guy she set on Keener might've left some evidence?"

"It's possible. Unlikely, but possible. We want to find the body, we want to catch this case because Keener's our weasel now."

"A con, Peabody," Roarke told her. "You have the case, you have the controls. And what they're banking on being an OD becomes a homicide investigation."

"If I can work it," Eve agreed. "Either way, she'll have to come out and ID him as her CI—that's procedure. If she doesn't, we can give her a nice slap for it. And we can be bitchy, just by-the-book sticklers and insist on details of their association, information, times, dates—which should all be in her files. Gosh, we're trying to find out who killed this asshole. A DB's a DB in my Homicide Division."

"You want to piss her off."

"I'm counting on it, and I'm going to enjoy it. Get me the probabilities, McNab, then we're going on a weasel hunt."

"You want the body before you go to Whitney and Webster."

Eve nodded at Peabody. "Now you're getting it. Keener's tangible, and dead he'll be corroborating your statement. With the connection of the arrest to Renee, we've got more. She's a decorated officer. She's a boss, and a respected, hell, revered, former commander's daughter. She's got eighteen years on the force without a blemish."

"And if I just blow the whistle on her, IAB may end up investigating me."

"You don't worry about that," Eve told her.

"I won't. I've leveled off now, and now I really want to pay her back for every second I was in that freaking shower. I mean, over and above bringing a dirty cop to justice."

"Naked in the shower," Eve reminded her.

"With nothing to do but give them an angry towel snap if they slapped open the door."

"We'll pay them back," Eve promised, and looked over to where Roarke and McNab worked together. Roarke in his tailored dress shirt and pants, McNab in pink, multi-pocketed knee shorts and a buttercup-yellow tank that sported E-DICK in screaming red letters across his skinny chest.

Geeks were geeks, Eve thought, whatever the wardrobe.

"Your map," Roarke announced, nodding to the wall screen. "And your most-likelies."

"Not bad. His type tend to stick to a certain area, to do their business within a handful of blocks where they know the score, the routes, the dodge points."

"If he was going to rabbit, wouldn't he move outside his usual turf?"

She shook her head, glanced at McNab. "Look at the time line from the conversation Peabody overheard. The heat's up, and that says this screwup was fresh. The kill recently ordered and executed. Garnet didn't even know about it. Add to that, ten thousand on the line. This had to move fast. From Keener's sheet, he's not a bright light. Smart enough not to go home, but not, most likely, smart enough to relocate outside his comfort zone. He hadn't rabbited yet, so he wasn't finished getting his shit together. We're going to find him within this area, just like his killer did."

She studied the map a little longer. "Eliminate anything he'd have to pay for. No tenanted apartments."

The map adjusted to Roarke's command.

She knew the area well enough, with its sidewalk sleepers, low-rent street LCs,

funky-junkies, ghosts, used-up chemi-
heads. Even the gangbangers had given
it up as not worth the trouble.

"I like these five locations. Two-man
teams. We'll get you a vehicle. A nonde-
script one," she added when she saw Mc-
Nab's face light up.

He shrugged. "I guess it has to be."

"It does. Roarke and I will take these
two, Peabody and McNab these two. If we
zero, we'll converge on location five. We
get nothing, we'll widen the map again. Do
either of you have a clutch piece on you?"

At the negative, Eve rolled her eyes.
"We'll get you that, too. There are some
people in this sector who just aren't very
nice.

"We'll seal up. I don't want to leave any
trace we've been there. Keep any distur-
bances to the locations to a minimum, and
don't talk to anybody. Don't ask questions.
Go in, go through, get out."

"If we find the body?" Peabody asked.

"Get out, signal me, and get gone. We'll
meet back here where I'll be getting an
annoying anonymous tip about a dead
guy. Records on, boys and girls, the whole
time, so keep the chatter down, too. Rec-

ords will be turned over to command and IAB."

She blew out her breath as she studied McNab. "You're not going on a covert op in that getup. Roarke, have we got anything we can put on this geek?"

"Actually, you're more his size."

Eve closed her eyes. "Jesus. I guess I am."

She found jeans and a black T-shirt, and after she'd tossed them at McNab, closed the bedroom door so both she and Roarke could change.

"I'm partially sorry," she said.

"Oh?"

"I'm partially sorry because I did start to tag you about being so late, then got interrupted and forgot. But I almost always remember, so I think I could get a goddamn pass on it."

"I wasn't angry, and I'm not angry about you not calling—particularly. I don't give you grief about that sort of thing, Eve."

"No, you don't, but I feel guilty about it because you don't."

"Ah, my fault again."

"Oh, shut up."

"There goes the truce."

"You could be partially sorry."

"But I'm not, not a bit, for enjoying the evening with Summerset and his very interesting friends—who I'd never met before either."

"You're better at that than I am. And I'm just saying if I'd known I wouldn't have come home with this other plan, and then had this to deal with."

"What other plan?"

"I just . . ." She felt stupid about it now, and dragged on her weapon harness. "I just thought we'd have dinner, that you'd have waited for me because that's what you usually do. And I was going to pick it out and fix it up."

"Were you?" he murmured.

"We haven't had much downtime in the last couple weeks, and I had this idea that we'd eat up on the roof terrace—the works, you know? Wine, candles, and just us. Then we could watch one of those old vids you like, except I'd put on sexwear and seduce you."

"I see."

"Then I come home and you're already having wine and candles and dinner on the terrace—not the roof one, but still. And it's not just us, and I've got asphalt crap on my pants, and former criminals in my house—I figured. A couple of people Summerset's probably already told I suck at the marriage thing, and come home with dirty clothes or trailing blood half the time. And I didn't want to have to squeeze in and end up being interrogated."

"First, you don't suck at the marriage thing, and Summerset never said anything of that kind. In fact, he mentioned to them at dinner, when it was clear you'd be late, that you were the first cop he'd had contact with who worked so tirelessly or cared so much about real justice."

He crossed to her now, cupped her face. "Second, that was a lovely plan you had, and I'd have enjoyed it, very much. And now, I am partially sorry."

She touched his wrist. "If we put those together, it would be one all-the-way sorry."

"It would, and that's a deal."

She kissed him to seal it, then stood for a moment, snug in his arms. "It's a good deal," she decided. "Now let's go find a dead junkie."

**4** Eve got behind the wheel so Roarke could do more research with his PPC.

"Let me ask you this," he began. "How many dealings have you had with Lieutenant Oberman?"

"None, really. I know *of* her, but we haven't had any cases cross so I've never worked with her. Illegals has its own unique setup. There's a lot of undercover work, some of it deep, some of it rotating. You've got squads who focus entirely on the big game—import/export, organized crime. Others stick primarily to street deals, others manufacturing and distribution. Like that."

"There has to be overlap."

"Yeah, and each squad is set up sort of like—what do they call it—a fiefdom?"

"I see, with its own culture and hierarchy."

"Like that," she agreed. "Uniforms and detectives reporting to a lieutenant heading that squad, with those lieutenants reporting to a smaller group of captains."

"Which means a lot of politics," Roarke surmised. "And when you have politics, you have corruption."

"Possibly. Probably," she corrected. "There are checks and balances, there's a chain of command. Screening—regular screening not only for burnout but for use and addiction. A lot of the undercovers burn out, get made, or get a little too fond of the merchandise."

"And would have fairly easy access to the merchandise," Roarke concluded.

It rubbed her wrong, not the statement but that he seemed to expect and accept cops on the take. She knew it happened. But she didn't, wouldn't accept it.

"Cops have access to a lot of things. Stolen merchandise, confiscated funds,

weapons. Cops who can't resist temptation don't belong on the force."

"I'd argue there's a gray area, but once
you step into the gray, it's a short trip to
the black. Still, easy access," he repeated.
"A cop busts a street dealer, pockets half
the stash. The dealer's not going to argue
about how much weight he was carrying."

"That's what the lieutenant's for. To know
her men, to supervise, assess. It's her
job—her duty—to stay on top of it. Instead
she's orchestrating it."

"She's betrayed her men, from your
view, as well as her badge, the department."

"In my view, she's a treacherous bitch."
Eve shrugged it off, but it burned in her
belly. "As for confiscated product, there's
an accounting division attached to Illegals
that's supposed to keep track of it, paraphernalia, payloads—as it comes in, as
it's used in trial, as it is subsequently destroyed. They have their own Property
Room to handle it."

"And a clever, ambitious woman like Renee could recruit someone from that accounting division to help her skim. Using
that, her own squad, her father's connec-

tions, to pluck the department's pockets. Resell product listed as destroyed."

"It's one way. Another would be to deal directly with suppliers, manufacturers, even street dealers—negotiate a fee to keep their business running smooth.

"Have to pick and choose," Eve considered. "You're not going to make rank, even with a daddy boost, if you don't close cases, don't lock up some bad guys. She has to keep her percentages up—arrests that lead to conviction."

She braked at a light. "How would you work it?"

"Well now, I'm not as schooled in the running of a division or squad as you."

"You run half the industrialized world."

"Ah, if only. But be that as it may, if I were looking for long-term profit—not the quick grab, but to establish a steady profit-making business in this area, I'd take a bit from each level. Street deals—that's quick and easy, and with the right pressure and incentives you could establish enough loyalty and fees in the low-level runners to finance and establish the next level. Runners get their junk from somewhere else unless they're self-reliant. And even most of those have to work within the system—fight for their turf or pay a fee to whoever runs the turf."

"You'd need soldiers to go out, establish that loyalty and fear. Negotiators to move it up the levels. Six years?" Eve shook her head. "She's got a network. Cops and crooks. Some lawyers she can flip if one of her crew gets squeezed, probably somebody in the PA's office, at least one judge."

"She needs a treasury," Roarke added. "There would be palms to grease, other expenses."

"It's not just the money. It's hardly ever just the money," Eve decided. "She has to like it. The kick, the power, the dirt, the edge. She's twisting and demeaning everything her father stood for. Stands for."

"That may be part of the point."

"Father issues? Boo-hoo. Dad was so busy being a cop he didn't pay enough attention to me, or he was too strict, expected too much. Whatever. So now I'll take my own badge and smear shit all over it. That'll teach him."

"I suppose you and I have little patience or sympathy for father issues that don't involve violence or real abuse." In understanding, he laid a hand over hers briefly. "But it may be part of this, and may be something you can work with."

"Once I inform the commander and IAB, I may be out of it."

"In a pig's eye."

She had to laugh. "Okay, I intend to fight—hard and dirty if necessary—to have a part in the investigation. I'm going to need Mira," she mused, thinking of the department's top shrink. "Her clearance will put her on board, and I want Feeney. We need EDD. McNab's already in it, but he'll need Feeney not only to give him the time and the space to work this, but to help."

She eased along the mean streets now, where streetlights—when they worked—shone on oily piles of garbage, and deals for sex, for drugs thrived in the shadows.

"It's going to be a fucking mess, Roarke. Not just the investigation, the media fallout when it hits. But the repercussions? They'll have to review every one of her cases, and the cases of whoever she sucked into this. Retrials or just being straightjacketed into springing bad guys because of the old fruit of a poisoned tree. Taking her and her network down means opening up cages.

There's no way around it. I could kick her ass for that alone—after I strip the skin off it for Peabody."

She pulled to the curb. Parking wasn't an issue here. If you didn't have weight in this sector, your vehicle would either be gone or stripped down to its bones if you left it for five minutes.

"Oh, forgot. The alarm works great," she told him. "Some mope tried to boost it—when I'm barely fifty feet away. Landed on his ass and limped away without his tools."

Like her he scanned the shadows, the deep pits of dark. "It's nice to know we won't be walking home from here."

"Seal up." Eve tossed Roarke the can of sealant, engaged her recorder.

"Dallas, Lieutenant Eve, and Roarke," she began, and listed the address. "Date and time stamp on record."

The building had likely been a small warehouse or factory at some point, and scooped up in the rehab-crazed pre-Urbans. Since, it might have served as sorry shelter for itinerants or a chemi-den—probably both at one time or another.

The rusted and broken chain and pad-

lock drooping from the door proved security measures had been half-assed to
begin with, and long since breached.

But the shiny new lock caught her interest.

"Cold weather hole," Eve said. "Nobody
much wants to be inside the dirt and stink
in high summer. Still . . ." She nodded at
the lock. "Somebody put that on recently."
She started forward, digging for her master.

The man who jumped out of the shadows boasted a half acre of wide shoulders.
He bared his teeth in an ugly grin that
demonstrated dental hygiene wasn't high
on his list of priorities.

Eve imagined it was his six-inch sticker
and what he took as a couple of easy
marks that put the grin on his face.

"Take care of that, will you?" she asked
Roarke.

"Of course, darling." He gave the man
currently jabbing playfully at him with the
blade a pleasant smile. "Something I can
do for you?"

"Gonna spill your guts all over the street,
then I'm gonna fuck your woman. Gimme
the wallet, the wrist unit. Ring, too."

"I'm going to do you a favor, as even if you managed to spill my guts all over the street—and odds are against you—if you tried to touch my woman she'd break your dick off like a twig then stick it up your arse."

"Gonna bleed."

When the man lunged, Roarke danced easily to the side, pivoted with an elbow jab to the kidneys. The responding *oof!* had the ring of surprise, but the assailant spun around with a vicious slice Roarke evaded with another pivot. He followed it by slamming his foot against the big man's kneecap.

"Stop playing with him," Eve called out.

"She tends to be strict," Roarke commented, and when the man—grimacing now—lunged again, he kicked the knife arm, sharp at the elbow. Even thugs can scream, he thought, and caught the knife as it flew out of the man's quivering hand.

"And here comes the favor." No longer pleasant, no longer smiling, Roarke's iced-blues met the man's pain-filled eyes. "Run."

As the footsteps slapped down the sidewalk, Eve watched Roarke press the mechanism on the sticker to retract the blade.

"If you're thinking of keeping that, you'd better dump it in an autoclave first chance. Ready?"

Roarke slipped the knife in his pocket, nodded as he joined her at the door.

She drew her weapon, rested it across her flashlight, angling away so the recording wouldn't show Roarke doing the same.

They went through the door, swept left, right.

She kicked aside trash to clear a path. Mold laced with stale urine and fresher vomit smeared the air. She judged the main source as a pile of blankets, stiff as cardboard and too hideous to tempt even a sidewalk sleeper.

"Clear the level."

They moved in, sweeping lights, weapons. Doors, wiring, sections of floorboard and stair treads—anything that could be used or sold—had been torn out, pulled down, and hauled off, leaving raw holes, toothy gaps.

She studied the open elevator shaft. "How the hell did they get the elevator door out of here, and what did they do with it?"

"Mind your step," Roarke said as she

started up the stairs, striding over the wide holes.

On the second level she shined her light over broken syringes, bits of utensils, and pots eaten through by chemicals and heat. She considered the splintered stool, the tiny, scorched table, the shattered glass and starbursts of burns on the floor, the walls.

"Somebody had a little lab accident," she commented.

She jerked her chin toward the bare mattresses stained by substances she didn't particularly want to think about. Remnants of fast-food containers lay scattered where she imagined they'd been picked over by vermin of the two- and four-legged varieties.

"Living where they worked, for a while."

Roarke studied the filth. "I can't say I love what they've done with the place."

She toed a discarded Chinese takeout container. "Somebody ate here in the last couple days. What's left in this isn't moldy yet."

"Still enough to put you off your moo goo."

"I think it used to be chow mein."

She followed the amazing stench to what had once been a bathroom. Whoever had attempted to rip out the toilet had fallen victim to impatience or incompetence so the broken bowl lay useless on its side. They'd had better luck with the sink, and some enterprising soul had smashed through the wall and managed to cut out most of the copper pipes.

They hadn't bothered with the tub, maybe daunted by the weight and bulk of the ancient cast iron. Chipped, stained, and narrow, it served as a deathbed for one Rickie Keener.

He lay curled in it, knees drawn up toward the bony chest coated with his own vomit. A syringe, a couple of vials, and the rest of his works sat on the lip of the windowsill.

"The victim matches the description and ID photo of Rickie Keener, aka Juicy." She drew the print pad out of her pocket, holstered her weapon. Crossing to him, she carefully pressed the pad to his right index finger. "ID is confirmed," she said when the pad verified the identification. "Roarke, signal Peabody. Tell them to break off. We've got him."

She stood where she was, breathing through her teeth, letting her light run over the body. "This corroborates Detective Peabody's statement vis-à-vis the overheard conversation in the sector-two locker facilities. Visual exam shows some minor bruising, arms, legs. Right elbow is scraped. A more detailed examination will have to wait until command clears the matter. My determination at this time is on-record verification only. To preserve clarity of investigation on Oberman, Renee, and Garnet, William, I cannot secure this scene, but will instead install a recorder for monitoring purposes."

She turned to Roarke. "Can you put it above the doorway?"

"Already done. If anyone comes through here, your comp and your PPC will signal. You'll be able to monitor the scene from any location you choose, until you officially open the investigation."

"That'll work." She glanced back at the dead. "Let's get out of here."

Out on the street she took a couple of breaths to clear out the worst of the stink, then checked the time. "The scene's as secure as we can make it, and there's no point in contacting the commander at this hour.

Better to get a couple hours' sleep, and start the process in the morning. Dallas and Roarke leaving monitored location," she said for the recorder, then shut it off.

"Fuck." She breathed it out.

"Did you think we wouldn't find him?"

"No, I knew we'd find him, but—like I said—a body's tangible. No getting around it now. No stopping it. We have to take her down."

She got in the passenger seat so Roarke could take the wheel. He gave her a few moments with her thoughts as he navigated the route back uptown.

"Have you decided how you'll structure this for Whitney?"

"Straight, start to finish. Once Peabody chilled, her statement of events was cohesive, so we have that on record. By tomorrow, she'll have steadied more, and she'll stand up when Whitney questions her."

"So you're taking a couple hours down as much for that as to give your commander a full night's sleep."

"Maybe. Yes," she admitted. "Off the record. We'll lay out the steps we took to locate Keener, and show Whitney the record of the discovery. It'll be up to him what comes next, but I'll be able to present him with the most logical and practical plan. We have to keep the investigation taut and tight. It's not just corruption, it's murder. And Keener's not the first."

"It's hard for you, going after one of your own."

"She stopped being one of my own the minute she went on the take." Deliberately Eve relaxed her shoulders. "I don't know how close Whitney might be with Commander Oberman. I know he served under him, and he took the chair when Oberman retired. That means something, the passing of command. Renee Oberman's served under Whitney, and that means something, too."

She sighed now. "We all know that we may be able to keep the investigation under a lid, but when it's done, when we bust it, the lid comes off. The media's going to rip into this like jackals on a fresh kill. I can't even blame them."

"When it makes you sad or discouraged, and it will, this process as you call it, think of Peabody in that shower stall, trapped, while two people who've exploited their badges to line their own pockets discuss the business of murder."

She sat in silence for a couple blocks. "That was well put," she said after a while. "Succinct, and all that. And good advice. Then there's Keener. He was probably a schmuck, almost certainly a very bad guy, but he's mine now. And the cop who left him choking on his own vomit in that filthy tub? He's going to be mine, too, right up until I slam the cage door on him."

Roarke had barely braked in front of the house when Peabody rushed out.

"You found him."

"First stop," Eve confirmed. "Luck of the draw. It's all on record, and the scene's being monitored."

"Set up like an OD?"

"Yes. It corroborates your statement."

"I don't know whether to be relieved or sorry," Peabody said as McNab ran a hand down her back. Strain shadowed her eyes, leeched her color.

"Be neither. Acknowledge it, then move on. We'll have plenty to deal with in the morning. Get some sleep. Take the room you usually take when you flop here."

"You're not going to contact Whitney?"

"It's nearly three in the morning, but you're free to wake him now if you're in a hurry."

"No, that's okay. Ha. A little sleep would be good."

"Then go get some." To make a point, Eve started up the stairs.

"Is there anything you need tonight?" Roarke asked them.

"No." McNab took Peabody's hand, gave it a squeeze. "We're set."

Roarke leaned down, kissed Peabody's brow. "Then sleep well."

He followed Eve into the bedroom, closed the door as she took off her weapon harness. The strain showed in her, he noted, as it had in Peabody. A rub on the back, a hand held might help a bit. But he knew what would shift her mind, at least briefly.

"You owe me makeup sex, but I'm happy to take your marker."

As he'd expected, she scowled at him. "Why do I owe the makeup sex?"

"Because you were partially sorry first."

She narrowed her eyes as she sat to pull off her boots. "That just means you lagged behind in the partially sorries. I think that means you owe me. I'll take your marker."

"I might agree with that, on the condition that your part of said agreement includes the far-famed sexwear." He watched her pull an oversized NYPSD T-shirt over her head. "Which I'm hoping that isn't."

"I can agree to those terms." She climbed into bed.

"Then it's a date." He slid in beside her, wrapped her against him.

"I have to program the alarm."

"What time?"

"Ah, I'm going to contact Whitney at six-hundred sharp. I should probably give myself an hour to prepare."

"Five then. Don't worry. I'll wake you."

Trusting he would, she closed her eyes.

She'd have sworn five minutes passed when she woke to the seductive scent of coffee. She slitted her eyes open and saw him.

He sat on the side of the bed holding a huge mug of coffee a few inches from her nose. He'd ordered the light on, about twenty percent, she judged, so the room held a soft dawn glow.

"You brought me coffee in bed?"

"You could consider me the prince of husbands—or just that I was awake before you. It's just gone five," he added.

"Ugh." She pushed herself up, muttered a thanks, then took the mug and glugged. Then she closed her eyes and let the beauty of caffeine slide through her system. "Good." Glugged some more. "Shower." She crawled out of bed, said, "More," and drained the mug before pushing it back into his hands.

Halfway to the bathroom she glanced back over her shoulder. Crooked a finger. And pulling off the T-shirt, let it drop to the floor as she walked the rest of the way naked.

Roarke set the empty mug on the nightstand. "Who am I to refuse such a gracious invitation?"

She'd ordered the jets on full, and—of course—brutally hot. He'd never get used to her love of boiling herself, and often himself as well, in the shower. Steam pumped, blurring the glass of the big, open area. She stood, sleek and wet, face lifted, eyes closed.

"A prince would probably wash my back."

Obliging, Roarke tapped a panel and, when it opened, cupped his hand to catch a creamy fall of soap. "You slept well, I take it."

"Mmmm."

Her back, narrow and smooth, with just a hint of gold from their days in the sun on their recent holiday, arched—just a little—at the glide of his soapy hands.

He loved the feel of it, the soft skin over tensile strength. The long length of it tapered to her waist then gave way to the subtle flare of her hips.

Lean and angular, his cop, built for both speed and endurance. And yet he knew her vulnerabilities, where a touch—his touch—would weaken or incite.

The delicate curve at the back of her neck, the little dip at the base of her spine.

He continued down, sliding, circling the silky liquid over slim, strongly muscled thighs. Up again, fingers teasing, advance and retreat, in lazy seduction.

She hooked her arm around his neck, arching back. And in a limber twist from that narrow waist, turned her head until her lips found his, until they parted for a long, deep mating of tongues.

She turned, her eyes glimmering like burnished gold through the water.

"You missed a few spots."

"Careless of me." He filled his palm with soap, swirled it over her shoulders, her breasts, her torso, her belly.

Every inch of her yearned, here in the heat and steam, with the pounding and pulsing of water against tile, against flesh. His hands were magic on her body, triggering needs, tripping sensations, finding—owning—her secrets. His mouth, when he used it on her, infused her body with a thousand aches of pleasure.

His fingers found her, opened her, and wet to wet stroked her through those aches and beyond.

She wrapped around him, a sleek, fragrant vine, her hands tangled in his hair, her mouth avid on his. Her heart beat wild and strong against his chest in quick, lusty kicks. And she filled her hands with soap, glided them over his back, his hips, slicked them between their slippery bodies to take him in that silkened grip.

To destroy him.

He all but heard the lead snap on his control and plunged into her. Trapping her against the wet tiles, capturing her cries even as her arms chained around his neck.

Hot jets of water pummeled their joined bodies. Drops glistened on skin, on the air. Steam rose and spread to blur them into one desperate form in that last mad rush.

She went limp in his arms. It was a moment he loved, when the pleasure overwhelmed her, left her weak. Just that instant of utter surrender to him, but more, to them.

Basking in it, she rested her head on his shoulder until he lifted her face, laid his lips on hers. Softly now, and sweetly.

He watched her eyes clear, watched them smile. "That wasn't makeup sex."

"Of course not."

"Just confirming."

"But it was an excellent prelude."

"Worked for me. Coffee in bed, sex in the shower—makes a solid wake-up combo."

She nuzzled another moment, then was gone—stepping out and into the drying tube.

While air swirled around her he ordered the water temperature to lower five civilized degrees.

When he walked into the bedroom with a towel slung around his waist she stood in a short robe doing something he rarely if ever saw her do. Actively studying the contents of her closet.

"This is weird," she said, "but I need to . . . Pick something out for me to wear, will you? I need to look in control, an authority, serious. Seriously in charge."

Frustrated, she circled her hands in the air. "But without looking planned or studied. I don't want it to come off like an outfit, but—"

"I understand you." He stepped in, studied the jackets first. He'd selected every one of them himself as wardrobe—much less shopping for wardrobe—was dead low on her list of priorities.

"This."

"Red? But—"

"Not red, but burgundy. It's not bright, not bold, but deep and serious—and transmits authority, particularly in this very tailored cut. With these pants—a serious gunmetal gray, and this top in a slightly softer gray—no fuss, no embellishments. The gray boots, as they'll give you one long line, with the jacket as the subliminal element of authority."

She puffed out her cheeks, blew out the air. "Okay. You're the expert."

Once she'd dressed she had to admit there was a reason he *was* the expert. She looked put together but not—how had she put it—studied. And the red—sorry, *burgundy*—did look strong.

Plus, if she got blood on it, it might not show. Much.

"Wear these."

She frowned at the little silver studs he held out. "I hardly ever wear earrings to work. They're—"

"In this case, just a bit of polish. Simple and subtle."

She shrugged, then put them on. Finished, she stood studying herself in the mirror as she sipped another cup of coffee.

"You're not giving this attention to your wardrobe for Whitney," Roarke said. "At least not particularly. It's true, that old saying. Women dress for other women. This is for Renee Oberman's benefit."

"If things go as I'm damn well going to make sure they go, we'll have our first face-to-face today. This is the sort of thing she'd pay attention to. She's going to know, on every level I can manage, she's dealing with power."

"You want to challenge her."

"I will challenge her. But that's for later." She glanced at the time. "I have to take the next step, contact Whitney. Christ, I hope his wife doesn't answer the 'link."

Eve picked hers up from the dresser, squared her shoulders. "Here we go."

Commander Whitney's wide face came on-screen after the second beep. She had a moment to be relieved he hadn't blocked video, which meant it unlikely she'd woken him. Still, she was pretty certain it was a sleep crease across his left cheek and not a new line dug by time and the stress of authority, so she hadn't missed by much.

"Lieutenant." He spoke briskly, dark eyes sober in his dark face.

She matched his tone. "Commander, I apologize for the early hour. We have a situation."

She laid it out with a military precision Roarke admired. Across the room, he dressed for the day, listened to Whitney pepper Eve with questions. Roarke thought you'd have to know the man and listen very well to hear the shock, but it was there.

"I want to review Peabody's statement, to speak with her myself, and to review your records."

"Yes, sir. Commander, if I could suggest we hold this initial review here rather than Central? Detectives Peabody and McNab are at this location at this time, and we would be assured of privacy until you make your determinations."

He considered a moment, then, "On my way," and clicked off.

"On your turf," Roarke commented.

"That's a factor, but he knows it's smarter to start this outside rather than with a major meeting in his office. I'm going to go prep for this."

"I imagine he'll have some questions for me, so I'll see if I can be available. I have a holo-conference in ten minutes. I should have it wrapped by seven or so. You did well," he added.

"It's just the beginning."

5 Eve prepared a packet for her commander with copies of all data, recordings, statements, and notes. While she worked she practiced, in her head, her pitch for the steps she hoped to take next, her reasons for each, her justifications for bringing in Feeney and Mira and connecting with Webster for the IAB aspect.

Tone, strategy, logic, confidence. She'd need them all, and in a seamless blend, to keep her hands on the controls of what would be a two-point investigation—one that put Marcus Oberman's daughter in the crosshairs where they met.

She glanced up as McNab came in. He wore his own clothes—probably for the best. Seeing him in normal attire might shock their commander senseless.

"Peabody's taking a few more minutes," he told Eve. "I think she just wanted a little time alone."

"What's her status?"

"She's pretty solid. I thought maybe she'd have nightmares, but I guess she was too wiped."

Wiped was how she'd describe him now. The bright clothes, the shine of the earrings crowding his earlobe didn't disguise the strain and worry clouding his face.

"Ah, you look . . . I guess the word's formidable. In a styling way," he added.

Score for Roarke, she thought.

"Anything I can do?" he asked her.

"There will be, but for now we're on hold. I checked the monitor. Everything's five-by-five there. Get some coffee," she said when he just stood in front of the board she'd set up, jingling whatever he had in his multitude of pockets. Then she remembered who she was talking to. "And some food."

"Maybe I'll put something together for Peabody." He started toward the kitchen, then stopped in front of her desk. His green eyes burned cold. "I want blood. I know I've got to get over, got to get straight, but fuck it, Dallas, that's what I want. It's not because—or just because—she was in a situation. The job puts you in situations, that's what it is. But it's not supposed to come from other cops."

"A badge doesn't make you a cop. Get over, get straight, McNab." She'd already told herself the same. "That's how we'll make this right."

While he fiddled in her kitchen, Eve rose to check the board again, to be certain she'd forgotten nothing. She heard Peabody come in behind her. "McNab's fixing food. Go get some."

"Stomach's a little jumpy. The idea of going through it with Whitney."

Eve turned. Not altogether solid, she noted. "Do you trust your commander, Detective?"

"Yes, sir. Without reservation."

She used the same brisk tone she had

with McNab as she gestured toward the kitchen. "Then get some food, shed the nerves, do the job."

Turning away, she checked the monitor again—unnecessarily, she knew, and logged the time as Peabody moved by her.

Moments later she heard McNab's voice. She couldn't make out the words, but the tone was sly, teasing. And Peabody laughed. Eve felt the tension in her own shoulders ease.

To satisfy her own needs she ordered Renee Oberman's ID photo and data on her comp screen for another long study.

Age forty-two, blond and blue, five feet four inches, one hundred and twenty pounds. Attractive, as Roarke had said. Flawless ivory skin with a hint of roses, classic oval face with sharply defined eyebrows several shades darker than her hair.

Dark eyebrows, Eve noted, and a dark forest of lashes—which probably meant Renee had a clever hand with facial enhancements. She'd left the face unframed, pulling her hair back for her official photo, but Eve had studied others with the long, straight-as-rain fall of it sleeked to the shoulders.

Vanity, Eve thought. Maybe another area to exploit.

The only child of Marcus and Violet Oberman, who'd been married forty-nine years. Father, police commander (retired) with fifty years on the job. Mother, a waitress, had taken six years as a professional mother after the daughter was born, then found employment as a sales manager in a women's upscale boutique until retirement.

Renee Oberman, one marriage that had lasted two years, one divorce. No offspring. Cross-reference had shown her that Noel Wright had remarried, and the second, six-year union had produced two offspring, a boy age five and a girl age three. The ex owned and operated a bar in the West Village.

She filed it all away. You never knew what might be useful, she thought.

"Lieutenant," Summerset announced through the house 'link. "Commander Whitney has just been cleared through the gates."

She'd already decided against going

down to meet him, to escort him upstairs made it more like home, less like a work space. "Send him right up. McNab! Program a pot of coffee. The commander's on site."

But she stood, deliberately flanking Peabody with McNab when Whitney strode in.

He wore command, she thought, on his wide shoulders, on his tough face, in the cold beam of his eyes.

He stopped at her board. She'd positioned it so he would see it immediately, so Renee Oberman's face, Garnet's, Keener's, the crime scene ranged together, connected.

And she saw a quick flare of heat flash through the cold.

Without asking, Eve poured him coffee, crossed over to offer it. "I appreciate your quick attention to this matter, Commander."

"Save it." He moved past her, zeroed in on Peabody. "Detective, I will review your statement on record, but at this time, I want to hear it from you."

"Yes, sir." Instinctively Peabody shifted to attention. "Commander, at approximately twenty hundred hours I entered the workout facilities in sector two."

Whitney went at her hard, hard enough to put Eve's back up, hard enough she had to shoot McNab a warning glare when she saw the temper light up his face.

Whitney questioned her ruthlessly, interrupting, demanding, forcing her to backtrack, repeat, overlap.

Though she paled, and Eve clearly heard the nerves skittering under the words, she never faltered, never changed a single detail.

"You were not able to make a visual identification of either individual?"

"I was not, sir. While I clearly heard the male subject refer to the female as Renee, and as Oberman, and heard her call him Garnet, I was unable to see either clearly. The female subject referred to as Renee Oberman was clear in her conversation that the male subject was her subordinate. I was able at one point to see a portion of her profile, hair color, skin color. I was able to determine her approximate height. With this information we have identified the individuals as Oberman, Lieutenant Renee, and Garnet, Detective William, of the Illegals Department out of Central."

"You are aware that Lieutenant Oberman is a decorated and ranked officer with a service of nearly eighteen years in the department."

"Yes, sir."

"You are further aware that she is the daughter of former Commander Marcus Oberman."

"I am, sir."

"And you are willing to swear to these statements in an internal investigation of these officers, possibly in a criminal trial?"

"Yes, sir. I am willing and eager to do so."

"Eager, Detective?"

"Eager to do my duty as a member of the NYPSD, as an officer who has sworn to protect and serve. I believe—correction, sir—I *know* these individuals have used their position and authority, have used their badges unethically, immorally, and illegally, and I am eager, Commander, to do whatever I can to stop them from continuing to do so."

He said nothing more for a moment, then—very quietly—sighed. "Sit down, Detective. Leave her be," he ordered McNab when the e-man started to go to her. "She doesn't need you hovering and clucking like a mother hen. She's a cop, and she's sure as hell proved it.

"Lieutenant."

Now Eve stood at attention. "Sir."

"You waited nearly eight hours to report this matter to command."

She'd expected this, had her response ready. "Six, sir, as it took time to acquire Detective Peabody's full and detailed statement, and to determine that the individuals she overheard were, in fact, NYPSD officers. At which time it was my judgment that this matter was best served by attempting to corroborate that statement and those details by locating Keener, and gathering all information possible to present to you."

She paused a moment, not a hesitation, but a beat to punch a point. "My detective had informed me of a possible homicide. I felt it imperative that I verify."

"That could work," Whitney murmured.

Would, she corrected in her head. She'd damn well make it work.

"All actions are on record, sir, for your review. I further determined after the body of Rickie Keener was located, both the scene and the body monitored, to wait approximately oh three hours before so informing you rather than contacting you with this information at three hundred hours. This is a delicate and disturbing process, Commander. I didn't feel it could be, or should be, rushed."

He nodded, then he, too, sat. "At ease, Dallas, for Christ's sake." He kneaded his brow, then dropped his hands. "Marcus Oberman is one of the finest cops I've ever served with. This *process*, as you call it, will smear his record, his reputation, and his name. And very likely break his heart."

And here, she thought, *may be the stickiest of the sticking points.* "I regret that, sir. We will all regret that. However, the daughter isn't the father." Her entire life, in many ways, had grown on that single fact.

"I'm aware of that, Lieutenant. I'm aware of that as Renee Oberman has served under me for several years. She is not the cop her father was, but few are. Her record has, so far, been excellent, and her work perfectly acceptable. Her strengths include a forceful personality, an ability to select the right person for the right job, and she's adept in accessing the details of a situation and streamlining them into a logical pattern. She is, I feel, better suited for administrative and supervisory duties than the street, and—in fact—prefers those duties. She runs her squad with a firm hand and gets results."

"A lieutenant running a squad should do work that's more than perfectly acceptable. In my opinion, sir."

He nearly smiled. "You would home in. In a department the size and scope of the NYPSD, it's often necessary to—accept the acceptable. There have been no signs, no forewarnings, no leading indicators of this corruption. Lieutenant Oberman is ambitious and has structured her career, has situated herself on a path to a captaincy. I have no doubt she has her eye on my seat, and very likely has a time line for when she'd drop her ass into it."

"She's going to be disappointed."

He did smile now, huffing out a half laugh. "Even prior to this, I'd have done whatever I could to keep her out of the commander's chair. She doesn't have the temperament for it. For the politics, for the grips and grins, for the paperwork and public relations, yes. She'd do well. But she lacks compassion, and she sees her men as tools, and the job as a means to an end."

He doesn't like her, Eve realized, and wondered if that made his part of the situation easier or more difficult.

"All that said," he continued, "we have an explosive situation, with the fuse already lit." He glanced over as Roarke stepped into the room.

"Jack," Roarke said with a nod.

"At this time only the five people in this room are aware of this situation. Correct?"

"Yes, sir," Eve agreed. "At this time."

"Show me the body. More detail."

"Monitor on-screen," Eve ordered, and the image flashed.

Whitney sat back, studied. "You chose not to establish TOD or secure any evidence."

"ID only, Commander. My thoughts were—"

"I know what your thoughts were," he interrupted. "Run the record, start to finish, on this location."

Eve followed orders, her face impassive as it played on-screen. Her recorder caught part of the scuffle between Roarke and the street thug.

"Prime move!" McNab's enthusiasm got the better of him. "Sorry, sir."

"No need. It was a prime move." Whitney nodded at Roarke. "Did you break that elbow?"

"Dislocated, I think."

"Sometimes I miss the streets." The record moved inside, into the filth. "Sometimes I don't."

He lapsed into silence, watching the rest. When it was done, the silence remained for several moments. "I'll review the rest, but assuming it's as you've already related to me, what's your next move? You have a next move, Dallas," he added. "You've had enough time to calculate several next moves."

"My first priority would be to officially discover the body and take the investigation. Through a tip from one of my CIs, or we'll run it so the record she sees plays that out. I believe that's less complicated and could be more useful than standard channels. She won't know who contacted me, and I'll have no obligation to inform her. In fact, it would be standard for me to protect my own weasel. She believes Keener's death will be seen and treated as an accidental OD. It won't be. I'll hardline it, give her something to worry about.

Or just be pissed off about. I'll be in her face, and by doing so will have the opportunity to observe her, her squad."

"How many of them are in this?" Whitney nodded. "It's not just Garnet."

"No, sir, that would be unlikely. Concurrent to that would be the Internal Affairs investigation. With your permission, sir, I would inform and fully brief Lieutenant Webster. I've worked with him before, and he knows Peabody. That connection would save time and should streamline the process."

"And you believe you can convince him you and your team need to play an active role, not just in the homicide but in the internal investigation?"

"There wouldn't be an internal investigation without Peabody, and it's very likely Keener's death would have been put down as an OD."

"You don't have to convince me. I'll also speak to Lieutenant Webster."

"I also need to inform and brief Doctor Mira. Her insights, opinions, and evaluations would be essential."

"Yes, agreed."

"And I need Feeney. I need EDD."

"IAB has its own e-men."

"We need ours. McNab is already in this, and his captain should be apprised. Every meet I have with Renee Oberman should, when possible, be on record. IAB will shadow her, sir, but if she's got any instincts it won't take long for her to smell rats. She hasn't gotten this far without good instincts, without taking precautions."

"Feeney and Mira. Your part of this investigation will have to be run, for the most part, from this location. We don't know how far her tentacles reach through the department. Through my house." Whitney looked at Roarke again. "Yours just became primary HQ."

"Apparently."

"You're a tolerant man."

"Not altogether. I have had, you could say, some experience with cops such as Lieutenant Oberman. If using my house helps remove her from yours, my door's open."

Whitney nodded, got to his feet. His gaze swept over everyone in the room. "Let's take the bitch down."

When the briefing concluded, Eve turned to Roarke. "I need that weasel tip, and it needs to look legit in case Renee manages to get her hands on the log."

"I can do that, but I need just one moment of your time first." He stepped back into his office.

"I'm really on the clock here," she began.

"Understood, and you'll have your tip come in—transferred to your 'link from your office unit—asap. I wanted to tell you I've just spoken with Darcia—Chief Angelo, Olympus."

"Okay."

"She's on planet, on holiday. We had a meeting scheduled for next week before her return, but she's come to New York early. She'd like to see Cop Central, and you."

"I'm a little pressed right now."

"And I could hardly tell her you're busy launching an investigation on a ring of dirty cops, could I?"

Eve shoved her hands in her pockets. "No. Guess not."

"Her main plan is to have a longer holiday in New York. I'll meet with her, take her to lunch or for drinks. But it's natural for her to want a look at your house, and to reconnect with you. You did work together, and well enough, during our little interlude on Olympus."

"Yeah, yeah. Okay." She considered, weighed, then nodded. "Maybe I can use it to my advantage. Once this rolls nobody who's sniffing is going to think I'd be spending time giving tours and having a girl-cop chat if I were tied into an internal investigation."

"I imagine, when it's all said and done, she'll be pleased to have been useful. I'll take care of the tip. Five minutes."

"Good enough." She walked back into her office. "We'll have the tip in five," she told Peabody. "I'll tag you on your 'link, tell you I'm swinging by to pick you up at your place to follow up on the tip. Could be nothing, so we won't inform Dispatch as yet. McNab, you need to get yourself to Central by your usual means. By the time you do, Whitney will have briefed Feeney. I want filters on all our electronics. Something that will not only show if anyone attempts a hack, but prevent one."

"We can do that," McNab assured her. "I'd go to the bank that Roarke already has filters and shields on everything in here. A couple minutes in Roarke's comp lab, and I can fix your pocket 'link, and Peabody's."

"We'll get to that after the tip. Speaking of which," she said when hers signaled. "He's fast, you have to give it to him." She held up a finger for silence. "Dallas."

"Don't use my name! Got me?" The voice was garbled, panty, and would never be mistaken for Roarke's.

"I got you."

"Somebody did him. Old Juicy. Did him bad, man, left him swimming in puke."

"Who's Juicy?"

"Juicy'd never pop heavy, man. They did him. The ones he was scared of. Fucker's dead."

"You're stoned, you asshole. Don't waste my time."

"Got stoned for Juicy. You gotta get him, Dallas, see? It ain't right. Stuffed him in the fucking tub. I ain't just doing weasel for you, Dallas. It's for Juicy."

The record would show her scowl, replay the warning in her voice. "Give me where, but if I don't find a body, I'm hunting you down and kicking your ass."

"You find him." The voice mumbled out

an address. "Poor old Juicy. You get me my twenty, right? I get my twenty."

"If I find a body, you get your twenty. If I don't, better find a hole." She clicked off, then walked to the door connecting her office with Roarke's. "How did you do that?"

"Oh, just a little voice-exchange program I've been working on. I used a blend of two actors in a couple of drug vids." He grinned, showing her he'd enjoyed himself. "Interesting, isn't it?"

"Hmm. You're up, Peabody," Eve said, and moved to step two.

"It seems kind of silly when I'm standing right here."

"By the numbers."

After the brief exchange Eve tossed her 'link to McNab. "Do your geek thing, then get down to Central—business as usual."

"I can give you a lift partway, Ian," Roarke said from the doorway.

"Iced. Give me a shake first."

"I'll go with you," Peabody told him, "get the 'links when you've done your magic. Meet you downstairs, Dallas. Thanks for everything, Roarke. Totally everything."

"Don't take him all the way," Eve began

when Peabody followed McNab out of the room.

"It's not my first time being sneaky." Roarke stepped to her to trace a finger down the dent in her chin. "I could beat you in a sneaky face-off."

"Probably."

"His respect for his predecessor weighs on your commander."

"Yeah, I got that. But he doesn't like the daughter. Didn't even before this. Sometimes that apple and the tree thing? Sometimes it does. Fall far."

Understanding she thought of herself and perhaps him as well, as much as Renee Oberman, he cupped her face, touched his lips to hers. "Sometimes the apple makes the deliberate choice to fall as far as possible. For good or ill, Eve."

"And sometimes it was rotten before it fell. And that's enough about fruit. I have to go find a dead junkie."

"Happily, this time I don't." He kissed her again. "Mind the live ones."

"Maybe I'll try your prime move." And she walked out sort of hoping she could.

Once they were in her vehicle Eve ran it

through again with Peabody. "We're going by the book. Sealed up, record on. Following a tip. We'll clear the first level before we move up. We don't know the vic by anything but Juicy until we ID him. Keep your recorder off me when I remove the eyes Roarke put over the bathroom doorway."

"Got it."

"We work the body and the scene exactly as we'd work any body and scene, and that's why we're going to give some weight to homicide. Regardless, it's a suspicious, unattended death, and in my department we don't brush that off because the vic is a loser chemi-head with a sheet."

"Damn straight. I was nervous with the commander."

"He came at you hard because IAB's going to come hard, and when we take her down, the defense is going to come hard."

"I got that, too." Peabody fiddled with her rainbow sunshades but didn't put them on. "And I got that there's going to be other cops who look at me like a traitor."

"She's the traitor, Peabody."

"I know. But I have to be ready for it. So whenever it comes at me, I'm going to see myself in that shower stall, and I'm going to think, 'Fuck you.'"

"It's a good thought. Time to set up the next step." She used her pocket 'link to contact Webster.

"Well, good morning, Dallas."

While his attractive face filled the screen she heard the sounds of traffic. "Where are you?"

"Walking to work on this fine summer day. Why?"

"Got company?"

"A few million New Yorkers." He sipped from a go-cup of coffee, but she saw his eyes change. Flatten. "No company."

"I need a meet. Remember where we met during a little federal matter?"

"I remember."

"There. In two hours. You'll need to take this as personal time."

"I've got a boss, Dallas."

"So does he, and so does his boss. This comes from the big chair, Webster. If you don't want it, I'll tag another rat."

"Funny. Two hours." He clicked off.

"Tag Crack," Eve ordered Peabody. "Tell him I need him to have his place open in a couple hours."

"You want me to tag a giant sex club owner at this hour of the morning, knowing I'll be waking him up?"

"Find your spine, Peabody," Eve suggested.

The neighborhood looked worse in the daylight, Eve decided, when every stain, every smear showed in sharp relief. A sad little convenience store sagged near the corner, papered with warnings.

NO CASH ON PREMISES!

MONITORED BY ON GUARD!

DROID OPERATORS ONLY!

A handful of people moved along the sidewalk, heads down, going about their business while it was too early for most thugs and toughs and troublemakers to hassle them.

"It's a hard life here," Peabody commented. "A couple blocks away, it's different, but here it's hard and mean. If you're born here, how do you get out?"

Eve thought of Roarke, a child, navigating the violent Dublin alleyways where hard and mean would have been a holiday. "Hook or crook," she murmured.

After parking, engaging all alarms and her On Duty light, Eve got her field kit out of the trunk. "Curtain up. Record on. Let's seal up." She tossed Peabody the can of Seal-It. "In case this turns out to be something other than a waste of time."

Peabody obeyed, tossed the can back. "We could've had some uniforms check it out."

"My tip. No point in wasting the resources until we take a look." She pulled out her master as they approached the building. "It doesn't look like anyone's lived in this place during this century, but see here—that's a new lock. Nobody's bothered to bust it yet."

"Looks like that's it for security. No cams, no pads."

"If it had them, they're long gone. Dallas, Lieutenant Eve, and Peabody, Detective Delia, bypassing lock, entering premises to validate or refute report of a body by a confidential informant."

She bypassed, drew her weapon. Then eased the door open. "Now, that's a lovely stench. If this is the flight of the wild goose, that weasel's going to get a serious scolding. Weapon and light, Peabody. Let's start clearing."

As she had hours before with Roarke, she swept the first level.

"This was probably a nice place once," Peabody commented. "You can see some of the original flooring and plasterwork."

"Sure. It's a real fixer-upper. Level one clear," she said for the record. "Crap, these steps better hold. If you fall through, I'm not hauling you out."

"I believe that's a comment on my weight. I may file an official complaint."

Eve snorted out a laugh. "You do that. God, the smell just gets better. It's like a shit pile bouquet perfumed with . . . crap."

"Shit is crap."

"For Christ's sake, Peabody, you've worked Homicide long enough you should be able to smell a DB even through this. Weasel said in the tub. Clear as you go," she ordered, and sweeping areas made her way back to the ruined bathroom. "This must be Juicy."

"I guess you owe the weasel an apology."

"He'll get his twenty." Eve approached the tub. "Swimming in puke. An exaggeration, but close enough. Let's ID him, call it in."

"Dallas, it's bad in here. If we don't want to spend an hour in the sanitizer, we should put on protective gear."

"Got a point." Eve stepped back, and as Peabody bent to remove the cover-ups from the kit, reached up and behind her for the cam Roarke had positioned. She slid it into her pocket, disengaged, then took out her communicator.

"Dallas, Lieutenant Eve."

Dispatch, Dallas acknowledged.

She reported the body, the location, the situation, requested uniforms to assist. Done, she unsealed the protective wrap Peabody offered her.

As before, Eve used her pad for ID. "Victim is identified as Keener, Rickie, age twenty-seven. Mixed race male, five feet and nine inches, one hundred and thirty pounds. Brown and brown. Vic is curled in a broken bathtub, empty needle syringe is in the tub with him. Other illegals paraphernalia also in evidence."

"TOD's coming in at oh four hundred yesterday, Dallas. It's reading approximate due to time lag and ambient conditions."

"ME to confirm TOD."

Peabody said what she believed she'd have said if they'd come across the body by a tip. "It looks like an OD. You can see his track marks. He went old school, but it's not his first trip to Neverland."

"Why the tub? There was a mattress in the next room, what could loosely be called a bed. He's got bruising, a scraped elbow."

"He could've gotten those seizing, banging against the tub. I think it's cast iron."

"Yeah. He's got a sheet, and wasn't a stranger to illegals. Maybe he screwed up his pop, or maybe he got something hotter than he knew." She shook her head. "He's got an address on record, and this isn't it. So why here?"

"Maybe he came to shoot with somebody, OD'd, and the somebody put him in here and went rabbit."

"Those are questions and possibilities. Well, Juicy's ours now. So we'll have to get the answers. ME will determine COD, but for now this is a suspicious death, and our case. Let's get to work."

6 She caught the Grimaces when she sent the uniforms out to canvass and knock on doors. It wasn't the type of neighborhood where cops were greeted with an offer of coffee, or even a pretense of respect. Nor was it likely anyone would admit to seeing anything or anyone even if they'd been a magical fly on the wall of the crime scene.

But it had to be done.

When the sweepers arrived, she hunted up the head CSI. "I'm going to want a full-level sweep, all three levels."

Eve got the beady eye. "Is this a joke?"

"No. And I tagged the lock on the front door. I need make, model, and an analysis of when it was installed."

"Petrie put you up to this, didn't he? He's got a sick sense of humor."

"Do you have a problem being thorough, Kurtz?"

Behind her goggles, the woman rolled her eyes. "Next thing you'll tell me is that isn't some dead chemi-head but the Prince of Monaco or some shit."

"No, I'm pretty sure he's some dead chemi-head. He's also my dead guy, and I need what I need."

"You'll get what you need, but it'd be better all around to just burn everything in here. Purify."

"Don't light the match until after the sweep."

That, at least, got a smile out of Kurtz before Eve left the scene to the sweepers and the body to the morgue team.

On her way out she sent a text to Morris, the chief medical examiner, requesting he take the body himself.

"There's going to be some muttering about going top level on this," Peabody

commented once they were outside, re-
corders off.

"Just what I had in mind."

She got behind the wheel and headed off
to a sex club to rat out Renee Oberman.

When she walked into the Down and
Dirty, Crack stood huge behind the bar.
His shaved head gleamed like polished
onyx, and his chest, his muscled arms,
bared but for a sleeveless vest, rippled with
tattoos.

He shot her a steely stare. "You screwed
my beauty sleep, white girl."

"Black man, just how much prettier do
you want to be?"

"Smart answer." He inclined his head
toward a corner table. "Got a rat in the
house."

"Yeah." She'd already spotted Webster.
"I've got reasons. I owe you one, Crack. I'll
owe you two if you keep the place shut
until I'm done."

"This time of day that ain't no thing. Figure one and a half. Want coffee?"

Experience told her the coffee here was
as lethal as the booze. "Maybe water?"

He snorted, but pulled two bottles from

under the bar, then after a moment's hesitation added a third. "Rats get thirsty, too."

"Appreciate it." Eve passed a bottle to Peabody, carried the other two across the room to Webster.

"Too early for entertainment," he commented.

She glanced toward the stage. In a couple hours a holoband would set the rhythm for the strippers on early shift, and the scatter of customers would insult their deteriorating stomach linings with hard drinks and cheap brew.

By midnight, the place would be ass-to-ass and elbow-to-elbow under swirling lights. Upstairs in the privacy rooms people—many who'd just met—would be humping away at each other like crazed rabbits.

"I could ask Crack to put on a couple virtual strippers, but I think what we've got for you is entertaining enough."

"It better be. How's it going, Peabody?"

"I guess we're going to find out."

"We're here with the commander's full knowledge and authorization, and with his directive that, at this time, the information we're about to give you isn't reported to anyone else."

"We're not lone wolves in IAB, Dallas."

She figured he had a recorder running. And also figured if he didn't agree to terms, she'd give him nothing to record.

"Yeah, I get that Bureau is short for bureaucracy, but that's the directive."

"My captain—"

"Is not to be apprised at this time."

He sat back, a good-looking man with cop's eyes even, Eve thought, if he'd traded the streets for internal sniffing. He'd thought he'd loved her once, which had been an embarrassing and . . . fraught situation.

But at the moment he studied her with cold impatience.

"Even the commander can't dictate IAB procedure."

"You don't want to play, Webster, I'll find somebody who does. There are reasons," she added, leaning forward. "And if you'd yank the red tape out of your ass, agree, and listen, you'd understand the directive."

"Try this. I'll agree, and I'll listen. Then I'll make the determination as to whether that directive holds."

She sat back.

"Dallas, maybe we should just wait until—"

Eve cut Peabody off with a shake of the head. Sometimes, she decided, you had to trust.

Besides, if push met shove, she'd get the recorder off him.

"I'm going to sum it up for you. I have a copy of the record of my partner's statement, and will have copies of all data pertinent to the homicide which relates. You'll get those records, Webster, when and if you give your word to adhere to Whitney's directive. To begin," she said, and laid it out.

She took him through it dispassionately, watching his reactions. He played a decent hand of poker, she remembered, but she recognized his shock, the calculation.

His gaze tracked to Peabody and back again, but he didn't interrupt.

"That's the nutshell," Eve concluded. "Your ball, Webster."

"Renee Oberman. Saint Oberman's baby girl."

"That's the one."

He took a long pull from the bottle of water. "Rough go for you, Detective," he said to Peabody.

"It was a moment."

"You've gone on record with these assertions?"

"I've gone on record with these facts."

"And it was your choice to, after this incident, inform your cohab, then your partner—and her civilian husband, then after considerable time passed, your commander. All of that prior to relating this information to Internal Affairs."

Eve opened her mouth, shut it again. Peabody would have to handle more than some deliberate baiting.

"It was my choice to get the hell out of the situation as quickly as possible without detection. I believed, and continue to believe, if I'd been detected I wouldn't have been in a position to inform anyone because I'd be dead. My cohab is also a cop, and I strongly believed I was in need of assistance. My partner is also my direct superior who I trust implicitly, and whose instincts and experience I rely on. Her husband is also a frequent expert consultant for the department."

She took a breath. "It was our decision to determine if the Keener referred to by Oberman and Garnet existed, and if so, if he was alive or dead. He's dead, and as Lieutenant Oberman asserted in the conversation I heard, his death was set up to appear as an OD. I went up the chain of command, Lieutenant Webster, and with that chain gathered and confirmed facts that are now reported to a representative of Internal Affairs. You can criticize my decisions, but I handled it as I deemed best. And would do exactly the same again."

"Okay then." He rubbed the back of his neck. "Renee Oberman, for Christ's sake. What are the odds of you proving Keener was murdered?"

"We will prove it," Eve told him, "because he was, in fact, murdered."

"I've always admired your confidence, Dallas. She's got, what, a ten-man squad?"

"Twelve."

"If she ordered this hit, as per Peabody's statement, it could be any of them, save Garnet."

"'Their boy,'" Eve reminded him. "Two of the squad are female. Which leaves nine. She also has a rotation of uniforms at her disposal, which adds. It's also possible, even likely, she's recruited beyond her own squad. We'll handle the homicide, Webster, but I can only access basic data on her, on her squad, or anyone else who might catch my attention without sending up a flag. I'm going to draw her off with Keener, focus her attention and concern on me, but I don't want her getting antsy, not right off the jump, thinking that I'm looking at her, specifically, or any of her people for it."

"We've got ways of digging without flags, but that's dicey without a nod from my captain."

"You'll have to work around that—and you can't use your own e-men," she added. "You'll have to work with Feeney and Mc-Nab."

"And you figure everybody will assume I'm hanging around EDD for the coffee and donuts?"

"There're more fizzies and PowerBars up there. My place is primary HQ on this. We have a comp lab as well-equipped as EDD's, and my home office is sufficient for our purposes."

"Yeah, I remember your home office."

She met his look equably. "Then you won't have any problem finding it."

"This process would move more efficiently with the full resources of IAB."

"You're so sure everyone in or associated with IAB is clean, Webster? Have you ever gone sniffing around Renee before—and because I'm betting from your reaction the answer's no, can you guarantee she doesn't have somebody inside looking out for her interests?"

"Nothing's guaranteed, but I know the people I've worked closely with, and that goes without a shadow for my captain."

"I don't know them. If you share the recording you've made of this conversation, and it gets back to Renee or Garnet, you've put Peabody's ass on the line."

She waited a beat, and now her voice was coolly matter-of-fact. "I'll break your arm if you try to walk out of here with the recorder you've got on you unless I have your word on this. If you take that broken arm to your captain or anyone else and repeat this conversation, if you do anything to jeopardize my detective, my partner, I'll bury you. You know I mean it."

His gaze locked on hers; he took another pull of water. "Yeah, Dallas, I know you mean it. And I mean this. I don't put a good cop's ass on the line."

"Then give me your word. I'll take it and we move from here. Otherwise I tag Whitney right now. He may not have the authority to directly interfere with IAB procedure, but he can sure as hell transfer you to fucking Traffic Control in fucking Queens."

He set the water down, leaned forward into her space. "Don't threaten me, Dallas."

She mirrored his move. "Too late."

He shoved away from the table, strode to the bar where Crack sat working silently in a notebook. In a moment Webster came back with a mug of coffee Eve knew would kick and burn like hot battery acid.

"You've got my word, not because you worry me, but because, I repeat, I'm no more willing to put a good cop's ass on the line than you are."

"Said ass appreciates it," Peabody muttered.

Webster drank some coffee, hissed, and swore. "Christ, this is bad. I need copies of every byte of data you've got, will get, hope to get."

"You'll have it."

"Every briefing's on record for IAB files."

"No. I can't agree to that, Webster," she said before he could argue. "All results, all operational and investigative plans will be written up and recorded, but I'm not having my people have to censor every word or risk a poke from IAB. My contacts and conversations with Renee Oberman, William Garnet, and anybody else I believe is potentially connected will be recorded and copied to you for IAB. I'll be wired, as will Peabody."

"You're going to get in her face with Keener."

"I'm going to crawl up her ass with Keener."

"How?"

Okay, Eve thought, she had him now. Invested, he'd not only assist, but he'd keep her team covered from any internal backlash.

"I've deduced he was her weasel by reading his file—which happens to be true. Plus, my mythical weasel knew him. I know how to handle that end."

"And I know how to handle mine. I have to tell my captain something. So . . . I've got a possible line on something major, but need some time to suss it out further before involving the Bureau. He'll press me some, but he won't box me in if I tell him I need the room."

She argued a little for form's sake. "How much room is he going to give you after you dangle a hint of something major under his nose?"

"Enough. I won't lie to my captain, Dallas—and more—by informing him to that extent, it puts my part of the investigation on record. That's going to matter when we nail her and her merry men."

"Okay."

"Now, since this coffee didn't kill me, I'm going to get started."

"Sixteen hundred, HQ," Eve told him.

"I'll be there." He stood. "You did the right thing, Peabody. Right down the line, you did right. That's going to matter, too."

Peabody sat another moment after Webster walked out. "God, I'm glad that part's over. Dallas, would you really have broken his arm? Or tagged Whitney and tried to get Webster transferred to Queens?"

"Yeah—maybe I'd've gone for his nose and Yonkers." She shrugged. "But I'd've been a little sorry about it."

* * *

Back at Central she told Peabody to start the board and book on Keener. "I'm going up to EDD, get wired, then pay Renee a visit."

"Shouldn't I go with you?"

"We're going to initiate this as a kind of courtesy call—LT to LT, weasel handler to weasel handler. I want her to know we're giving the case our best effort, and my detective is laying the foundation before we check in with the morgue."

"Do you think she already knows we found him?"

"It's going to be interesting to find out. Get it started, Peabody, then take one of your little 'breaks' with McNab and get wired up."

All innocence, Peabody widened her eyes. "What little breaks?"

"Do you really think I don't know what goes on in my own department?"

Eve split off, took the glide up to EDD.

She ignored the noise, the eye-searing colors, the incessant movement as best she could and ducked into Feeney's blissfully normal office.

He sat at his desk, comfortably rumpled, stoop-shouldered, alternately tapping his fingers on a screen, and raking them through his bush of wiry ginger red hair.

His basset hound eyes tracked to hers.

"I've got to close out that noise. How the hell do you stand it?" She shut the door, and for a moment neither spoke.

His face, as comfortably rumpled as his shirt, went grim. "This is a hell of a thing."

"Yeah."

"I've crossed with Oberman's daughter plenty. Everybody needs EDD. I wouldn't have figured it."

"You're not alone."

"I took a look at her when she came out of the Academy. Had a shiny record there, so I thought about asking if she wanted Homicide, wanted me to train her."

Connections, Eve thought. You never knew where they'd come from. "Why didn't you?"

"Just didn't seem the right fit. I can't put my finger on it, even now, except you know when you know. Like I looked at somebody else who came out of the Academy with a shiny record a few years later and knew." His saggy face moved into a smile. "That was a pretty good fit."

And if he'd taken Renee, would he have still taken her? Fate, she decided, you never knew where that came from either.

"You'd be running Homicide still if you hadn't gone over to the dark side."

"I trained you to run it." He tapped a finger in the air at her. "Besides, you never did understand or appreciate the power of the geek."

"Enough to know when to use them." She sat on the edge of his desk, dipped a hand into his dish of candied almonds. "Fuck, Feeney, I just put us in bed with IAB."

"No choice, kid." He opened a drawer. "And no regrets. I've got your eyes and ears here. High grade. They won't show on a scan or a sweep. Running a network like this, she's probably hooked in for scans. You want to be careful with these. They're worth double what we make in a month, combined."

He rose, blew out a breath. And his ears pinked a little. "You gotta strip off the jacket and shirt."

"Yeah, yeah." They avoided looking at each other as she did.

"That one, too."

"Jesus, Feeney, I'm naked under here. It's a support tank."

His color spread from his ears to his cheeks; his gaze stayed pinned over her shoulder. "I don't want to see your tits any more than you want to flash them, but this has to go against skin. So you should've thought of that and worn one of those other things."

"Man." Mortified, she stripped to the skin, shoved the diamond she wore behind her back.

"You got some tan."

"Jesus, Feeney."

"I'm just saying 'cause I'll need to adjust the tone, blend it in. I can make it damn near invisible even when you're naked. Stop fidgeting. Talk about the murder."

She put herself back in the filthy bathroom, which was somehow better than thinking about standing half naked in EDD.

"I think the killer put the new lock on the front door. Why would Keener do that? New locks just dare some asshole to break it and see what's worth locking up inside."

"Wanted him to be found."

"Yeah. Not this fast, but yeah. If some asshole found him, it's probable they'd have messed up the crime scene, riffled through Keener's junk. He had some clothes, a little cash, a toss-away 'link in the room he'd flopped in. And shoes. They always take the shoes. If it had gone that way, we'd have less to work with. I have a source, which I made up, telling me Keener wouldn't OD. I play that against his record, his experience with his recreation of choice."

"How are you going to work her?"

"I've got some ideas, but I need a face-to-face to refine them. And I need to talk to Mira. I have to make first contact now, but I want a run-through with Mira."

"Done." He immediately turned his back. "Put something on, for Christ's sake." He picked up an earbud the size of a baby pea. "When and if you need it, one of us will be able to communicate with you through this."

"How do I turn the recorder on and off?"

"I'll set you up key phrases, whatever you want."

"Ah. Cinnamon donuts. I missed breakfast," she told him. "I could go for a cinnamon donut."

He sat, keyed the phrase into a control panel. "That's on. I could go for a cinnamon donut myself."

"Who couldn't?"

"And it's reading five-by-five. Off phrase?"

"Down the block."

He keyed it in, tested it. "Those phrases, your voice print. That's a go. It'll record into this." He tapped a mini-monitor. "I'll be bringing this to Roarke's lab. We'll set up another in your office. Peabody will be keyed in the same. The kid okay?"

"Yeah. Can you have McNab hook her up? They can use one of their rendezvous closets and everybody'll just think they're groping."

"I like to pretend I don't know about the closets and the groping. Yeah, I'll tell the boy."

She nodded. "Sixteen hundred, HQ, initial full briefing."

"I'll tell the wife not to hold dinner."

She started out, hesitated. "Do you always remember? To tell her?"

"She doesn't complain if I have to work a seventy-two-hour stretch, if I crash in the crib because I'm too beat to get home.

She's a damn good cop's wife. But if I don't tell her I'm going to be late for dinner, my life isn't worth living."

"I guess that's fair. So, we'll provide the chow."

"That's fair, too," Feeney told her.

She walked out and headed for the Illegals division.

She made her strides brisk as she passed through the warren and angled off toward Renee Oberman's squad. Engaged the recorder. She scanned the squad room, noted the case board, the assignments listed, the open cases, the closed ones.

Like any squad there was noise and movement, the tap of fingers, the beep of 'links, but it was muted—more to her mind like a droid office pool than a cop shop. And unlike her division every cop at a desk wore a suit. Nobody worked in shirtsleeves, and every man wore a tie. The smell was off, too, she decided. No hint of processed sugar or burned coffee.

No personal clutter either, mixed in with the files and disks, the memo cubes—not even in the cubes where a couple of uniforms worked.

A female detective with a short crop of curls and toffee-colored skin swiveled in her chair. "Looking for somebody?"

"Your boss. Lieutenant Dallas, Homicide. I need to speak with Lieutenant Oberman."

"She's got somebody in with her. Shouldn't be long." The detective wagged a thumb at the wide window and door— both with the blinds down and closed.

"I can wait. Any problem letting her know I'm here?"

"No, ma'am."

"It's sir in my unit."

"Sir. Hold on." Rather than go to the office, the woman tapped the keys of her interoffice com—added, Eve noted, the privacy mode. "Lieutenant, pardon the interruption. There's a Lieutenant Dallas from Homicide here to see you. Yes, ma'am. One minute," she said to Dallas. "Coffee in the break room if you want it."

"I'm good, but thanks, Detective—"

"Strong."

"Quiet in here," Eve commented. "And clean."

"Lieutenant Oberman commands an orderly space." The detective added a small, humorless smile, then went back to work on her comp.

A moment later the office door opened. Eve recognized Garnet as he came out. "You can go right in," he told her. "Bix, we're rolling."

As she crossed the room, Eve noticed a big blond rise from his desk, check the knot of his tie before following Garnet out.

Then she entered the sanctum.

It was the word that came to mind. The desk was wood, deeply grained, highly polished. It held a top-flight data and communication center, an engraved nameplate, and a small white vase of pink and white flowers. A mirror in a slim frame and a painting—some moody seascape—rode the walls in a space that tripled Eve's office.

And dominating it on the wall across from the desk stood a full-length portrait of Commander Marcus Oberman standing militarily straight in dress blues.

Eve wondered how it felt to have him watch her every move—and why she'd chosen to.

Renee rose—a crisp white shirt under a fitted jacket with tiny black-and-white checks, the shining blond hair sleeked back into an intricately braided knot at the nape. Jet earrings dangled, and one of the pink and white flowers graced her lapel. When she skirted the desk to greet her, Eve noted Renee wore high black heels.

"Lieutenant Dallas, it's a pleasure to finally meet you." Renee extended a hand, her bright blue eyes smiling. "I'm sure you know your reputation proceeds you."

"Likewise, Lieutenant."

"Please, have a seat." She gestured to one of the two plush black visitor's chairs. "Can I get you some coffee, or something cold?"

"No, thanks. I wish I was here under better circumstances, Lieutenant, but I have to inform you one of your CIs is dead."

"One of mine?"

"From what I found in his file, I have to assume Rickie Keener, aka Juicy, was yours."

Eve let that hang while Renee walked back around her desk, sat. Calculating, Eve thought, but she had to figure it's smarter to admit it, acknowledge it.

"Yes, for a few years now. How did he die?"

"We're working on that. Were you aware he used a hole off Canal?"

Angling her head, Renee frowned. "No. That's his territory but not his flop. Is that where he was killed?"

"Looks that way, and it looks like he'd holed up there. Any reason you know of why he'd go to ground?"

"He was a junkie." Leaning back in her desk chair, Renee swiveled slightly, side-to-side. "A lot of CIs are when you work Il-legals. He might've had some trouble on the street, with a supplier, a customer."

"He was still dealing?"

"Small-time. Mostly zoner, and low grade at that. It's the sort of thing we have to offset against potential information with a resource. You know how it is."

"Yeah, I do. When's the last time you had contact with him?"

"Let me check my log." She turned to her comp, began to tap as she spoke. "You don't have COD?"

"He's at the morgue, and I'll be heading over there shortly."

"I'd appreciate it if you could give me your opinion, or the basic facts. He was mine, after all."

"Understood. It looked like an OD."

Renee pressed her lips together. "Something we're always prepared for around here."

"But I'm not buying it."

The tapping stopped; an eyebrow quirked. "Oh? Why?"

"Some variables. A few details I want a closer look at."

"You think he was murdered?"

"It's a strong possibility, in my opinion, at this time. You got that last contact?"

"Yes, sorry. I spoke to him via 'link on July eight from fourteen-ten to fourteen-fourteen regarding a tip on a Zeus kitchen on Avenue D. It was good data. We shut it down two weeks ago."

"Could this have been a possible reprisal for passing the tip?"

As if considering, Renee sat back, swiveled in the chair again. "I had some concerns in the last couple of months that he was using heavier, and when he went up too far, he lost his filter. He'd brag. If it turns out it wasn't an OD, he might have said the wrong thing to the wrong person."

"You didn't pay him off? On the tip?"

"He hadn't contacted me for payment

yet. Which, yes, wasn't usual. He'd normally be hot for payment. I can't say I gave it much thought. We're always busy here, and paying him wasn't high on my to-do list until he made contact."

"You said he mostly dealt zoner. What did he tend to use?"

"Whatever came to hand. He liked the needle." Renee's brow creased, her fingers tapped on her desk. "If he'd gone to ground, he was either working something or he'd gotten his hands on something prime and didn't want anybody trying for a share until he'd had enough. How did you find him?"

"I've got weasels of my own. One of them knew him, and the information I was given indicates Keener didn't do that last pop on his own. I could use any information you can give me on him."

"Of course. But you understand I'd like to hold off on giving you his CI file until the ME determines COD. I don't want to compromise confidentiality or any ongoing investigations if it turns out it was an OD."

"It wasn't," Eve said flatly. "If you'd prepare the data, I'll expect it once I get COD."

The blue eyes frosted at Eve's no-bullshit tone. "You're very confident of your informant."

"I'm confident of my gut, and my gut says Keener crossed somebody who didn't like being crossed." Eve pushed to her feet. "I'll find them. Thanks for your time, Lieutenant. I'll be in touch."

She strode out. The hard smile didn't spread until she was out of Illegals and on the way back to her own turf.

Start scrambling, bitch, she thought, because I've got your number now.

7 Eve went straight down to Mira's office. Time, she thought, to get to the meat of the pathology. Understanding the enemy could be, in Eve's opinion, as deadly a weapon as a fully charged blaster.

She paused in the outer office to steel herself for the expected confrontation with Mira's dragon of an admin.

"I need to see her."

"Yes. One moment." The woman tapped the headset tucked over her ear. "Lieutenant Dallas is here. Yes ... Absolutely." She tapped it again. "She's ready for you."

"You're telling me I can go right in?"

The admin tipped her head, making Eve wonder how she managed to move it at all under the impressive helmet of hair. "That's correct."

"Seriously?"

"Lieutenant, Doctor Mira is waiting for you. Her time is valuable, and you're wasting it questioning me."

"Okay, that's more in line." Satisfied, Eve gave the door a brief rap, and walked in.

Mira wore one of her pretty summer suits, this one cool as a pitcher of lemonade. She'd swept her hair back in a clip of deep blue—matching the strappy heels that showed off toes painted dusky gold. She stood at the AutoChef, her back to Eve—programming, Eve had no doubt, cups of the herbal tea she favored.

When she turned, Eve saw she'd let some trails of her deep brown hair curl around her face. And there was tension in the curve of her jaw, the set of her lips.

"Have a seat," she invited. "I've been expecting you."

Saying nothing—letting her take the lead—Eve lowered into one of Mira's blue scoop chairs. She took the tea she didn't actually like and waited.

"The commander briefed me on the situation, and I've reviewed the files on Lieutenant Oberman and Detective Garnet." Balancing her delicate cup and saucer, Mira sat, crossed her legs.

"Okay."

"It's not possible to have this discussion with you without saying that I know and respect Marcus Oberman."

"Join the crowd."

Mira sighed, sipped. "It's difficult. This is difficult. I feel that respect, and a preconception that stemmed from it, might have influenced me in regard to Renee Oberman's screening. I'm asking myself, Eve, if she'd been someone else would I have pressed harder, would I have looked deeper, would my evaluation have taken a different tone."

"What's your answer?"

"I'm afraid, in hindsight, it's yes." Mira's soft blue eyes met Eve's. "And that's very difficult. If I hadn't been influenced by who she was, whose daughter she was, she might not have been cleared for command.

She might not now be in the position of power and authority she holds."

Eve frowned, nodded. "So we can blame you—and the commander, the review board, all her immediate supervisors along the way for boosting her up the ranks."

Mira smiled a little. "I'm aware I'm not responsible—solely responsible—for her position in the department. But thank you for that."

"She's good. She's closed a healthy number of cases and now runs a squad that does the same. She's got no bumps, that show anyway. Which tells me something right off because if you're a cop for going on eighteen years and don't have a single bump, you're not doing the job. You're manipulating the job, your record, sliding around the tough stuff, holding back. Or greasing the right palms.

"But on paper," Eve concluded, "she's good."

"I agree. It could be said she uses intellect, intimidation, and cajolery—whichever the situation calls for—as her primary tools. And those are valuable tools in police work. She's never wounded or terminated a

suspect or any individual on the job. Therefore, she's never been through Testing,
required of any officer who terminates."

"But's she's been screened, and she's
gone through the required psych evals."

"Yes. I conducted her initial screening
and have done several of her annual evals.
In the past several years, her evaluations
have been conducted by Doctor Addams."

"Why?"

"Practically speaking, the size of the department requires the use of multiple psy-
chiatrists, psychologists, profilers, and so
on. At the time, I thought nothing of it. In
fact, didn't notice. I see a great many officers and techs and department personnel,
for a variety of reasons."

"I get that. I'm asking why she opted to
trade in the best, the head of the line, for
somebody down the ladder."

Mira took a moment to drink and, Eve
thought, to consider her answer. "I can
speculate she didn't like my analyses, my
questions, my style. I can further speculate she preferred a man."

"Because she believes she can more
easily manipulate or influence or deceive
males."

"Yes. She sees her sexuality as a tool. Again, it can be one, a useful one. Women are a threat, competitors. She prefers the company of men."

"No crime."

"No. No crime," Mira repeated, "but perhaps a signal I should have heeded more closely. As she's implicated in corruption, illegal activities, and a homicide, I can give you opinions, a profile, a broad analysis. I can't, however, give you specific details gleaned from sessions."

Eve set the tea aside, tapped her fingers on her knee. "Let me try this. Hypothetically, a child—particularly an only child—whose father is revered in his profession. Demanding, time-consuming profession. He's, in a very real sense, the gold standard in his field. That child might feel compelled to follow in his footsteps."

"Yes." Relaxing a little, Mira leaned back in her chair. "Love for and pride in the parent, a lifetime of exposure to excellence and dedication. The need to feel love and pride reflected from the parent."

"Alternately, some might feel compelled to do exactly the opposite. Say the parent was a hugely successful businessman.

One who acquired wealth and position through hard, honest work, long hours, skill, and dedication. The kid might decide to sit around on his lazy ass, or join a Free-Agers commune and grow tomatoes."

Mira smiled again. "Yes. Pressure to succeed, the child's urge to rebel against parental expectation and authority, a desire to forge one's own path."

"And another choice might be to go down that same path, but without the same skills, the same purity of purpose, say, the same innate dedication, or whatever it takes, the child might take some shortcuts. Still wants the pride, the glory, the status, but can't get it Daddy's way. Or just doesn't especially want to. Saints can be hard to live up to. Gold standards tough to reach. That's a pisser. But there are ways to get what you want, ways to build authority, to use that gold standard as an entree, even a shield, while smearing it."

Eve leaned forward now, punching her point. "There's some satisfaction there because the fucker shouldn't be so hard to live up to. Or shouldn't have expected, demanded so much from the child. Got a saint for a father? Why not be a sinner, reap the rewards, while using the same path, and staying shiny on the outside."

"That's an excellent thumbnail," Mira said after a moment. "There would be more, of course, under the surface, rooted in child-hood, in dynamics, in disposition. Some, in this hypothetical theory, would both revere and detest the source—the father. Some would crave the authority and position, and the power and privilege—the respect—that comes with it. Even be willing, perhaps ea-ger, to expend the time and effort to achieve it. In their own way."

"Okay." Eve set her hands on her knees. "Let's get down to it. She's dirty. Daddy's the excuse. You can think of a reason if you want," she said before Mira interrupted. "That's not how I see it. Maybe she started off sliding on his name, using her brand of manipulation, putting in the time while she figured the angles, searched out the openings. Sucking up to or sucking off whoever was more useful."

Mira choked a little on her tea. "To put it bluntly," she managed.

"Sexuality as a tool, prefers the com-pany of men. She wears a girly suit that shows off her tits, mile-high heels to show off her legs. To work."

Mira brushed lightly at the skirt of her girly suit. "Hmmm."

"You're not a cop," Eve returned. "It's highly unlikely you'll be drawn into a foot-race today. And okay, neither will she because she sticks to her desk. She's above the streets in her big, perfect office closed off from her scarily ordered squad."

"Scarily ordered?" Mira repeated.

"Everybody's in suits. Nobody's got their jacket off. Every one of the men is wearing a tie—and none of them loosened. She's shined, hair combed. Like any minute some-body's due to come in to take a squad photo.

"Everybody's desk or cube or worksta-tion is in perfect order. Nobody has any junk sitting around, or personal clutter. No photos, no toys, no empty coffee cups. No full ones either. And there's no chatter. Nobody's yelling across the room, no-body's ragging anybody. I've never seen a squad room that clean, or cops so pressed, so quiet."

She pushed to her feet. "You could put it down to the boss's style, sure. She likes order and expects her cops to be turned out in suits. Illegals cops, for God's sake, who're going to be going out at some point and pushing at chemi-heads and dealers. But their shoes are nice and shined. More."

Eve glanced at Mira.

"Yes, go on."

"She keeps the blinds down on her office. Big window, big door, with the blinds down and closed. She dresses like a CEO, one who secretly wouldn't mind getting laid during her lunch break. Her desk's clear, and there's a fresh vase of flowers on it. Flowers, for . . ."

She spied the flowers on Mira's desk.

"You're not a cop," she said again. "And your desk is tidy, but not clear. You have family photos and little bits of stuff sitting around. Your space has a feel to it. It's welcoming, comfortable. Which it has to be, sure, given you have to put people at ease. But it's also who you are.

"And I should probably think about what my office says about me, but that's not important."

"I could tell you," Mira murmured, but Eve was already moving on.

"She's got a painting on the wall, a good one. I have to admit I liked it. All moody, beach and ocean. She's got a mirror. A cop with a mirror on the wall of her office? Says vanity to me. And a big picture of her father—full dress blues, commander's rank. Formal shot."

"Where's the picture situated?"

Eve smiled, nodded. "Good question. On the wall opposite her desk."

"I see." Mira nodded. "Using his status so anyone coming into her office would feel the connection. And she can look up, see him. So he can, symbolically, see her. What's she's doing, how she does it."

"Look at me. I'm a boss, too—and before much longer I'll have captain's bars. How do you like that, Dad? Oh, excuse me a minute, I have to order one of my men to go kill a pathetic junkie who tried a double cross. Stick that one up your perfect ass, Commander."

"I don't disagree with anything you've just said." Mira balled a fist in her lap, stared down at it a moment. "I'm so angry. I'm so damn angry I didn't see what I should have in her. That I let myself be manipulated and influenced so I brushed aside the little niggles of doubts. So I told myself it was because I was holding her to a higher standard because of her father, and that was unfair and unprofessional."

"Well, I guess your ass isn't perfect."

Mira set her cup aside. "That's a very comforting thing to hear right now." On a breath, Mira drew her shoulders back. "Factoring in Peabody's statement, your impressions, my own belated analysis, I would conclude Renee Oberman is a very organized woman, one skilled in compartmentalization. She runs her squad with a firm hand and insists they meet her personal standards in appearance."

"Spit and polish. Pressed and shined."

"Yes," Mira agreed. "It's important to impress. Important, too, to be obeyed, even on the smallest detail. She is concurrently running what is purported to be a full-scale and illegal operation that utilizes at least some of her squad, at least some of their street contacts and CIs. She is, absolutely, in charge and in control of both. She accepts no less. When threatened, she doesn't hesitate to take action, up to and including conspiring to murder.

"Money, like her father's picture, is a symbol," Mira continued. "It represents power and success. No doubt she enjoys it to acquire what she likes, but I would speculate she hoards the bulk of what she's earned illicitly."

Eve's brows lifted. "Why?"

"Because the acquisition—with the method she's chosen—the having, is the success. It's the purpose."

"She was pissed about the ten K," Eve recalled. "As much as anything else. Keener and ten K, that's small-time. Yeah, the having, the money and the obedience. I get that."

"She's very intelligent, understands thoroughly the workings, the politics, the pecking order of the NYPSD. She focused on Illegals, I believe, because it's an area rife with the potential for corruption, for weaknesses, for backroom deals, all of which she can exploit. She seeks success on the job to please her father, and pursues her criminal business to punish him."

Daddy issues, Eve thought again. *Boo fucking hoo.*

"She's vain," Mira went on, "she's confident, she's highly intelligent, and she's ruthless. She views her name as her legacy and her right, as a stepping stone she doesn't hesitate to use when it suits her.

And also as a dragging weight around her neck."

"I can use all of that."

"She won't like you. Even outside this situation, she wouldn't like you. You're every-thing she's not, as well as an attractive—younger—woman in power. That makes you a threat. She's disposed to eliminate or crush those who threaten her."

"I'm hoping she'll try. Focused on me, she's less likely to get any buzz about the internal investigation. Right now, it's all about me and the homicide. She's worried about that. I think she knew we'd found Keener be-fore I told her, and was, I'd say, already dis-cussing it with Garnet. She had to think on her feet when I talked to her because she was sure it would be passed off as an OD. Quick skim, who cares, over and done. Now she's got to worry because I made it clear I smell murder, and I'm going to push it."

"She won't come at you directly, not yet," Mira said. "She'll need to weigh the situation, you, see what you do, what but-tons you push, what doors you open, if any. But make no mistake, Eve, if she con-cludes you're in the way, you're too big a threat, she'll try to take you out."

"Yeah, probably with this big, blond detective. I need to check on him." She glanced at her wrist unit. The day was moving too damn fast. "But now I've got to go to the morgue."

"Don't underestimate her, Eve."

"I don't intend to. I've got a briefing at my home office—sixteen hundred."

"Do you want me there?"

"I can take the team through Renee's profile, but you'd be valuable. We're going to have to work through her squad, so any insights you've got on any of them would help."

"I'll be there."

"Thanks." Eve went to the door, hesitated, turned. "She should be a good cop. She's got the foundation, the resources, the brains, the training. It's nobody's fault but hers how she chose to use them."

The day's moving, Eve thought again as she went quickly back to Homicide. Several things checked off, and that was good. But she wanted to squeeze in time to study the murder board Peabody should have set up in her office, time to peek into the data on the members of Renee's squad.

And maybe let it show, she considered.

Yeah, maybe send a flag or two there. Give her something to think about.

She paused at the bullpen, took a good look around.

The noise level hit somewhere between EDD and Renee's squad—which she judged as normal. Cops worked in shirtsleeves, and there were plenty of hard shoes and boots showing wear and tear. It smelled like really horrible coffee, a hint of sweat, and somebody's veggie hash. Which meant Reineke was probably on a diet again.

Desks weren't especially tidy, photos, printouts—some of them likely bad or obscene jokes—papered cubes and workstations.

Jacobson sat kicked back in his chair juggling three colored balls—his thinking mode, she knew. Someone had recently hung a rubber chicken over the new guy's desk, which meant he—Santiago—was sliding into the team and the rhythm.

To her mind it looked, sounded, smelled, and felt like cop.

She walked into her office, nodded at the murder board, hit the AutoChef for coffee.

Skinny window— she thought the cleaners occasionally wiped it down. Overloaded desk—but she'd clean up the paperwork. Ancient file cabinet because she liked the backup—plus it was an excellent hiding place. Old AutoChef that still did the job, fairly new C&D that wasn't yet giving her grief. The recycler worked, and as far as she knew was still a successful secret spot for her personal cache of candy.

She had her roster, rotation, case status on a wallboard because she liked being able to glance at it quickly rather than calling it up on the comp every time she had to change or check or adjust.

Deliberately horrible visitor's chair, because who had time for chatty sessions anyway? Her desk was old, scarred, and serviceable, and like Jacobson she liked to think with her boots up.

The office didn't open into the bullpen—there was a little jog first. But unless she was catching ten of downtime stretched out on the floor or needed absolute privacy, her door was always open.

She took the time to drink her coffee, to study her murder board, to consider her next steps. Before she took them she texted Roarke rather than tagging him in the middle of his workday.

Briefing HQ, 1600. Promised food. OK?

There, she thought, that covered the marriage rules, plus shifted to Roarke—she hoped—the obligation to inform Summerset he'd be feeding a bunch of cops.

"Peabody," she said as she crossed through the bullpen again, "with me."

Peabody scrambled to catch up as Eve hit the glide. "Murder book and board in your office."

"I saw. I informed Lieutenant Oberman of the death of her weasel."

"How'd she take it?"

"Always tough to lose a CI. She'll pass me all data on the vic, after we verify COD. She doesn't buy homicide." Eve shrugged carelessly for whatever eyes and ears might catch any part of the conversation. "Then again, she's a desk jockey who doesn't work murders."

"And we're the kick-ass murder cops."

"We are. We'll see what the ME has to say. We could get lucky and find the sweepers report waiting for us when we get back."

"I admire your optimism."

They talked shop in general until they

were in the garage, in the vehicle, and driving out.

"Did you get wired?" Eve asked her.

"Yeah, I'm set. What about Renee, really?"

"She's smooth, hard, cold. And she's quick. She had to decide on the spot whether to admit Keener was her weasel, then how to play me when I said I was looking at murder instead of OD. Her squad room looks like the reception area of a big-shot office, and her office is the big shot. We'll go over it all at the briefing, including Mira's analysis and eval, but the upshot is she's a stone bitch with daddy issues and a thirst for power, status, and money."

"I got the stone bitch part from the locker room."

"There was a detective Garnet took out with him right after he came out of a meet with Renee—in her big, fancy, shuttered office—which was right after she was told I was there to see her. Blond and blue, early thirties, about six four, maybe two-thirty. Garnet called him Bix. See what you can get."

"All over it. You think he's her muscle."

"Odds are. There was another, female, mixed-race, also early thirties. Detective

Strong. My vibe was she isn't a big fan of her boss."

May be able to use that, Eve thought, turn that.

"Bix," Peabody announced, "Detective Carl, age thirty-two—you got the height dead on, two pounds under on the weight. Ten years on the force, out of the Army where he served from age eighteen to age twenty-two. Born in Tokyo where his parents—both also Army—were stationed at the time. Has a sib, a brother, four years older. Assigned to Illegals under Lieutenant Oberman for the last four years. Did a year in Vice after making detective. I'd have to go deeper to get any more," Peabody told her.

"Hold off on that for now. Army brat, older brother, four years in the military. Used to taking orders from his superiors. Combat training, worked the streets if he had time in Vice and Illegals."

"Strong, Detective Lilah," Peabody continued when Eve parked at the morgue. "Age thirty-three, five-six, a hundred and twenty-two. Born Jamaica, Queens, to single mother. No father of record. Two sibs, older brother, younger sister. Brother listed as dead, 2045—age seventeen. Partial scholarship aided with education assistance to NYU. Major law enforcement. Ten years on the job, seven in Illegals. Recently transferred from out of the one-six-three to Central, and Lieutenant Oberman. Like six months ago."

"New then. Yeah, maybe an asset. How'd the brother die?"

"Ah, wait." Peabody ran it as they walked down the familiar white tunnel. "Killed during what looks like a drug deal gone wrong. Multiple stab wounds. He's got a sealed juvie."

"Dealing or buying the junk," Eve concluded. "Likely a user, and dead before he can vote. Sister turns this into a career working against what killed her brother. Yeah, if that plays out, she could be an asset."

She pushed through to Morris's suite.

He had a laser scalpel in his hand, blood on his protective cloak, and still managed to look stylish in a collarless suit of midnight blue and his hair braided in a looping queue.

"We're having a two-for-one sale," he told her. "Yours is right there." He lifted his chin toward the body with its neatly closed Y cut. "Just let me finish removing this brain, and I'll be right with you."

"No problem." Eve walked to Keener.

They'd washed him, so he actually looked better on the slab than he had in the tub. Old track marks ran lividly down both arms, circled his ankles. Comparatively, the bruising he carried was minor.

Eve put on a pair of goggles and began to search the body for any signs of stunner marks, pressure syringe. But there were other ways, lots of ways, for a man trained in combat to incapacitate a man he outweighed by more than a hundred pounds.

She sealed her hands and probed his head, his scalp, ignoring where Morris or one of his techs had stitched it back together.

"Doing my job now?"

"Sorry." Eve glanced over. "There's a knot back here, just behind his left ear."

"Yes." Morris weighed the brain, recorded it, then walked to the sink to wash. "He has several bruises, some knots, as you say. He would have seized with that much in him. His system was loaded with what they call Fuck You Up. Have you heard of that one?"

"Horse tranquilizer base, right?"

"Yes, and he had enough to take down a four-hundred-pound stallion. And just for the hell of it the Zeus lacing was barely pushed. The combination was absolutely lethal—as we all can plainly see."

"This knot. If he took a blow here, by someone who knew how and where, it would take him down, put him out."

Morris lifted his eyebrows. "It could, done properly. You prefer murder to overdose."

She wished she could lay it out for him. "I've got questions, yeah. Why the tub? You said he had enough in him to kill him a couple of times. Look at his tracks. He's a junkie, but he's a junkie with experience. Why take so much of something so risky— and even if you're an idiot, wouldn't you want to spread out the high? He's not in his flop, but locked in this hole instead, and it looks like he made himself a little camp there. And that says he's hiding. So maybe somebody found him."

"Perhaps. He'd eaten a decent enough

meal, around midnight. Pizza with sardines."

"You call that decent?"

Morris smiled. "He ate hearty, we'll say, and washed it down with a couple beers."

"There weren't any takeout pizza boxes or brew bottles on scene. Maybe he ate out. We can work that. I wonder why he'd eat hearty, then a couple hours later hole up, crawl in a filthy tub, and jab himself with what he should have known, given his history, was a lethal dose."

"So noted. I haven't as yet made my determination, so it stands that COD is the overdose—all other injuries were nonlethal. But I cannot, at this time, with this data, determine accident, suicide, or homicide."

"Just what I wanted to hear."

"I believe I'll need to do a further analysis of the wound below his left ear."

"Couldn't hurt."

"You've something up your sleeve. Quite a nice sleeve today, I might add."

"Just doing the job. We'll let you get back to your brain."

8 "Here's what we're going to do." Eve pulled out in front of a Rapid Cab, zoomed through a yellow light—and had Peabody gripping the chicken stick.

"Are we doing in a hurry?"

"What? I had plenty of room. We're going to update the book with Morris's preliminary findings, copy the commander as usual. You're going to contact Renee and inform her of those findings and tell her I need the data and files we discussed, asap."

Hand still gripping the chicken stick,

Peabody blanched. *"I'm* going to talk to her?"

"I'm much too busy and important to trouble myself with this kind of follow-up. That's how she thinks. I'm going to see if Morris has a spare spine lying around you can borrow if you're scared to speak to that high-heel-wearing, smug-ass bitch, Peabody."

"Not scared. Uneasy. I admit to uneasy." To prove to herself she had that spine already, she loosened her grip on the stick. "So I tell her the chief medical examiner has determined COD, but cannot, at this time, determine self-termination, accidental overdose, or homicide. Therefore, Lieutenant Dallas requests—"

"Requires," Eve corrected.

"Lieutenant Dallas requires the data and files on the victim, as discussed. What if she balks?"

"You courteously inform her that Commander Whitney has, per procedure, been copied on all notes and files, including your lieutenant's notification to her, the vic's handler, and the requirement for data."

Peabody mulled it. "Courteously adds a dig."

"You bet it does. If she carps after that, I'll deal with her. But she won't," Eve added. "She wants this to go away, and the potential of me going over her head and bringing this more fully to Whitney's attention spotlights her."

"Better to cooperate and keep it low-level." Peabody's fingers crawled back to the stick when Eve swerved around a slow-poking maxibus.

"That's how I'd play it in her place. Next, we get everything we need for the briefing, and spend a little time at it. If she's got feelers out, and she damn sure does, I want to be seen working this. We'll do a run by the vic's flop on the way to HQ."

"Why aren't we doing that now?"

"Want to be seen—and I want to make sure her dogs have had time to go by, go through, look for anything that might tie them in." She glanced over. "If Garnet and Bix weren't heading to Keener's flop when they left the squad room, you can bet your ass she tagged them and sent them there after my conversation with her."

"But . . . If there was anything, they'd get rid of it."

"Maybe there was—unlikely, as Bix should have hit the flop already and ditched anything that tied in. But maybe." Eve shrugged it off. "I'm more interested in following their tracks." She pulled into the garage at Central. "You should yammer like always in the bullpen about the case."

Peabody tried on a mildly offended look. "I don't yammer. I respectfully object to the term *yammer*."

"All of you yammer, that's how it's done." Eve turned into her slot. "Yammer and bitch, and with the yammering and bitching you play angles off each other. You handle this with the rest of the men just like usual. If you clam up, evade, they'll smell something off. Bunch of cops get a scent, they can't help but start digging for the source. And there's no harm in mentioning our vic was Renee Oberman's weasel. Someone might have some dish on her, an opinion, an interesting anecdote."

"So I'd actually be doing the digging. It's like spy stuff."

"It's like cop work," Eve corrected, and got out of the car.

"It's interesting about that welt behind the vic's ear." Peabody scanned the garage as they crossed to the elevator, lowered her voice. "Is it okay to talk about that?"

Eve just nodded. "It strikes me, given the location and angle of the wound, it could have come from a blow. Somebody, who knows what they're doing or gets lucky, clips him at that spot, side of the hand."

"Like a karate chop," Peabody said as they loaded on, other cops loaded off.

"And it seems a little too good to be luck. If you didn't know what you were doing, you'd use a sap, or a bat. Either would do more damage."

"There wasn't any indication the vic had been in a fight."

"Exactly." When the elevator stopped, more cops lumbered on, Eve got off. "Blow from behind—a strong and heavy one, and pretty precise. The other scrapes and bruises are minor," she added as she jumped on a glide. "Might have happened when the vic was dumped in the tub, might have happened when the vic seized during the OD. If he suffered this blow, if it knocked him out or even dazed him, it would give the killer—should there be one—time to inject the lethal dose. Vic's flying now, helpless. Dump him in the tub, set up the rest of the works. Now it looks like the vic was hallucinating, as you would in the early stages of Fuck Me Up, and decided to take a nice bath."

"Why not leave him on the mattress?"

"The tub's more humiliating, and that says the vic and killer were previously acquainted. It's a kind of flourish," Eve decided, "and flourishes are always a mistake in murder."

She got off the glide, made the turn to take the next. And spotted Webster strolling toward her. "Goddamn it," she said under her breath.

"Lieutenant, Detective. How's it going?"

"Well enough, up until now."

"Always pleasant. We're heading in the same direction." He stepped on the glide with her.

She channeled her irritation. "If the rat squad's going to chew at Homicide, I expect to be informed."

"Not Homicide, so relax." But he stepped off the glide with her.

"For Christ's sake, Webster," she said under her breath.

"Relax," he said again, in the same undertone. "I've got some business on this level, then a meet with the commander. I heard you took some time off recently."

She stopped at Vending. "It's nice IAB's got time to chat."

"As much as murder cops do. Keep it clean, Dallas." He started to back up, then his face changed as he stared down the corridor. For a moment he looked . . . reverent, Eve thought.

And he said—reverently, "Oh, yeah."

She followed his direction and spotted Darcia Angelo. She wore a summer dress, a breezy one covered with hot pink flowers that showed strong golden shoulders and a lot of smooth skin. Her mass of black hair tumbled to those golden shoulders, curling wildly around her face. Dark, sultry eyes warmed when she saw Eve, and the wide, bottom-heavy mouth curved in a smile.

Eve supposed it was the high, needle-thin heels adding to the already statuesque figure that caused the hips to sway as if to an internal rhythm.

Or maybe not.

"Dallas! It's so good to see you again. And Peabody—Detective Peabody since I saw you last. Congratulations."

"Thanks. I didn't know you were on planet, much less in the city, Chief Angelo."

"A little holiday, a little business." She turned that smile, those eyes onto Webster, who simply stood staring as if he'd just witnessed a miracle. "Hello."

"Yeah, Chief Angelo, Olympus PD; Lieutenant Webster, IAB," Eve supplied.

"Internal Affairs?" Darcia offered a hand. "Are there many?"

"Enough to keep us busy. Is this your first time in New York?"

"The first with any vacation time. I had lunch with your husband," she told Eve. "And since I was downtown, I couldn't resist coming in and seeing how things are done here. It's an impressive facility, from what I've seen."

A couple of cops perp-walked a skinny, struggling man down the corridor.

"I was just trying to get his attention!" the man protested at the top of his lungs.

"If he'da listened, I wouldn'ta had to bash him."

"And full of such interesting people," Darcia added.

"Yeah, we're loaded. My office is down this way," Eve began.

"Yo, LT!" Jacobson hailed her from the bullpen doorway. "Got a minute?"

She signaled an affirmative. "I'll show you around," she told Darcia.

"I'd love it. Go ahead and speak to your man. I'm just going to get something cold to drink. It's awfully hot out there. I'll be right along."

"Good enough. Peabody, make that tag. I want that data asap."

"Yes, sir. Nice seeing you, Chief. Enjoy New York."

"I intend to." Darcia gave her hair a little toss when Eve and Peabody walked away, then turned to study the offerings. "Hmmm."

"Buy you a drink?" Webster offered, and she smiled.

"Yes, please."

"So, Chief Angelo . . ."

"Darcia. I'm off duty."

"Darcia. I should've known the name would suit. What'll you have?"

"Surprise me."

In the bullpen Eve listened as Jacobson ran through the angles he'd come up with through juggling. She did some juggling of her own, keeping the balls of murder, Renee, Darcia Angelo, and now Jacobson's brainstorm in the air.

When she'd finished with Jacobson, she was half inclined to go out and see if Darcia had gotten lost on the short walk to Homicide.

Then Olympus's chief of police glided in.

Eve distinctly heard Baxter's—the words were reverent again— "Oh, Mama," as she passed his desk.

"Don't drool on those fives," Eve muttered, and walked over to Darcia. "Our bullpen. The way the unit's set now, the detectives work with a regular partner or a permanent aide—whom they're responsible for training—or they can snag one of the uniforms assigned to the unit. Case board, closed in red, open in green. There's an excuse for a break room in the back. I don't go there unless I have to. Occasionally somebody may take a wit back there if they want serious privacy, but it's more usual to interview right at the desk if the wit comes in, or in the lounge—a communal break room for the level. Lockers and showers through that way."

"An efficient space," Darcia commented. "And a busy one."

Eve noted Baxter easing up from his chair. She sent him a warning look that had him sighing and sitting again. "Meaning crowded and overworked, and yeah, we are. It's a good unit. My office is down here."

She made the turn, let Darcia in.

"It's separate?"

"That's the setup, and I prefer it. When the LT's space is attached, window, door through to the bullpen, it's like the boss is watching their every move. A guy can't even scratch his balls in comfort. Door's open unless I need it shut. They know where to find me."

"You prefer a small space, too, or you'd have bigger. And it suits you," Darcia decided, doing a tight circle. "Spare, lean, unsentimental." She lifted a chin to the murder board. "And you're working on something now."

"Caught it this morning. Vic's a longtime

chemi-head—and the weasel of an Illegals lieutenant. Found in a broken bathtub in an abandoned building—not his personal flop. Looks like he OD'd on a massive dose of what the street calls Fuck You Up."

"I've heard of it." She might have been dressed like a fashion plate, but Olympus's chief gave the death photos a thorough, cool-eyed study. "And since you say 'looks like,' you don't think he OD'd of his own volition."

"There are extenuatings."

She watched Darcia sip from what looked like a lemon fizzie and scan the board. "Ugly. Hard and ugly. There was so much of that when I was on the job in Colombia."

"And now?"

"Now I'm enjoying the shiny and new of Olympus." Darcia moved to Eve's window. "But this, this city. It's so layered and varied, so exciting, so full of energies, passions. I'm going to treat myself and wander, and buy myself several frivolous things."

"How far can you wander in those shoes before you cry like a baby?"

Darcia laughed, turned back. "I'm tougher

than that, and I liked putting on a pretty dress to have lunch with your very handsome, very charming husband. Maybe before I go back home, you and I could have a drink, talk shop."

"I'd like that," Eve said, realizing she actually would.

"Then we'll make it happen. I'm going to let you get back to work, and I'm going to go find something frivolous to waste my money on."

"There's this place." Eve wound the location through her head, relayed the simple directions. "Stupidly expensive handbags and shoes. Like that."

"Sounds perfect—and not at all your style."

"I broke up a catfight there when two women tumbled out onto the street at my feet. They were ready to kill each other over some purse."

"That sounds like your style—and it's going to be my first stop. I'll talk to you soon."

"Have a good time—and watch out for the hair-pullers."

With a laugh, Darcia strolled out.

Eve checked the time, then began to

gather the files, the photos, the reports she'd copied to take home. By the time she'd finished, her incoming signaled. She nodded in satisfaction at the name of the file and the brisk accompanying message.

To Lieutenant Dallas, Homicide
From Lieutenant Oberman, Illegals
Confidential data re Keener, Rickie
As requested.

I bet that hurt," Eve murmured, then copied and saved the file.

Peabody was already getting up from her desk when Eve came out. "I was just coming in to check if—"

"Got it. Let's move."

"Hey, hey, hey!" Baxter leaped up. "You've got to tell me about the amazing skirt."

"She's out of orbit, Baxter. Literally."

"I'll say—in the best of all ways. Who—"

She kept walking. "And she outranks you."

"Do you think women like that are born like that?" Peabody began. "Chief Angelo. I mean, so they pump out hot and sexy with every breath, but in a really classy way?"

"There are probably training courses."

"Sign me up."

"If you wouldn't mind putting your hot and sexy aspirations on hold, we could actually focus on our current investigation. Just for the hell of it."

"I think everybody has hot and sexy aspirations," Peabody considered, "except those that already are. But I am totally focused on our current investigation. I assume Lieutenant Oberman sent you the required data."

"She did."

"I don't think she was too happy about it." Peabody shrugged. "I guess some handlers are pretty territorial about their weasels, even when the weasel's dead."

"Maybe even more so. Did the lab ID that lock?"

"I've got the make and model. The report says it hadn't been installed more than a couple of days. It's actually an interior lockset—cheap and available in pretty much any place that deals in locks. It hadn't been picked or tampered with," Peabody continued. "I've got the full report."

"Sweepers, interior?"

"Not in yet. You asked for a second level."

"Right. How pissed was Renee?" Eve asked when they got in the vehicle.

"I'm going to say controlled fury. She didn't like getting the nudge, and my take is liked it less getting it from your subordinate. What she really didn't like was my very courteous—as directed—statement that you had copied and informed the commander."

"Good." Perfect, in fact. "She'll be stewing over that for a while."

Pleased with the idea, Eve drove through thickening traffic to the ugly slab of a building squatting between a low-rent sex club and a windowless bar.

"Not much better than the hole he died in," she decided. "And less than three blocks away. Not a bright bulb, our Juicy, even when he was breathing."

The lock on the entrance of the building was still intact. No point busting it, she thought. Who'd want to break into a place where nobody had anything anyway?

She mastered it open, started up the stairs directly across from the door.

The tags on the walls were all sex or

drug related, and the scent hanging in the overheated air reeked of both, with a sticky thread of old garbage weaving through. Someone's choice of music banged on the walls like hammers against someone else's choice of a screaming game show. On the second level a rail-thin cat hardly bigger than a rat sprawled.

"Oh, poor little kitty." Even as Peabody reached out a hand, the cat leaped to its feet, arched its back, bared its teeth with a throaty hiss.

Peabody missed having her hand raked open to the bone by inches.

"Jesus. Vicious little bastard."

"That'll teach you to be so soft-hearted and friendly."

Eve moved up to the third level, down the grimy corridor—taking her time for the benefit of anyone peering through a peep.

"Record on." She bypassed Keener's locks.

His flop was a few shaky steps up from his final resting place. But even that was a vast improvement. It stank of sweat, rolled with heat, and carried the added perfume from the mostly empty takeout cartons and boxes.

"Chinese, Thai, pizza, and what I think used to be a gyro. A regular U.N. of disgusting, undiscarded food. Juicy was a pig." She eyed the unmade daybed. "Still that looks more comfortable than the ratty mattress in his hole, so he definitely made a few sacrifices to hide out."

Single room, Eve thought, no bigger than her office. No AutoChef, no Friggie, no bathroom attached—which meant the flop and all or most of the others on the level shared one, likely at the end of the hall.

Still he had eight locks and bolts on his door, another set on the single window.

"Okay, let's toss it."

"Yuck" was Peabody's opinion.

"I bet you're not the first cop in here today with that sentiment."

They found ancient underwear, one of a pair of holey and amazingly smelly socks, several pounds of dust, enough dirt to plant roses, empty brew bottles, broken syringes, the torn empty baggies dealers used to store their wares.

"There's nothing here." Peabody mopped

at sweat. "If he was getting ready to rabbit, he must've taken everything he had—except for dirty underwear—with him."

"I'll tell you what we found," Eve corrected. "Rickie lived like a rabid rat. Lived with this smell rather than dumping his trash. Probably because he stayed high as much as possible. The locks inside the door aren't new, so he probably kept some of his junk in here, whatever he made off dealing and weaseling. And he stuck to his territory. It's also interesting what we didn't find, here or at his hole."

"A minimal level of hygiene?"

"That's missing, and so is any kind of client book, memo book—nothing like that on his disposable 'link. He might've dealt on the lower levels, but he had contacts. He was a weasel, and a weasel's useless without them. I'm not buying he kept names, locations, numbers in his rabid rat head."

"Shit. I hate when I miss something like that. He'd have taken it with him."

"More valuable to him than clean underwear, I guarantee. And Bix relieved him of it. He and Garnet had to come through here today, just to make sure Bix didn't miss something after I put a little heat on the deal. We're going to make that their mistake."

"We are?"

"Let's knock on doors." She stepped out, rapped on the one directly across the hall. No answer, which wasn't unexpected even if there'd been a crowd of twelve inside. But she heard no sound.

The music lover's unit was a different matter. She pounded, then pounded and kicked, until she finally beat out the banging of drums.

The man who answered couldn't have seen his twenty-fifth birthday. He carried the pasty-white complexion of a shut-in, or prison inmate, and that peppered with pox and acne scars. Stringy ropes of hair hung to the shoulders of a sleeveless tee that had perhaps once been white. With it he wore a pair of underwear not much more reputable than those discarded in Keener's apartment.

"'Zup," he said with the blissed-out smile and glassy eyes of the seriously stoned. Eve could smell the zoner smoke—hell, she could see it hanging in the air.

She held up her badge.

He smiled at it for a while, then some

level of its meaning eked through. "Aw, c'mon. Just getting my buzz on. Not hurting anybody, check?"

"Is that what you told the other two cops who came by today?"

"Didn't see no cops but you. Just hitting the music and buzzing. Too hot for else."

"You know Juicy?"

"Sure, man, he'll tell you I'm no deal."

"When did you see him last?"

"Dunno. It's hot, man. Every day's hot. All the same."

"Yeah." It was when you were in a permanent state of stupidity.

She heard approaching footsteps and turned to see a man coming down the hall, head down, fingers snapping. At the door across from Keener's he pulled out a set of keys.

She stepped his way. He saw her, made her in the flash of an instant. And turned to run.

Perfect, she thought, and sprinted after him. "Police! Halt!" She judged the distance, bent her knees, and jumping up took him in a mid-body tackle.

"You think I want to chase you in this heat?"

"I didn't do nothing." He humped under her. "Get off me!"

"Why'd you run?"

"I . . . forgot something."

"Right. I'm going to let you up so we can have a civilized conversation. When I do, if you run, I'll catch you—and I'm going to be really unhappy when I do. Understand?"

"Yeah, yeah. I didn't do anything. Cops can't just go knocking people down."

"File a complaint." She eased off, nodding as Peabody positioned herself to block the stairs. "Name?"

"Jubie, not that it's any of your business."

"Peabody, in a ball-breaking contest between me and Jubie the asshole, who's your money on?"

"You, sir, but I've seen your work and the many broken balls resulting from it."

"True. Where you been, Jubie?"

"Look, I just went out to pick up a pack of herbals." He continued to aim for insulted as he shoved the hair out of his eyes, but nerves jittered through the corners. "Herbals are still legal in a guy's own place."

"Then you were in your own place earlier today."

"Yeah, so what? What's with you cops today, crawling all over the place. My lip's bleeding." He swiped the back of his hand over it. "I hit my lip when you knocked me down."

"File another complaint. Tell me about the other cops."

He crossed his arms over his chest, accenting his saggy little potbelly. "Don't have to tell you dick."

"Well, that's true." Eve offered an agreeable nod. "Just like I don't have to tell you to assume the position so I can search you as I suspect you're carrying illegal substances—since I can fucking see the bag sticking out of your pocket."

He shoved at it hastily. "What bag?"

"Jubie, Jubie, let's let bygones be. You tell me about the other cops, I walk away and you get to enjoy your herbals, since that's what we're calling them, in peace and privacy."

His eyes narrowed, shifted. "How do I know you're not doing some entrapment shit?"

"You watch too many cop shows. The cops, Jubie, where were they?"

He transferred his weight from foot to

foot. "Okay, but if you screw with me, I know a lawyer."

"God, that sure strikes fear in my heart. Did you hear that, Peabody, Jubie knows a lawyer."

"I feel my feet trembling in my shoes."

He scowled at both of them, but had to be considering pushing it and getting hauled in. "Couple of dudes, sharp suits. One's a really big guy. They went in Juicy's place. There."

He pointed across the hall.

"Didn't even bother to knock. Fucking cops. I heard them coming up the stairs, looked out the peep in case it was Juicy coming back."

"Juicy usually supply you with the herbals?"

"Maybe. So I make them as cops, and they go right in. That's a violation of civil rights."

"Your knowledge of the law astounds and impresses. Describe them."

"Like I said, one's a big guy. Got blond hair. Other's got dark hair. I didn't take a freaking picture. Stayed in about a half hour maybe and came out all sweaty, looking pissed. That's it."

"Peabody, would you please show this gentleman a selection of freaking pictures since he didn't take one."

"Happy to." Peabody pulled several copies of ID shots out of her bag, mixed Bix's and Garnet's with them. "If you'd take a look at this, Mr. Jubie, and let us know if you recognize any of these individuals."

"Christ's sake, don't you cops know each other? Him. Him. Those are the ones broke in to Juicy's place and violated his civil rights."

"You're sure?"

"I said so, didn't I?"

"When's the last time you saw Juicy?"

"Couple days ago. Three, maybe. Who keeps track?"

"Okay. Thank you for your cooperation."

Before she could change her mind, he jammed his key in the lock and did a fast turn into his flop.

"Got them," Eve murmured. "One more stop. Pizza."

"It's rare for me to say, but I'm really not hungry. Between that flop and this heat, food holds no appeal."

"We're not eating. We're going to visit the scene of Juicy's last meal."

"Oh. Listen, when we finish there, is it okay if I go to my place, grab a shower and change? Even before that fun-filled search in garbage hell I was feeling a little grungy."

"Be at my home office by sixteen hundred—thirty sooner's better."

"No problem. And . . ." Peabody pulled her sticky shirt away from her breasts. "I think everyone will thank you."

True to form, the pizza joint was in Keener's territory—and, in fact, between his hole and his flop.

"Did I say not the brightest bulb? This one was burned out for a while."

Counters lined one wall and the box-sized window. A couple people enjoying a slice rolled eyes toward her, then hastily away. She could almost hear the relief slide out of them when she walked past.

"What'll it be?" The woman behind the glass-fronted counter rolled her shoulders as if to dislodge an ache. She was black, with thin, tough-looking arms, her hair tied back in a blue kerchief and a single hoop piercing her left eyebrow.

"Questions." Eve showed her badge.

"Look, I don't want trouble so I stay out

of it. I'm clean. I've got a kid at home, and I've got to work to pay the rent."

"I've got no problems for you. Do you know Rickie Keener? Juicy?"

"Everybody knows Juicy."

"Who was on the counter last night?"

"I was." She glanced toward the back with a look of avid dislike. "Gee made me work the late shift, even though he knows I gotta get a sitter costs more than I make when it's night work."

"Was Juicy in?"

"Yeah, he came in. Got a whole damn pie—with sardines. That's his usual—the topping, not the whole pie. Whole pie, couple of brews, so he had to be flush." She pulled another kerchief out of her apron pocket, dabbed at her sweaty throat. "In a real good mood, too."

"Is that so?"

"He tipped me. I get a tip about once every ten blue moons, but he laid a five on the counter, and says, 'That's for your own sweet self, Loo.' Says how he's settling his accounts, closing up shop, and going where there's cool, sea breezes. Full of bull."

Then she shrugged, stuffed the kerchief

back in her pocket. "I guess you know what he does, but he was always polite to me. Always said thanks—and he never did business in here. I guess he's in trouble."

"He's dead, Loo."

"Oh." Loo shook her head, cast her eyes down a moment. "I guess it's hard to be surprised when somebody lives that life."

"How about this guy?" She gestured for Peabody to show Bix's shot.

"Haven't seen him in here. He'd stick out, that's for sure. Big, healthy white guy. Seen him somewhere, maybe. Maybe . . . yeah, I think I saw him—somebody big and white anyway, hanging around down the block when I walked home."

"What time did you get off?"

"Not till damn near three. Half the street-lights out, and I don't stroll, if you get me, when I've got to walk home at that time of night. I caught a glimpse because I keep my eyes open. Mostly the assholes leave me be because they eat here, but you never know. So I caught a glimpse, like I said. Could've been this guy."

"Good enough. Thank you."

"I'm sorry about Juicy. I didn't like how

he made his way, but he never did me any harm."

Not a bad epitaph for a junkie, Eve thought as she left.

 Eve calculated she had time for a quick shower and change herself. She'd feel better and would be able to turn all the data, statements, and observations over in her mind while she scraped off the grunge from a dead man's flop.

She began to turn them over even as she walked into the house, into the cool, into the beady stares of Summerset and the cat.

"Have I missed a national holiday? There must be celebrations in the streets for you to be home at this hour of the day."

"I'm calling it Summerset Goes Mute Day. The city's gone mad with joy." She angled for the steps, stopped. "I've got a team coming in for a briefing."

"So I'm informed. You'll be serving pulled pork barbecue, a cold pasta salad, fresh tomatoes with mozzarella, and green beans almondine."

"Oh."

"Followed by peach pie à la mode and a selection of petit fours."

"We'll never get rid of them."

"How is Detective Peabody?" he asked as she started up the steps.

She stopped, shoulders tense. "Why?"

"I'm neither blind nor insensitive, Lieutenant. She was very obviously shaken when she and Detective McNab arrived last night."

"She's steady. She's fine. I also figure you know what goes on in this house, so you know we all went out, two separate vehicles, and came back late. You know Peabody and McNab stayed here, you know Whitney was here early this morning. The circuits are closed on this, closed tight."

She might've been on the steps above

him, but Summerset managed to meet her eye and transmit the impression he looked down his nose.

"I don't discuss your professional or personal business."

She ordered herself to throttle back. She knew he didn't gossip. He'd hardly be the man Roarke trusted with, well, everything, if he was a blabbermouth.

"I know that. This is an extremely sensitive and layered investigation."

"Involving Detective Peabody."

"You could say. And that's all I can say."

"Would you tell me if she's in trouble? I'm very fond of her."

She knew that, too—and this time didn't have to tell herself to throttle back. "No, she's not in trouble. She's a good cop. That's why she's involved." Crap. Now she felt obliged. "Listen, I'm sorry I couldn't spend more time with your friends last night."

His eyebrows lifted, ever so slightly. "Perhaps it is a national holiday."

"Anyway." Leaving it at that, she continued upstairs.

"Go on," Summerset told the cat. "I expect she'd like the company whether she knows it or not."

Galahad padded, as briskly as his bulk allowed, after Eve.

In the bedroom, he bumped against her legs as she stripped off her jacket. So she crouched down to give him a rub that had his bicolored eyes slitting in ecstasy.

"I'm going to wrap her up," Eve told him. "Wrap her up like a smelly fish. Wrap her up, put her in a box, and tie down the lid. Put her in a cage, her and every one of her murdering, cheating, lying, corrupt cops. Jesus, I'm pissed."

She took a breath, another, as the raw anger she'd managed to cage the entire day threatened to break loose.

"Treacherous whore-bitch *cunt* using everything and everyone to feed her own pathetic needs. Abusing what she'd promised to honor. Twisting everything she'd been given, everything entrusted to her so she could stroke her bank account and her goddamn sick ego."

She tried another couple breaths. "Really pissed," she admitted, "and that won't help. I should be more like you, more like my cat. Cool and sneaky."

She gave him a last pat, then removed her weapon, the rest of her clothes. In the shower she let her mind empty, just empty out. And in that calmer space began to test the pieces, calculate the angles, arrange the steps.

Cool and sneaky, she thought again. Good tools when you were planning to take down all or most of a police squad.

Once she'd dressed, she strapped her weapon back on. Hardly necessary inside her own house, but wearing it would be more official. Another symbol, she supposed. And maybe, as silly as it sounded, it offset the casual tone of peach pie à la mode.

She hauled up her file bag and headed to her office.

The door to Roarke's office stood open. She heard his voice, moved to the doorway. Whoever he spoke with, and whatever they spoke about, utilized the short speak of high-tech that eluded her. It was, she thought, like listening to a conversation in Venusian.

Whatever it was had to do with, she assumed, the weird schematics flashing on-screen—and if she was following the Venusian, the changes Roarke wanted to them.

"Put them in and run a new analysis. I want to see the results tomorrow afternoon."

"I didn't know you were here," Eve said when he'd finished. "What was that thing?"

"What will be the new generation laundry unit."

She frowned at him. "Like for washing clothes?"

"It'll do a bit more than that. One self-contained, multi-compartment unit." In his beautifully cut suit, he leaned back against his desk, studied the schematics with obvious satisfaction.

"It should do everything but tuck your clothes in your drawers and hang them in your closet. And if you want that as well, you could purchase the droid attachment."

"Okay. I guess it seems a little mundane for you."

"You wouldn't say that if you ran out of clean underwear." He crossed to her, gave her an easy hello kiss. "And people need the mundane every day."

"I used to take all my stuff to Mr. Ping's place around the corner from my apartment," she remembered. "He was good at getting bloodstains out."

"An essential service in your line of work. I don't see any today."

"Day's not over. I've got to set up for the briefing. Things are rolling."

"I've got a few things to finish up, then you can fill me in."

"Okay." She paused at the doorway. "You know, I guess there was somebody a few hundred years ago, beating a dirty shirt against a rock in a fast stream, who thought there's just got to be a better fucking way. If he hadn't found it, we'd all be wading in rivers on laundry day. Mundane's got a point."

She moved into her office. She arranged two boards, one for the murder, one for the investigation on Renee Oberman's operation, adding data on every cop in Renee's squad she'd acquired through low-level runs.

She grabbed the sweepers report the instant it came through, studied it and the lab analysis on the illegals taken from the crime scene.

Little pieces, she thought. Tiny little pieces—mundane, you could say.

Once she'd input everything in her computer, she sat back with coffee and considered her approach.

When Roarke came in he went to her

boards. "You've made considerable progress."

"I know what she's doing. I have some ideas on why. I even know how to some extent. I know some of the other players, but not all. I know who killed Keener, why and how and when. But it's not enough. Yet. I had some face time with her today, got to fuck with her a little."

"I imagine you enjoyed it."

"I'd have enjoyed smashing my fist into her face more, but yeah, it wasn't bad."

He walked to her desk, took her coffee, drank a little. "Sometimes we just have to make do."

"I had Peabody contact her, fuck with her a little more. Not only because it's good strategy, but . . ."

"You can't beat the monster in the closet unless you open the door. Our Peabody won't be as unnerved by the woman now."

"Plus Renee lost that round, so even better. Renee's overplayed her hand, but doesn't know it."

Eve looked at the board again, and again thought, *little pieces*.

"I'm going to say this first, get it out of the way while it's just you and me."

"All right."

"I've got this terrible hate on for her—so many levels of it. It's Peabody, it's Whitney, even Mira after I saw her today. It's the department, and it's the badge and everything it means."

"I know. And it's more."

He would know, she thought. He would see. "Cop's daughter. Can be rough, I guess. But screw that. She had two parents, a decent home. No hint of anything under that, and you don't get to be commander of the NYPSD without making enemies. If there'd been anything, somebody would've found it."

"I'd agree with that. And I imagine you spent some time today looking for any hint of that."

"Yeah, I did," she admitted. "No traumas, not one that shows—and I think by now, especially with Mira taking a hard, close look—it would. Normal is what she had. Well, a cop's house probably has its own brand of normal, but—"

"She was housed and fed, educated, very likely loved, certainly tended to," Roarke continued. "Her father set an example, held to a code. He didn't lock her in dark rooms."

Roarke touched Eve's cheek, just a brush of fingertips. "He didn't beat her, didn't rape her, didn't terrorize a helpless child night after night, year after year. Rather than value what she was given, she chose to dishonor it. She made a choice, and that choice betrays everything you believe in, everything you've made yourself."

"It sticks in me. I need to get over it."

"No. You're wrong. You need to use it. And when you end this, you'll know that what you made yourself from a nightmare beat what she made herself from normal. More, Eve, you'll know that's why you beat her."

"Maybe." She laid a hand on his. "Maybe. But right now I feel better, just getting that said. So."

This time when she took a breath, it worked. "She's not really worried about me, but more pissed off. More annoyed at the inconvenience, at having me bump up against her authority. She handed me this homicide because she got sloppy, because she surrounds herself with people without ethics, without any respect for the job."

"That would be key." Roarke took an-

other sip of her coffee. "To run a successful business, it's an advantage to hire
people with a similar vision, or at least the
ability to adapt to your vision."

"Yeah, I think she's got that down. But
when your business is living a lie, you have
to take what you get. Hotheads like Garnet,
brutes like Bix. Plus, her ego's a problem.
She doesn't look for the smartest, but the
most malleable, the most easily corrupted.
It's most important for her to stay on top, to
be in charge. To her way of thinking, as I see
her, if she recruits the best and the brightest,
somebody might outsmart her, out think her,
maybe figure *Why should I listen to her*?"

"If she can't grasp or accept it's not essential to be the smartest person in the
room, but to be sure the smartest person
in the room is working for you, she was
destined to fail."

"She's had a good run up till now." Eve
took the coffee back. "She runs her squad
precisely—dominating by forbidding any
sort of personality. No personal items, no
genuine partnerships. Every man for himself," Eve murmured. "That's what I felt in
there."

She rose to walk to the board, to tap her

finger on Bix's photo. "She recruited him, and I'm going to bet she helped work his transfer to her unit—because of his skill set. Military, combat trained. Both parents also military. He takes orders, he'll kill on command. He's her dog."

"How does she turn him?"

"I want Mira's take, but I see it could be done a couple of ways. Maybe he was a good soldier, and good soldiers are often ordered to do harsh things for the greater good, or good or not, the mission. Illegals is an endless war. She could convince him this is another way to fight it. Or she recognized in him a need, a predilection to hurt, maim, kill, and channeled it to meet her requirements."

"It could easily be both."

"Yeah, it could. Garnet? She used sex and greed, and likely appealed to a *Why the hell shouldn't we get ours?* That's her play for a lot of it, I think, with variations on *Why the hell should we do what we do, risk what we risk, step in what we step in, and settle for a cop's lousy pay? We're the ones holding the line. We deserve more.*"

"She couldn't play on the weaknesses if they weren't there."

"Everybody's got weaknesses. You give in to them, you cross the line and do exactly what you've taken an oath to stop?"

The anger bubbled up again, the hot surge of it.

"You don't deserve to be a cop, and you need to be taken down harder than the assholes the rest of us risk what we risk to stop. I've been up against wrong cops before. Something the size of the NYPSD? It's inevitable. But she's more."

Eve drilled a finger into Renee's photo. "She's worse. A choice, you said, and that's a goddamn bull's-eye. It's not that she's weak, not that she's greedy or needy—or not just. She chose to be a cop, then she chose to be dirty. To make a fucking *business* out of it. Deliberate. Calculated.

"I want to hurt her for it. I want to make the choice—just as deliberate, just as calculated—to burn her for it."

He smiled at her. "And that, Lieutenant, is how you use it to beat her."

Peabody and McNab arrived first.

She handed off some new runs to Peabody, gave McNab the same names.

"I want a property search—one that

doesn't show yet. Just a standard inventory check. What you're looking for are check-ins of these illegals. I want who was on the property desk, who generated the invoices for them. I want those crossed with the officers who confiscated, and with their reports. Just Central for now. We'll keep it focused."

"What can I do for you, Lieutenant?" Roarke asked her.

"Garnet has property in the tropics— which covers a lot of area. I need to find it. I need to find it without sending up any flags—and not using unregistered equipment," she added, lowering her voice. "I figure if you've got nice beach property, you go there whenever you can manage it, which means you have to use transportation."

"You would, yes. That's quite an interesting puzzle. I believe I'll enjoy it."

"He'll have a vehicle at that location— something high end. Probably a boat. And almost certainly an alternate ID to cover all of it. I figure it's a long-term project, picking out the pin in a pretty massive haystack—"

"That would be needle."

"Whatever. It would be good information to have at some point."

"I'll get started."

"The rest should be here in about twenty. I guess I'll have them chow down first, so they're not distracted by the thought of food. Might as well have them temporarily distracted by actual food."

Since Peabody and McNab were on her comp and auxiliary, she went into the kitchen and used the mini on the counter to run a few probabilities.

Sneaky, calculating, deliberate. Could she be all that, she wondered, and drive it through with this fire of rage and loathing burning in her belly?

"I guess we'll find out," she murmured.

When she heard voices, she stepped out again.

Time to get the party started.

Damn good chow," Feeney commented, and chomped into a pulled pork sandwich. "I hear there's pie."

She wondered if there was a cop in the universe, including herself, who didn't have a weakness for pie. "Pie's for after the formal briefing."

He gave her a sorrowful look. "That's harsh, kid."

"Yeah, yeah." She moved to the front of the room. "I'm going to begin while all of you finish licking your plates clean. If you'll direct your attention to the boards, and the two separate but connected cases."

It was brief, as most of the team had already been updated on the steps and progress. She called on Mira to present personality profiles on Renee Oberman, William Garnet, Carl Bix, and the victim.

"What is your opinion, Doctor Mira, in determining if the Keener case is homicide, accident, or self-termination?"

"Self-termination isn't consistent with any of the victim's actions. He moved himself and his possessions to another location. On the night of his death he had a meal and spoke with his server. According to her statement his mood was pleasant, even expansive, and he spoke about relocating.

"Accidental overdose is always a risk with an addict," Mira continued. "However, the massive dose injected isn't consistent with the victim's previous habits. In my judgment, based on facts, statements, and personality, this was homicide."

"Renee's going to have a hard time arguing with that," Feeney put in.

"That's the plan. I'm going to have to ask her opinion on how her weasel, a low-rent street dealer, got his hands on that much of a high-grade illegal substance. And I'm going to want to know who deals in that substance. I'm going to need to talk to anyone in her squad—then the department—who made a bust involving that substance.

"Which takes us to Property. McNab."

He swallowed pasta. "At the lieutenant's direction, I initiated an inventory run on specific illegals invoices in Central's property room. Do you want to see the work, or just the results?" he asked her.

"The work'll go into the file, be copied to all team members. Let's have the results here and now."

"Illegals squad under Lieutenant Harrod. Detectives Petrov and Roger had a pretty nice bust about six weeks ago. They confiscated a number of illegals, including a large batch of street name FYU. I should add that Detective Roger and two uniformed officers were injured during the bust. In Detective Petrov's report, he estimated the FYU at thirty keys. That's a street value of about two hundred and fifty thousand. They also bagged what he estimated to be ninety keys of Dust and five hundred capsules of Exotica.

"I took the majors first, Lieutenant," Mc-Nab explained. "I haven't had time to do a thorough run. Petrov checked the confiscated substances into Property for weighing, registering, and invoicing. On-site estimates are over a lot of the time. They're just eyeballing them and, well, who doesn't like bigger numbers? The official count after check-in was twenty-two keys of FYU, eighty-four of Dust, and three seventy-five caps of Exotica."

"That's quite a discrepancy."

"Yes, sir, it is. Roger was being transported to the hospital, so Petrov didn't wait for the weigh-in."

"Who received and weighed said substances?"

"Runch, Sergeant Walter."

"Computer, display on-screen data on Runch, Sergeant Walter. I conducted a standard background and ran an analysis of Property officers," Eve continued when the data came up. "She needs a man on the desk or else she's limited to her own men, and watching all that profit swim right by her. An analysis of Runch in the two years, four months he's been on the desk shows that his weigh-ins are regularly under the estimate—his percentages of those discrepancies increase when said estimate is outside Renee's squad."

"When the cop on the bust is one of hers," Feeney put in, "he takes the weight off the estimate before weigh-in."

"That's what plays," Eve agreed. "Not every time, not even most of the time, but with regularity and most particularly when dealing with major busts.

"As you see, Runch was assigned to Property after receiving a rip for busting up a bar while beating the hell out of his bookie after he lost five large over a three-point spread in Arena Ball. Runch has a little gambling problem and was given the opportunity for counseling and reassignment, which he accepted."

Eve picked up the photo she'd already printed out, added it to Oberman's board.

"You already had him?" McNab asked.

"I had the probability. You put the bow on it. What does IAB have on Runch?" she asked Webster.

"I didn't work him, but if there's more, I'll find out. I have interviewed her detective Marcell, regarding a termination. He and a Detective Strumb, both under Lieutenant Oberman, were covering an undercover, Detective Freeman. Freeman was up as a buyer, had been working this deal for a couple weeks, and it was due to go down. It should've been a play-by-play, but it went south. Dealer brings along his muscle, and his woman. The woman makes Freeman, screams how he's a cop, how he busted her for possession. Everybody draws down, Marcell and Strumb move in to assist. Freeman's wounded, Strumb and the dealer end up dead. Muscle's wounded according to Freeman and Marcell, but he and the woman managed to get in the vehicle and escape—with the money and the product."

"Handy," Eve commented.

"It added up. Freeman's and Marcell's statements meshed. Freeman ID'd the woman, and he had busted her for possession six months prior. Crime scene reconstruction played out as the officers reported. Marcell acknowledged terminating the dealer, citing self-defense and defense of his partner as Strumb was down. He went through Testing, and the results corroborated."

"What did you think?"

"What I thought was he probably terminated the dealer out of revenge for his partner—but I didn't have it on him. Three days later, the bodies of the muscle and the woman were found in a motel off the turnpike, throats slit. No money, no product. And I thought he might have gone after them. We looked at him for it, but he had a solid alibi. He was with his lieutenant, Detectives Garnet and Freeman at TOD, in the back room of a bar, holding a private wake for their fallen comrade."

Webster nodded at the screen. "Put it together with what we know now? It smells."

"Peabody, generate Freeman's and Marcell's ID shots, put them up. That's four in her squad, one in the property room. Generate Lieutenant Harrod's Detective Roger."

"The wounded officer?" Peabody asked.

"I'm wondering if the estimate would've been so far off the weigh-in if he hadn't been wounded and therefore unable to do the estimate himself. He's a possible. She's got more," Eve added. "Weighing Mira's personality profile, I did an analysis on her history as boss of the squad. Within six months of her assignment, three officers were transferred to other squads or divisions. In two of the cases, Renee was able to request specific detectives to replace them. One of those was Freeman, the other Detective Armand, who came in from Brooklyn PD, where he'd worked in their E-Division."

Eve added his ID shot. "She needs an e-man. The third detective transferred out in under a year, as did another from the original squad. One of the later replacements who transferred in, female—went down in a multi-squad bust eight months after joining the squad. Another remains under her command. Detective Palmer previously worked three years with a squad focused on organized crime. She needs the contacts," Eve said, and added his photo.

"How many are you looking at?" Whitney demanded. "How many of that squad?"

"It won't be all of them, Commander. She needs scapegoats, fall guys, sacrifices—

as it may turn out both Strumb and the female transfer were. She has to have at least one man in Accounting, for the same reason she needs one in Property. The numbers have to add up to keep her squad under the radar. It's likely she has at least one in another squad—and I'm looking at Roger—or has someone who she's cultivated who'll just gossip—somebody who passes information about investigations, planned operations."

She glanced at Mira. "I'm adding Doctor Addams, as she requested him for her psych, and my check indicates her entire squad now uses him.

"The homicide investigation puts pressure on her, and it infuriates her. Keener was supposed to be a speck of lint she flicked off her sleeve. Now he's a stone in her shoe. I'm going to insist, as is my right as primary, to interview everyone in her squad. I expect she'll file a complaint with command."

"Yes," Whitney agreed. "I expect she will."

"I request permission, due to the evidence so far compiled, for EDD to install a tracer and recorder on her vehicle. It's department issue, sir, and not her personal property."

"So we slip around the need for a warrant."

"Slip's the word," Webster put in. "She can give you grief on that at the end of the day. It's questionable, and lawyers love questionable."

"How about this? Her current vehicle experiences some mechanical problems. She has to requisition a replacement. When she accepts said replacement, she signs a waiver. Who reads those things? We cover it—carefully—and if she signs, she's agreed to accept said vehicle as it comes to her."

"That'll work."

"Feeney, who can you glad-hand in the vehicle pool to find out what gets earmarked for her?"

"I've got a couple guys. That's not a problem."

"Can you and McNab get to the vehicle, wire it up so it doesn't show on a standard sweep?"

He tipped his head down, eyes narrowed on her. "I'm insulted you'd even ask."

"Fine. Peabody, generate a standard

vehicle waiver, and we'll make a few amendments."

"How are you going to decommission her vehicle?" Webster demanded. "Much less slip her the doctored form?"

"I'll take care of it," Eve told him, careful not to so much as glance at Roarke. "Feeney, just let me know, asap, when you nail down the vehicle—and you could use your geek magic to get me the exact location of her old one."

He loved to watch her work like this, Roarke thought. How she laid it out, ran it through, timed it—even down to giving the nod for pie to relieve some of the tension in the room.

He looked at her board now, thought of how deliberately she'd added one name, one image at a time so each had its own specific impact. So each mattered as much as the next. Not one melded group of bad cops, but individuals.

Now, with the pie lending a less formal mood, she brought him into it. Clever girl.

"From the conversation between Renee and Garnet Peabody overheard, we know Garnet owns property—tropical, beachy. I've asked Roarke, as expert consultant, civilian, to try to locate that property. If Garnet owns a little tropical paradise and has gone to any lengths—perhaps illegal lengths—to conceal that ownership, it'll help wrap him up. It may help flip him, if and when we need one of her crew to flip on her."

"Not that I don't think that's a good idea," Webster began, "but anything that scratches too deep at his financials, his assets—without the filter of a warranted search or IAB status, is going to alert him. Even with those, if he's taken the precautions, he could catch wind of a sniff."

"Which is why I'll have to be very quiet about it," Roarke returned.

"Listen, if you obtain any data by questionable means, the data becomes questionable when the lawyers start on it."

"I'm aware of that." Roarke angled his head. "I'm married to a cop. Would you like me to tell you how it might be done, Detective?"

"Go ahead."

"One might, particularly as a businessman with many interests and investments in transportation, generate a kind of survey. And as an example, we might collect data on how many men, with a certain demographic, travel from New York to a tropical location more than three times a year—the same location. It might be worth our while to increase our transportation services to those locations, and offer incentives to that specific demographic."

"Yeah." Webster began to smile. "I could see it might."

"As our services include private transports, and it always pays to offer perks to those who could afford them anyway, we'd look at those individuals, particularly if we found those individuals owned property. People who own multiple homes and can afford to travel to them regularly are excellent customers."

"I bet they are. It's a good angle. If you get a hit, let me know. I could work a filter from there, so you could take it down a few levels." When Roarke lifted a brow, Webster nodded. "A filter sanctioned by IAB keeps it from edging into questionable."

"Understood."

"If that's all for tonight, I've got to take off." Webster pushed to his feet. "I'm meeting someone."

"As pertains to this?" Eve demanded.

"No, as doesn't pertain to this." He shot Roarke a quick grin. "Thanks for the pie."

"I'll thank you, too." Mira stepped up as Webster left. "I'll have profiles on the other officers, get them to you tomorrow. I'd suggest you find a way to talk with members of the squad prior to Renee's command there, get a sense from them."

"It's on my slate," Eve told her.

When the room finally emptied of cops, Roarke leaned back on Eve's desk. "Alone at last. And I suppose we'll be leaving shortly so I can decommission Renee's official vehicle."

"I figured you'd enjoy it. A nostalgia thing."

"It would be more enjoyably nostalgic if I stole it."

She actually considered it for a moment. "No, it's better to just take it out. But you need to do it so it looks like a regular—but severe—mechanical problem, not tampering. I don't want her to be able to use it for, say, a week—and I want diagnostics to see it as a normal breakdown."

"Well then, at least there's a tiny challenge involved. I'll need to change. While I do you can tell me how you plan to fix it so Renee signs your doctored waiver."

"You should know when you need to run a con, you hire a grifter."

**10** Vehicular tampering wasn't something she did every day, particularly with departmental approval. She wondered just how she'd write it up in her report.

Assigned expert consultant, civilian (former thief), to debilitate the official vehicle of a ranked NYPSD officer.

Probably not quite that way.

"She doesn't deserve to be a ranked NYPSD officer," Eve muttered.

Roarke glanced over as he drove. "You're not actually feeling guilty about this?"

"Not guilty. Uncomfortable," she decided. "It was my idea, and it's a good step. It's department property, so the commander can order or approve said step, and we have tacit IAB sanction with Webster's attachment. But I'm still a cop deliberately and covertly disabling another cop's ride. So I have to remind myself she doesn't deserve to be a cop."

"Whatever gets you through, darling. You might try to enjoy it, as I intend to." He flashed her a grin, gave her a playful finger in the ribs. "Criminal activity does have its appeal. Otherwise there wouldn't be so many criminals."

"It's not a criminal activity. It's department sanctioned."

"Pretend."

She only rolled her eyes. "The building has—as you'd expect with a cop, and a dirty one at that—solid security. Underground parking for tenants is assigned—"

"Which you already told me, and is the reason I took a little walk through the records for said garage and identified her slot. Level two, slot twenty-three."

"I'm just going over it." Because, she admitted, it made it seem less criminal.

"Visitor parking is limited to level three. Visitors have to clear garage security. The simplest way is to key in a name and corresponding apartment."

He tipped her a glance, quick and full of humor. "No, there are simpler."

"Which I have here," she added, willfully ignoring him, "from your little walk-through. Apartment 1020, Francis and Willow Martin. There'll be cams at the entrance to the garage, and on all levels."

"Mmm-hmm."

"They'll document the vehicle and tag going in and out," she continued. "But Renee will have no reason, if you do the job right, to suspect tampering and request a review of the discs."

"I've often wondered what sort of partner in crime you'd make, should we have met back in the day. Now I see, sadly, it would never have worked. I fear, darling Eve, you're much too tight-assed."

"I take that as a compliment," she said between her teeth.

"Which proves the point."

"Listen, smart-ass, I don't want to give her any reason to question the disabled ride, or to take too hard a look at the new one."

"Trust me," he said simply, and turned to the gated doors of the garage.

"Apartment 1020," she reminded him.

He said, "Mmm-hmm," even as the gates lifted.

"How the hell did you do that?"

"I could cite professional secret, but since I'm among friends, I activated a jammer just before I pulled up. It released the gate while it briefly disabled the cam. They'll have a bit of a video snag—the cams flicking for a time. On the way down," he continued as he snaked the downward curve. "Then when we're done, on the way up."

Slick, she thought. Pretty damn slick. But still. "I don't know why that's simpler than just keying in some data."

"Well now, we don't know Francis and Willow, do we? Whether they've got a visitors' block up, or are off in Saint Maarten's having manic sex on the beach."

"I checked their data—I'm not an idiot. She's an OB, and she has regular office hours tomorrow. They're not in freaking Saint Maarten's having any kind of sex."

"More's the pity for them. Maybe they're out for the evening. Perhaps she's delivering a baby as we speak, and taking advantage of her absence, Francis slipped out to visit his young, nubile mistress for a bit of that manic sex."

He stopped the car, aimed his PPC out the window. "Point being, we don't know what Francis and Willow are up to, so why risk it?"

"What are you doing?"

"Just a minute."

She shifted in her seat. He'd tied his hair back—work mode—and was keying a series of numbers, letters—who could tell—into his handheld. He had a half smile on his face, but she knew those eyes. He was focused on whatever the hell he was doing.

"That should take care of it."

"Of what?"

"For the next five minutes the cameras on this level will record the area as it is now—without us in it." He drove on. "It's not the Royal Museum, but still it would be awkward if a security man decided to check the garage and saw me fiddling with Renee's vehicle."

He pulled in longways behind it. "This won't take long," he told her as he got out.

Frowning, Eve shoved open the passenger door. She followed him around to the hood. She started to remind him the hood would be secured, but was glad she saved her breath. He had it open in seconds.

"How did you deactivate the alarm without—"

"Quiet."

He took another of his little toys from his pocket, attached it to something under the hood with a thread-thin wire. He keyed in a command that had numbers and symbols flashing by in red on the miniscreen. He watched them, then paused the sequence. He keyed in another command, generated another series of codes.

Smiling, he held out the device. "Here, push ENTER."

"Why?"

"Partners in crime."

"Crap." She pushed ENTER and distinctly heard several sharp electrical snaps.

"Nicely done. You're a natural."

"Bite me."

"One of my favorite activities." He

entered yet another series, another command, then detached the device. Secured the hood.

"That's it?"

"It is. I put the extra time blocking the cams in case you want to search the vehicle. Would you like me to get you in?"

She would. Oh boy, would she. "I didn't get clearance for that."

"Stickler—which is much the same as tight-ass." He waited, watching her fight her internal battle.

"No. If I need to toss her ride, I'll do the new one. With a warrant or at command directive. Let's go."

"That was fun." Roarke got back behind the wheel, made the turn to curve up to the exit. "But vaguely unsatisfying."

"What did you do to it?"

"Identified, copied, then countermanded the mainframe system code with an incompatible command issued by a diagnostic clone issuing feed directly into . . ." He trailed off, smiling at her. "I do love it when you get glassy-eyed over tech. It's not altogether dissimilar from when you come."

"Oh, please." Deliberately she darkened the look with a scowl.

"I'm the one privileged to look in those eyes of yours at such moments. Basically, I fried a number of chips, which will disable the starter. I issued a second command so when she get in, tries to start it, the action will set off a further reaction, and essentially completely bollocks the engine."

"Okay. That's good. Will it pass diagnostics?"

He sighed, long, deep, exaggerated. "I wonder why I tolerate such abuse and cynicism? Ah yes, it's those glassy eyes. It'll read like a starter defect, which, in turn, compromised the engine."

"That's perfect. Thanks."

"My pleasure. On to our favorite grifter?"

"Yeah. They're expecting us."

Lieutenant Renee Oberman clipped into the squad room in a very bad mood.

"LT," Detective Strong began, and received a furious shut-the-fuck-up glare.

"Officer Heizer, contact Requisitions and tell them I want the damn paperwork on my vehicle asap."

"Yes, ma'am."

"And I don't want to see that piece of crap they hauled out of my garage this morning again. If they replace it with a similar piece of crap, I'll make their lives a living hell."

"Yes, ma'am," he repeated even as she stormed into her office. Renee pulled up short when she saw Eve in one of her visitor's chairs.

"Lieutenant. Nice hours you have here in Illegals."

"Don't start on me." Renee strode around to her desk, opened a bottom drawer, tossed her purse inside. "My vehicle rolled over and died this morning."

"Sympathies," Eve said with no sincerity whatsoever. "They are crap."

"Now I'm dealing with those idiots in Requisitions and the Vehicle Pool."

"Pain in the ass," Eve agreed. "I'm here to give you a bigger one."

"Look, Dallas, you put me in a corner regarding sensitive data and files generated with the use of my CI."

"Your dead CI."

"Dead or alive, that data remains sensitive. Several of those cases are either in trial or yet to come to trial. If the information's compromised, those trials could be compromised."

Eve's face went stony. "Are you insinuating, Lieutenant, that I might apprise a defendant or said defendant's legal rep of that data?"

"I'm not insinuating anything, I'm stating a fact. I don't know how you run your division, who might now have access to that data. But you left me no choice. Now you've got it, and as far as I'm concerned, that's the end of it."

"You'd be wrong. To start, Keener's COD was an overdose of FYU, sweetened with barely pushed Zeus. I'm wondering how a low-level chemi-head who dealt primarily in zoner managed that one."

"I told you." Renee spoke deliberately, as if to a child. "He used whatever he could get."

"Yeah, and I'm wondering how he managed to get the high grade. I need to know who in your squad worked on anything involving FYU, who they busted on it, and so on. I'll need those files."

"That's bullshit! Are you standing there, in my *office*, implying one of my people passed my weasel high-grade illegals?"

Perfect, Eve thought. Simply perfect. "I wasn't implying that. Should I be? In fact, given my next order of business with you, that's a very interesting angle."

Renee slapped her hands on her desk. "Now you listen to me—"

"'Scuze." A tiny woman with shoe-black hair in hooking pigtails poked her head in. She snapped bright pink gum and gave the two lieutenants a bored look out of chocolate brown eyes. "Either of you LT Renee Oberman?" Brooklyn drenched her voice.

Renee gave the woman a quick sweep, from the pigtails, over the cheap white polo shirt, the baggy pants, the dull gray skids. "I'm Lieutenant Oberman."

"Candy, Requisitions." Candy's ID badge bounced between enormous breasts as she walked to the desk.

"It's about time."

"Yeah, well, we get backed up, you know. Cops're hard on their rides. Gotcha a spank-new Torrent. That's an upgrade, as requested. Got your codes and what-not here."

Renee held out a hand. "Well?"

"Jeez, can't hand 'em over till you sign. Whatcha think? We just pass out rides? Sign, date, initial both pages—that's in dupe." Candy laid the forms on the desk, tapped them with a bright—and chipped— pink fingernail. "Said you were in a big-ass hurry, so they sent me up. Nice office."

"Just give me the codes," Renee snapped as she dashed her signature on the forms.

"Don't have to get huffy about it." Candy passed her a sealed card. "You want to change the codes, you gotta notify—in trip—so's we got it on record."

"Fine. That'll be all."

"Nope. You gotta sign my screen here, verifying acceptance of the new vehicle and codes. You don't verify, somebody could say I boosted the ride, turned it on the street."

Renee snatched the little screen, scrawled her name on it with the attached stylus. "Get out."

"Jeez." Candy gathered the forms, sniffed. "You're fucking welcome."

"It's hardly a wonder they're so disor-ganized over there," Renee said when Candy strolled out. "Hiring people like that."

"You got your new ride, Oberman. Now if you're all set, why don't we continue this fascinating discussion with you telling me why two of your detectives were in my victim's flop yesterday?"

"Excuse me?"

"No, I won't excuse you. What I will do is file a formal complaint against you, your detectives, and this squad for interfering with and potentially compromising a homicide investigation."

Renee's eyes burned hot as she took two challenging steps toward Eve. "You think you can come into my squad, into my office, and threaten me and my people?"

"Yeah, because that's just what I'm doing." For the hell of it, Eve closed the distance until they were nearly nose-to-nose. "And I will, I promise you, follow through if I'm not satisfied with your explanation of why Detectives Garnet and Bix entered Keener's flop yesterday without my authorization. I'll do more than follow up if I find out either or both of them hooked my vic up with illegals."

"And I *demand* to know on what grounds you're making that assertion."

Eve twisted her lips into a sneer. "I don't have to tell you squat. This is my case, my investigation, my vic. And I'm wondering just why you're trying to stall it, to interfere with it, to compromise it."

"That's ridiculous, and insulting. I don't take those kinds of accusations lightly, so believe me, *I'll* be following up."

"I don't take a couple of your men tromping through my vic's flop, screwing with potential evidence and undermining my authority and investigation in the process lightly. In fact I don't fucking take it at all. You don't want to talk to me, no problem. We'll both talk to Whitney."

"Is that how you solve things, Lieutenant? Jumping to the commander?"

"When it's warranted, you bet your ass." Deliberately Eve glanced over her shoulder at Commander Oberman's portrait. "I'd have thought you'd understand and respect that, particularly since Dad used to hold the chair."

"You don't want to bring my father into this."

Sore spot, hot button, Eve thought when Renee's voice vibrated. "You don't want to stonewall me. I can, and I will, write both your men up for this, drag both your men into formal interview. I can and will charge them with trespassing, illegal entry, obstruction of justice—for a start—if I don't get some answers."

Renee swung around to stand behind her desk. "I'll speak with my detectives on this matter, and get back to you with my findings."

Oh, you're pissed, Eve thought, and trying to convince both of us you're in charge. "You're not following me, Oberman. You will speak to your men, in my presence, now, or they will speak to me in my interview room, on record. Make a choice, and stop wasting my time."

In the moment of heated silence, Eve thought if Renee believed she could get away with using her weapon on a fellow officer, she'd have drawn and fired.

Instead, she flicked on her squad room com. "Detectives Garnet and Bix. My office. Immediately. I won't have you harassing my men, Lieutenant."

"Harassing's the least I have in mind."

Garnet came in a step ahead of Bix. Both wore dark suits, carefully knotted ties, and a mirror shine on their shoes.

Are these cops or Feds? Eve wondered, and got a hard, cold look from Garnet.

"Close the door, Detective Bix. Lieutenant Dallas, Detectives, please sit down."

"No. Thanks," Eve added after a beat.

"Suit yourself." Renee sat behind her desk in what Eve assumed she considered her position of authority. Shoulders back, hands clasped together, face stern. "Detectives, Lieutenant Dallas is asserting that the two of you entered the residence of Rickie Keener, now deceased, at some point yesterday. The lieutenant is primary in the investigation of Keener's death."

"Murder," Eve corrected. "It's a homicide investigation."

"Lieutenant Dallas is approaching it as such, though as yet the ME has not determined homicide, self-termination, or accidental death."

"You're behind the times there, Lieutenant Oberman, as the ME has determined homicide as of this morning. But that's not the point."

"This matter has been determined a homicide?" Renee demanded. "I want to see the ME's report."

"I'm not here to give you information, but to get it. These two men entered Keener's flop yesterday, between the time I informed you of the death of your CI and the time my partner and I went to Keener's place. Which means, Lieutenant, you were aware of his death and my investigation when your men so entered—in violation of procedure, in violation of my authority."

Renee held up a finger. "Are Lieutenant Dallas's assertions accurate?" she asked the men. "Did you, in fact, go to Keener's residence and enter same?"

Not going to cover for them, you spineless, calculating bitch, Eve thought. *Going to let them swing for it.*

Garnet kept his eyes on Renee's. "Could I talk to you in private a minute, LT?"

"Not going to happen," Dallas told him before Renee could speak. "I hear it now, from you, or I'm charging you both—as I've already informed your lieutenant. And I will be informing command."

"Detectives, I know you've been focused on the Geraldi investigation. I fail to see how that would take you to Keener's residence, if indeed the lieutenant's information is correct."

"We had some intel. We had a tip." Garnet glanced toward Eve, then back at

Renee. "LT, the investigation is at a sensitive point."

"I understand that, but the investigation will stall, or worse, break down if the lieutenant files a complaint, or worse, charges. For God's sake, Detective, did you go in to Keener's?"

"We got wind he had some juice on—" He broke off, glanced at Eve again. "Some information on an individual with a connection to our investigation. So we went over to talk to him. We weren't aware, at that time, he was dead. We didn't find him in his usual locations, so we went to his flop. He didn't answer. Everybody knows Juicy enjoys his own product and has a habit of zoning out."

She'd thrown them a hook with this Geraldi angle, Eve concluded. Now Garnet was spinning his line from it.

"Let's say," he continued, "if we're going to make it official, we believed we smelled an illegal substance emanating from the residence. Bix was uncertain whether it was an illegal substance or smoke. Bix?"

"Affirmative. Might've been smoke."

"Therefore, we obtained entry in order

to determine if the occupant was in need of assistance."

"That's your story?" Eve asked.

"That's how it was," Garnet insisted.

"And it took you thirty minutes to determine a flop the size of a utility closet was empty, there was no smoke either from an illegal substance or fire?"

"You want to come hard because we took a look around? We didn't know the little prick was dead, and we've got a major investigation coming to flashpoint. Maybe he had something on it. I don't know how you work it in Homicide, but—"

"Obviously not. Did you or your fellow officer remove anything from the area?"

"Nothing there but garbage. He lived like a pig, and from what I hear he died the same."

"The little prick who lived like a pig is my victim," Eve said coldly. "And by violating procedure you may very well have compromised the chain of evidence needed to bring his killer to justice."

"I heard he OD'd." Garnet shrugged. "There's no reason for anybody to kill the little asshole."

"Really? Even if the little asshole had

information about an individual connected to a major investigation that is at flash-point?"

Caught in that little hole in the web of lies, Garnet shut his mouth. Eve turned back to Renee. "In addition to the other data already required, I'll need a copy of all files and data on this Geraldi investigation."

Now Garnet surged to his feet, and his face blotched with angry color. "There's no fucking way you're sticking your nose in my case. You're looking to bust our balls over some dead weasel because you've got nothing else."

"You'd better stand down, Detective," Eve warned.

"Fuck you!" He snarled it out even as Renee said his name. "Fuck her." He whirled on Renee. "She's not coming in here telling me how to run a case, screwing up my work over some useless dead junkie. You better back me on this, god-damn it, or—"

"Detective Garnet!" Renee's voice sliced through the air, cut off his words so his breath heaved in and out.

"You'd better back me," he repeated.

"I'm going to have that data, per procedure, Detective. Deal with it." Eve stepped
a little closer, angled, lifted a hand. "You've
already crossed over into insubordination,
so—"

He spun around, and as she'd hoped,
his forearm smacked sharply into hers. To
make it a little more dramatic, she fell back
a step.

"Get off my back. You're not in charge
here."

"From where I'm standing, nobody is."
Eve spared Renee a brief, disgusted look.
"And you, Detective Garnet, just earned
yourself a thirty-day rip. Another word
comes out of your mouth, it'll be sixty," she
warned, then gave Bix a cold stare as he
got slowly to his feet. "Sit down, Detective
Bix, unless you want the same."

"Bix." Renee spoke quietly when he didn't
move. "Take your seat."

Good dog, Eve thought when he obeyed.

"Detective Garnet, sit down and calm
down. Not another word," Renee added.
"Lieutenant Dallas, obviously we have a
situation where emotions ran hot. My detectives are running a difficult investigation
that appears to have bumped into yours.

There's no reason why we can't work this out, reasonably, and without any undue interference to either investigation, right here in this office."

"You want a *favor* from me?" Eve looked amazed. "You're going to stand there and ask me to do you a solid when you failed to control your own detective, when you failed to take any action when he spoke to me with extreme disrespect, even after I warned him. When he laid hands on me?"

"In the heat of the moment—"

"My ass. I'll be writing him up because, frankly, I don't trust you to do so. I'll also be writing up the incident regarding my vic's residence. I will be speaking to any member of your squad who's involved in this Geraldi case. Further, as already detailed, I want all data on any busts or investigations that involved the substance known as FYU."

"That's absolutely—"

Eve stepped closer, let her own heat show. "You don't know how we do things in my division? I'll tell you this, if one of my men displayed such extreme disrespect to a superior officer, I'd be the one who took him down. Because it's my command. I

want the data and files on the investigation within the hour."

Eve strode out, pleased to see every
eye in the place follow her out—and enjoyed the faint smirk Detective Strong
didn't quite mask.

Part of her wanted to break out in song,
but she kept cold, controlled fury on her
face as she stormed back to her own level,
her own bullpen.

"Reineke!"

His head snapped up, eyes wide at the
tone. "Sir!"

"What would happen if you said 'fuck
you' to a superior officer in my presence?"

"If I said it in my head or out loud?"

"Out loud."

"My ass would be extremely sore from
the repeated and forceful application of
your boot thereto."

"Fucking A. Peabody, my office." She
kept that pissed-off look in place until Peabody came in, obeyed Eve's signal to shut
the door. "Watch this, because you won't
see it often."

Eve swiveled her hips, pumped her
arms in the air.

"Would that be your happy dance, sir?"

"It's restrained, I know, but this is serious business and requires some restraint. I just creamed Renee, embarrassed her, pissed her off, and undermined her command—and as a bonus maneuvered Garnet into behavior that earned him a thirty-day rip. Which I will write up forthwith."

"You did all that without me?"

"I didn't know going in I was going to hit the jackpot. I need to write him up, file the rip. I have to do it asap, in my righteous fury and all that. I'll fill you in as soon as possible. Meanwhile I'm expecting a case file from our pals in Illegals—the blind Garnet tried to use to justify going into the flop."

"They admitted it?"

"Had to. Geraldi investigation's what he used to excuse going into the flop. I want you to pick through the file. Odds are they're planning on doing a nice skim when it goes down. Let's see who and what we can use."

"Did you scare her? I'm good with the embarrassed, pissed off, and undermined, but I'd really like her scared."

Eve's smile spread wide even as her eyes burned. "Peabody, I put the fear of God into her."

"Good. Good. The guys are going to ask what's up with you."

"And you tell them—discreetly—that one of Lieutenant Oberman's detectives got in my face, used obscenities, and struck me."

Peabody's eyes widened, rounded, all but glazed. "He *hit* you?"

"Well, technically I made sure my arm got in the way when he did his furious whirl around to me, but there was contact. Renee stood there ineffectively—pass that on—then tried to talk me into letting it go. That's enough to get it growing on the Central grapevine."

"I'll say." In a mimic of Eve, Peabody swiveled her hips, pumped her arms, then strolled out.

An hour later, Eve answered a summons to Whitney's office.

He leaned back in his chair. "I just had a long conversation with Lieutenant Oberman."

"I'm not surprised, sir."

"She wished me to countermand your thirty-day suspension of Detective Garnet. I read your report on him. How did you manage to incite him to . . . basically tell you to get fucked and to make physical contact?"

"It was surprisingly easy. He's got a temper, and once the right buttons are pushed, feels entitled to use it. Bix is more controlled, sir, and I found it interesting that her tone with him is almost maternal. Garnet does the talking, Bix the listening. Bix immediately obeys an order, Garnet ignores them, at least when he's hot."

"Lieutenant Oberman cites a current investigation, in which both Garnet and Bix are involved, as the necessity for me to countermand, or failing that, to postpone the rip."

"The Geraldi matter. My opinion, sir?" She waited for his nod. "Renee pulled that out of the air, and they tried to run with it. But without time to plan and coordinate, it tripped them up."

"She relayed what happened—her version of what happened during the time you were in her office, assures me she will discipline her detectives and order Garnet to issue an apology to you."

"Not accepted."

"Nor would I accept in your place. But . . ." He lifted his big hands. "Don't you think it would be more useful to the investigation if Garnet remained on active duty?"

"He's a hair trigger, Commander. He's already steamed at Renee, already questioning—even ignoring her authority, her strategies. Now he's taken this knock and she didn't fix it. His dissatisfaction with the status quo just increased. He's going to find trouble in his current mood and situation."

"There's a crack," Whitney said with a nod, "and you use him to widen it."

"I think he'd shatter it. When we take him down, he'll flip on her. As much as making a deal with him leaves a bad taste, Commander, Garnet will flip on all of them for a decent deal. Bix won't flip. He's loyal. But I can flip Garnet."

"Compromise, even with a bad taste, is something command routinely swallows. All right, Lieutenant, the suspension holds. Has Renee copied you on the investigation?"

"The data came in right before I received

your request to meet, sir. I've got Peabody going through it, and I'll do so myself."

"As will I. You've made an enemy of her, Dallas."

"She always was, Commander. She just didn't know it."

II Eve kept her stony face on as she traveled back to her division. From the few glances shot her way, the occasional murmur, she was assured the Central grapevine was spreading the gossip.

She needed to close herself off in her office awhile, do some probabilities, and use her instincts to select the next step.

Peabody started to hail her, but Eve shook her head and kept going. She heard the squeal when she was a few short steps from her door.

There was baby Bella decked out like a

daffodil with her sunny curls, her chubby body tucked into a bright yellow sundress decorated with pink candy hearts.

The hearts matched her mother's hair. Mavis Freestone bounced her baby girl and giggled at the squeals of delight. She'd scooped her hair back into a trio of stacked ponytails. What there was of her summer dress exploded with interlacing circles in vivid purple and pink.

Green eyes sparked with laughter in her pretty face as Bella bapped her hands together.

"Applause, applause!" Mavis gurgled, and the baby slapped her hands together again. "Now take your bow!"

On cue—and how the hell did a brain that tiny know—Bella pushed her feet—in shiny pink sandals that were a mini version of her mother's—and rose up to stand on Mavis's lap. She lowered her chin to her chest.

"Kisses to the crowd!" Mavis switched her handhold to Bella's waist so the baby could smack her palm against her lips, then wave it.

Eve had to admit it was a pretty good routine.

"You brought the baby to a cop shop?"

Mother and daughter both turned, and big, happy smiles spread. "She wanted to visit."

Bella threw out her arms, babbled.

Eve inched back. "What does she want?"

"You. Which is great." Mavis popped up. "'Cause I absolutely have to pee. BRB," she added, and shoved the baby at Eve.

"Hey! Hey!" But Mavis's shiny pink sandals were already skipping away. "Jesus Christ."

Bella giggled, patted her drool-dewed hands on Eve's cheeks, then got a Herculean grip on her hair. She tugged then slurped her wet lips on Eve's cheek.

"Slooch!"

"Yeah, yeah, I remember." Smooch, Eve thought, and eyed Bella's lips—and more drool. "On the mouth?"

"Slooch!" Bella pursed like a guppy and made kissy noises.

"Fine, fine." Eve gave her a little peck, then stared into her big blue eyes. "Now what?"

Bella widened her eyes, and looked, to Eve's mind, very serious as she babbled and garbled, head turning side-to-side, little butt bouncing on Eve's forearm.

"Nobody understands that. Anybody who tells you they do is just stringing you, kid."

She decided to sit—safer and closer to the floor if the kid wriggled free. Plus maybe she could start on the probabilities. But the minute they were down, Bella pushed up.

"God! I wish you wouldn't do that. Sit."

In response Bella pumped her legs and danced on Eve's knees. She grinned like a maniac and squealed, "Das!"

"Sure, sure." Eve eyed the mountainous purple bag taking up most of her desk. "Probably something in there to keep you occupied. One of those plugs, something." Hooking an arm around Bella's waist, she pulled out things at random—shaking things, beeping things, singing things.

But all the kid wanted to do was dance.

She pulled out a box highlighted with a baby's cherubic face. Bella danced harder, cried, "Yum!" and made a grab for it.

"Hold it, hold it." It was a struggle, but Eve managed to hold the box out of reach and peek inside at what appeared to be thick crescents of stale bread.

"Those look disgusting."

Bella narrowed those big blue eyes, slitting them into what looked suspiciously like a warning. "Yum!"

"Is that a threat? Do you see how much bigger I am than you? Do you really think that's going to work?"

Now the little mouth quivered, and the big blue eyes filled with tears. "Yum," she sniffled. A single fat one slid down the rosy cheek.

"Okay, that works." Eve dug one out. The box wouldn't have a baby on it if it wasn't *for* babies, she reasoned.

Bella clutched it and brought the biscuit and Eve's hand to her mouth to gnaw. Tears miraculously vanished into a sunny smile.

"Yum!"

"You're a player, aren't you? I have to admire that. But turning on the waterworks to get what you want? That's weak. Effective, but weak."

Still smiling, Bella pulled the gnawed biscuit from her mouth and shoved it at Eve's.

"No. Thanks. Oh, God, it *is* disgusting."

"Yum," Bella insisted, then plopped her

butt on Eve's desk and happily gnawed away.

Eve looked around quickly as Mavis bounced in. "If she's not supposed to have that thing, you shouldn't have left it here."

"No big deal, those are her yums."

"So she told me—I guess."

Mavis pulled a heart-covered bib out of the bag, whipped it around Bella's neck. "They're kinda messy."

"You did that on purpose, didn't you? Dumped her in my lap and poofed."

Mavis giggled, lifted her shoulders. "Busted. But I did pee."

"Why?"

"Because my bladder asked me to."

"Mavis."

"Because she loves you, and because you've pretty much stopped holding her at arm's length like she's a boomer full of poop."

"Poop is sometimes involved."

"True." Mavis took a quick sniff. "But not now. She can say your name." To prove it Mavis gave Eve a kiss on the cheek. "Dallas."

"Das!" Bella squealed and stroked a gooey hand where her mother had kissed.

On a strangled sound, Eve started to swipe the goo off with the heel of her hand, but Mavis pulled a damp wipe out of a packet.

"That's my name?"

"It's the closest she can come to Dallas right now. She can't manage Peabody, but she's got McNab."

"Nab!" Bella waved her dripping biscuit in triumph.

"And she's got Roarke."

"Ork!"

"Ork." That tickled a laugh out of Eve, and the sound had the baby sending out a chant.

"Ork! Ork! Ork!" Then damned if the kid didn't take a bow.

"Jesus, Mavis, she's you all over."

"With her daddy's sweet, sweet heart." Mavis pulled a rainbow-hued blanket out of the apparently bottomless bag. After spreading it on the floor, she took Bella, plopped her on it.

"Okay if I close the door? In case she starts to motor."

"Good idea."

Mavis shut the door, then dropped down in Eve's visitor's chair. With the baby at her feet, she crossed her legs. "So, how'd I do?"

"Good job, Candy."

"Not too OTT? Over the top," Mavis translated. "I decided to plug in the Brooklyn and the tits when I was putting it together this morning. Just a little jazz."

"Both were impressive. I barely recognized you myself. You haven't lost your skills."

"Felt mag, too, gotta confess. Sliding back in and duping a mark. Temporarily," she added, "and for a righteous cause."

"Check."

"I guess you still can't tell me what the righteous cause is?"

"Not yet."

"Doesn't matter, because I so totally didn't like the mark. Pushy b-i-t-c-h. Hard a-s-s, and not in a good or frosty way."

"You're actually spelling swear words now? The kid's not even listening."

"You never know. This Oberman is the b word and the a word and a whole universe of other words I don't want to say in front of my Bellamina. And, Dallas, she'd like to rip your heart out of your chest with her bare hands."

"I've given her cause. That's part of it."

"Just watch your as—a-s-s. I was back in my grifter's skin, you know, and man, the vibes. Cold and dark. Belle and I want our Das to stay safe, and to kick the b-word's you-know-what."

"I plan to do both."

After Bella waved bye-bye, Eve got coffee, settled down to review the data she'd already accessed on the detectives who'd transferred out of Renee's squad, crossed that with what Baxter had dug up for her.

She studied their records before, during, and after Renee's command, their records after transfer, and in one case retirement.

She took a hard look at Detective-Sergeant Samuel Allo. Thirty-five years in before he'd turned in his papers—thirty-one years and five months of that prior to Renee's command. A full seventeen in Illegals before Renee, and he'd finished up the last of his thirty-five years in Illegals as well, only in the six-eight out of the Bronx.

She juggled him in with a couple others who looked strong to her, ran a variety of probabilities. In the end it satisfied her to see the computer agreed with her gut.

She walked out into the bullpen. Before

she could signal Peabody, Carmichael strolled over with a little box. "Got something for you, Lieutenant."

Noting the cops on desks watched, she opened the box.

"Okay. Why are you giving me a cookie shaped like—is it a dog?"

"Yeah. See, it says Top Dog. My sister works in a bakery, so she made it."

"Nice. Because?"

"A little token for taking Garnet down a peg. I had a case cross with one of his awhile back," Carmichael explained. "He's an asshole."

"I can confirm that assessment. Why do you say so?"

"Struts," she said with a little sneer. "I don't like strutters. Likes pushing his weight around and acting like he's doing you some big favor for sharing info when you're working angles on the same case. Doesn't like getting his pretty suits dirty either. Roasted a rook uniform in front of God and everyone for asking a question, and when I objected he told me to stop being a little girl."

"How long did he limp?"

Carmichael smiled. "I was tempted to bust his balls, but deemed it more appropriate to secure the scene, preserve evidence. So, in the spirit of what goes around, a token for the Top Dog for busting his balls now."

"Happy to so bust. Thanks. Peabody, with me." Eve bit the dog's head off as she walked out, then glanced back at her men. "Tasty."

As Eve chewed the dog, Peabody sent her a puppy-dog look.

"Jesus, here." She broke off a foreleg, handed it over.

"Thanks. It is tasty. Everything chill with the commander?"

"Completely. I want to recanvass the area around the crime scene, try to hook with my weasel, see if he's got any more I can squeeze out of him."

Since there was no weasel in this case, Peabody just nodded. "He was pretty rattled about what happened to Keener. He may have gone under for a while."

"Then we'll have to dig him up."

When they were in the vehicle, Peabody asked, "Where are we really going?"

"We'll take a swing by the scene. Maybe we'll be able to squeeze out more juice on Juicy. After, we're going to the Bronx."

"I guess it won't be to catch a Yankees game."

"DS Samuel Allo, retired. All data indicates he was a solid cop. Probability confirms my analysis with a ninety-four-point-seven."

"I recognize the name. He was with the squad before Renee got promoted. He transferred out."

"About seven months after she took command," Eve confirmed. "Out of her squad, and out of Central. He put in another three-plus with Bronx PSD. Did thirty-five. He has a few bumps, and a lot more commendations. One rip—under Renee—for insubordination. Her evals of him over the seven-month period were not stellar. Coasting, she claimed, just riding out his time. Questioning her authority, balking at doing OT when deemed necessary.

"Oddly, his evals and records with the six-eight in the Bronx did not reflect his previous lieutenant's opinion."

"She squeezed him out."

"That's my take. I'm interested in his."

Detective-Sergeant Allo had a modest house in a neighborhood of modest houses. And in the short driveway sat a huge boat.

Allo stood on the deck—the bow, Eve thought—polishing the brightwork with a rag. He took a long look when they pulled in, then laid the rag over the rail.

He had a sturdy, broad-shouldered build and carried a little extra weight in the middle. He wore a backward ballcap—Yankee blue—over hair he'd let go gray.

Retired or not, he had a cop's eyes and gave Eve and Peabody a good once-over as he climbed off the boat, and they stepped out of the car.

"Is there a problem in the neighborhood, Detectives?"

"Not that I'm aware of. Lieutenant Dallas, Detective Peabody. Got a minute, Detective-Sergeant?"

"Got a lot of them since I retired. Put a lot of those into this baby here." He patted the hull affectionately. "I've got you now," he added with a nod. "Out of Central. Homicide. Somebody dead I know?"

"Again, not that I'm aware of. You were assigned to Illegals out of Central for a number of years, and a few months of that under Lieutenant Renee Oberman."

"That's a fact."

"Would you mind telling us why you transferred out, and into the six-eight?"

His eyes stayed on Eve's. "Can't say why this should interest Homicide. Our son had his second kid, moved out here. My wife and I decided we wanted to be close, enjoy the grandchildren. We bought ourselves this place. The six-eight's a lot closer to home than Central."

"Nice house," Eve commented. "Big boat."

He grinned at it, very much like Mavis grinned at Bella. "I always wanted a boat. I'm shining her up. We're going to take the family out this weekend."

"Should be a nice one for it. Would it be fair to say, Detective-Sergeant, that you and Lieutenant Oberman didn't mesh well?"

His face shifted back to neutral. "That would be fair."

"Lieutenant Oberman notes in your file you had difficulty with her authority, with taking orders from a female superior."

His jaw tightened. "What cause do you have to check my service records?"

"They're of interest to me."

His stance shifted, combative now. "I served thirty-five years, and I'm proud of every day I spent on the job. I don't like an LT I never met coming to my home and questioning my record."

"It's not your record in question."

His jaw remained tight, but his eyes narrowed in speculation. "You want me to dish some dirt on Lieutenant Oberman? I don't much like you coming to my home for that either."

She'd have been disappointed if he'd launched into a series of complaints, and trusted him more when he didn't.

"I'm asking for your opinion. Thirty-five years on the job, solid record—and a single rip. Under Oberman. I have reasons for coming to your home, reasons for asking you about Lieutenant Oberman."

"What are they?"

"I'm not free to give you that information at this time, but can tell you we're on an active investigation."

"What, do you think she killed somebody?" When Eve said nothing, he blew out a long breath. With his hands on his hips he looked away, just looked away for a space of time. "It's a hell of a thing," he murmured. "A hell of a thing. Have a seat on the porch. My wife's off with some girlfriends. I'll see what we've got cold to drink."

He had iced tea, cold and sweet. They sat in the shade of the little covered porch and drank.

"I keep in touch," Allo began. "Talk to or hook up with some of the guys I worked with. And I keep up with what's going on. I know your rep, Lieutenant. Yours, too, Detective."

He paused, drank again. "Let's be clear. I never had a problem working with a female officer, or taking orders from one who outranked me. I served my last three years with a damn good detective, who happened to be female. I'm still pissed about that rip," he admitted. "All this time, and it still eats at me. Insubordinate, my ass."

He shifted, angled more directly toward Eve. "I argued with her, sure. But I never disrespected her. She says we all have to wear suits and ties, even on the desk, I put on a suit and tie. She wants us to clear off our personal items, even family photos. I clear them off. It's her squad. I don't like it—and I'm not the only one—but it's her squad."

He brooded a moment. "Her squad, that's the thing. When you have a new boss, you expect changes. In how things are done, in the tone. Every boss has a style, and that's the way it is."

"You didn't like hers," Eve prompted.

"Cold, nitpicky. Not picking nits over an investigation, but your fricking shoe shine, your haircut. She played favorites. If you were down on her list you got the shit assignments. Every time. All-night stakeouts in the middle of the winter because somebody got a tip maybe something was going to go down. But the somebody who'd be one of the favored was too busy with something else to sit and freeze his ass off all night."

He puffed out his cheeks, released the air. "Maybe all that sounds like picking nits, too."

"I don't think so."

"Every boss has a style," he commented, and looked at Peabody. "We pick up the style, learn to work with it so everybody gets the job done."

"That's how I see it," Peabody agreed. "The job's the thing."

"The job's the thing." He nodded. "But she'd question the direction of an investigation, pull you off one and stick you on another. Dump somebody else's petty case on you. That happened to me twice. I'm this close to making a bust, and she pulls me in, reassigns. When I argue it, she sits there behind her fancy desk and tells me she's not satisfied with the quality of my work, or with my attitude."

"That's not style," Peabody put in. "That's not making the job the thing."

"Sure as hell not."

"Did you complain up the chain?" Eve asked him, though she had the answer in the file.

"No. I don't work that way. The boss is the boss, and hell, the squad was closing cases. Plus this is Saint Oberman's daughter, and when she came on as boss she was the golden girl."

"And she hung a life-sized portrait of her father in the office, in case any of you forgot."

Allo smiled at Eve. "You sure as hell

couldn't miss it. Anybody paying attention could see she was weeding out the old, sowing in the new. Handpicking when she could."

He shrugged. "Boss's privilege. But it got so I hated going in to work, hated knowing I'd be sitting in that squad room. It wears at you, makes you hard to live with. Hard enough to live with a cop, right?"

"No argument."

"It wore me down. She wore me down. I knew she wanted me out, and I knew— after the rip—she was going to find a way. I wasn't going to go out that way. I wasn't going to have her put another mark on my record. The boss is the boss," he said again, "but I'll be damned. I might as well add my wife put her foot down, and I can't blame her. So I put in for the transfer. I had another three years with a good squad, a good boss. And when I put in my papers, Lieutenant, it was my choice."

"I'm going to ask you something, Detective-Sergeant."

"Allo," he said. "Just Allo."

"Was she on the take?"

He sat back, shook his head from side-to-side. "I knew this was coming. Goddamn it." He rubbed a hand over his face, shook his head again. "Did you see the name of my boat?"

"Yes, I did. *The Blue Line.*"

"Being retired doesn't shift the line."

"From where I stand that line breaks for a wrong cop, or it means nothing. For a cop who uses her badge, her authority to fill her own pockets, and worse, the line breaks."

He kept his gaze hard on her face. "And if I say hell, yeah, you're going to believe me after everything I just told you?"

"Yes, I am. I came to you because I believe you're a good cop—fuck retirement, Allo, you're still a cop. You'll always be a cop. I came to you because I believe you respect the badge, and because I believe I can take your word, even your opinion, to the bank."

He took a long drink, let out a long breath. "I'm going to say hell, yeah, but I couldn't prove it, couldn't give you one solid piece of evidence. Not then, not now. She liked her closed-door meetings with her chosen few. And I know damn well with a couple of the busts I managed to stick on, somebody skimmed. No way I underestimate junk by the amounts it came back to after weigh-in. My mistake there was going to her on just that. Telling the boss I suspected somebody'd skimmed some off the top. That's when things got bad for me. Or worse, I guess you'd say."

He shrugged. "Coincidence? Maybe if you believe in coincidence. I never did."

"Neither do I. I bet you still have your notebooks. I bet you still have your records of the investigations and busts you took part in under Lieutenant Oberman."

"You'd win that bet."

"I'm trusting you, Allo, to keep everything said here to yourself. Not to share it, at this time, with the friends you talk to, hook up with. I'm not going to insult you by saying if you do that, if you trust me with those records I'll see that rip is expunged from your record. But I will tell you, either way you go, I'm going to look into that."

"I'm not asking for a favor, but I won't turn this one down." He sat another minute. "She's done murder, too?"

"Her hands are bloody."

"I'm sorry to hear it, sorry because of

her old man. You're going to take her down."

It wasn't a question, but Eve answered anyway. "To the ground."

He nodded, rose. "I'll get my books."

He paused at the door, turned back. "There was an officer—female officer— who went down in the line under Oberman."

"Detective Gail Devin."

He nodded. "She was a good cop. She was the daughter of an old friend of mine. My oldest friend. We went to school together in the old neighborhood. She had some concerns about Oberman and came to me with them."

"What concerns?"

"How Oberman tended to have regular closed-door meets with certain members of the squad. How invoices for confiscated illegals and cash were usually under the estimate. Same as me. I looked into it after it happened, as best I could. It looked clean, but I always wondered. I had this place in me that wondered, and it still does. If you look into that, Lieutenant, if you look into what happened to Gail, you can forget about the rip."

"I'll be looking into both."

Driving back to Manhattan, Eve considered angles, approaches, timing.

"I want you to take the lead on Devin."

"Take the lead?"

"Approaching it like a cold case, an unsolved. Dig into the files. Have McNab and/or Webster help you if you need to shovel anywhere that might send Renee a flag. She's not thinking about Devin—that's old, settled business to her."

"You think Renee had Detective Devin killed?"

"Fact: Devin wasn't one of Renee's handpicks. She was a newly minted detective, and according to our source—DS Allo, who strikes me as very grounded—she was solid. In my scan of her records, her evals were the same. Solid. Until assigned to Renee where they took a dip."

"And that's pattern with Renee."

"Add in Mira's profile, which says Renee has a problem with females. Conclude with another fact. Less than a year under Renee's command, Devin goes down in a raid. The only officer to go down."

"How did she go down?"

"The official report states she got separated from her team during the confusion and was found with her neck broken. Read the file, examine the evidence. Dig. Then I want you to tell me if Renee had Devin killed."

"It could've been me. If they'd found me in that shower stall."

"And you have to put that to the side and study, access, investigate objectively. If there was a cover-up, you uncover it."

Eve engaged her 'link and contacted Webster.

 **12** Webster clicked off the 'link he'd put on privacy mode and looked across the table where he'd been enjoying a late lunch. "Sorry about that."

"It's not a problem." Darcia smiled at him. "Do you have to go?"

"Soon." He reached over, took her hand. "I'd rather stay."

"There's tonight. If you're free, and interested."

"I'm both. What would you like to do?"

"I happen to have two orchestra seats for a play—a musical. Broadway musical is on my New York checklist." She lifted the glass of champagne she'd indulged in. "You weren't. But I made an addendum."

"Luckiest day of my life." He was still riding on the thrill of it. "If I were to visit Olympus, what should I put on my checklist?"

"Hmmm, drinks rooftop of the Apollo Tower. The view is stunning. Horseback riding along Athena Lake, with a picnic in its young forest. Me. Will you visit Olympus?"

"Will you have drinks with me on the rooftop, ride with me along the lake, picnic with me in the forest?"

"I will."

"I have some time coming. There's something I have to wrap up first. Once I do, I'll put in for it."

"Then I'll show you my world." She looked down at their joined hands. "Is it foolish, Don, what we're doing here, what we may be starting here?"

"Probably." He tightened his grip on her hand. "I don't care, Darcia."

"Neither do I." On a half laugh, she shook her head. "It's so unlike me. I'm a practical woman."

"And the most beautiful woman I've ever seen."

She laughed fully, delightedly. "Your eyes are dazzled—I suppose mine are, too. I'm sitting here in this lovely restaurant in this exciting city, and all I can think is I'm sitting here with this handsome man who can't take his eyes off me."

"There's nothing I'd rather look at."

"Handsome, charming man," she added. "But looks, even charm, are only the surface."

"You've got an amazing surface, and I like everything I've found under it so far."

"It's only our second date," she reminded him, and her eyes sparkled like her wine. "There's more."

"I'm looking forward to discovering you, Darcia. We don't have to rush it. Well, hard to rush it anyway when we'll be on two different planets—or a planet and a satellite—in a few days."

"I like to take things slowly, carefully. The job, as you know, can be difficult, demanding, so in my personal life I prefer the uncomplicated."

She lifted her champagne again, smiling at him over the pale gold bubbles. "I didn't ask you into my hotel room last night because this—you and I—this will be complicated."

"I've been taking a break from complicated myself, in the personal area. But I want to see you again, spend time with you. I want to see what happens next."

"I've given some thought to what happens next. And since I know what I'd like that to be, I'll be asking you into my room tonight."

He smiled back at her. "I was hoping you would."

With the data Webster passed to her, Eve ran an analysis of Accounting for Renee's squad. Then an analysis of the analysis. The flood of numbers, the puzzlement of percentages gave her a headache. And still she couldn't see a clear pattern. She couldn't see enough to point a finger at anyone in charge of the accounts.

She toggled away from that—maybe if she let the numbers rest they'd make more sense to her—and took another sweep through Renee's squad. There she believed she saw a pattern, where Detective

Lilah Strong, a rookie uniform, and two other detectives stood as abnormalities.

She needs clean cops, Eve calculated. To handle the piddly stuff, to turn in legit reports—and as fall guys when she needs or wants them. Use them, then lose them. One way or another.

She thought of Gail Devin, glanced at Peabody.

Her partner was in it deep and would stick, Eve knew, no matter how long it took, no matter how many layers needed to be shifted through.

She looked at her board.

On one side, Rickie Keener. Loser, criminal, junkie, low-life pig. But he was hers now.

On the other, Detective Gail Devin, by all reports a good cop with good instincts— and with the moral code to talk to an older, experienced cop she respected about her concerns over her boss.

Two sides of the scale, Eve decided, but she knew—she *knew* that while Renee may not have plunged the syringe or snapped the neck, she'd killed them both.

Added to one side of that scale, Detective Harold Strumb—stabbed to death in an alley while his partner and a squad mate walked away unharmed.

They wouldn't be the only ones. And unless Renee went down, they wouldn't be the last.

She opened Allo's case notes, began to read.

She liked his style—terse, even pithy, but thorough. She noted he'd questioned Sergeant Runch's invoices regularly. And when she correlated with Allo's file under Renee's command she found the lieutenant's notations citing him as malingering or conflicting with fellow officers.

Eve started her own file on Allo's cases during the seven-month period, the invoices, the evals. Not wanting to disturb Peabody, she sent her a memo to do the same on Devin, and to follow it, as she was with Allo, with a probability analysis.

While it ran, she began to study the Geraldi files she'd forced Renee to send her.

She put it on hold when Webster came in.

"You've got something?" she demanded.

"Nothing major. Why?"

"You look like you've got something. You look happy."

"I'm a happy guy."

She waved that away. "What have you got that's minor then?"

"Marcell—partner of Strumb, the one who went down. IAB's got a file on him."

"Over Strumb?"

"No. Deals with before that. They interviewed and investigated him over a questionable termination—five years ago. There were witness reports claiming Marcell fired on full, twice, after the suspect had dropped his weapon and surrendered."

"The determination?"

"Cleared him. The witnesses were two other dealers, so their statements were given the fish-eye. The suspect did have an illegal weapon and had discharged it. Marcell stuck to his story. The suspect remained armed and was again preparing to discharge. Reconstruction couldn't disprove. However, there's a note in the file— the one I had to slide out without notification. A big, fat question mark. Updated after both wits met violent ends."

"Like Strumb and those wits."

"Yeah. Marcell had an alibi in both cases. Solid."

"For the wits on Strumb, yeah," Eve

agreed. "Solid but bogus. What did he use on the wits on the older deal?"

"He was on a stakeout with another officer. Freeman, coincidentally."

Webster dropped into a chair. "I know he's wrong—Freeman, too. You know it. The pattern's saying they're wrong in big, shiny letters. But we're not there yet."

"More there than we were twenty-four hours ago."

"Can't argue. In other news. I've started my own file on everyone currently in Renee's squad—including her. There's plenty of shadow there, Dallas. If I could take this to my boss, we'd break it open, and we'd damn well be there."

"People slip out of shadows, Webster, just like Marcell. I'm not jeopardizing slamming this lid down so IAB can make a big bang."

"I don't give a shit about the bang, Dallas."

"I wouldn't have asked you if I thought you did. I contacted and spoke with DS Allo and have his case notes from the seven months he was with the squad under her. It's no wonder she needed him gone. He doesn't miss anything."

"You brought him in?"

"I made a judgment call. He knew Runch was skimming and reported it to his lieutenant."

"Did he document?"

"He has detailed notes, times, dates. I doubt we'll find them corroborated in her files. What he got in return was the first rip in a thirty-year career. He suspected Renee. I've written up my conversation with him, and I've got a copy for you. Attached to it is the file on Gail Devin."

"The other officer in her squad who went down."

"Allo knew her, and she came to him with concerns about their lieutenant and the squad that mirrored his. But, I think, instead of transferring out, she not only stuck but she might've pushed it. She talked to somebody else or started documenting— something—and they took her out."

"If you're right, and fuck it, Dallas, it feels right, that makes two cops she's killed."

"I'm betting more. Peabody's working the Devin angle. She'll copy you on what she finds or concludes. Contact you if she needs any cover with the digging."

He nodded. "So . . . you went a round with Garnet today, and he lost. Did you set him up or did he just fall into it?"

"Some of both. He tried to cover why he and Bix accessed my vic's flop by some bullshit about a connection to a major investigation they're working. That was a stupid move, because it handed me the files. The thing is, the files aren't complete. She did some deleting, rearranging. There's something off. I've read enough of her reports by now, her style there, to know she slid things around. Things she didn't want me to see."

"Do you want me to find an IAB angle on the investigation?"

"Not yet. I've got a way around her game. But a little whiff of IAB nosing around Garnet wouldn't hurt."

"More pressure on him."

"That's right. He'll blow. If I can get him in, he'll turn on her to save his own ass. Last thing, I'd like you to dig around, see if there's been any dirt or accusation of dirt on Strong, Detective Lilah, in Renee's squad. She's new there, and her record reads solid. And my read of her is she doesn't like the boss or the setup."

"Clean cop, female cop." Webster weighed it out. "You're looking for a mole."

"If I use her, if she's clean and she agrees, I want her protected against an IAB hit if she needs to do or profess herself willing to do what would earn her one."

"I'll look at her, and if it goes, I'll have it all documented. She's undercover, sanctioned. Whitney needs to sign off."

"It won't be a problem." She held up a finger when her 'link signaled. "It's Feeney. What ya got?" she answered.

A thin smile lightened his hangdog face. "I thought you'd like to hear this. Renee's in her vehicle, and just had a 'link conversation."

"Roll it out."

"One sec. Patching the recording on."

"What the hell," Eve decided. "Incoming 'link transmission on wall screen." She glanced over, saw Peabody grin.

"Thanks."

She saw Renee first, behind the wheel, fingers tapping, shoulders swaying to the beat of the music she'd selected.

"Likes her new ride," Eve murmured. "Nice upgrade."

When Renee's 'link signaled, she cut

her eyes down—dash screen readout, Eve concluded. Her face went hard. "Goddamn it. Transfer transmission to pocket 'link two." She snatched it up, shoved it into its on-dash slot. "Garnet."

The angle blocked the pocket 'link's screen, but his voice came through loud and clear.

"You said you were going to fix it. Fuck this, Oberman. I'm not taking a thirty-day rip from that cunt because you can't figure out how to slap her down."

"Calm down. And don't contact me about this or anything else unless it's on the safe 'link. You know how I feel about that."

"I'll calm down when you do what you're supposed to do. You'd better have my back on this."

"Bill, I went directly to Whitney on your behalf. I explained the situation, that in my view it was simply a heated exchange between you and the lieutenant. That you were, very understandably, protecting an investigation you've put considerable man-hours, considered effort into—and which is at a tipping point. I went to bat for you, Bill, just as I said I would. And because I did, Whitney called her up. She won't budge."

"I'll budge the fucking whore."

"You listen to me. You listen to me," Renee said with a whip in her voice. "I'll handle her. I'm going to try another approach. You stay clear, do you read me? If you have to take this rip, I'll make it up to you. Jesus, Garnet, if it sticks, look at it like a month's vacation. Go to the beach. You know how you love the beach."

"Fuck that, and fuck you if you think I'm going to let this cut me out of the Geraldi deal."

"Nobody's cutting you out of anything. If you'd get yourself under some damn control we wouldn't be in this situation."

The tone shook with anger, accusation. Not, Eve thought, the right way to handle a man whose fuse was already lit and running.

"Goddamn Dallas wouldn't be in your face, or mine, if you hadn't screwed up in the first place. And you wouldn't be facing a rip if you'd held it together. You went at her, for Christ's sake, in *my* office, under *my* nose. You made physical contact."

"She got in my fucking way."

"And you're getting in mine. I'm putting myself out for you, and I don't like putting myself out. Remember that."

"And you remember just what I can do if you try to fuck with me. Remember who knows where the bodies are buried, where the dirt's stored. If you want to keep what you've got, Renee sweetie, you make damn sure I keep mine."

"Asshole!" she spewed, pounding a fist on the wheel when he broke transmission.

Feeney came back on. "Pretty, huh? After she pulled into her garage. Sat there stewing in her vehicle for a while. Didn't make any more contacts."

"Very sweet. No actual admissions of wrongdoing, but plenty of insinuations. He's on the heat, and she knows it."

"He's still useful to her," Webster put in, "so she wants to keep him."

"Definitely," Eve agreed, "but more than that, he works for her, she took him on, and she damn well needs him to remember who's . . . top dog."

"She loses it when her authority's questioned or threatened." Peabody waited for Eve's nod. "Under it, I don't think she's as confident as she wants to be, even thinks she is. She's scared of losing the controls because holding the controls is what matters most to her."

"I believe you'd do Mira proud with that analysis," Eve told her.

"Fear makes her dangerous."

"Then we're going to make her very, very dangerous." And, Eve thought, she would personally revel in it. "We'll have to see how she intends to *handle* me. On the Giraldi investigation, according to the file, Garnet and Bix have been tracing a shipment coming in within the next two weeks for the Giraldi family—specifically for Anthony G. She's altered some in the file, but I'm going to take care of that. My research indicates Anthony Giraldi deals primarily in Zeus and hard-line sex drugs like Whore and Rabbit."

She frowned as her 'link signaled another incoming. "Oh, look here. It's Renee sweetie. Stay on, Feeney, answering as conference trans, blind incoming to current contact.

"Dallas," she answered with an edge of impatience.

"Lieutenant." Renee gave her a sober look through the screen. "I understand I'm not your favorite person at the moment."

"You hit down the list."

"I think we got off on the wrong foot, and that was just exacerbated by what transpired in my office today. I'm hoping we can come to terms, find a middle ground. I'd like to buy you a drink, to apologize, and to talk this out. Lieutenant to lieutenant."

"I'm working a case, Oberman."

"We're both busy women. This friction between us is disruptive. I'm trying to reach out, Dallas, so we can smooth this over and both do our jobs."

Eve leaned back as if considering. "You want to buy me a drink? Fine. O'Riley's Pub, Upper West on Seventh. In an hour."

"That's perfect. I'll see you there."

"It could be a setup," Peabody said immediately after Renee clicked off. "She could have Bix or another of her gorillas lie in wait for you."

"She can't afford to take me out now. Not when we're having this 'friction.' When everybody at Central's talking about us butting heads. Shines another light, and she wants to dim them."

"She could let Garnet know where you'll be and when," Feeney put in. "Stir him up so he goes at you. It all falls on him."

"If it fell he'd start talking, and she knows it."

"He can't talk if she takes him out. He goes for you, takes you out or at least puts you down. And she rides to the rescue, has to take out one of her own officers in your defense. It'd be a good play."

Eve had to agree. "Yeah, but I don't think she's as smart as you, Feeney, or has time to set it up. She's not desperate yet. She's pissed off and she's off balance."

"I'm going with you," Peabody insisted. "I'll back you up."

"Peabody, she's researched me, so she knows who you are, knows you're my partner. If she spots you, this could fall apart."

"I'll do it." Webster glanced at his wrist unit. "She doesn't know me—and in any case, IAB's good at blending. She won't make me."

"She's not going to try for me. It's not her play, not now."

"Regardless, I'm backup."

"Backup for what?" Roarke asked as he came in.

"For nothing I need it for. I'm having a drink with Renee, at her request. I told her

O'Riley's, in an hour. I heated things up some today, and she wants to cool them down."

"She's already killed—or had two cops killed," Webster told him. "That we know of. Sometimes you know what you can't yet prove," he said before Eve could speak. "I'm going to back her up. I've got soft clothes in my vehicle," he told Eve. "She won't make me."

"I'll be backing the lieutenant up," Roarke said. "Or I should say Webster and I will."

"She knows Dallas," Webster pointed out, "so she sure as hell knows you and that you're married. She won't talk with you around."

"She won't see me, will she? Tell Webster why you selected O'Riley's."

"Because it's close, and because he owns it."

"There's a snug behind the bar. A room," Roarke explained. "We can monitor them from there."

"I'm already monitored." Eve tapped her chest. "You put the damn thing on me this morning."

"So I did," Roarke agreed. "And very

pleasant duty it was. We'll be monitoring from on site. Would you still like to change, Detective?"

"Yeah. In case I need to go out of the back room for any reason."

"Summerset can show you a room for that then."

"I'll get on that."

"This is over the top," Eve insisted when Webster walked out.

"She's a cop killer. You're a cop." Roarke tapped her chin. "You're my cop."

"If you're going to get squishy, I'm closing off," Feeney said. "We'll have you covered from here, Dallas."

"I'm going to be so covered I might as well be smothered."

"I feel better," Peabody commented.

"Oh well, then it's all worth it."

"While you're having your drink, I'm going to ask McNab to come in, work this with me from this point."

Still miffed, Eve shrugged.

"You can drive me over," Roarke said. "When you're in and clear, I'll take Webster in through the back of the snug. And on the way, we can fill each other in on how we spent our days."

* * *

You might as well ride with us," Eve said to Webster.

"Actually, I'll need to take off after the meet—if we're clear. I have a life outside the job, Dallas," he added when she frowned at him. "And I'm going to get back to it once we're clear of the meet."

"Fine. Suit yourself."

Roarke slid into the passenger seat. "So, what have you done today that persuades Renee she needs to buy you a drink?"

"I maneuvered Garnet into a thirty-day rip, which didn't take much—and to do the mouthing off in her office, in front of her face. So that makes her look bad—like she can't control her men."

"That must've been satisfying."

"Oh, yeah. Among other things I did today, I went to the Bronx."

She filled him in on the conversation with Allo as she drove.

"You gave Peabody that angle of the investigation because of her experience in the locker room."

"Partly. She's good with the tiny details, and I want the answers on Devin but don't

have time right now to dig in. Not the way
Devin deserves. And if Peabody's able to
gather the evidence that points to Renee,
or her command, on that officer, it's going
to outweigh that locker room experience.
It's not payback. It's justice. She'll have
helped get justice for another cop, and it'll
matter a lot to her."

"Which shows, my darling Eve, the difference between a strong, intelligent,
and—though you won't like the word—
sensitive leader and one who aims to lead
only for gain."

She'd have preferred intuitive to sensitive, but let it go.

"How did everybody miss it, Roarke?
Start with her father—but I guess there
are times a father doesn't see or has to
pretend he doesn't. Her trainer. I looked at
him. Sterling record, trained good cops. It
feels to me like her father had a hand in
picking him for her—they were partners
for eight years—about the same age. Mira
missed it, Whitney missed it, her captain,
her previous LTs. She slid right through."

"She wasn't always dirty."

"Fuck she wasn't," Eve said with some
force. "She may not have started her 'busi-

ness' until a few years ago, but she was always dirty. Some cops who work under her, she gives them a buzz, and at least two of them end up dead.

"You know why she didn't get between me and Garnet today—and that's just what she should have done, clean or dirty. Why she didn't move to control him quick enough? Because having him go at me gave her a nice little tingle. She liked it, and I'm damn sure she would have loved it if he'd beat me bloody in front of her. She's got the brains to know she can't have that, had to maintain, but she's got the belly for it. I screwed up her orderly pile, so she'd love to watch me bleed."

"And you didn't want backup?"

"She'd love it," Eve told him, "but she can't afford it. Not yet."

She found a spot a block from the pub, snagged it. "Since Webster's got a life, you'll need to wait for him to find a spot, walk him in."

"I'll be walking my wife in first—or at least to the point where I can watch her go in. They've got a corner table ready for you."

"Did you put muscle in there?"

"Darling." He tapped her chin. "I always have muscle in there. It's an Irish pub, after all."

Her 'link signaled again. "It's Darcia. You can watch me from here—and I'll be talking to another cop while I walk half a block. I think I'm covered if some bad guy jumps out, and I faint from fear."

He had to grin at her as he watched her walk away.

"Dallas."

"Hi. I was hoping we could make good on that drink."

"Actually, right now . . . would be good," she decided. "Or say in thirty? O'Riley's Pub," Eve said, and gave Darcia the address. "Can you get here?"

"I'm loving getting around in New York."

"Great. Listen, I'm actually walking into the place now. I have a meet—another cop. You could do me a favor."

"Sure."

"Don't come over to the table unless I signal you. If I don't, I've still got to work it a little. When I do, you could stroll on over. Like you've just come in and spotted me— but we had a meet set."

"No problem. Are you going to tell me why?"

"One of these days."

"All right then, half an hour."

"Chief Angelo?" The title made Darcia smile. "You're easier to work with than I remember."

"But I'm not working, am I?"

Eve tucked her 'link away and strolled into O'Riley's.

Fiddle music piped out of the speakers, a backdrop to conversations among the grab-a-drink-after-work crowd. In a few hours, she knew, musicians would settle into one of the booths with their instruments, pints at the ready, and fill the place with bright reels and sad songs. The bartenders would hustle, pulling pints, pouring glasses for the crowd that invariably packed in.

The little redhead waved to her, gestured to a table for two. Eve remembered her from when she'd joined Roarke and a couple of his out-of-town business associates who'd wanted a taste of an Irish pub, New York style.

"Get you a drink, Lieutenant?" the

redhead asked, and balanced her tray on her hip.

"Not yet, thanks."

"Just give me a sign when you're ready."

Eve sat down, back to the wall, scanned the customers. Coworkers winding down, some tourists, a guy doing his best to hit on a couple of twenty-somethings who were stringing him along.

Cop didn't blip on her radar.

And Renee came in.

She'd changed from her power suit into a little black number that showcased her body, left toned arms bare. She'd paired it with hot red heels so her toes, painted the same color, could play peekaboo, and left her rain of blond loose. The complex series of sparkling links around her neck held a round red pendant.

She did her own scan, Eve noted, a slow sweep with eyes expertly shadowed and smudged. Then sent Eve a friendly smile as she walked toward the table.

She likes knowing she's caught attention, Eve thought, that men are checking her out and women are wondering who she is.

"Thanks for meeting me." Renee slid onto her chair. "I hope I'm not late."

"No."

"Do you come here a lot? It looks like a nice, friendly place. Unpretentious. A working man's bar."

Eve wondered what the reaction might have been if she'd set the meet at the Down and Dirty. "Now and then," she said, and caught the waitress's eye. "Nice outfit," she commented. "You didn't have to dress up for me."

"Actually I'm meeting my parents for dinner later. Have you—"

She broke off as the redhead came to the table. "What can I get you, ladies?"

"Pepsi, on ice," Eve told her.

"Oh, come on, Dallas, live a little." With a bright, beaming smile, Renee tossed back her hair. "We're off duty, aren't we? And I'm buying."

"Pepsi," Eve repeated, "on ice."

"Well, I'm off duty. I'll have a vodka martini, straight up, two olives."

"I'll get those right to you." The waitress set a snack bowl of pretzels on the table, then went to put the order in.

"I was going to ask if you'd ever met my father."

"Not formally, no."

"I'll have to introduce you sometime. I'm sure you'd enjoy each other." Renee took a pretzel from the bowl, broke it in half, nibbled. "We should have dinner. You, your husband, my father and I. Roarke's certainly a man I'd like to meet."

"Why?"

"Like my father, he has a strong reputation, and it would seem, a gift for command. He'd have to, to have reached his level of success. It must be fascinating, being married to a man who commands that much power, with so many varied . . . interests. I heard you vacationed in Europe this summer."

"You want to talk about my summer vacation?"

"I don't see any reason you and I can't be friendly, do you?"

"Do you want a list?"

Renee sighed, sat back, and continued to nibble on the tiny piece of pretzel. "We really did get off on the wrong foot, and I'm willing to take responsibility for a great deal of that. I was upset about Keener, and I admit, territorial. So we butted heads when it would've been more efficient, and certainly more productive, to work in tandem."

She paused again when the waitress returned with their drinks. "Anything else I can get you for now?"

"We're good," Eve told her. "Thanks."

Renee lifted her glass. "Why don't we drink to a fresh start?"

Eve left her glass where it was. "Why don't you define fresh start?"

In the snug, Webster watched the exchange. "She's chapping Renee's ass."

"She's good at it," Roarke agreed. "She'll wind her up. The more Eve rejects the overtures, the more Renee will push."

"It's a good play. Garnet's hammering her on one side, Dallas is blocking her on the other. You know Dallas is trying to get Renee to come at her—to set Bix on her."

"I know my wife very well."

The faint emphasis on *my wife* had Webster shoving his hands in his pockets. "I thought you and I were settled."

"It's hard to resist giving you the needle now and again. See the body language there," Roarke pointed out. "Eve, slouched, kicked back. Disinterested. Renee tipped forward a bit. Working hard to engage. But her foot taps under the table—hard rhythm. She's angry."

Roarke glanced over, smiled at Webster. "Fancy a beer?"

"Yeah, but until this is done, I'm on. You go ahead."

"Ah well, we'll wait on it."

At the table, Renee sipped her martini. "I'm apologizing for not giving you my full cooperation over Keener. He'd been my CI for a long time, and though I didn't use him often in the last few years, we had a history. I felt, right from the start, you were shutting me out. I reacted to that. You and I have different styles, Dallas, obviously. And they've clashed. I'd like to put that behind us."

Eve shrugged, and at last picked up her glass. "My investigation of Keener's murder may require more information from you, may require me to question members of your squad who knew him, had dealings with him."

"Understood. But I can tell you neither I nor anyone in the squad used Keener much. He'd occasionally feed me some small change, and I'd see he got a twenty. But I kept him as a CI mostly out of sentiment. He used more than he should have, and his information had become less and less reliable. He didn't have solid contacts anymore."

"Then why did somebody kill him, and go to so much trouble to stage it as an OD?"

"I can't answer that. Hopefully your own CI has some information that will give you some lines there. I'm asking that we cooperate with each other on this. I'll give you whatever I can to aid your investigation. I want to be in the loop. I want to know what you've got."

"I'll copy you on all data I deem appropriate."

"That's a start." Obviously pleased with that, Renee put on the earnest. "Now, about my detective. Dallas, I want you to understand when Bix and Garnet went into that flop . . . it was just bad timing. If they'd known he was dead, you were investigating, I promise you, they'd have come to you with full disclosure."

"I'm curious. If Keener didn't have solid contacts, only fed you small change and so on, why did your detective feel he had some connection to or information on the

Giraldi matter? And feel so strongly enough to illegally enter his residence? I never got an answer to that."

"They followed a tip, and frankly, I think it was a blind. I agree they acted hastily, and I've spoken with both of them about it. If they'd informed me before following the tip, I could have told them Keener was dead. We'd have avoided all this. I promise you it won't happen again.

"About Garnet—"

"You don't want to go there."

"I have to." Renee spread her hands in appeal. "I'm his lieutenant. He was absolutely and completely in the wrong. There's no excuse."

"Fine, we agree. Subject closed."

"Do you ever bend?" Renee snapped. "He lost his temper. You were in his face, and he lost his temper. He's put a lot of OT in on the investigation, done miles of legwork. He was on edge, and the confrontation with you pushed him over."

"He damn near knocked me over," Eve reminded her.

"And that's regrettable. You have my file, and you know how essential he is to closing this case. I'm asking you for a little consideration. I'm asking you to let me discipline my own man, my own way. You can't tell me you've never had one of yours snap back at you, or another superior officer."

"If one of my men behaved in the way yours did today, I'd write him up myself. And I wouldn't make excuses for him, much less whine about needing him on an investigation he's obviously too strung out to work efficiently."

Eve watched Darcia step into the pub as Renee's hand fisted on the table.

Well shit," Webster muttered when Darcia moved into the range of the monitor. "What are the odds?"

Roarke arched an eyebrow at Webster's reaction. "Very attractive, isn't she? The sultry brunette. She's Darcia Angelo, Chief of Police on Olympus."

"Yeah. We've met."

"Really?" Roarke's smile spread slowly as he added two and two into four. "This just gets more and more interesting."

"Christ" was Webster's opinion. "I'm really going to want that beer."

* * *

In the pub, Darcia wandered to the bar, shook her head at the bartender, and settled down to watch the table.

"I take responsibility," Renee began.

"It's a little late for that."

"Goddamn it. I *do* need Garnet. You pushed. He pushed back. He was wrong, and he's earned a good, hard slap for it. I'll give him one. Two weeks without pay after the investigation closes, and he'll have to ride a desk for another two. I'm just asking you to pull the rip."

Now Eve shifted, eased forward. "You've got the nerve to ask me for a solid when you stood there, did nothing, while your man insulted me, while he threatened me, while he struck out at me. And you want to give him a slap on the wrist for it—when it's convenient for you? You dangle dinner with Dad at me to pave the way, like I'd sit up and say 'yes, please.' Your man's a hothead, one with no respect for authority. Including yours. Nobody talks to me as he did today and walks away smiling. If he were mine, he'd get the boot."

"He's not yours."

"Exactly." Eve shrugged, sent a subtle signal to Darcia. "He's your problem."

 **13** "The commander isn't the only one I can speak to about this," Renee said.

"Speak to whoever you want." Eve added a shrug and a bored glance at her watch. "Garnet earned the rip. It stands. Hey, Darcia."

"Dallas." Darcia stopped at the table, beaming smiles. "Sorry, am I early? I'm interrupting."

"No, you're right on time. Chief Angelo, Lieutenant Oberman. The lieutenant and I are finished."

"For the moment." Her rage palpable,

Renee shoved back from the table. She turned her back without acknowledging Darcia and stormed out with a sweep of hair and an angry click of heels.

"My, my, my." After following the drama of the exit, Darcia turned back to Eve, batted her lashes. "Something I said?"

"No, it's on me—and so, apparently, is her drink. Have a seat. Give me a second." Eve pulled out her com, tagged Feeney. "She'll be coming back to you. You might want to adjust your volume down a few notches, spare your ears the blast."

"Copy that."

Eve tucked her com away again, smiled, said, "So."

"So indeed. You made her very angry, then put some lace on it by making her think you double booked."

"The last was just the whims of fate when you got in touch about a drink."

"And she didn't even finish hers."

"Yeah, let's take care of that." Eve started to signal the waitress, spotted Roarke and Webster coming out of the snug. "I guess we need a bigger table."

"Oh?" Darcia glanced over her shoulder. "Oh," she said again, but with a kind of purr that had Eve's antennae quivering. "Roarke." She offered a hand. "Isn't this fun? Detective."

"Chief."

Eve looked from Webster to Darcia, back again. This time she said, "Oh."

"They've a bigger table for us," Roarke announced with the glint in his eye of a man anticipating an interesting time. "You can have that beer, Webster, if you're set on it, but I think this calls for the bottle of wine I took the liberty of ordering."

"I'd love it." Darcia stood, shifted to Webster. "Let's see, an NYPSD lieutenant being monitored by EDD, and IAB on the scene. It appears the whims of fate had me walking in on some of your official business. I hope it's not a problem."

"No. No problem." He pulled back her chair at the table for four.

"We enjoyed the show," Roarke commented as he sat beside Eve.

"I came in just at the finale—but I believe I follow the story line. You're looking at this Lieutenant Oberman for something— and as Dallas is involved, something must include murder." She tipped her head to the side. "I'd vote for a dead junkie. Since Don's here, it also involves an internal investigation."

Don, Eve thought. Christ.

"We can't really get into it," Eve told her.

"Understood. But obviously we don't like her. Though I did love her shoes. By the way, I bought three pairs at that fabulous little boutique you sent me to yesterday, Dallas."

"Why?" Eve leaned forward. "Sincerely. I've always wanted to know why anyone buys multiple pairs of shoes at a time."

"If I have to explain it, the joy is lost."

"And how have you spent today?" Roarke asked her as the waitress brought four glasses and a bottle of red to the table.

"Shopping—I can't stop myself—and I spent a wonderful two hours in the Metropolitan Museum. Had a late lunch." She smiled at Webster when she said it.

A hot beam of a smile, Eve thought. Like a tropical sun.

Roarke sampled the wine, approved. "Plans for the evening?"

"The theater. My first Broadway musical. I'm looking forward to it. To all of it," she added, then lifted her wine. "Since we're about to enjoy this lovely wine, I assume both lieutenants are off duty."

"Looks like it," Eve murmured. "For now."

"Good." Darcia angled over, leaned in, kissed Webster—light, soft, like that tropical sun through palm fronds. "Hello."

He grinned like a moron—in Eve's opinion. "Hi."

Eve raked a hand through her hair. "This is just weird."

"I think it's delightful." Roarke lifted his glass. "To new friends."

Roarke took the wheel for the drive home. "Are you sulking, darling?"

"I'm not sulking. I'm thinking. I have a lot on my mind." Sulking, she thought. What a crock. And speaking of crocks. "What the hell are they thinking, starting this up? They don't even live on the same planet."

"Love finds a way."

"Love? Jesus, they met five minutes ago."

"A bit longer than that, obviously."

"Like a day. And now they're all shiny-eyed, late lunch, theater going, and if they haven't banged each other yet, that's the entree on the after-theater menu."

He swallowed a laugh, barely, and sent her a pseudo-sympathetic glance. "A little jealous, are you, watching a former flame light up for someone else?"

"I'm not jealous! I didn't have any flame. He had the flame, and I never wanted him to have any flame. You damn well know I didn't—" She broke off, and the sound she made was nearly a growl. "You did that on purpose, to trip me up."

"Irresistible. I thought they looked wonderful together—and happy."

"Happy-sappy, that's not the point. I need Webster focused. This whole thing's going to break, and soon. And he's busy falling for somebody—somebody completely inappropriate given their situation."

"Ah, that takes me back."

"What?"

"How two other people who could have been considered completely inappropriate for each other, given their situation, fell in love when you needed to be focused on a difficult investigation."

He took her hand now, brought it to his lips. "Love found a way. And justice was served."

He made it hard to argue—and the old

standby *that was different* sounded stupid even in her head. "You have to think it's weird."

"I think possibilities often come unexpectedly, and what you do with them, how much you're willing to risk for them, can change your life and make it more than you ever imagined it could be. You changed mine."

"This isn't about us."

"If you'd followed logic, *a grha*, if you'd followed the part of your head that said no, this is inappropriate, and impossible, you'd never have let me in."

"You'd have broken in," she muttered.

"I would have, yes, being mad for you from the first instant. But I wonder if it would be as it is between you and me if you'd shut down your heart and only listened to your head."

He kissed her hand again, turning the palm to his lips.

"We found each other. We recognized each other—our two lost souls—when logic says we shouldn't have. The choices we made once we did brought us here."

And here, even now, she thought, his touch, the stroke of his voice, could turn her insides to jelly.

"I like them both. And okay, maybe I have a little speck of guilt about Webster because I didn't see the damn flame until he practically scorched me with it, and you followed that by kicking his ass."

"Ah, good times."

She cast her eyes to the ceiling and really tried not to smile. "It's that I can't see how this can work. If they were just going for the bang, the vacation whoopee, fine. But that's not what I was looking at across that table."

"And who doesn't enjoy the vacation whoopee? And no, that's not what it is—or that's not the potential of it. They're adults, Eve, and they'll figure it out, one way or another. Meanwhile, I enjoyed our little interlude—and watching them enjoy each other."

"And now he's going off to watch people sing and dance, and I'm going back to work."

"Do you think he's derelict in his duties?"

"No." She let out a long breath. "No, I know he's on top of it. And I know when I'm being pissy."

He made the turn to home. "Would it

help if I tell you how very entertaining—
even arousing—it was for me to watch you
metaphorically grind Renee into fuming
dust to the tune of 'Whiskey in the Jar.'"

"Maybe. It was fun." She rolled her shoulders. "It was satisfying. More fun, more
satisfying when it stops being metaphorical,
but pretty damn entertaining."

"And arousing?"

She shot him a quick, cocky grin.
"Maybe."

They got out of the car, and he caught
her hand before she could start up the
steps. "Come with me."

"No, you don't. I've got to—"

"Take a walk with me on this bright summer evening. Love's in the air, Lieutenant."

"You mean watching me be a bitch got
you stirred up."

"It did. Oh, it did." He gave her arm an
easy swing with his. "When we go inside,
we'll work. But just now? There's a bit of a
breeze—finally—and it's stirring in the
gardens, and the woman I love has her
hand in mine."

He broke a blossom from a bush—she
couldn't have named it—and tucked it behind her ear.

It didn't feel foolish, but sweet. So she left it there and walked with him.

They paused a moment at the young cherry tree she'd helped him plant in memory of his mother.

"It looks good," she commented.

"It does. Strong and healthy. And next spring it'll bloom again—we'll watch it bloom again, you and I. It means a great deal."

"I know."

"She thinks you married me for power," he said as they walked on. "Renee. As that's what she'd have done. The power and the money is one in the same to her."

"She's wrong. I married you for the sex."

He grinned. "So sure of that am I that I work diligently to hold up my end of it."

They wandered into a small orchard, perhaps a dozen trees, branches heavy with peaches.

"Does Summerset actually use these to make pie?"

"He's a traditionalist." Roarke searched out one that looked ripe, twisted it free. "Have a taste."

"It's good. Sweet," she said when she had.

"He's after adding a few cherry trees."

"I like cherry pie."

Roarke laughed, took a bite of the peach when she offered. "I'll give him the go."

It smelled of summer, of ripe fruit and flowers, and green, green grass. The walk in the warmth and the scent, her hand in his, served to remind her she had what she'd envied of Renee's childhood.

She had her own normal.

"See that spot there?" Roarke gestured to a sparkling roll of green. "I've been toying with the idea of having a little pond put in. Just a little one, maybe six feet in diameter. Water lilies and willows."

"Okay."

"No." He skimmed a hand down her back. "What do you think? Would you like it? It's your home, Eve."

She studied the space—thought it was fine as it was. It wasn't as easy for her to imagine little ponds and water lilies as it was for him. "With those weird fish in it?"

"The carp, you mean. We could, yes."

"They're a little creepy, but interesting." She looked at him now. "You stay home more than you used to. Don't travel nearly as much as you did before. It would probably be easier for you to handle some of the stuff on site—wherever—but you don't unless you have to."

"I have more reason to be home than I once did. I'm glad of it. Every day, I'm glad of it."

"I changed your life." She looked down at the peach they shared. "You changed mine. I'm glad of it." And back up, into his eyes. "Every day, I'm glad of it. I'd like a little pond, and maybe something to sit on so we could watch the creepy, interesting fish."

"That would suit me very well."

She linked her arms around his neck, laid her cheek on his. Love finds a way, she thought.

"I didn't follow logic," she murmured. "Even when I told myself it was inappropriate, it was impossible. I couldn't. Everything inside me needed you, like breath. No matter what I told myself, I had to breathe. I'd been loved before. Webster thought he did even if I didn't recognize it, even if I couldn't give it back. And I had a different kind of love with Mavis, with Feeney. I loved them. I had enough in me for that, and I can look back at who I was and be grateful I did."

She closed her eyes, drew him in. Like breath. "But I didn't know how much there was, what there could be. What I could be, before you.

"Before you, there was no one I'd want to walk with. No one I'd want to sit by a little pond with. No one," she said again, easing back to look at his face, "before you."

He took her lips softly, letting them both sink into the kiss, into the moment. Into the tenderness.

Sweet, like the peach that rolled out of her hand as they lowered to the ground— and quiet, like the air that whispered around them with the scents of ripened peaches, summer flowers, green, green grass.

She rested a hand on his cheek, tracing down to the strong line of his jaw. His face, she thought, so precious to her. Every look, every glance, every smile, every frown. The first time she'd seen it something had shifted in her. And everything she'd closed off, maybe to survive to that point, had begun to struggle free.

Love shimmered through her, and joy followed.

She gave, offering him her heart, her body, moving with him as elegantly as in a waltz. Not a warrior tonight, he thought, but only a woman. One with a flower in her hair, and the heart she offered in her eyes.

And the woman moved him, unbearably.

"*A grha.*" His lips roamed her face while the words he murmured came through his own heart, through his blood, in Irish. Foolish words, tender words she wouldn't understand, but would only feel.

"Yes," she said, when their lips met again. "Yes. And you're mine."

She touched him, sliding his jacket aside, loosening his tie. And smiled. "Always so many clothes."

He slid her jacket off as well, released her weapon harness. "Always armed."

"Disarm me." In a gesture of surrender she raised her arms over her head.

He watched her as he shoved her weapon aside, as he drew her shirt, her tank over her head and bared her to the dapple of evening sun.

Watched as he skimmed his hands over her skin, as he rounded them over firm breasts. She sighed out her pleasure as her eyes went heavy. Then he lowered his head, sampled her, savored her. Stirred her toward moans as he traced his tongue down her torso.

She felt those nimble fingers unhook her belt, and her breath quickened at their touch, at the anticipation of more. He stripped her, inch by inch, using those nimble fingers, his lips, his tongue to saturate her in sensation—slow, steady waves that rolled over her, rolled through her until she was drenched.

Dazzled, dazed, she reached for him, found his lips again with hers. Struggling to take her time, as he had, she touched, and bared. She sampled and savored.

Undid him, he thought. She undid him. She always could. She could make him feel weak as water, strong as a god all at once, and more a man than he'd ever hoped to be. With her, it was more than the thrill of flesh against flesh, more than the heat and beat in the blood.

Love was a gift shared.

When he eased into her, the gift was sweet, and tender. Again, her hand rested on his cheek. Again he watched her heart fill her eyes. Watched until his own flew into them.

She lay quiet for a time, stroking his hair, content to stay pinned under his weight.

"It was a really nice walk," she said at last.

"Good, healthy exercise, walking."

She laughed. "I feel pretty healthy right now. Hungry, too."

"I'm with you there." He eased up, smiled down at her. "You look healthy, my darling Eve, lying naked in the sunlight."

"If you'd have suggested a couple hours ago I'd be lying naked in the sunlight I'd've called bullshit. But I don't feel pissed or pissy anymore, so I guess it was healthy."

She sat up, reached for her tank, then her eyes popped as she tapped a hand on the wire camouflaged between her breasts. "I forgot about the wire."

"Well, one hopes it's off or we've given Feeney and/or McNab some unscheduled entertainment."

"It's off—I cued it in the pub. But, Jesus, I'm not supposed to forget it's there."

"You were busy walking," he said when she dragged the tank over her head.

"It's a damn good thing I didn't call out for cinnamon donuts while you were busy walking with me."

After they'd dressed he took her hand as he had before, gave her arm a little swing with his. "I expect you fancy pizza for dinner."

"It'd be easy. I've got some digging to do, and I need to check Peabody's progress on hers. Plus you haven't given me an update on yours—on the finances."

"We'll get to that."

"Problem?"

He wound back through the garden. "There wouldn't be if you'd bent a bit, given me the go to look into it my way. I've got some surface right enough, but I can't reach under the layers with my hands cuffed, Eve."

"And if you use the unregistered, I'd have the data, but I couldn't use it."

"The unregistered would simplify it."

"I guess I didn't realize you could only do simple."

He stopped, shot her a narrow, frustrated look. "I know damn well you're aiming at my ego, and well played. I can do it without the unregistered. There are ways, but they're still my ways. If I do it yours, it could take weeks. I'd think you could trust me to know how far over the line I can go and keep the data clean. Otherwise, you should do it yourself."

She made a rude face behind his back as he opened the door. Childish, she knew, but it felt good. "If I can get proof Renee has secret accounts, that Garnet does, or Bix, I can clear Webster to open that part of it to IAB. He's hamstrung, too."

"Then unstring us, damn it."

"You don't have to get mad about it," she said as they both strode past Summerset and up the steps.

"I'm not a cop," Roarke reminded her.

"Alert the media."

"Mind yourself, Lieutenant. I'm not a cop," he repeated, "and it's annoying to be asked to perform minor miracles while toeing the line you set."

It was her turn for frustrated, with a pinch of temper. "I've moved it plenty, and you know it."

"So move it again."

"Every time I do, I worry I won't remember where I left it."

"You couldn't forget that if you had amnesia. Added to it, I know where. I may not

agree, but I know where you put it, and
how far you can nudge it and feel you've
done the right thing. You ought to know
the same of me."

She opened her mouth, prepared to
punch back a little, then closed it again. "I
do," she realized. "I guess I do. This is . . .
a situation. If I had the data, I could pass it
officially to Webster for IAB. If IAB could
officially open an investigation, they'd find
the damn data. I'm trying to find the way
between, and what I'm hearing is you can't
get it with the way I've set this up. I don't
get why, but—"

"I can bloody do it."

Insult reared up in his eyes. Not just insult, she decided. *Geek* insult.

"But it'll take more time—considerable
time." He lifted his brows, his voice coolly
pleasant. "Would you like me to explain all
the technical reasons, roadblocks, fail-
safes, and so on as to why?"

"Really, no. I don't get why," she began
again, "but if you tell me you can't do it this
way in good time, it can't be done this way
in good time. My way," she corrected. "So
do it yours. I mean, not all the way yours.
Not the unregistered on this, Roarke."

"I understand that. I'll work it as close to your line as I possibly can. All right?"

"Yeah."

He rocked on his heels as he studied her. "That was a quick spat."

"Probably because there's still a little sexual haze."

"You wouldn't be wrong. Start your digging. I'll get the pizza."

She walked to her board first, circled it, studied it. She rearranged a couple of the photos fanning out from Renee, cocked her head and considered.

"I have to go out," she told him when he came back in with the platter. She walked over, snagged a slice of the pie. "Ow. Hot."

He shook his head as she shifted the slice from hand to hand. "Try this," he suggested, handed her a plate. "Where are we going?"

"Not we. I need to talk to a cop—a female cop in Renee's squad. Probability is minimal she's involved in this. Renee doesn't work with women. She intimidates or eliminates."

"She hasn't had any luck intimidating you."

"Yeah, and that's a pisser for her. She's

going to face a bigger one when she doesn't have any luck eliminating me. Strong, Detective Lilah," Eve told him. "I had a feeling about her the first time I walked into that squad room, and I need to follow my gut on her. And it needs to be a one-on-one."

"You could tag Peabody rather than go this alone."

"Then it's ganging up. I don't want to intimidate her—mostly because it wouldn't work unless I put a lot behind it. What I need to do is give her an opening. It'll give you time to play your geek games without me bugging you."

"There is that. You'll engage your wire."

"Yeah. Everything on record. She's the new guy," Eve mused, "but in six months, if she's any kind of cop, she knows, or senses something's off. I'm going to give her a chance, and a reason, to talk about it."

"And if she doesn't take that chance?"

"I've wasted some time. But I've got a feeling."

"Best to follow it then."

And come back, he thought. *To me.*

"Couple hours, tops," she said. She gave him a quick kiss, and he could see

her mind was already on her approach as
she left.

He stood for a moment, studying the
best part of a pizza, and toyed with the
button he kept, always, in his pocket.
Trust, he reminded himself, was a two-
way street. So he'd trust her to do her job,
her way. And he'd go do the one he'd agreed
to take on, in his.

Eve made the tail in under five blocks.

They were a little sloppy, sure, but she
had the advantage of the superlative camera system built into the vehicle Roarke
had designed for her.

The tail employed a standard two-
vehicle leapfrog, which told her two things.
First, she'd worried—or had just pissed
off—Renee enough for the woman to order two men to sit on her. And second,
Renee wasn't worried or pissed off enough
to delegate a more effective shadow.

Eve engaged her recorder. "I've got a
tail, a two-point switch-off. Both departmental issues—for Christ's sake, do they
think I'm a moron?"

Really, it was a little insulting.

She read off the makes, models, licenses,

then ordered her cams to zoom in on each to document before requesting a standard operator run.

The vehicle currently two blocks behind her was assigned to Detective Freeman. The one breezing by her to circle around the block and take the rear again was assigned to a Detective Ivan Manford.

"We'll add you to the list, Ivan. Now, let's play."

She cut over to Fifth, continued downtown, deliberately falling into a nice little knot of traffic. She faked a couple of attempts to thread through, watched Freeman's vehicle swing by. Timing it, she pried her way between a Rapid Cab and a gleaming limo, bulled by, and nipped through a light as it went red.

Manford would pass her to Freeman, she knew, until he could move back into position. But that would be a problem as Freeman had cut west. Eve hit vertical, skimmed over a lane, and to the music of angrily blaring horns, flashed east to play her own brand of leapfrog, nipping in front of a lumbering delivery truck whose driver stabbed up his middle finger.

She couldn't really blame him.

She swung downtown on Lex, punched it, enjoying the speed and the occasional vertical lift, until she headed west again, shoving her way crosstown.

"Chasing your own tails now," she murmured, and though she preferred street parking, decided on an overpriced lot two blocks from Strong's building.

She tucked her vehicle between a couple of bulky all-terrains, engaged her security.

Renee, she thought as she strolled through the warm summer night, would be very displeased.

Working-class neighborhood, she noted, with plenty of people also out for a stroll, or hanging out at one of the tiny tables squeezed in front of tiny cafés or sandwich bars. Traffic rumbled by on its way somewhere else. Some of the shops remained open, hoping to entice some trade from the residents who were too busy earning a living to spend their pay during the day.

She followed a Chinese delivery guy straight into Strong's building, catching the door on the backswing. He angled off on the second floor of the walk-up, but the scent of kom pao chicken lingered while Eve climbed to three.

Outside Strong's apartment door Eve caught what sounded like a high-speed car chase. Watching some screen, she concluded. Tucked in for the night, security light a steady red. She flicked her gaze up, spotted the dark eye of a minicam.

So Strong took security precautions, which to Eve's mind made the detective smart enough to guard her own.

Now, she supposed she'd see just what kind of cop Lilah Strong turned out to be.

She lifted her fist and knocked.

**14** She heard the yap-yap-yap of what sounded like a small canine, then the slide of bolt, the click of opening locks.

The man who opened the door was big—Arena Ball-tackle big— with massive shoulders, tree-trunk legs, and bricklayer biceps.

He gave her a friendly smile as he stood with his bulk barring the entire doorway.

"Hi. What can I do for you?"

"I'm looking for Detective Strong." She shifted her gaze down to the puffball with teeth dancing at his feet. "Lieutenant Dallas, NYPSD."

"She doesn't bite," he said. "She just wants you to think she's fierce." Bending, he scooped the puffball into his hand and made shushing noises. "Lilah! Cop at the door."

"Yeah? What cop?"

Strong looked around the man's mass, and her eyebrows lifted in surprise. "Lieutenant Dallas."

"Detective. Can I come in?"

"Ah, sure . . ." Obviously off guard, Strong looked around the room the way people did when unexpected company made them wonder how big a mess they had lying around.

In Strong's case it was minimal in a simply furnished living area set up for comfort.

"Tic, this is Lieutenant Dallas, Homicide, out of Central. Tic Wendall."

Tic offered a hand the size of a meat platter, and the careful way he took hers made her think of Mavis's Leonardo. Big men with gentle ways.

"Nice to meet you."

"The same. Sorry to interrupt your

evening. Detective, I'd like to talk to you for a few minutes."

"Why don't I give you ladies the room," Tic began, "and take Rapunzel out for her walk?"

At the word *walk* the dog wiggled in Tic's hold and did her level best to lap the skin off his face. He set the dog down. "Get your leash, girl."

At the command the tiny dog scurried off in a storm of delight.

"Thanks, Tic."

"No problem." He took a poop bag out of a box near the door, and when the dog came back with a bright pink leash clamped in the tiny teeth, he clipped it on her jeweled collar.

"Back soon," he told Strong, and kissed her in a way that told Eve they'd been together long enough to be casual.

Eve waited until the door closed behind them. "You have a dog named Rapunzel that's the size of a well-fed rat?"

"Tic has the dog. She's all hair, so, she's Rapunzel. He takes her everywhere—even to work."

"What's he do?"

"He's a lawyer—tax attorney."

"I figured him for Arena Ball, plowing the field."

"Tic lacks the killer instinct. Sweetest man I've met in all my life, and I don't think you came here to talk about my guy."

"No. Can we sit?"

"Okay." Strong switched off the screen, pointed to a chair. "Tic does some home-brew," she said, nodding at the bottles on the coffee table. "Do you want one?"

"Wouldn't say no," Eve told her, knowing sharing a couple of short brews indicated the visit wasn't official.

She took her seat, then the bottle Strong offered. She sipped. "Good. Smooth."

"He's got a knack." Strong dropped down on the couch but didn't relax. "What are you after, Lieutenant?"

"You know I'm investigating a homicide that crosses with your squad."

"That's no secret."

"Did you ever meet my vic? Keener?"

"Never had the pleasure."

"Did the squad give him space because he was the boss's weasel?"

"Maybe." Strong took a hit of brew. "Myself, I never had any reason to roust him."

"You're mostly riding a desk now."

Her face remained absolutely neutral. "A lot of work gets done at a desk."

"It can. You're a street cop, Detective, and your previous record on the street's solid. It makes me wonder why your lieutenant has you doing follow-ups and writing up reports."

"You'd have to ask her."

"I'm asking you."

Strong shook her head. "If you think I'm going to whine and bitch about my LT, you're going to be disappointed. It's no secret either, sir, you and Oberman are butting heads. You want dish? I'm not serving it."

"You don't like how she runs the squad. You don't have to say anything." Eve gestured casually with the brew bottle. "I'm just stating my personal observations. You don't like being behind a desk when you know damn well you'd do more good on the street. You think it's bullshit—the suits and ties, the shiny shoes—and the tone of the squad, that always reflects the boss, precludes any personality, any sense of partnership. You don't like the closed-door meetings behind the shutters, or her daily fashion parade, or the fact that she acts like a CEO instead of a cop. It's not a squad, it's her personal kingdom—and her next stepping stone to captain's bars."

When Strong said nothing, Eve nodded, sat back. "I know something else. If another cop slammed me like that to one of my men, there's not one in my division who'd sit there and say nothing."

Strong shrugged. "I bet there are a whole bunch of people in the city who don't especially like their boss."

"Like doesn't mean dick. Respect does, and you don't respect her. Giving her respect," Eve expanded, "isn't the same as feeling it. She knows you don't. It's only one of the reasons your evals have gone down since you joined the squad."

The first sign of anger rippled over Lilah's face. "How do you know about my evals?"

"I know a lot of things. I know Oberman isn't just a lousy cop. I know she's dirty."

Strong shook her head, stared fiercely across the room.

"Your gut's told you the same," Eve continued. "You're too good not to have caught a whiff. Too good not to wonder why so many weigh-ins come in light."

"If there was a problem with the weigh-ins, there'd be questions up the line."

"Not when she's got somebody covering the numbers in Property, in Accounting. You've got experience, contacts—valuable ones. But who gets the heavy cases? Bix? Garnet? Marcell? Manford? Manford and Freeman tried to tail me here tonight."

Strong's gaze snapped back to Eve's.

"I'm better than they are," Eve told her. "No worries. They tried because earlier to-day Oberman finally figured out I'm not going to play ball. Shutting me out hasn't worked. She has to think about shutting me down, has to figure out where I'm go-ing, and why I'm going there."

Eve took out her PPC, called up a file—then handed it to Strong. "That's my vic."

Lilah studied the crime scene shot. "That's a bad end."

"Bix ended him, on Oberman's orders."

With some force, Lilah shoved the PPC back at Eve, pushed to her feet to pace away. "Goddamn it. Goddamn it."

"I know this for a fact. I have a witness who overheard Oberman telling Garnet just that, who overheard her discussing *business*, the dirty money."

"Fuck, fuck, fuck." Lilah leaned her hands against the narrow kitchen counter that separated the living space from a kitchenette.

"She's built her organization over years." Eve rose as well. "Using her father's name, sex, bribery, threats, guile—whatever it takes. Including killing other cops."

At the statement, Lilah's face went blank.

"Not herself—I don't know if she's got the stones for it. Bix seems to be her primary weapon. But she has others. Marcell and Freeman ambushed Marcell's old partner. Detective Harold Strumb. I'm moving to prove she was also responsible for the death of Detective Gail Devin, who served under her briefly. Devin's record, her style—a lot like yours. If she can't weed out cops who aren't useful to her, or who start looking too close, she eliminates them."

"You can't prove any of this." Lilah's throat rippled as she swallowed. "If you could she'd be in a cage right now."

"I will prove it. Count on it. You're not with her, Detective. I'm not wrong about that. She's got a twelve-man unit. Garnet,

Bix, Freeman, Marcell, Palmer, Manford, Armand. That's seven out of twelve I know or am damn close to knowing are on the take—and worse—with her. I put you on the other side. What about the other four?"

"You want me to pimp out my squad, my boss?"

"How many more cops have to die before somebody stands up and takes her down?" The fury edged through now, couldn't be contained. "You know she's dirty, Lilah. You were hot when I said it, but you weren't surprised."

"I can't prove anything. No, I don't like the way she runs the squad. There's a lot I don't like. But I worked hard to get into Central. It's where I want to work. In another six months, I'm going to put in for a transfer to another squad. If I do it now, it looks like I can't stick."

Lilah picked up her brew, rubbed the chilled bottle over her forehead as if to cool it. "I want to do the job. I need to get back out and do the job so I know it matters if I get up in the morning. She gives me some raps in my evals, I can take it. I can sit a desk for a year as long as I know at the end of it, I'll be back doing what I'm trained to do. Who's going to work with me, Lieutenant? Who's going to trust me if I turn on my own?"

"Okay. I appreciate the time."

"That's it?" Lilah demanded. "You come here, lay all this on me, then you appreciate the *time*."

"I'm not going to try to talk you into something that's against your instincts. Mine brought me here. If they're wrong, and anything I've said here gets back to Oberman, I'll know where it came from. Otherwise, I've got no problem with you. I may not agree with where you stand, Detective, but I understand it. I can't promise you a damn thing. I can't tell you if you cooperate here it'll all be roses when it's done. I can't promise other cops will pat you on the back."

"I don't give a shit about that."

"Yes, you do. We all do. Because if we can't count on each other, we can't count on anyone, or anything. And that alone makes Renee Oberman the worst of the worst.

"Thanks for the brew."

"Asserton's not in it."

Eve paused at the door, turned back. "Why?"

"She gives him mostly bullshit assignments—which is more than she usually gives me. Has him doing a lot of PR with schools, playing Officer Friendly. He's a street cop. He's riding it out. His wife had a baby a few months ago, and the assignments, the hours make it easier to deal. But he's starting to get itchy. I know he's thinking about transferring—out of the squad and Illegals.

"He sneaks pictures of his kid in to show me. He hates Oberman's guts."

"Okay."

"If Manford's in, so's Tulis." On a sigh, Lilah pressed fingers to her temple. "They're practically joined at the hip. Tulis likes to hassle the street LCs into giving him free samples. He tried to cop a feel on me in the break room."

"How long before he could use his hand again?" Eve wondered.

Lilah's smile flickered, but died. "I punched him in the face, and I reported the incident to Oberman, immediately. The upshot was Manford swore he was in there, too, and Tulis never touched me, only told a dirty joke and I overreacted."

"Tulis makes eight."

"Brinker's sleeping his way through until he gets his twenty. He's looking at private security so he can sleep his way through that. I'd say Oberman's setup is too much effort for him. Sloan, she keeps her head down and her mouth shut. She wants the desk. She got roughed up pretty good during an altercation with a couple dealers last year. The fact is, Lieutenant, Sloan lost her belly for the street."

"It happens," Eve agreed.

"Maybe she knows or suspects, but I don't think she'd be involved. I don't think Oberman would trust her."

"I agree. That's all good to know."

Lilah sat, rubbed her hands over her face. "She carries a disposable 'link. I opened her door once, poked my head in without waiting for her come-ahead, and she was on it. She reamed me—you'd've thought I'd walked in on her having sex with the commander."

Lilah dropped her hands. "I think she's got a hide in her office."

Interesting, Eve thought, as she suspected the same. "Why do you think that?"

"She keeps the place locked like a fort most of the time. The only reason I could

poke my head in that day was because
Garnet had just come out, and she hadn't
locked the door again. That door is locked
more than it's not, and the blinds are always closed. Always. But I think maybe
she's got eyes and ears on the squad
room."

Blinds down so she can't be seen, Eve
mused, but wants to keep the hawkeye on
her men.

"Back when I first transferred," Lilah told
her, "I got a couple prime tips. Before I
could move on them, she dumped a bullshit
assignment on me. Both times I told her I
had something hot, and she ordered me
to pass the heat to Garnet. One time?
Maybe. Not twice.

"Same deal for Asserton," she added.
"She's dumped him into something crap
just when he hit on hot. I'm pretty sure the
break room's covered, too. Asserton
showed me a picture of his kid in there,
right after he was born. Ten minutes later,
Oberman's calling him in to remind him of
her policy against personal items in the
squad."

"Will he talk to me? Asserton?"

"I think he will. But . . . I know he'll talk

to me. We grab lunch together sometimes. He's the only one in the squad I feel a connection to."

"You be sure, absolutely sure, before you do. You don't talk in the squad room, or in Central. You don't talk by 'link or e-mail. Face-to-face, somewhere you can be sure nobody's listening."

"You already figured he wasn't in it. You wouldn't give me the go like this just on my take."

"He was my next stop if you said no. But you confirmed my take on him. Don't be so sure Brinker's sleeping—he's still an unknown for me. People who look like they're not paying attention are often the ones who are."

"I wouldn't put him with her. I can't see it."

"Maybe he's not," Eve said. "But he's been in the squad nearly as long as she's had command. Nobody lasts that long unless they're in it, or she has another use for them. Sloan, she's probably going to be clear because Oberman doesn't like to work with women—but we're not moving there as yet either. Sloan took a hard knock. Hard knocks can convince people to go along."

"Can you tell me how far you're into this?"

"I'm hoping to access some data tonight, tomorrow latest that will put some serious weight on it—so you could wait another twenty-four before approaching Asserton."

"Yeah, I'd rather wait. This is a lot to lift." Misery on her face, Lilah pressed a hand to her belly. "He's got the new baby. It could hold, maybe, until you get that serious weight."

"Use your best judgment," Eve told her. "When I'm sure we've got that weight, I'll be notifying IAB."

"Ah, shit."

"They're going to want to talk to you."

Lilah closed her eyes, nodded. "I've wanted to be a cop since I was a kid. My brother . . ." She opened her eyes again. "I guess you've read my file, so you know."

"Yeah."

"I wanted this, and I worked for this. I wanted to do something—to maybe do something so somebody's mother didn't get her heart broken, somebody's sister wouldn't ask herself, again and again, if she could've done more, if she could've stopped it, saved him."

Lilah's eyes took on a fierceness that reminded Eve of Mrs. Ochi.

"Every time I pick up my badge, that's why. Even if I don't think about it, it's why."

"The why's a big part of making us the kind of cops we end up being."

"Maybe." Lilah blew out a breath. "This isn't what I signed on for, Lieutenant. Sitting on my ass in a dirty squad isn't what I signed up for."

"She's exploiting somebody's mother, somebody's sister, somebody's brother every time she takes—the junk, the money—every time she makes a deal. I can promise you, Detective, she thinks about what she's going to cash in every fucking time she picks up her badge."

"If I can help you take her down, and the rest of them with her, I will."

"I'm asking you to be my eyes and ears inside. Watch, listen." Eve took out a card. "If you need or want to contact me, use a disposable or a public 'link. No point taking chances. My personal number's on there."

"Lieutenant?" Lilah said as Eve opened the door. "I knew—some of it anyway. I knew in my gut, but I didn't do anything."

"Now you are," Eve said simply, and closed the door.

Pleased with the progress, Eve took a zig-zagging route home, watching for shad-ows. No one followed her, but as she approached the gate, she realized some-one was waiting for her.

The car flashed across the road, directly in her path, and angled broadside to block the gates as she hit the brakes.

Fury came first, but she engaged her recorder as she watched Garnet slam out of the driver's side.

No one with him, she noted, using her cams to be sure no other vehicles made any move to corner her. She'd be *damned* if she'd be trapped at the gates to her own home. Her own normal.

Garnet wanted another confrontation? she thought. It might prove interesting.

She slammed out of her own vehicle.

"You don't come to my house, Garnet. Do yourself a favor. Move your vehicle and keep going."

"Who the fuck do you think you are? You think you can come into my squad and push me around? You think you can set IAB on me?"

So Webster let him have a sniff, Eve thought. Fuel to the fire she'd built.

"I think I'm your superior." She said it coolly, braced to defend against what she saw wasn't just a ride on temper, but a little chemical help to amp the speed.

"You're nothing. Anybody can marry money and use it for the climb. You're just another whore with a badge."

"I still outrank you, Garnet. And you're about to double that thirty-day rip."

"Nobody here but you and me, bitch." He gave her a taunting little shove, both hands to her shoulders. "You're going to find out rank doesn't mean dick."

"Touch me again, Garnet." She knew she was baiting him now. She wanted to. "Put hands on me again, and you lose your badge for good. You've been using. You've confronted, threatened, and assaulted a superior officer—again. Get in your vehicle and drive away, or I take you all the way down."

"Fuck you." He backhanded her; she let him. She went with the blow, let it propel her around as he moved in, fists raised.

She slammed hers into his face. "No, please. Fuck you."

The unexpected punch knocked him back a step, had blood trickling from the side of his mouth.

"Now, back off," she warned, but he charged.

His fist glanced off her shoulder, but had enough behind it to sing down her arm. Still she knew in that moment she could take him one-on-one. He was bigger, had more of a reach, but he was consumed by his fury, and sloppy with it.

She blocked, hit him again with a hard, short-armed punch to the face. "Back the fuck off!"

From behind her she heard the roar of an engine and knew Roarke was barreling down the drive. *Time to end this,* she thought, *before somebody got seriously hurt.*

Even as she thought it, she saw the move. On instinct she kicked out, kicked hard so her boot connected with Garnet's forearm. The weapon he'd drawn flew out of his hand, clattered against the iron gates.

"You've lost your mind." There was a

tinge of genuine wonder in her voice.
"You've completely lost your fucking mind."

As if to prove it, he started toward her.
Then the gates swung open. Like her, he
could hear the slam of a door, the rush of
footsteps.

"I've got this," Eve said to Roarke as he
bent to pick up Garnet's weapon. "I've got
this."

His eyes burned as cold as his voice.
"Then you'd best get rid of it before I do."

Garnet, mouth bloody, left eye already
swelling, looked from one to the other.
"This isn't over." He stormed back to his
car, wrenched the door open. "I'll bury you,
bitch!" he shouted before he jumped in,
sped away.

"You're letting him go?"

"For tonight." Eve rolled her shoulder
where Garnet's fist had hit. "I want to see
what he does. He's sure as hell off his
leash. I'll report this—and it's on record,
my wire, your surveillance. Things go right,
they can pick him up tomorrow, charge
him with assault, assault with a deadly. It'd
be enough, I think, for him to bargain, for
him to flip on Renee for a deal."

"You could take him in now, same

results." Roarke handed her the weapon. "You don't want a deal."

"You're damn right I don't. I want all of them, all the way—and maybe I'll have enough for that by tomorrow." She flexed her fingers, shrugged at the scraped knuckles. "But punching him in the face a couple times didn't suck."

Roarke tipped her face up, dabbed gently at her lip with a fingertip. "Your lip's bleeding."

She disengaged her recorder. "I let him get one in. The fucker can have the rep of all reps, but that recording, showing him hitting me, drawing first blood, moving in to draw more? Rat in a trap, and no way out of it."

"I wish you wouldn't so often use your face as an investigative tool. I'm very fond of it."

She grinned, then winced as it smarted. "You ought to be used to it. Anyway, thanks for riding to the rescue. You need a white hat. Good guys wear white, right?"

"I look better in black."

"Let's go on in. I have to report a rogue cop—and what I'm going to bet is his unregistered weapon."

"It's turning into quite a day," Roarke commented.

It wasn't over for anyone.

The last thing Renee Oberman needed after suffering through an endless meal that included a lecture from her father was to find Bill Garnet pacing outside her apartment.

One look at his face told her he'd looked for trouble and found it, and he'd brought it to her door.

"Go home, Bill, and put an ice pack on your face."

He grabbed her arm as she shot her key card in the slot. She'd expected it, but it didn't make her yank away any less testy.

"I'm not in the mood for this."

"I don't give a shit what you're in the mood for." He shoved the door open, pushed her inside.

She whirled around, outraged, shocked. "Don't you *ever* put your hands on me again."

"I'll put more than my hands on you. I'm done, Renee, done doing this your way. Your way got me suspended."

"You got yourself suspended. You're out

of control, and the way you're behaving right now only proves it. I told you I'd deal with the rip."

"Then fucking *deal* with it." Under the bruising his face burned, red and livid.

Not just off the leash, Renee realized. He'd snapped it. She tried for a combination of understanding and weariness. "I'm doing everything I can. For Christ's sake, I went to the bitch personally to plead your case. And I had to humble myself tonight and ask my father to intervene."

"And will he?"

"He'll talk to Whitney tomorrow." But wouldn't, she knew, interfere with command's decision. Saint Oberman had made that crystal.

She turned away, crossing over to her kitchen. She pulled a bottle of whiskey from a cupboard, two short glasses from another—and poured two fingers in each.

Her father wouldn't back her up, and she wondered why she continued to let herself think he would. Not perfect Commander Oberman, oh no. Not by-the-fucking-book Oberman.

But she put a cool look on her face as

she turned with the glasses. No point in letting Garnet know the score while he was on a rampage.

"Have a drink and calm the hell down."

"I'm not swallowing a suspension, and I'm not getting cut out of the Giraldi deal. I'll fuck you up, Renee."

"Understood. So . . . who punched you?"

He tossed back whiskey. "Fucking bitch."

She lowered her glass, had to set it down because the hand holding it shook with rage. "Are you telling me you got into it with Dallas? Are you telling me, goddamn it, Garnet, that you hunted her up and got physical? Again?"

"She earned it. IAB sniffing around me—I got word on it. That whore set them on me, and she'll get more than what I gave her tonight before I'm done with her."

IAB—it was a slap in her face, and a singular threat to her business.

Goddamn Garnet. Goddamn Dallas.

"In the fucking name of God! I'm surrounded by idiots. I put Freeman and Manford on a standard tail, and she goes out, and they lose her in five damn minutes. Then you go after her? How the hell did you . . ." Fury wanted to choke her. "Freeman told you. You got Freeman to tell you she went out. What the hell did you do, Bill? Don't tell me, fucking Christ, you went to her house?"

"The house everybody knows she whored herself into." His knuckles went white on the glass as he gulped down the rest of the whiskey. "So what? Her word against mine, and Freeman will back me. He'll swear I was with him tonight, and nowhere near that cunt."

It was falling apart around her, she thought. Men. Goddamn men. She'd be damned if she'd let any of them screw her out of what was hers, what she'd worked for. What she'd built.

What she *owned*.

She turned away again, struggled for control. And picking up her glass again, her brain went ice cold.

"All right. We'll deal with it. We'll deal with her. She's gotten in the way once too often."

"About fucking time."

"I need to set it up. Go hook up with Freeman, make sure you're seen. Then go home, wait. I might be able to work something tonight to get her off our backs. All the way."

"I want to do it. I want to do her."

"Fine, but it's going to take me awhile to work it. A couple hours, maybe three. Go hook up with Freeman, have a couple of drinks, make it public. Then go home, Bill, and wait."

"If we don't clean this up tonight, I'm taking care of it myself. My way."

"It won't be necessary." She took his glass. "Get out."

"You're going to give me one too many orders, Renee, and regret it."

But he got out.

She took the glass into the kitchen, deliberately and viciously smashed it in the sink. "Fucking asshole!"

Everything that had gone wrong in the last few days had started with him. Keener slipping his collar, with the 10K? Direct line to Garnet's screwup. If not for that she wouldn't have Dallas on her back, in her face, in her squad. Wouldn't have had to swallow the commander's refusal to push the bitch out. Wouldn't have had to humiliate herself to her stiff-necked, unbending father.

He'd become a liability. Calmer, she poured herself another short whiskey. Liabilities needed to be corrected, and if correction proved impossible, eliminated.

Thinking, she circled the living area of the apartment she'd furnished with care, with some style, and within a strict budget.

She wasn't a fool like so many who worked for her.

Her home in Sardinia, now, that was a different matter. There she could indulge herself in the lush. She could buy art, jewelry, clothes—everything and anything she wanted. And keep the highest of high-end droids on staff to maintain the house and grounds immaculately.

Nobody was taking that from her, much less an ex-lover who'd lost his edge, and all his appeal.

Time to fix it, once and for all.

She opened her purse, took out her disposable mini-'link, and contacted Bix on his.

"Are you alone?" she asked him.

"Yes, ma'am."

"Good. Bix, I'm afraid I have a serious

problem, and you're the only one who can handle it as it needs to be handled."

He said nothing for a moment, just looked into her eyes. "What do you need me to do, Lieutenant?"

15 When Eve finished her oral report with Whitney on the incident with Garnet, she settled down to write it up, with the attached record.

"Perhaps when you've finished that you'd be interested in hearing what I accomplished while you were out getting in fistfights."

"He was waiting for me when . . ." She pushed up, jabbed a finger at Roarke. "You got her."

"Not quite, but I'm closing in there. I'll want a bit more time to tie that knot. But I

have Garnet and can serve him to you—or
IAB, I suppose—on a platter."

She sat down, grinned—and made her
lip throb again. "I love you."

"Excellent news. You can prove it with
lots of sex."

"We had sex a few hours ago."

"No, we made love a few hours ago—
angels surely wept. I want sex for this job,
as it's given me a buggering headache
trying to straddle your far-famed line. I
want mad sex, with costumes—maybe
props—and an intriguing story line."

"Milking it, pal."

"Until it runs dead dry." He tossed her a
disc. "He owns property in the Canary Islands under the name Garnet Jacoby—
Jacoby being his maternal grandmother's
maiden name. Amateur."

"What kind of property?"

"A house to start, with two acres. It's ap-
praised at five and a half million, and some
change. Jacoby paid cash. His ID has him
as an entrepreneur, with Brit citizenship.
He also owns two vehicles kept there, and
a boat. A yacht, you could say. Jacoby is a
few years younger than Garnet, has green

eyes rather than brown, and lost his first and only wife in a tragic climbing accident."

"That's very sad."

"He has a healthy account in that name, and another, smaller—I'd say backup money—in another under Jacoby Lucerne— the street where he lived as a child. Lucerne is Australian. Between the three—Garnet, Jacoby, Lucerne—they're worth in the neighborhood of sixty million. Not bad on a cop's pay."

"And he called me a whore," she murmured.

Roarke eased onto her desk. "I'd be very sorry if that hurt you."

"It doesn't hurt me. It's a pisser of biblical proportions to be called a whore by that motherfucker."

"All right then."

"Renee?"

"A bit more time there. She's smarter, and a great deal more clever than Garnet. I think I have her, but I want to finish verifying and gathering it up. You're not going to ask how I came by the data on that disc?"

"No. You told me you straddled the line, so you straddled it. Sorry about the headache."

"That's what blockers are for. I have Bix on the disc as well. That took some doing, and I'm really going to want costumes. He's not smarter than Garnet, necessarily, but his ass was surely more covered."

"That's interesting."

"It is. He doesn't really spend the money, but banks it. Several accounts, various names, nationalities. He has a little place in Montana. A cabin, really, worth a fraction of his partner's home away from home. And an all-terrain. Collects weapons under several of his aliases, so none of them cause much of a ripple. Added together, it's quite the arsenal. Still, nothing flashy for Bix."

"It's not about the money for him. It's about the chain of command."

"I've started on the others, made considerably more headway tonight. But I thought you'd be most interested in those three."

"You'd be right. Anything on Brinker?"

"Brinker." Roarke's eyes narrowed in thought. "Ah, yes. He's the little chateau in Baden-Baden—going back to his roots, I'd say—the manor house in Surrey, and the three mistresses."

"Three? No wonder he's asleep at his desk." So, Lilah's instincts were off there. "Asserton or Sloan?"

"No, nothing as yet—and as I haven't had a single hit on either, there's likely not to be."

"Agree. Shift them over, push the rest. We serve Garnet up to IAB tomorrow, garnish him with the charges stemming from tonight's temper tantrum with me. He's cooked. What you've got? It's the sauce."

"The clever cooking analogy doesn't distract me from the fact you don't want to serve him up alone. You want Renee sharing the platter."

"Be tastier," she admitted, then waved a hand. "We've got to get off the food stuff. I'd rather have her nailed before I take Garnet in. Her, and the rest. But it's not an absolute. He'll flip if I need him to flip, and he'll still go away a good, long time. If you're done with this for the night, no problem."

"And I look like the weak sister?"

"Don't make me smile again. It hurts."

"I'll finish it. If I get further along, I should be able to program it to complete the task while we both get some sleep."

"I need to contact Webster."

"Eve," Roarke said as she reached for her 'link. "He's with Darcia."

"Yeah, so? He needs to . . ." She broke off, winced as she had when her lip throbbed. "You think they're having sex?"

"Oh, at a wild, what-the-hell sort of guess? Yes. Very likely."

"I can't think about that. I don't want to *know* that. I know what he looks like when he has sex."

Roarke flicked a finger on the top of her head. "I wonder why I need to be reminded of that."

This time she pressed her fingers to her lip to hold it as it throbbed since she couldn't quite swallow the laugh. "I'm just saying. I like how you look having sex better."

"Darling, how sweet of you."

"I need to scrape off the sarcasm you just piled on me, then I'll contact him—but straight to message. I want him and the rest here by oh seven hundred."

Bix picked Garnet up at one A.M.

"It's about fucking time," Garnet said.

"It took awhile for the LT to get it set up. Nobody wants any mistakes on this. Like

she said, you and Dallas had a confrontation. Don't want this to blow back on you."

"Freeman's got me covered." Resentment oozed out of his pores. "If Oberman
had done the damn job, I wouldn't need to
be covered."

Bix said nothing, then glanced over.
"Dallas do that to your face?"

Color—anger and humiliation—stained
Garnet's cheeks. "She's not looking so
pretty either. Cunt sucker-punched me."
The lie came so easily, as it had when
he'd told Freeman the same, he nearly believed it himself. "Pulls her weapon on me.
Says she's going to take my badge. Maybe
go after Oberman next," he added, knowing Bix's loyalties. "She's jealous of the LT,
that's what it is. Bitch wants to take her
down, cause trouble. If she causes enough,
the whole thing's going to break down.
We're all in the shit can then, Bix."

"I guess so."

"What's the plan? You didn't lay it out
before."

"The boss is using a bogus weasel to
tag Dallas with a tip. A big one, deals with
Keener. The boss says how Dallas is hot
to close Keener, really wants to tie it to use

that to discredit her. So we draw her in tonight, back to the scene."

"That's good." Garnet nodded, tapped a
little of his go-powder on his hand, inhaled
it. He wanted the buzz, fresh and rising,
when he sliced the bitch to pieces. "What's
the tip?"

"I didn't ask; don't need to know. The
lieutenant said she'd get Dallas there,
she'll get her there. We take care of business, and that's that."

"She might call it in." Garnet tried to figure the angles through the rush in his
head. "Tag her partner anyway."

"So what if she does?"

"Yeah. We do them both." He was eager for it. "Maybe better that way. Better
yet if we have somebody to pin it on. The
whole thing—Keener and the two bitches."

"The boss is working on it," Bix said
simply, and pulled to the curb.

"Dallas is mine." Garnet patted the
sheath on his belt. "You remember that."

"If that's how you want it."

"Did you bring me a piece? Bitch took
mine."

"We'll take care of it inside."

Bix didn't speak as they walked the short

distance to the abandoned building. He knew there were probably some eyes on them—on two men in black—but it was unlikely they'd be approached. People rarely approached him looking for trouble. His size backed them off.

If anyone did, well, he'd do what needed to be done. He had orders, he had a mission. He would follow orders and complete his mission.

He unsealed the door, opened the locks.

"Dark as a tomb in here. Smells worse." Garnet reached in his pocket for his penlight. "It's a good place for her to die."

He played the light around the ruined space, calculating the best kill spot. "I want her to see me do it. I want her to see me when I cut her."

Bix said nothing. He simply yanked Garnet's head back by the hair and dragged the keen edge of his knife over Garnet's throat.

And it was done.

He took a moment to be sorry when Garnet fell to the floor, blood and breath gurgling. He hadn't liked the man, not particularly, but they'd been partners. So he took a moment for a little regret.

Then he pressed the master he'd used to unseal the doors into Garnet's hand, slipped it into Garnet's pocket. Removed Garnet's disposable phone, his wallet, put them both in a bag, along with the knife he'd used. He'd dispose of them elsewhere.

He drew out the baggie of the powder Garnet had grown too fond off, dipped the dead's thumb and index finger in it to leave more trace, then added it to the disposal bag.

It would look, in a way, very much as it was. Garnet had come to the scene for a meet, and the meet had gone south. His killer had taken whatever was of value from the corpse, and let it lie.

Bix straightened, cleaned the blood off his sealed hands. He turned and walked away, leaving the door open as a man might when running away from murder.

Back in the vehicle he drove north, putting some distance down before he contacted his lieutenant. "We're clear, Lieutenant."

Her acknowledgment—a nod as if she'd expected no less—rewarded him. "Thank you, Detective. Be sure to dispose of the

weapon before you go to Garnet's and remove anything that needs removing."

"Yes, ma'am."

While Bix circled around to dump the contents of the bag in the river, Roarke stepped
into Eve's office.

She was, he noted, starting to fade. And
he imagined if he drew blood from her and
ran it through an analyzer, it would register
outrageous levels of caffeine.

"Marcia Anbrome."

Eve looked up, blinked. "Who?"

Yes indeed, fading fast. "Take a moment," he suggested.

"Who the hell is Marcia Anbrome? I just
need to finish this backtrack on the— Shit.
You got her?"

And she's back, Roarke thought. "I want
to put a bow on it, so I've got it running on
auto to tie the ribbon, but I'd say I—or
we—have her."

"Anbrome—that's a—what is it—
anagram. Oberman, Anbrome. Marcia—
Marcus. It's a goddamn testament, or
finger in the eye, for her father."

"And I imagine Mira will have considerable to say about it." He walked over, put

her current work on auto himself, shaking his head even as she started to protest. "You have a briefing in less than six hours. She has a home in Sardinia," he continued, drawing Eve to her feet. "And a flat in Rome. Her passport is Swiss. They're excellent credentials, by the way," he added, leading her toward the bedroom. "She must have paid a hefty sum for them. I've found properties and accounts worth upward of two hundred million. I think there's a bit more tucked here and there."

"I don't get it. If she's accumulated that much, why the hell isn't she in Sardinia rolling in it? Why is she still pushing her way through the department, aiming at captain—and maybe commander? Why is she still on the job when she could be lying on the beach fanning herself with her own dirty money?"

"I'm probably the wrong one to ask."

"No, you're exactly the right one." She sat on the arm of the sofa in the bedroom, pulled off her boots. "And I know the answer. It's the rush, the challenge, *the business*. And hell, if you can make a couple hundred mil, you can make four hundred.

She'll never give it up. It's not just what she does, it's who she is."

"As I've picked my way through her life—lives, I should say—I'd agree. She does spend time as Marcia. She keeps a private shuttle in Baltimore, flies over once or twice a month, depending. She generally spends an extended time there in the winter, sometimes in the summer as well. But she spends a great deal more time here, running that business.

"And here," he told Eve, "she lives precisely within her means. A bit too precisely. Every bill paid upon receipt, and no purchases—that show—that would squeeze her very strict budget. No luxuries, none. So I'd say when she indulges herself, it's in cash."

"Everything's precise with her, which means the books for her business will be very accurate, very detailed. Strong thinks there's a hide in the office. I'd bet she has a copy there, another at her apartment. That's control. That's being able to open them up and gloat over all those tidy columns while her father watches her from the wall."

After dragging on a sleep shirt, she

rolled into bed. "It's all the same. Money is power, power is money, control holds both, and command opens doorways for more. Sex and command are tools for creating more money and power, and the badge? It's a gateway. Killing? Just the cost of doing business."

"There are others like her." Sliding in beside her, Roarke drew her close. "I've known them. Even used them when it seemed expedient, though I preferred, until more recently, to avoid cops altogether."

"There's more of us than them. I have to believe that."

"Since I've been exposed to how real cops work, think, what they'll risk and sacrifice, I can say one of you is more than a dozen of them. Let it go now." He brushed his lips over hers. "It's smarter to go into a fight rested."

"You gave it up for me. You were mostly out of that kind of business when we got together, but you gave up the rest for me."

"The rest was more a hobby by that point. Like coin collecting."

She knew better. "I don't forget it," she told him, and closed her eyes to sleep.

* * *

Her com signaled at four-twenty and, cursing, she groped for it.

"Dallas."

"Lieutenant. Detective Janburry from the one-six. Sorry to get you up."

"Then why are you?"

"Well, I've got a dead body here, on your crime scene. Your name's on the seal."

"Off Canal?"

"That's the one. I'm on the DB, Lieutenant, but wanted to give you the heads up. Especially since the vic was on the job."

Her belly contracted. "ID?" she demanded, but already knew.

"Garnet, Detective William. Illegals out of Central."

"I need you to hold this until I get there. I'm on my way now. Don't transport the DB."

"I can hold it. I'm primary on this, Lieutenant. I didn't inform you to pass this ball."

"Understood, and the tag is appreciated, Detective. I'm on my way."

She tossed the com down, pushed out of bed to pull at her hair, to pace, to curse. "I set him up; she took him out. Goddamn it, goddamn it. I could've taken him in. I could've slapped him in a cage, put the pressure on with what I had. But I wanted more. I wanted to make them sweat. I wanted more time to put it together, to see what she'd try next. Now he's dead."

"Don't you stand there and take the blame for one dirty cop killing another."

"I made a choice. The choice killed him."

"Bollocks to that, Eve." Roarke said it sharply enough to stop her, to make her turn. "His choices and Renee's killed him. Do you think she couldn't have gotten to him in a cage, had him done?"

"I'll never know now. I miscalculated. I didn't think she'd risk bringing this kind of attention to the squad, adding another avenue of investigation. She outplayed me on this."

"I disagree. You're angry, and foolishly guilty, so you're not thinking it through."

"I'm thinking it through—Garnet's dead."

"Yes, and killing him requires another tale spun. More lies, more cover-up. If *she'd* thought it through, she'd have found a way to placate him, to keep him level. Failing that, kill him, certainly, but get rid of the body, lay a path that indicates he packed up, left."

She stopped dressing to frown at him. "Hmm."

"Hmm? He'd been suspended, and after tonight, he'd lose his badge. He'd be disgraced. Christ, I can write the script myself. Eliminate him, destroy the body. Meanwhile, go into his apartment, pack what a man who's angry, who's fed up, who's humiliated might pack. Toss a few things around—temper, temper—and so on. In a day or so, tap his account, use his credit—send a message to his lieutenant, maybe to you, telling you all to go to hell. You can keep the bloody badge. He's done with it, with you, with New York."

"Okay, I can see how that would work. It's a little unnerving just how easily you came up with it, but I can see it."

And calmer, Eve saw it clearly.

"Keep tapping the account," she considered, "tapping the credit awhile, making it look like he's traveling or gone to Vegas II, whatever. Then transfer the money out."

"Basically. A few finer details to tie it up, but basically. He's not dead. He's just gone."

"But she didn't think of that—and she

should have. Hell, I should have. But she wanted him dead *and* gone. She went with impulse—she may not see it that way, but that's what it was. And what I didn't expect. She went with impulse rather than planning. So there'll be mistakes in there. One of them was not arranging for one of her crew to get the tag on this. No way Janburry contacts me this early if he's with her."

"Now you're thinking. I'll drive."

"No. I'd appreciate the other set of eyes, and the scary brain, but if I'm hung up I need you here to start briefing the team."

Those fabulous eyes stared right through her. "You want me to brief a room of cops? That's appalling, Eve, on so many levels."

"Nobody knows how to run a meeting as well as you. I'll try to be back, but I have to follow this out."

"I'm definitely going to want the costumes. I may have them designed for you."

"One of us is worth a dozen of them," she said, repeating his words. "You're one of us."

"I realize you see that as a compliment, but . . ." He trailed off, sighed. "Thank you."

"I'll be back as soon as I can."

Roarke watched her rush out, sighed again. "Bloody hell."

Since he was up, he'd get some work done—of his own, thank you—before the cops came to his door.

She went in hot. She didn't want to give Janburry time to change his mind, and did a quick run on him on the way.

He looked solid. Fourteen years on the job, into his tenth as a detective—and recently promoted to second-grade. He was thirty-seven, on his second marriage— four years in—with a two-year-old kid.

Good service record, from what she could see. No big highs, no big lows. She knew his lieutenant a little. She could tug some lines if she needed to.

First, she'd see how Janburry wanted to play it.

She nosed in behind a black-and-white, hooked her badge in the breast pocket of her jacket.

A lot of cops, she noted, tapping her badge before ducking under the barricade. That's the way it was when word went out one of their own had gone down.

How many here, she wondered, would

consider Garnet one of their own if they knew?

Janburry stepped out as she approached.

He had a strong, dark face, with deep brown skin stretched over hard bones, deep brown eyes. Cop's eyes, she thought, and held out her hand. "Detective Janburry, again I appreciate you contacting me."

"Lieutenant. It was your scene first. Dead junkie. My vic worked Illegals. One and one add up to two in my book."

"Yeah, mine, too. Is it okay with you if I take a look before you fill me in?"

"Sure."

"My field kit's still in my vehicle. Can I borrow some Seal-It?"

He nodded, and she saw he understood she didn't intend to step on his toes. "Hey, Delfino. Toss me some Seal."

He caught the can, tossed it to her.

"What time did you get the dispatch?" she asked as she sealed hands and boots.

"It came in at three-fifty. My partner and I arrived on scene at oh four hundred. Uniforms doing a drive-by saw the broken seal—the door open—and investigated.

They'd secured the scene by the time we got here."

"That's good."

She stepped inside, into the glare of cop lights.

He hadn't gotten very far, Eve noted. Maybe six paces inside the door. He'd fallen on his back, so he lay faceup, arms and legs sprawled out. The long slice across his throat had pumped out blood that soaked his jacket, shirt, spread a lake on the dirty floor.

She noted the knife and sheath on his belt, and the lack of a sidearm. His penlight lay a few feet away, its beam still shining like a little white eye.

"What have you got so far?" she asked Janburry.

"No money, no ID. We ran his prints and identified him. My partner—Delfino!"

His partner, a small, spare woman with curly dark hair fought back in a tail, moved to join them. She nodded at Eve.

"Detective Delfino ran the vic while I worked the body."

In a rhythm that told Eve they worked well together, Delfino picked it up. "I got his squad, his CO, and he just got a rip this afternoon. Ordered by you, Lieutenant."

"That's correct. Your vic didn't like my investigative style on Rickie Keener. Keener was Garnet's LT's weasel, and it was necessary for me to . . . discuss that relationship and any cases involving my vic with Lieutenant Oberman. However, Garnet and his partner took it upon themselves to access my vic's flop, without authority. On learning this I had a further discussion with Lieutenant Oberman and Detectives Garnet and Bix. During the discussion, Garnet used abusive language, made threats, and even after being warned, made physical contact."

Delfino glanced down at Garnet. "That wasn't very bright."

"It was less bright for him to accost me in front of my home tonight. You may suspect that the facial bruises on your victim are a result of an altercation with his killer. I put them there."

Janburry pursed his lips, ever so slightly. "Is that so?"

"Garnet laid in wait, blocked the entrance to my home with his vehicle. He subsequently threatened me again, again made physical contact. I reciprocated that. At that time, Garnet drew his weapon— one which has proven to be unregistered. I disarmed him. All of this is on record, both on my home security and my recorder, which I engaged before exiting my vehicle. And all this was reported, immediately, to Commander Whitney. I'll make sure you get copies of everything for your file."

"That'd be good."

"Lieutenant." Delfino gave her a clear-eyed stare. "I have to say, if some guy tries to bust on me twice in one day, draws down on me, I might want to do more than give him a black eye."

"I can give you a statement on my whereabouts at TOD, if you tell me when TOD was."

"Just after oh one hundred."

"Okay. I was home, up, and still working. There'll be a log of that on my comp. I can't, at this time, give you the contents of the work. I can tell you Garnet was going to be dealt with tomorrow—today," she corrected. "He was going to lose his badge and face criminal charges. You can confirm this with command. I wanted that a lot more than I wanted him dead."

"Yeah," Delfino said after a moment. "I'd like that better myself. Vic's got some interesting trace on his right thumb and index finger."

"I believe he made use of the product he was bound by duty to get off the streets. I believe I could have made a case on that. I believe he was a wrong cop—I know he was. But whatever he was, he's your victim, and whoever slit his throat has to pay for it. I'll give you all the information I'm authorized to give, as I'm authorized to give it."

"Is he tied to your vic? To Keener?" Janburry asked.

"Short answer is yes. I'm not free to give you the long one. I'm not blocking you on this. It's all I can tell you at this time."

"Are there rats in the house?"

Eve nodded at Janburry, acknowledged IAB involvement.

He blew out a breath, said, "Shit. We're still not passing the ball."

"Understood. If I have any influence over the matter, I'll do whatever blocking may be necessary to keep that ball in your hands."

She watched the look that passed between the partners, and saw the tacit agreement.

"It reads like the victim entered, using a master. It was in his pocket. We'll re-verify the time the seal was broken, but at this point, given the read is so close to TOD they're stepping on each other, we'd say the vic and killer entered together. Killer took him from behind—quick and dirty."

"He had his back to the killer," Eve said.

"That's how it reads. Somebody punched me in the face a few hours ago, I'm not turning my back on them. Added to it, you're a tall woman, Lieutenant, but not tall enough to have inflicted this wound at this angle unless you were standing on a box. We'll take the comp log, the record-ing, and so on, but I can say Delfino and I aren't looking at you for this."

"Always good news. Did he have any-thing else on him?"

"The knife—still sheathed. Illegal length on the blade. Didn't have a 'link, a wrist unit, a memo book, wallet. You might think, looking at it, it was some kind of deal that went bad. Killer took him out, grabbed what he could use or sell, and fled the scene. Left the door open."

"You might think," Eve agreed.

"I'd be interested in what you think," Janburry told her.

Eve crouched down for a closer look at the body. No defensive wounds, she noted—and she could smell booze on him. She lifted his right hand—bagged now—by the wrist. No user would leave that much candy on his fingers. *That,* she thought, *was overkill.*

"I think he and his killer entered together. Why, I can't say, but I'd bet my ass Garnet believed they were here to screw either with me or my investigation. He not only knew his killer, but trusted him. Walked in ahead of him, got his light out, turned it on. A slice like that?"

She wished she had her gauge, but eyeballed it.

"I figure the killer pulled Garnet's head back, exposed the area—gives him a wide, clear target, makes a wide, clean slice. The killer came here for that purpose, and then took the ID and the rest so it might appear to be a meet gone bad, followed by a robbery of opportunity.

"Keener's OD was staged," she continued. "This is more of the same."

Janburry crouched down, kept his voice low. "You think another cop did this."

"I think people who kill for expediency, for profit, for any reason other than self-defense or in defense of another aren't cops. They just have a badge in their pockets."

"How much muck are we stepping into?"

"I can't tell you—yet—but I'd bring spare boots."

 When Peabody and McNab walked into Eve's home office, McNab's heart, mind, and body arrowed directly to the breakfast buffet.

"Morning eats! Told ya."

"I just said you shouldn't count on it." Peabody shifted her file bag and wished the scent of grilled bacon didn't wrap around her system like a lover.

But since it did, she dumped the bag and surrendered to temptation, crunching into the first slice as Roarke came in.

"Morning," she managed. "Best briefings ever."

"No point in solving murders on an empty stomach. You're looking rosy this morning, Peabody."

"It's the bacon."

"Woot! French toast." McNab grinned as Roarke poured himself some coffee. "Thanks for the spread."

"Feeding cops has its rewards."

And this one, Roarke assumed, had the metabolism of a manic chipmunk to eat as he did and remain thin as a wafer.

"We got here a little early," McNab told him, "so Peabody could help Dallas set up."

"And I want to go over some things with her on the Devin investigation."

"While they're at it," McNab continued, heaping a plate, "I wanted to bounce this idea off you. Feeney and I kicked it around some last night."

"Bounce away."

"I think we could use the bugs we planted in Oberman's vehicle to narrow in on the frequency of her disposable. We'd need to tweak and enhance the remote, narrow the focus to the disposable's signal when she's on it. It'd take some luck to lock it in, but if we could, we should be able to use it to triangulate."

"Coordinate the plants and remote, boosting output while narrowing range, re-direct, and trap her signal. Trap it," Roarke considered, intrigued, "and clone it."

"Yeah. If we pulled it off, we could— theoretically—use the clone to pick up her signals and conversations whenever and wherever she used the disposable."

"Like a conference call," Roarke mused. "Interesting."

"Theoretically."

"By boosting the strength, you'd run a risk of her picking up the bug on a full sweep, particularly during triangulation. But timed right, and with the right adjustments, it could work."

"If you want to play with that idea," Pea-body interrupted, "I could hook with Dallas on my end."

"She's not back yet." Roarke glanced at the time. "She responded to a second hom-icide at your original scene. Garnet's dead."

"Shit, that balls things up." McNab stuffed a bite of French toast dripping with syrup into his mouth. "Feeney and I were going to start on his electronics today, and if we got the go, slip into his place and wire it up. No point now."

"Why didn't she tag me?" Peabody demanded. "If Garnet's down, I should've gotten the tag."

"It's not her case—your case," Roarke amended. "The primary on it contacted her early this morning, as a courtesy I'd say, and likely because he hoped she'd give him a lead."

"It should be ours," Peabody began, then settled down, backtracked. "No, it can't be ours. She had two confrontations with him yesterday. McNab was monitoring when the asshole tried to jump her right out front here. We can't work the case. Do you know who the primary is? How much she's going to tell him?"

"Detective Janburry, but as to the rest, I couldn't say."

"Renee did this, because he went outside the box, became a negative factor. I have to run this Janburry." Peabody forgot her love affair with bacon and moved off.

"Garnet made some bad moves," McNab commented. "Too bad he's dead because he earned a long stretch in a cage. But . . ." With a shrug, McNab shoveled in more food. "How'd he buy it?"

"I don't know that either. She hoped to

be back to run the briefing." Christ knew he'd hoped it. "If she doesn't make it, and she's cutting it close, I'll lead things off."

"Solid."

Feeney came in, smiled at the buffet. "I told the wife I'd get plenty of the most important meal of the day. The boy tell you about his brainstorm?"

"Yes," Roarke answered. "It would be interesting to program."

"I've been playing with it—in my head," Feeney said as he filled a plate. "It'll come down to catching the waves."

For the next ten minutes they discussed options, alternatives, possibilities.

"Morning, all." Webster strolled in, looking relaxed and a little sleepy-eyed. "Man, I could use some fuel, and that looks prime."

"I imagine you could use it," Roarke said smoothly when Webster hit the buffet, and couldn't help enjoying Webster's lazy grin. "How was the play?"

"Unforgettable."

"Darcia goes back soon."

"Couple more days. I've got some time coming." Webster scooped eggs onto his plate, spoke casually. "I'm going to check out this off-planet resort of yours personally."

"You couldn't have a better guide than the chief of police."

Mira and Whitney came in together. Whitney scanned the room, then focused on Roarke. "She's not back yet?"

"No. She asked me to begin the briefing if she was delayed. You can take the floor if you prefer."

"No, we'll follow Dallas's line." He poured coffee but skipped the food.

"You look tired, Charlotte," Roarke said to Mira.

"I am a little. Long night."

"Have some food. Get your energy up."

"I don't think that will help. It's clear my colleague's involved in this. A man I've worked with, a man I trusted."

"I'm sorry." Roarke touched a hand to her shoulder. "It's a deeper kind of treachery, isn't it, when there's trust?"

"When I think how many police officers have trusted him with their secrets, their fears, their feelings, yes, it's a very deep kind of treachery. All of this is, isn't it?" She looked at the board. "On the deepest level. Doctor to patient, cop to cop, to the public, daughter to father."

"You'll stop it, all of you. Treachery only

thrives in the dark. You'll bring it into the light."

"It weighs on him." Mira glanced toward Whitney as he took a seat, alone with his coffee. "On all of us, but it's his command. And what this small and, yes, treacherous, percentage of all the good men and women who work and risk and fight every single day has done to diminish that work, that risk, that fight, it weighs heavy."

She walked over to take a seat beside Whitney.

And so, Roarke thought, he couldn't put it off any longer.

He moved to the front of the room. "The lieutenant's been delayed."

"Dallas isn't here?" Webster interrupted. "Where the hell is she?"

"At the scene, or hopefully on her way back from the scene, where Garnet was murdered."

"Garnet? What the—" Webster broke off, and the relaxed body, the sleepy eyes vanished. "When the hell did this happen, and why wasn't I apprised? She can't investigate Garnet's murder. Commander—"

"If you'd take your seat." Roarke handled the outburst as he would at any meeting he conducted. Coolly. "You'll be thoroughly briefed on this matter, and all others pertaining to these investigations. The lieutenant isn't assigned to this last murder, but consulting with the officers who are—at their request.

"Now, as I have the floor, we'll begin with some progress I made regarding the finances of three of the subjects. Data one on-screen," he ordered, and the image of Garnet's passport, with photo, came on.

"As you see, this is Detective William Garnet, aka Garnet Jacoby. Though they're both dead now, it's of interest that Garnet, under this assumed name, has amassed over thirty-five million dollars in cash, stocks, bonds, and property. He has quite a lovely home in the Canary Islands. Had, that is. Data two with image, onscreen."

"How did you dig this out?" Webster asked him. "You never tagged me for a filter."

"Carefully, tediously, and within the law. Barely," Roarke added, "but within, as the lieutenant ordered and expected."

"We could've hung him out to dry on this," Webster muttered as his angry gaze scanned the screen, the image of the lavish house, the numbers. "Out to fucking dry."

"A bit late on that. However, if you'd prefer we can move on, come back to this. It might improve your mood to see another stream of data. One-A, on-screen. Meet Marcia Anbrome, currently of Sardinia, Italy."

"Oh yeah." Though he said it between his teeth, and his face hardened further, Webster nodded. "That improves my mood."

"Maybe the idea of taking her down on graft, on corruption brightens your day, Lieutenant," Peabody said as she swung around. "But she's killed cops. Not all of them were like Garnet. They're dead because they weren't like Garnet."

"Understood, Detective. We all want the same thing here."

"Detective Peabody." Roarke's tone was more gentle than the one he'd used on Webster. "I understand you're pursuing a side investigation on the death of Detective Gail Devin. It might aid you in that investigation to know that Renee Oberman—as Marcia Anbrome—deposited two-point-eight million USD in her account two days after the operation in which Devin was killed. Garnet also made a large deposit at the same time. One-point-two. As did Bix, under his assumed identification."

The hell with the screen, Roarke thought. He had all of it in his head. "As John Barry, Bix holds accounts in Montana—where he's also purchased a cabin and fifty acres—in the Philippines, where he was once stationed while in the Army, and in Tokyo, where he was born. While we began with these three, we're working through the squad. I have Freeman, Palmer, and Marcell complete. I should have the others within hours."

"You'll need to add Doctor Addams to your list." Mira sat, hands folded in her lap. "As I've already informed the commander, in reviewing all the case files, testing results, evaluations, and history of each member of Lieutenant Oberman's squad, I've found troubling inconsistencies, and what on closer study appear to be amended results in those squad members Doctor Addams examined, tested, or treated."

"Of course." No point in telling her he'd already added her colleague, already found some of the pots the man had buried.

"Detective Peabody," Mira continued. "You should be aware that a few weeks before Detective Devin's death, Lieutenant Oberman, according to Doctor Addams's notes, expressed concern about Devin's state of mind, citing the detective had difficulty focusing on her work, adhering to procedure, took excessive personal time. Addams arranged for sessions with Detective Devin. He saw her twice a week for seven weeks, until the time of her death."

"She would have trusted him."

"She may have come to, yes," Mira agreed.

"If she did, she could have told him she thought something was off in the squad, and why. What she was going to do about it."

"It's possible." The fatigue on Mira's face deepened. "If she did, I believe Addams was certainly complicit in her death."

Eve came in, her strides long and brisk. "Apologies for the delay." She glanced at the screen, nodded. "I see you've been briefed on the financial angles. This gives us proof Renee, Garnet, and Bix procured false identification and with that hid property and funds."

"Add Freeman, Palmer, and Marcell," Roarke told her. "Others to come."

"Good. This alone is enough to remove them from the force, to arrest them, charge them, try and convict them. We have to take Garnet out of that process as I've just come from examining his body, but the data on him weighs on all involved."

"I'd like a report on Garnet's homicide," Whitney said.

"Sir. Detective Janburry is primary, and with his partner, Detective Delfino, is investigating. The detective contacted me, allowed me on scene. At which time I gave them a statement regarding both my altercations with the victim."

"What do you mean 'both'?" Webster asked.

"The second occurred at approximately twenty-two hundred last night when Garnet confronted me outside the gates of my home—where he had lain in wait for my return. My assumption is he was informed I left the residence by Detective Manford and/or Freeman who attempted a two-point tail on me some ninety minutes earlier."

"What the hell is this, Dallas? Why wasn't I kept informed?"

"You were busy," she snapped at Webster. "And you're being so informed. My altercation with Garnet is on record, and that record and my report on same was given to my commander."

She paused a moment. "Moving on. Detective Garnet entered the building where Keener was killed at one this morning, breaking the seal, bypassing the locks. Or his killer did so and left the master on him. About six paces in the door, Garnet was attacked from behind. His throat was slit. There were no other visible injuries other than the bruises I put on his face at approximately twenty-two hundred."

"Jesus Christ."

"Read the report, Webster. Watch the record. Garnet's valuables were removed—except for the knife he had sheathed on his belt. The detectives have agreed to keep me informed of their progress."

"What did you have to give them for that?" Webster demanded.

She rounded on him now, every bit as angry as he. "Not everything comes down to payment, to quid pro quo. I have an interest in their case—their vic is connected to mine and was killed in the same place. Since they're cops with brains, they can follow the dots. I told them I couldn't share certain details and areas of my own investigation with them, at this time. Which, again since they're cops with brains, tells them it's bigger than a dead junkie. Which they were smart enough to have already figured out. It will be the commander's decision as to whether the officers investigating Garnet's murder will be so informed."

"I'll review it," Whitney told her.

"Yes, sir. From my own examination, from the angle of the wound, the killer was taller than the vic. The vic was a solid six foot. He was also taken from behind, indicating he entered ahead of his killer, had his back to his killer. Indicating this was someone he knew, trusted. I believe Bix killed Garnet, and given his pathology and profile, he did so on orders from his lieutenant."

"A little housecleaning," Feeney said.

"Yeah, Garnet was mucking up her tidy area. I suspect in the period between his altercation with me and his death, he contacted her or went to see her. He knew IAB was sniffing," she added with a nod to Webster.

"I put out the scent, as agreed."

"It worked. He'd turned on her before, put the muscle on her the night Peabody overheard them. He lost control, twice, with me. She had no control over him in her office yesterday—and she knew it. Her attempts to clean up after him went no-where, and added to her embarrassment. He came at me again last night, and would lose his badge over it. He was not only no more use to her, but a threat. She acted quickly—too quickly, I think. Heat of the moment. A cooler head would have found another, quieter way, to get rid of him."

"Yes, I agree," Mira said when Eve looked her way. "Garnet and Renee were once lovers. She took away whatever power he had in the relationship by ending the sexual connection."

"Which was probably why she started and ended it," Eve suggested.

"Very likely. He took orders from her on two levels, and did so because it was prof-itable, and because she continued to see he had meaningful assignments on both levels. She reprimanded and punished him for whatever mistake he made with Keener. Then he was confronted with another female superior, one who did not show him the respect he deemed himself due, nor did she placate him as Renee would. Now he's punished again, reprimanded again. And snaps.

"Oberman can't control him, which reflects poorly on her, on both levels again. His actions demand that she do so, and since she can't, she eliminates him. The ultimate control, proving she is in charge. Proving it," Mira added, "to herself as well as those under her command."

"And that's priority for her," Eve put in. "To be on top, in command, in charge."

Mira nodded. "If she's not in charge, she's nothing. Nothing more than the daughter of an important, revered man, one she can in no way live up to. Except by treachery and deceit. She acted quickly, decisively, because she saw it as command. When, in fact, it was fear and loathing."

"Why that location?" Eve asked.

"I suspect you know. Not only would it serve as a place Garnet would go, if properly enticed, it's a slap at you. Here's another body when the first is hardly cold. It was a way to use him against you, particularly if she was aware you'd fought with him earlier, and the results of that would show."

"Yeah, I left some marks on him," Eve agreed.

"It was your scene. You and the victim had an altercation earlier in the day. She has no way of knowing you recorded and reported the second incident, but can be assured the investigating officers would be obliged to question you regarding Garnet.

"She has to prove she's better than you. You've shaken her command and her confidence in it. She can't tolerate that."

"She'll have to tolerate a whole lot more before it's done. Anything fresh from EDD?" she asked Feeney.

"Now that you mention it."

Before he could continue, Webster stood. "This is IAB's now. I'm obligated to take this to my captain and initiate an official investigation. The financial data and falsified docs are enough to bury them."

"There's a small matter of murder," Eve reminded him.

"Which we'll also pursue."

"IAB isn't taking my case. Keener's mine."

"The Keener homicide's a direct offshoot of internal corruption and malfeasance, which involves all or most of a squad and spirals out."

"Which IAB would know nothing about if I hadn't brought you in. Why is that, Webster? Just why didn't the rat squad have fuck-all on Renee and her crew?"

"I don't know. But we have it now."

"And if she's got a man inside IAB, and he lets her know a storm's coming? She'll poof. She's got the means to do it in style. Or she'll find a way to twist it so the lightning strikes another head. She didn't get this far by being stupid."

"There's another body on a slab, Dallas. Dirty cop or not, he's dead, and she's responsible. She has to be shut down before she decides to clean house again."

"He's right." Whitney spoke before Eve could snarl at Webster. "And so are you, Dallas. I want both of you, and your captain, Webster, in my office at eleven hundred. He will then be fully briefed on this matter. And we'll damn well hash it out. On the matter of the two homicides now known to be involved, IAB will have to go through me to yank them from their current investigating officers. You'd be unwise to take me on, Lieutenant."

He nodded when Webster shook his head.

"I have contacted and fully informed Chief Tibble on all areas of these matters. I will request he attend as well. Lieutenant Dallas, I'll need you in my office at ten hundred. Commander Oberman has requested some of my time today, and has further requested to meet you."

"Renee's asked him to intervene. Commander—"

"Intervention will hardly help Garnet now," Whitney interrupted. "If he asks me to influence or order you to ease off his daughter regarding the murder of Keener, he will be disappointed."

Whitney got to his feet. "Ten hundred, Lieutenant."

"Yes, sir."

He looked at the screen again. "It's good work you've all done," he said. "Good work on an ugly business."

Mira rose. "Would you mind giving me a ride in?"

"Of course."

She's worried about him, Eve thought. And she's not the only one.

She faced the room again. "Dismissed."

"Hold on, hold on." Obviously disgusted, Webster shook his head. "You think you can push me out? Get me out of the way before you're updated by your EDD team and your partner?"

"They have nothing on which to update me. Is that correct?"

"Not a thing," Feeney said easily.

"They're having a sale on cashmere sweaters," Peabody announced. "Not that I can afford one anyway. Naturale—all locations. But that's probably not what you meant by update."

Eve gave Webster a cool stare. "It seems we're done."

He simply shook his head again, folded his arms.

"If you'd excuse us, Lieutenant Webster and I need a few minutes."

Feet shuffled. And Roarke continued to lean against the wall. Eve sent him a look that managed to be apologetic and annoyed at the same time. Roarke pushed off the wall.

"Mind your hands, boyo," he murmured as he passed Webster. "Otherwise, this round I'll let her have a go at you. And she's meaner than I am."

Webster rose again, scowled. But stuck his hands in his pockets.

"You're not cutting me out of this, Dallas."

"Me, cutting you out? You just stood there and tried to grab my case."

"Bad cops fall under IAB."

"Don't give me your bureaucratic bullshit. If I didn't expect, and fully understand, that IAB needs to have a hand in this, I wouldn't have asked for your assist, and you'd still know squat."

"At which time I played it your way instead of immediately informing my captain. I'm sick to death of this attitude that we're not cops, not real ones."

"I never said you weren't a cop. But you're sure as hell not Homicide, not anymore. You made your choice there, Webster. You've got a job to do. Accepted. So do I, and you're not making a grab for my investigation."

"You need the collar? No problem. I'll make sure you get the credit."

"I ought to kick your ass for that." Indeed her hands fisted at her sides. "Fuck you. Fuck you sideways if you think this is about a collar, about credit. If you think—"

"I don't. I don't," he repeated, and rubbed

a hand over the back of his neck. "And that was a cheap shot, Apologies."

She swore again, paced away. "I could have done this without you."

"Yeah, and it feels like you are. Give lip service to the rat, but don't keep feeding him any new cheese."

She turned back. "What?"

"Why don't I hear until this morning that Garnet came after you? I don't hear he got the chance because you'd gone to talk to one of Renee's people."

"Lilah Strong isn't one of her people."

"She's in the squad," he reminded her, "and I should've been consulted on it. I didn't hear until this morning there's a tail on you. I didn't hear about Garnet."

"I informed the commander," she began.

"Now who's bullshitting?"

"It's not bullshit. That's my first duty. And I didn't contact you at every turn because you were . . . involved, in the thing. Darcia."

"Now you've got a problem with me and Darcia?"

"No. God." Frustrated, she raked her

hand through her hair. "I wasn't holding out on you. I didn't contact my own partner because I didn't deem it necessary. I didn't contact you, same reason, and also because I thought I was doing you a solid. Giving you the night to . . . to go to the theater. The musical theater."

He stared at her for a moment, then his body lost its fighting stance. "I guess you were, doing me that solid. It's appreciated. But I'm a cop, and so's Darcia. You know interruptions of . . . musical theater are part of the deal."

"What would you, or could you, have done about any of it, if so interrupted?"

"Nothing, really. But I'd have had it worked out in my head better, been clearer on the lay of the land."

"Fine, I'll interrupt you next time. And if you're in the middle of the big production number, it'll be your own fault."

He laughed. "I always had a thing for you."

"Oh, for—"

"Not that way, not that way." Cautiously, he took a step back. "Don't punch me, or call out the dogs. I worked with you a few times, and I like the way your mind works. Even when I don't agree. I like how you can chomp at a case until you spit it out, your way. You're a hard-ass, Dallas, but that's one of the reasons for the thing. You weren't much of a team player back the couple times we worked the same cases."

Maybe not, she thought. No, definitely not. "I wasn't in command. Command changes things because your men depend on you to head that team. I wasn't . . . a lot of things for a lot of reasons."

She thought of walking with Roarke on a summer evening. "I'm not the same person now I was then."

"No. I guess I'm not either." He held out a hand. "Bygones?"

"It depends." She took his hand. "If you go after my case, I'll take this hand again. And I'll break it off at the wrist."

He grinned at her. "Go, team."

"I'm going to trust you, because I've gone through doors with you before. If you want to stay for the rest of the briefing, take a seat. I'll be right back."

"No, but I appreciate it. I've got things to do before we meet with the commander."

"I'll see you then."

She walked to Roarke's office, opened the door, shut it behind her. "Thanks for the space."

"You're welcome. And?"

"We worked it out. Mostly a combination of parallel but not quite meshing goals and a misunderstanding of motivations." She went to his AutoChef for coffee. Closed her eyes, rubbed the space between her eyebrows.

"Take a minute, Eve. Sit."

"Better not. I need to get this briefing finished, shut down for some thinking time. Then gear up for these meetings. Christ— Oberman, Tibble, and IAB." She opened her eyes again. "It's going to be a rough morning."

"You've already had one." He moved to her to gently rub that spot between her eyebrows himself.

"Opened him up, ear to ear. He was dead before he hit the floor. Fast, fast way to go, and he'd earned slow and painful, in my book. And even so, it's not up to her to decide who lives, who dies. How. When. It's not her call."

Because she wasn't who she'd been

before, she laid her aching brow on his shoulder. "He'd probably have done the same—to Renee, to me, to whoever. Odds are he walked in there thinking he'd be opening me up, ear to ear. He was an open, festering wound on the department."

She straightened again.

"And Keener? Maybe harmless in the big scheme, maybe he gave his pizza server a nice tip when he was flush. But he lived his life on junk, and peddling it. I don't imagine he'd have had a quibble if the buyer was twelve, as long as the kid had the scratch. He was a pig, looking for the easy way in and the easy way out."

She drank some coffee, set it aside. "But none of that matters. Festering wound, pig, she doesn't get to decide."

Roarke cupped her face. "He'd have killed you if he could, and enjoyed it. Another cop may be primary on his murder, but Garnet's yours now."

"That's just the way it is."

"For you, yes. That's why Renee Oberman will never understand you."

"I understand her."

"Yes, I know you do." He kissed her lightly. "Let's get this done."

With a nod she walked to the door connecting their offices.

**17** Eve listened to her e-men explain, in their way, McNab's idea for a tap and trace. She listened until her ears began to ring.

She waved a hand in the air to cut off the geek-fest. "Bottom line. If you can do this, we'd have Renee's disposable—incoming and outgoings on record."

"Bottom line," Feeney agreed. "But that doesn't credit the juice in the concept or execution—and this one's loaded with it."

"Kudos all around. If you can take it from concept to execution, we need a warrant."

Feeney puffed out his cheeks. "Yeah,

that would be a little hitch. We've got enough for one, Dallas, starting with Peabody's statement, going right on through your meet with Renee, the financials, the tail last night to dead Garnet. It's your call whether we go there. IAB could work one."

Her call, she thought, and every decision angled off another path. "I'll get the warrant and inform IAB—after you've pulled off your juicy concept. I'll need to meet with Reo," she said, thinking of the ADA she trusted. "And before I meet with the commander again. Privately meet with her. Peabody—"

"Oh man, you want me to tag Crack again."

"Him, then Reo. Tell her to meet me there in thirty. Say it's urgent and confidential. You know what to do."

"Yeah," Peabody said on a sigh.

"Roarke, Peabody's going to need a vehicle."

"I am? Aren't I with you? You need me for Reo, then, Dallas, I should be with you for the meet with Commander Oberman, to push with you with IAB."

"No. I've got your statement for Reo. Dealing with Commander Oberman and

IAB, that's my job. You need to pursue your investigation. You need to stand for Detective Devin, Peabody. You need to get justice for her, and that's what you'll do. I have every confidence that's what you'll do."

"I'm not even sure I'm going down the right roads," Peabody began.

"You'll find out." She glanced at Roarke, and he nodded.

"I'll see to the vehicle. Feeney, why don't I meet you and McNab in the lab here? I'll be right along."

McNab gave Peabody a quick, supportive shoulder squeeze before he went out with his captain.

"Don't give her anything flashy," Eve called out to Roarke.

"Maybe just . . ." Peabody held up her thumb and forefinger, a half inch apart.

Roarke sent her a wink and left them alone.

Eve pointed Peabody to a chair, then walked to the buffet, poured coffee.

"You brought me coffee."

"Don't get used to it."

"It's usually my job."

"Because I'm the lieutenant." Eve sat. "I

pulled you into Homicide because I looked at you, and I thought, that's a cop. Solid, a little green, but solid. And I could help her be a better cop. I have."

Peabody stared into her coffee, said nothing.

"You have a cop's work to do for Devin. I put that in your hands because, well, I'm the lieutenant. I have to know my men— their strengths, weaknesses, style. I have to know them, and I have to trust them to do the job. Or I haven't done mine."

Eve sipped her coffee, considered her words. "Meetings like I've got set up? That's cop work, too, but it's the drag of command, Peabody. It's the politics and deal making, the pissing contests. It has to be done, and I have to do it."

"Because you're the lieutenant."

"Damn right. I've thought a lot about what it means to be in command, to have rank since Renee Oberman. Not just about what it means to be a cop, but to be a boss. The responsibilities, and the influence, the obligations to the badge, to the public, to the men and women under your command. I wanted it, and I worked for it. I had to be a cop. It's all I could be. I'd

been a victim, so I knew I could stay broken, or I could fight. I could learn and train
and work until I could stand for the victim.
We all have our reasons for being a cop."

"I wanted to make detective, so bad.
Being a cop . . . it meant I could help people who needed it, and that was important.
Making detective, well, for me, it meant I
was good, and I'd get better. You got me
there."

"I helped get you there," Eve corrected.
"I didn't want the rank for the office, for the
pay raise."

"You've got one of the crappiest offices
in Central," Peabody told her. "It makes us
proud."

"Seriously?" Surprised, then foolishly
pleased, Eve shook her head.

"You don't care about the fancy, you
care about the job. And your men. Everybody knows it."

And that, Eve realized, didn't merely
please. It warmed her, in the deep.

"Anyway," Eve continued, "I wanted it
because I knew I could do it. I knew I'd be
good, and I'd get better. I know when I
walk into that bullpen I can depend on
every man there. But it's just as important,

maybe more, that every man there knows he can depend on me. That I'll stand for them and with them, and if necessary, in front of them. If they don't know that, have absolute faith in that, in me, I've failed."

"You haven't failed." Peabody sniffled a little. "We've got the best damn division in Central."

"I happen to agree. Part of that's me, and I'll take credit for it. I'm a damn good boss, and the boss sets the level. Renee set hers, Peabody, and some cop who maybe—maybe—would have done the job, would have respected the badge chose to use it and to dishonor it because the person responsible for them said it was okay. Because the person responsible for them dug down for the weakness and squeezed it."

"I never thought of that, or thought of it like that, I guess."

"Other cops, good cops like Devin, died because the person responsible for her, the person she should have been able to have absolute faith in, made that call.

"You're going to bury her for it."

Peabody looked up again, blinked at the sudden fierceness in Eve's tone.

"I'm the lieutenant, and I'm telling you you're going to stand for Detective Gail Devin, and you're going to get her justice."

"Yes, sir."

"Now, set up the meet with Reo."

"Can I just run a couple things by you, on the avenues I'm taking?" Peabody smiled a little. "Because you're the lieutenant."

"Make it quick. I've got politics and pissing contests on my slate."

"You advised me to treat it like a cold case, so I've studied the file, the reports, the wit statements. The investigation was minimal because there were statements from cops—Renee's cops—that Devin peeled off during the raid, lost her cover. And during that time was assaulted and killed. She got some streams off, took down a couple of the bad guys before she went down."

"And?" Eve prompted.

"It reads like a cover, Dallas. An obvious cover. Like she screwed up, but her team edged from that so she'd get the posthumous honor. It reads blue line. No point putting she fucked up in her record since she's dead—but it's there, you know?"

"Yeah."

"I can't reinterview the wits without alerting them and Renee. So I'm reinterviewing the victim."

Eve kept her smile inside. "Okay."

"Her record previous to Renee's command, her instructors in the Academy, cops she worked with when she was in uniform, after she made detective. Her family, friends, DS Allo. I'm working down the line. I told them, except for Allo, I'm working on something that crosses with the raid, so I'm just back-checking."

"Good."

"She wasn't a fuckup, and hearing what Mira had to say in the briefing, I can follow the dots on how they set her up to look like one."

"Where are you going from here?"

"I wanted to talk to her mother," Peabody told her, "but her mother doesn't want to talk to me. She doesn't want to revisit, and has a serious hard-on for cops. She had a breakdown after it happened, and from what I've got she's never come all the way back. They were tight. I think she might have something and not know it. Something Devin said or did that could bounce me to the next step. I don't know how hard to push."

"If your gut tells you she's got something, you push. You find a way. You know how to work people, Peabody, how to relate, empathize, slide into their skin a little. Your eyewits are liars, so you're looking for people who have no reason to lie. That's good strategy."

"I'll go see her this morning. But . . . it's possible that if we can flip this doctor, put some pressure on the cops in the raid, we could get her for Gail Devin without anything else."

"Possible. Do you want possible?" Eve demanded. "Listen, you may not be able to wrap it all the way, but you keep going, and you'll know you did your best by her. That's what she deserves, it's what I expect, and it's what you'll be able to tell yourself when it's done. One way or the other. Now set up my damn meet."

"All over it." Peabody rose. "You were my hero."

"Oh, Jesus."

"When I was at the Academy, when I got into uniform, I studied you, your cases like you were some mythical figure, and I was on a quest. I wanted to be like you. When you took me on as aide I was so happy, and I was so fucking scared."

Remembering, Peabody let out a half laugh.

"Those were the days," Eve said, and made Peabody's laugh full.

"It didn't take long for me to learn you weren't a mythical figure, or the kind of hero who stun streams bounce off of. You bleed just like the rest of us, but you still go through the door. That makes you, and the rest of us who do the same, damn good cops. I learned I'd rather be a damn good cop than a hero. I learned I didn't want to be like you. You taught me to want to be me. You taught me and helped make me a damn good cop because you're the lieutenant."

Peabody pulled out her 'link to set up the meet.

In short order Eve stood outside studying the spiffy little compact in sapphire blue.

"What part of not flashy did you miss?" she asked Roarke as Peabody let out a happy *woo-hoo*.

"You consider anything this side of ugly

flashy. This vehicle is serviceable, handles very well, and has an excellent electronics package Peabody might find useful."

"Woo-hoo!" Peabody said again. "It's uptown mag! For a serviceable vehicle I will treat with great respect," she added.

"Wait ten minutes after I'm through the gate before heading out," she told Peabody. "If they've set up a tail, they'll follow me, and you'll be clear."

"Do you think I can't shake a tail?"

"How many times have you done so?"

"Okay, but there's always a first time. Which isn't this time," Peabody continued, "due to the delicacy of the investigation."

"That would be correct. Update me when you have something worth telling me. I appreciate the loaner for my partner," Eve told Roarke, "and apologize if she drools on the upholstery."

"Go get your warrant." He kissed her lightly. "I want to go play with my friends."

"Well, enjoy." She got into her vehicle, shook her head as Peabody stroked the shiny blue fender and purred. "I like mine better," she muttered, and drove off in her ugly but loaded DLE.

When Eve walked into the sex club,

Crack gave her what she could only interpret as the stink eye. Reo sat at the bar, chatting with him, looking like a lost ray of sunshine in the dim and dinge.

"Sorry." Eve set down the box she'd loaded from the buffet table in her office. "I brought you pastries—and real coffee."

Crack opened the lid, studied the contents. "Not a bad payoff, white girl. Plus, lucky for you, I like Blondie's company. Give you some room." He set another bottle of water on the bar and took his payoff box down to the other end.

"I don't get pastries?" Reo demanded.

"Maybe he'll share. Sorry I'm a little late. I got hung up."

"It better be good. I had to reschedule my nine o'clock. So, what's urgent and confidential?"

Eve opened her water. Reo was a curvy little blonde with a hint of Southern in her voice. She looked and sounded like a lightweight, a fact she used expertly to disarm, then skewer, defense attorneys, defendants, and opposing witnesses.

"If you can't move on what I tell you respecting that urgency and keeping a seal on the confidential, I can't tell you."

"I can't suck up urgent and confidential unless I know what I'm sucking up."

"Yeah, that's the trick, isn't it? Give me this. Do you trust your boss without qualification, without hesitation?"

"Yes. He's a good PA, a good lawyer, and a good man. Do I agree with him a hundred percent of the time? No. But if I did, it wouldn't say much about either of us."

"That's a good answer." In fact, Eve decided, she couldn't think of a better one. "If I ask you if you'll speak to no one but him about what I'm going to tell you, what I need from you, can you agree to that?"

"Yes. But I can't promise to agree with what you need, or to recommend to him he agree."

"You will." Eve took a long drink of water, then laid it out, start to finish.

It took time. When dealing with a lawyer, Eve knew, everything tangled with questions, arguments, points of law. Reo took out her book, made notes, demanded Eve backtrack and go over already covered ground.

And all of that assured Eve she'd gone to the right person.

"This is going to be a massacre," Reo murmured. "And the blood that stains the ground is going to sink in deep. Everything she's touched, Dallas, everything her squad's touched is going to carry that stain. The legal ramifications . . . arrests, confessions, plea bargains, convictions. Every one will go in the sewer."

"I know it."

"Oh, she's going down. We're going to take her down hard. I've had her on the stand. Her, Garnet, Bix, some of the others. Had them on the stand—witnesses for the prosecution. I've put people away who damn well deserved to go away, and because of this, those people get the door opened. She's going down," Reo repeated, her eyes like blue steel. "How many cops do you suspect she's had executed?"

"If you count Garnet—"

"I don't," Reo snapped.

"Okay then, two I'm sure of. I have what we've got for you." She pushed a disc across the bar. "You're not just here because the e-geeks want to try a new angle and we need the warrant. You're here because I wanted you to be prepared, to give you time to start putting your end of it together."

"Believe me, we will."

"Reo, I'm not trying to tell you how to do your job, but I have to say it. You have to be absolutely, unquestionably sure of the judge you go to on this. She could have one in her pocket, or have a bailiff, a clerk. She could have somebody in your office."

"God, that pisses me off. It pisses me off that this makes me worry that might be true. I'll go to my boss, and we'll work this out. That has to be done first, so it'll take some time to get that warrant."

"The e-work's probably not a snap anyway."

"I'll get back to you."

Alone, Eve sat at the bar for a minute, turning the water bottle in circles. Crack walked back down, took a long look at her.

"Still working the hard one."

"Yeah. I want to be pissed off—mostly am. But now and again I lose that edge, and then I just feel sick."

"Maybe I say something, piss you off. Give you the edge back."

She shook her head, smiled a little. "No. I already owe you three and a half."

"Friends don't keep score. Not when it

matters." He put his huge hand over hers on the bar, patted it. "Want a pastry?"

She laughed this time. "No, thanks. I've got to get back to the hard."

Peabody approached the little house in the Bronx with trepidation. She wasn't afraid she'd walk away empty—though that was a possibility. She was more afraid she'd push the wrong way and break what she believed was a brittle hold on survival.

She thought of her own mother, what it would be like for her to be told her daughter was dead. Dead because she'd made the choice to be a cop. Dead because she'd been ordered to put herself at risk, and had done so.

Her mother was strong, Peabody thought, but it would put cracks in her. It would damage, and there would be fissures that would never fully close again.

So she thought of her own mother as she knocked on the door of the little house in the Bronx.

The woman who opened it was too thin—brittle again—with her hair pulled back in a tail. She wore cutoff sweats and a T-shirt and studied Peabody with annoyance out of shadowed eyes.

"Mrs. Devin—"

"I told you yesterday, when you got me on the 'link, I've got nothing to say to you. To any cop about Gail."

"Mrs. Devin, if you could just hear me out. You don't have to say anything. Just hear me out. I wouldn't disturb you if it wasn't important."

"Important to who? You? I don't care about what's important to you. You're cleaning up your files? That's all she is to you, a file. Just a name in a file."

"No, ma'am, she's not. No, ma'am." The emotion in her heart, in her belly rang clearly in her voice. "I apologize more than I can say if I gave you that impression. I've gotten to know Gail a little. I know she liked to sing, and she had a strong alto. I know her father taught her to fish, and even though she didn't really like it, she went with him because they liked the time together. I know you and she had a strong and loving relationship. I know even after she moved to Manhattan, the two of you got together every week. For girl time. Lunch, dinner, a vid, the salon, shopping. It didn't matter."

Peabody's stomach clenched as tears began to roll down the woman's cheeks. But she didn't stop. "She called you her best friend. You didn't want her to be a cop, but you didn't stand in her way. You were proud of her when she graduated from the Academy, with honors. When she made detective you had a party for her. She knew you were proud of her. I think it meant a lot to her to know you were."

"Why are you doing this?"

Tears burned in Peabody's eyes. She didn't let them fall, but she wasn't ashamed to let them show. Not here, not with a dead cop's mother.

"Because I have a mother, Mrs. Devin, and she didn't really want me to be a cop. I know she's proud of me, and it means a lot. I love her so much. And some days, because she lives out West, I miss her until it hurts."

"Why did you do it then, why did you leave her and do this?"

"Because I'm a cop. It's what I am as much as what I do. Gail was a cop. She was your daughter, and she loved you. She was a cop, and she tried to make things better."

"It killed her."

"I know." Peabody let a little of the anger clutched inside her show, let it mix with the sympathy. "When I was coming here, I thought of my mom, and what it would do to her if she lost me. I wish, for her, I could be something else. But I can't. You were proud of Gail. I would have been proud to know her."

"What do you want from me?"

"Could I come in, please?"

"Oh, what does it matter?"

When the woman turned away, leaving the door open, Peabody stepped inside. She noted the clutter on a table—items that had obviously been on shelves, caught the scent of cleaner, polish.

"I'm sorry I upset you so much yesterday. You didn't get much sleep last night. Now a cleaning binge to help you work it off." She tried a small smile. "My mom does the same."

It wasn't quite true, as it was her father who used that route, but sticking with mothers seemed best—and not altogether a lie.

"Ask what you want to ask and go. I want to get back to my housework."

Won't have her long, Peabody calculated, and skipped over the groundwork she'd intended to lay. "Gail had a good record. Her evaluations from her supervisors were excellent. There were some notes in her file during the period she served under Lieutenant Renee Oberman that indicated she was having a difficult time."

"So what?" The resentment, the instinctive defense of her child charged out. "It's difficult work, and she worked hard. Too hard. She barely did anything but work those last weeks."

"Did you see her during that period, during those last weeks?"

"Of course I did."

"Did she tell you why she was stressed, or what she was working on that was particularly difficult?"

"No. We didn't talk about her work. She knew I didn't like it. Being proud of your child doesn't mean you want to be reminded how dangerous the work is they've chosen. I know she was tense. On edge. She'd lost weight."

"You were worried about her."

"I asked her to take some time off. Said we'd take a little trip, a few days at the shore.

She said she'd like that, could use that. But she had to finish something first. Finish something important, then she'd really want to get away for a while. It was work. If it had been a man, or anything else, she'd have told me."

"Is there anyone else she would have told?"

"One of you. Cops talk to other cops."

Peabody nodded, felt it slipping away. "Did she keep a notebook, a diary, any sort of journal?"

"No."

"You're sure?"

"Of course I'm sure." Anger fired through grief again. "And if she had kept one, I wouldn't let you see it. It would be personal. But she didn't keep a diary. I have all of her things, and there's nothing like that."

"You have her things?" A little bubble of excitement, of hope opened in Peabody's throat. "Can I see them?"

"Why should I—"

"Please, Mrs. Devin. I can't explain everything, but I promise you I want to do right by Gail. I swear to you, that's my only purpose in being here, in asking you."

"You're like a dog with a bone." The woman turned her back, strode through the living area to a dining nook, through that to a room off a kitchen that gleamed and smelled of lemon.

It was like a small bedroom without the bed. Clothes hung neatly in the closet— Peabody imagined more were neatly folded in the small dresser. Pieces of Gail Devin sat here and there. Whatnot boxes, scarves, a bright pink vase. Photos, framed posters, a Little League trophy, a fishing rod.

A slim case held discs. Music discs, music vids, Peabody noted. All arranged by category, alphabetized.

She got a little buzz.

"That's a nice collection."

"It was how she relaxed, let loose."

I know her now, Peabody thought. She was smart and determined. A good cop. Where would a smart, determined, and good cop hide a record she wanted to keep handy, keep safe?

"Mrs. Devin, I have to ask you to let me borrow Gail's music collection."

Hot pink color stained cheeks already wet with tears. "Do you think I'd hand over

what was Gail's, one of her most important things, to a stranger?"

"She's not a stranger to me." Peabody
looked in Mrs. Devin's eyes and repeated,
"I want to do right by Gail. If she were
standing in front of my mother, I know
she'd do the same for me."

On her way back to Manhattan, Peabody had to pull over, rest her head on the
wheel.

"Please, God," she murmured. "Let me
find something. Don't let me have done
this to that poor woman for nothing."

18 Eve had a short window to check in with her own men, so she hit the bullpen between meetings. After a quick scan, she gestured to Trueheart.

"My office."

She went in, grabbed coffee, downed half of it.

"Where's Baxter?" she asked when Trueheart stepped in.

"He's working a wit in the lounge, Lieutenant. I'm verifying some information via 'link. We're—"

"Is there a reason I need to know what

you're working on?" she interrupted. "Any humps, bumps, problems, questions?"

"No, sir. Not at this time."

"Good. Is there anything anybody's got going that requires me? You pay attention, Trueheart," she said when he hesitated. "You know what's moving out there. I don't have time for a rundown unless I need a rundown."

"Um, no, sir. I don't think your attention's required on anything current."

"Get the word out. If I'm needed leave a memo. If it's urgent, contact via 'link."

"Yes, sir."

She eased down on the corner of her desk, a deliberate move to take some of the formal out of the exchange. "What's the buzz out there, Trueheart?"

He looked at her, spiffy in his uniform. "Sir?"

"Jesus, Trueheart. I know damn well Baxter's clipped some of the green off of you, and as I said previous, you pay attention. You know what the talk is. Let's hear it."

"Well, um. Everybody knows something's going on, and it's more than the dead junkie. Word's out one of Lieutenant

Oberman's men went down, at the same scene."

"And being cops they're speculating," Eve added. "And laying money on various scenarios."

He flushed a little. "It's very possible, Lieutenant."

"Get the word out I consider speculation the natural order of things, and would be shocked, Officer, shocked and appalled to discover gambling was going on in my bullpen."

He gave her a sober nod, spoiled a little by his struggle to control a grin. "Yes, sir, Lieutenant."

"I can be contacted, but only on urgent matters, for the next two hours. Understood?"

"Yes, sir."

"Dismissed."

Alone, she stood a moment, finishing her coffee and studying her board. When her 'link signaled, she saw Peabody on the display.

"Dallas."

"I think I might have something," Peabody began.

Eve switched her to privacy mode and

took the communication on the way to Whitney's office.

Whitney opened the door personally. There were new lines dug into his face, she noted, more gray threaded through his hair than there had been even a few days before.

Command, she thought, could be a harsh master.

"Lieutenant."

"Sir."

He gestured her into his office with its wide windows to the city he was sworn to protect.

Commander Marcus Oberman stood in front of one of them—tall, sturdy in his serious gray suit and steel blue tie. He'd let his hair go white, kept it shorn short, military style. Command had left its mark on him as well, but he remained a handsome man, striking and fit at eighty-six.

"Commander Oberman," Whitney said, "Lieutenant Dallas."

"Lieutenant." Oberman extended his hand. "I appreciate you taking the time to come in to meet with me. I understand the value of your time."

"It's an honor, Commander."

"And for me. You have an impressive reputation. Your commander speaks highly of you."

"Thank you, sir."

"Can we sit?" Oberman asked, deferring to Whitney.

"Please." Whitney gestured to chairs.

Oberman took one. "You were barely out of the Academy when I retired from this office," Oberman began, "but I've followed some of your investigations in the media, and heard the buzz at the trough where we old warhorses gather."

He smiled when he said it, the bright blue eyes he'd passed to his daughter friendly on hers. But Eve felt herself being summed up.

She had no quibble with that, as she did the same with him.

"Of course, now with the success of Nadine Furst's book, your work on the Icove case is well documented. It's been good for the department, wouldn't you agree, Jack, the interest in that case? How it was pursued, investigated, and closed?"

"I would."

"From what I'm told and, observed, Lieutenant, you've butted heads with fellow officers during the course of investigations."

"I'm sure that's accurate, Commander."

His smile widened. "If you're not butting heads now and then, you're not doing the job—in my opinion."

He leaned back in the chair. Taking the formal out, Eve judged, as she had with Trueheart.

"It takes confidence, even bullheadedness, as well as training, talent, dedication to stick with the job, and to move up the ranks. I understand you and my daughter are butting heads at the moment."

"I regret if Lieutenant Oberman sees it that way."

He nodded, his gaze pinned on hers. Still cop's eyes, Eve thought. Shrewd, probing, the sort that could peel away the layers and expose what was hiding beneath.

"Your commander will attest to the fact I don't make a habit of interfering with departmental business. I no longer have the chair, and hold nothing but respect for the man who does."

"Yes, sir, as do I."

"But a father is a father, Lieutenant, and from that job no man retires. I expect you and Lieutenant Oberman would have some certain friction between you as you are different types, have different work styles. But you're both still ranked officers of the NYPSD."

"Absolutely understood, Commander."

"I hadn't intended to become involved in this situation, in any way." He lifted his hands, spread them. "Even when I had the chair, I believed my officers should settle their own differences."

Daddy refusing to grease the wheels? Eve thought. That had to chap Renee's ass. "Yes, sir. I agree."

"I reconsidered this only after learning early this morning that one of my daughter's men had gone down. The officer who was at the center of the friction."

"It's very regrettable Detective Garnet lost his life, sir."

"Every man lost can and does affect us all, but most particularly his commanding officers. You've lost men under your command, Lieutenant."

"Yes, sir." She could list their names. She knew their faces.

"It's my hope, Lieutenant, that given these new and tragic circumstances, you will agree to expunge the mark you placed on the fallen officer's record. Deservedly placed," he added. "But I would reach out to you now on this, for Lieutenant Oberman and her man."

"No, sir. I regret I'm unable to accommodate you on this matter."

He sat back, obviously taken by surprise. "It's so important to you, Lieutenant, that this rip stands? On a dead man?"

"Dead or alive, he earned it. I apologize to the father, sir, but hope the commander who held this chair, and who served this department honorably for more years than I've been alive, will accept my stand when I say Detective Garnet's lieutenant, present throughout that incident, did not intervene. Did not control the situation."

"Are you directing the rip at Garnet or his lieutenant?"

"I'm not in the position to discipline his lieutenant. Respectfully, sir, I will not expunge his suspension. And in fact have already begun procedures that will result, I believe, in his expulsion from the force. Posthumously."

"That is a harsh stance. A harsh line."

"Yes, sir, it is. You may not be aware,

Commander, that last evening Detective Garnet came to my home, did in fact lie in wait at my home. He attempted to assault me. Did, in fact, make physical contact. Did, in fact, draw his weapon."

"No." Oberman's face went to stone. "I was not aware. I was not apprised."

"The incident is on record, sir, and was reported immediately after it occurred. I believe Lieutenant Oberman will have been made aware of it."

She waited just a beat to let that little gem shine.

"Detective Garnet's death is regrettable, Commander, but it is my opinion he didn't deserve his rank, his badge. I will continue to do whatever I can to see he's stripped of them. His death doesn't make him any less of a bad cop."

"No, it does not. I withdraw my request, Lieutenant Dallas. And I apologize for making it."

"No apology necessary, sir."

Eve rose as he did.

"I'll let you, both of you, get back to your work. Thank you, Commander Whitney, for giving me the time. And you, Lieutenant."

"It was an honor to meet you, sir."

As Whitney led Oberman to the door, the former commander paused, turned back to Eve. "Do you believe Garnet's death comes out of the murder of this Keener?"

"I'm not working Garnet's case, sir, but am cooperating and will continue to cooperate fully with the officers assigned to that investigation."

"I see." He looked at her for a long moment, then walked out without another word.

"He's embarrassed." Whitney closed the door. "Angry and embarrassed to have put himself in this position. And there's a place in him now, twisting inside as he wonders, worries, considers what position his daughter might be in."

"Yes, sir," Eve agreed. "It's going to be worse for him, and soon."

And as Whitney walked to the window to look out at his city, Eve understood he, too, was angry and embarrassed.

"All the years he gave this job, this city. All the years he sat in command. All the work he put into helping rebuild and reform this department after the Urbans? And his name will always carry this."

"Her name."

Whitney shook his head as he turned back. "You don't have children, Dallas. It will always be his name. And it will always be his shame."

She waited until Whitney returned to his desk, sat heavily behind it.

"Permission to speak freely, sir."

"So given."

"I can't and won't say that none of this will fall on you. You're in command, so it will. But I can and will say you're not responsible."

"Being in command makes me responsible."

"No, sir. Taking responsibility and being responsible aren't always the same thing. You'll take it because you'd never do otherwise. But Renee Oberman is responsible, and in a way that's deeply unfair, so is her father. His name and his reputation, the awe he inspires, allowed her room, inclined some to turn a blind eye, influenced others to go along."

"Including me?"

"I can't answer that, Commander. But I know when I brought this to you, you didn't turn a blind eye or give her room. You acted as a commander, because you'd never do otherwise. And you acted, knowing full well what would fall on you. You could've done it differently."

Obviously intrigued, he sat back. "How so?"

"You could've found a way to get her off the job. You could've found a way to pressure her off, to keep it internal, to weed out her squad. And, sir, you could have covered it up. Kept it inside, called on the blue line. Dead man's just a junkie. Sure, cops are dead, but you can't bring them back."

She paused a moment, watching his face. "You probably considered it, weighed it out, for about five minutes. You could've made it work—I can see how you could've made it work. But you'd never take that out. Because you're in command. Because you're a cop, sir, and you'll never be anything else."

He pressed his palms together, tapped his index fingers on his chin. "You assume you know me, Lieutenant."

"I do know you, Commander." She thought of what Peabody had said to her. "I have had the opportunity to study some of your work as a detective, as you moved up the ranks. I have studied and observed your methods and manner since I've served under you. I respect how you sit the chair."

"Do you consider how you might do the same? How you might sit this chair one day?"

"That's a terrifying thought."

She made him laugh. He rose, walked to the AutoChef. And sighed. "Christ, I wish I had some of your coffee."

"I can have some sent up."

He shook his head, made do with what he had—then brought her a cup, once again reminding her of her earlier session with Peabody.

"Sit down, Dallas. Tibble will be here any minute, and IAB will be right behind him. We're going to stick there, you and I, not only in your proprietary role in the Keener homicide, but in your integral role in the Oberman investigation. I believe Tibble will agree. If not, we'll convince him."

"Yes, sir, we will. Commander . . . contact Nadine Furst."

He lifted his eyebrows, said nothing.

"She will agree to and proceed by stipulations of timing, off-the-record statements,

of confidentiality. She won't release anything until you give her the green."

"You want me to use her to spin this off
me?"

"Not precisely, sir, no. Nadine likes to
get her teeth in red meat as much as any
reporter. She's just better at seeing the
real story—not just the jazz that pulls rat-
ings. That's why, I think, she pulls them.
She digs for the truth, not just the juice. I
know we have our PR people, media liai-
sons, mouthpieces, but in my opinion,
she's worth ten of them."

He nodded slowly, watching her now.
"Go on."

"Sir. Renee Oberman's actions will hurt
the department once they become public. More, they'll hurt the public as cage
doors will certainly open. I see the value
in using whatever is at our disposal to
minimize that damage. With truth. Corruption existed. When uncovered it was
ruthlessly, systematically, and unhesitat-
ingly cut out."

"I'll consider it."

"Sir . . ."

"You're still in the speak freely zone,
Dallas."

"Go on her show. You, the chief if he'll agree. Me, Peabody. Especially Peabody. The situation she was in, the actions she took, who she is, will play well." Eve pushed, hard, surprising herself how fiercely she wanted to convince him. "A good cop—a young female detective trapped in a deadly situation—who turned that and spearheaded the exposure of corruption, of murder and treachery.

"We're the blue line, sir, and that will resonate on-screen. But Peabody is the face, the very human element. And she would symbolize who we are, contrast sharply against what Renee Oberman is."

He rubbed his chin, and his lips curved a little above his fingers. "You can carve out an angle like that, an excellent angle, and believe the idea of your ass in the chair someday down the road is terrifying?" He waved off her response before she could make it. "I should have thought of it myself, should have thought it through exactly that way. I'll contact Furst."

Something inside her unknotted. "Thank you, sir."

"Don't thank me. I'm wondering why I haven't assigned you to Media and PR."

"Because, sir, I hope I've done nothing to deserve that kind of punishment."

Both he and Eve rose when Whitney's admin announced Chief Tibble.

He was dark, long, and lean, and wore a suit well. A good look, Eve knew, for media conferences and screen time. But there was considerably more under the surface.

He studied Eve a moment, then addressed her directly. "This avalanche was precipitated by a dead junkie in a bathtub."

"No, sir, this avalanche was precipitated by Renee Oberman's corrupt and illegal use of her badge, her name, her rank, and this department."

"Point well taken, and well expressed. But I wasn't talking about the goddamn shit rolling down the goddamn hill, but what set off the roll."

"That would be a dead junkie in a bathtub, sir—technically."

"We're going to use him, everything and everyone that came before and after him, to bury her in it. When we do, the department's going to stand on top of that shit pile and claim victory. We're going to work on that, Jack."

"The lieutenant has just given me a solid suggestion on just that."

"We'll talk about it, after we're done with IAB. We'll talk about that, work on that, and we will goddamn deal with that because she's not going to take any part of this department down with her. You take her down," he said to Eve in a tone that told her he'd prefer to do it himself. With his bare hands.

"You take her down hard. Hard enough she can't get up again. I don't want her limping away from this, turning it so the department takes more hits."

"That's my intention, Chief Tibble."

"Make it your mission in life," he snapped, then turned to Whitney. "We'll handle the fallout. Goddamn it, Jack, how the hell does a woman like this get rank, get power, get a free fucking pass?"

Before Whitney could speak, Tibble waved a hand in the air, spun away. He stalked to the window, stood staring out, his hands linked behind his back.

"I should know. I've had her in my office. I've entertained her along with her parents in my own home. My own home," he said more quietly. "I've probably given her a few of those free passes myself. Goddamn it. Lieutenant Dallas, did Renee Oberman order the assassination of police officers?"

"I believe she did, sir."

He whirled around, led with absolute fury. "I don't want your beliefs. You *prove* it. You prove it so the PA can take it to a jury without a reasonable doubt. Your beliefs mean nothing in a court of law, and without—"

"Chief Tibble." Whitney moved until he stood between Eve and the chief. "Renee Oberman is under my command, and her actions have taken place under my watch."

"When I want you to throw yourself on your sword, I'll tell you. This department can't afford to lose you, and I'm damned if Renee Oberman will cause us to shed more blood. But I know it's taken a Homicide lieutenant and a dead junkie to bring you and me, IAB, and God Himself into the light on this. That's a hell of a thing."

"Chief Tibble," Eve began, "it was, in fact, my partner overhearing the damning conversation between—"

"Don't interrupt me when I'm complimenting your work, Lieutenant, and blowing off steam I need to finish blowing off before dealing with IAB."

"Sir."

He pressed his fingers to his eyes briefly. "Your partner did well, Lieutenant, as did you. As have you, Commander. We're going to make damn sure at the end of the day that outbalances a corrupt cop and a blemished squad."

He stopped when IAB's arrival was announced.

"Let's go with pecking order, Jack. Let me take the wheel first. Lieutenant, have a seat."

Apparently, Eve thought, the steam had blown as now Tibble stood, cool and contained, as Webster and his captain entered.

"Captain, Lieutenant. Be seated. Here," he said when they had, "is how we want this to go."

He laid it out concisely, reasonably, and in a tone that said this was already so. Eve admired the style, particularly since she'd just finished being singed by the furnace blast of his temper.

She would continue to head the investigation into Keener's death, providing reports and data to IAB, who would, in turn, keep her apprised of all actions and progress in their internal investigations relating to Oberman.

There was debate, disagreement, but it was clear to Eve that Tibble had the controls. A good general, she thought, looks at the whole battlefield—and the ground beyond—then chooses where and how to fight.

"IAB's investigation of Renee Oberman and the others involved with her remains essential, necessary, and will have every assist, every cooperation from my office, the commander's, from Lieutenant Dallas and her people. But the murder of police officers, and civilians, outweighs even that."

"The murder of police officers is part of IAB's investigation," Webster pointed out.

"Which is why this has to be a coordinated effort. You agree, Commander?"

"Unquestionably."

"Lieutenant Dallas?" Tibble asked.

"Absolutely, sir. The fact is, my team and our investigation have made considerable progress on the officer-involved homicides. I received an update from my partner on that end a short time ago, and have not yet updated the commander or passed that information to IAB. I'd like permission to do so if we're all agreed on how these matters will proceed. Otherwise, I would be obliged to follow the letter of procedure, reporting only to my commander and leaving it to him what information he deems proper to relate to Internal Affairs."

"Don't get slippery, Dallas," Webster warned.

"Don't get greedy, Webster."

Before he could snap back at her, his captain shot him a warning look. "There are points all around. While we may not be on the same page, I think we all want this book to close the same way. IAB will cooperate, stipulating that if any information regarding any other officer is uncovered during the outside investigation, we are given that information. No surveillance, no e-track, no meets involving any tentacle of these investigations takes place without IAB knowledge."

Tibble kept his face neutral, turned to Whitney. "Commander?"

"Agreed. Lieutenant Dallas, your report."

"Detective Peabody interviewed Detective Gail Devin's mother this morning.

Mrs. Devin has been resistant to speaking with the police on any matter, and particularly about the death of her daughter in the line of duty. As you know, Commander, Peabody has a way of softening hard lines. Through her efforts, Mrs. Devin allowed Peabody to take a collection of what appear to be music discs. All of Devin's possessions are now with her mother and have been held there. We're aware Devin suspected her lieutenant of something from previous statements already shared with IAB through Lieutenant Webster. Peabody's assessment is Devin was an organized cop, a detailer, a sharp observer—which we believe led to the order for her execution. Peabody believes, and I agree, it's very likely Devin kept a record of observations, a record she would have been smart enough to hide until such time that she felt justified in reporting those observations, or had proven her suspicions."

"Music discs?" Webster repeated, but Eve saw him calculating.

"Lieutenant Oberman sent two men to toss Keener's place the morning after his death, when she learned the case had fallen to me and was being pursued. If she worried enough about Devin to order the hit, she sure as hell found a way to search Devin's apartment, her electronics."

"And may very well have found, taken, and destroyed any documents or files," the IAB captain commented.

"May have. But Peabody believes Devin was smart enough not to have anything on her comp, on her 'link, in an obvious file. A collection of music discs, ordered and in plain sight, could easily have been ignored. Maybe you check out a couple, then move on. Peabody is—or has by now—transported them to my home office, which is set as HQ—for examination and analysis."

"Even if Devin made a secret record of her suspicions, they're still suspicions," Webster pointed out.

"It goes to pattern, to motive. Leave the homicide investigating to me. It's what I do. We can and will build a case against her, for Devin, for Strumb, for Keener, even for Garnet."

Eve shifted so she spoke more directly to Whitney. "Commander, it's my opinion she's had relatively smooth sailing in her little venture, all this time. She's had damn good luck, and she's got skills along with the power of her father's name. And she got cocky—she mishandled Garnet, and had been mishandling him for a while. She didn't play him right because she simply got used to having him dance when she said dance. She's more lucky than smart," Eve continued. "Cop smart," she amended. "She's ridden on Daddy's coattails whenever possible—and that's something she resents. She does it, resents it, so she has to keep reaching for more. You've got her from Mira, that's how she's made.

"Garnet not only slapped back at her authority, he turned on her, and he caused her embarrassment, caused her to lose a round with me. She ordered him gone as much for pride and revenge as expediency."

"How does that connect to Devin?" Webster insisted.

"Jesus, Webster, you haven't been out of murder that long."

The impatience burning through only added impact to her theory.

"It's how she deals when she wants to shed a problem—and when the problem touches something personal. Devin, female, questioning her—or asking questions about her. Pushing where Renee didn't want her pushing. Devin's mentor is a vet, a retired cop—who was on the squad when Renee took over. He didn't like her, and he transferred."

"Allo," Webster said. "Detective-Sergeant Samuel."

"Yeah. She'd know Devin was talking to him. Devin's trouble, and isn't falling in line or transferring out even with bogus crappy evals. Peabody may find more, something specific, the hair on the camel's back—"

"Straw." Webster smiled a little. "It's the straw that broke the camel's back."

"What would a camel do with a straw? Whatever. Renee needed Devin gone, she made her gone. We'll find the same with Strumb. It's pattern. She ordered Bix to do Keener. Could've scared a weasel like him off, but that's not enough for her. Dead means safe. And he can't screw with her, her plans, her tidy system. Dead, they're out of the equation."

Eve got to her feet. "Commander, I'd like to get back to work, with your permission, and trust you to work out any further details on coordinating with Internal Affairs.

Commander Oberman will have had sufficient time, I believe, to speak to her."

"Commander Oberman," Webster began.

"A moment, Lieutenant, and you'll be apprised. Permission granted, Lieutenant Dallas."

"Thank you, sir. Chief, Captain, Lieutenant."

"Is it permissible to ask where you're going?" Webster asked.

"I'm going to kick more dirt in Renee Oberman's face," Eve told him. "It's the fun part of the job."

And looking forward to it, she went out, closed the door.

19 They wore black armbands in Lieutenant Oberman's squad. Other than that, as far as Eve could see, it was business as usual. Then again, the mood here struck her as depressing in any case.

As usual, Renee's blinds shuttered her window and the glass of her closed door.

Eve's glance flicked over Lilah Strong, just long enough for their eyes to meet. Then she moved directly to the lieutenant's door.

"The boss isn't available."

Eve turned to Bix. She'd been hoping

for a confrontation there, but hadn't expected it to be so easy. "Were you speaking to me, Detective?"

"The lieutenant isn't available."

"As you are addressing a superior, Detective, that would be, 'The lieutenant isn't available, sir.'"

"Sir." He kept his seat, his eyes cold as a shark's. "Lieutenant Oberman's orders are she is not to be disturbed at this time. We lost one of our own last night."

"I'm aware of the loss, Detective—Bix, isn't it?"

"That's right."

"That's right, sir."

"Sir."

"You partnered with Detective Garnet?"

"When so assigned by my lieutenant."

Eve waited a beat. "And it appears you share his difficulty in showing the respect due to superiors. Or is that a theme that runs through this squad? As I hold the opinion the boss sets the tone, this gives me cause to wonder if Lieutenant Oberman has difficulty showing respect to superiors."

"You're not her superior."

Eve took a step closer to his desk, well

aware the focus of the room had narrowed on them. "You want a pissing contest with me, Bix? Then get on your feet for it. On your feet, Detective," she ordered when he didn't move.

He started to rise, slowly. His face never changed—cold eyes, hard jaw. She wondered what it would take to goad him into taking a shot at her. Just one shot, she thought, and she'd have his badge, threaten Renee with a full disciplinary review, and send her squad into chaos.

The door behind her burst open—and told her one of the things she wanted to know. Renee had the squad room monitored from her office.

"Dallas. I don't appreciate you coming into my squad and harassing my men."

"Is that what I'm doing?" Eve kept her eyes on Bix as she spoke. "Do you consider it harassment to expect and demand respect due rank? Your men are a disgrace."

"In my office!"

Now Eve turned, and her tone brought winter into the room. "I don't take orders from you, Oberman. You're on the edge of having me file a formal complaint against you, against this detective, and requesting a full review of your command."

Angry color slashed across Renee's cheekbones. "I would prefer to discuss your *grievances* in the privacy of my office."

"Sure," Eve said, and strolled inside. She had to fight a satisfied smile when the door slammed.

And it was just plain fun to see, even with the heels Renee wore, that she retained the advantage of height. She tried a Summerset-style look down her nose.

"Who the hell do you think you are? Coming into *my* squad, threatening me, abusing my men? Do you think because you're Central's golden girl you can come here, aim and fire at me? Today of all days. You bitch, I lost a man last night—and you want to talk to me about respect? Where the hell is yours?"

"Are you finished?" Eve said smoothly. "Or do you have more?"

"I don't like you."

"Ouch."

"I don't like your attitude, your interference, or your habit of muscling in on my command. You're not the only one who can file a formal complaint."

"Be my guest. I think we both know, especially since Dad's no longer in the chair, who'd come out on top on that one. Speaking of your father . . ." Eve glanced at the portrait. "It was a pleasure meeting him earlier."

"Fuck you."

This time she didn't bother to control it, and just laughed. "Wow! That really stings. Now, do you want to keep shooting your spitballs, or do you want to get down to it?"

"I've already wasted more than enough time on you."

"Oh boy, I have to say right back at you. However, I actually make it a policy to do my job, even when it's annoying. I'm here regarding Garnet. I see you've been informed of his death as you're decked out in mourning black. Nice suit, by the way."

Renee's withering stare only gladdened Eve's heart. "I'll be documenting your sarcasm and disrespect toward a fallen officer."

"Document your ass off. It has yet to be determined if he went down in the line, and in fact is leaning hard otherwise. And that's not considering he was on suspension at the time of his death. It's further not considering he'd have certainly lost his badge and faced criminal charges had he lived."

"What the hell are you talking about?"

"Well, gee, I'd say I guess you didn't get the memo, except we both know otherwise." Eve pulled a disc out of her pocket, tossed it on Renee's desk. "That's a recording from my home security that clearly shows Garnet ambushing me at the gates to my home, threatening me, striking me, and drawing his weapon on me with clear intent.

"Your man was rabid and rogue, Renee, a fact I have no doubt you and your father discussed quite recently. No wonder you're in such a bad mood."

"What my father and I discuss is none of your business."

"On the contrary, you've made it mine. You went crying to Daddy about mean old Lieutenant Dallas, and it backfired on you. Instead of disciplining your detective for his behavior, you took steps to attempt to sweep it under the rug. And that detective, fully aware you would not and did not discipline him, escalated into drawing down on a fellow officer—with an unregistered weapon. He'd been using when he did it, and it will very likely be determined he'd been using when he died."

"I—"

"I'm not done," Eve snapped. "If you don't immediately request and recommend a random test for your squad for illegals, I will—with cause."

"What do you know about Illegals work?" Renee demanded. "Garnet had been under a great deal of pressure the last weeks. He'd been working on a lead on the Giraldi case, and it fizzled on him. He'd been working to revive it when you showed up here, pushing your weight around."

"I fail to follow how my coming to you over your dead weasel somehow incited Garnet to abuse illegals, threaten me, and end up dead."

"He was on the edge. I was fully aware of his problems and had discussed them with him. I wanted him to take some time off, get some counseling—and he asked for more time, asked to have a couple more weeks on Giraldi. I gave it to him, and I believe he was making progress on it, and on his personal problems, until you insisted on the suspension."

"It's amazing," Eve said in sincere wonder. "Really, it is. You can justify the outrageous, even criminal behavior of your detective, and consider my actions in response not only as unfair but as a contributing factor. Your man was a fuckup, a dangerous fuckup. Now he's a dead fuckup. You bear some weight there, and how you deal with that's on you.

"One thing I know," Eve continued, "is in a couple of days you've lost a weasel and a detective. Since I do know how Homicide works, I'll be actively pursuing that connection."

"It's obvious Bill was using Keener," Renee said wearily. "I don't know why he didn't tell me. I know he wanted to prove himself to me since I'd made my concerns known, and he was on notice. Whatever he'd been able to tap out of Keener, or whoever Keener had tried to tap, got Keener killed. Bill followed that up, searching Keener's flop, then—it certainly seems apparent—arranging a meet at the location where Keener had gone to ground, had died. And that cost Bill his life."

"That'd be nice and tidy. Except for the fact that you had a detective out there pursuing leads, taking actions that don't show up in his reports or case files—or in those of the detective working with him on the case. Or in yours."

"You said it yourself. He'd gone rogue."

Easy to toss him in front of the runaway train, Eve thought, since he was already dead. But she had another, a live one. "I'll need to interview Bix."

"Damn it, you've just said there's nothing in Bix's notes or reports. Garnet went lone wolf on this—it's clear. Bix never met with Keener."

"How would you know?" Eve pumped derision into the question, watched Renee's jaw clench. "If you had one detective writing his own score, you could have two." She glanced at her wrist unit. "I've got time now."

"I'm not going to allow you—"

"You don't *allow* me," Eve interrupted. "I'm primary on an active homicide, and consulting on a second, believed connected homicide, which involved a police officer. Bix is entitled to his rep or a lawyer, but I will have him in Interview."

Eve pulled her com out of her pocket. "This is Dallas, Lieutenant Eve, Homicide, requesting an interview room—"

"You can interview him here, in my office," Renee objected. "There's no need to take him into a formal."

"The pissier you get, the pissier I get," Eve responded. "Interview B," she confirmed, and closed the com. "Have him report within fifteen minutes. My division, Interview B."

"I'm coming in with him."

"You're welcome to watch from Observation." She started for the door, paused. "You know, it's weird. I would think you, Bix, everyone on the squad would not only be willing but anxious to cooperate on every level with an investigation that may lead to the identification, apprehension, and arrest of the individual responsible for Garnet's murder.

"But . . ." Eve shrugged. "That's just me."

She strolled out of the squad room as she'd strolled in. And considered her luck rolling along when she ran into Janburry and Delfino on their way in.

"Detectives."

"Lieutenant," Janburry acknowledged.

"I've just finished meeting with Lieutenant Oberman. I'm sure she'll inform you, as she did me, regarding her actions on

Garnet's illegals use, and his apparent working off book on an investigation, his use—in her opinion—of her CI, Keener, as an informant. I'll copy you on my report on these details, in case the lieutenant misses any in her discussion with you."

"We appreciate that, Lieutenant." Delfino's eyebrows lifted, just a hair. "Lieutenant Oberman states she was aware Garnet was using?"

"And took actions—or didn't take them—as she deemed best. I'm going to interview Detective Bix of her squad, as he was Garnet's most usual partner and was involved in this investigation. He may have additional information that may prove helpful to your case, and mine. You're welcome to observe."

"That's mighty cooperative of you," Janburry commented.

"I'm in a mighty cooperative mood. My division, Interview B, in about fifteen."

"In the tit for tat department," Janburry added, "Garnet's tox screen confirms he'd consumed illegal substances, and alcohol. The alcohol is corroborated by Detective Freeman, also of this squad, who states he and Garnet were together between about ten and midnight at the Five-O Bar. The details will also be in our report, which we will copy to you, but Freeman states Garnet was in an excitable and edgy mood—and had considerable uncomplimentary things to say about you."

"Oh, golly."

Janburry smirked. "He also claims Garnet received a tag on his 'link around that midnight hour, which he took outside before returning to finish his drink and tell Freeman he had a fresh line to pull."

"But though drinking, excitable, edgy, and running high, I bet he didn't give his pal any details about said line."

"Nary a one."

"Nary." Now Eve grinned. "I like that. Nary a one."

"He reads a lot," Delfino supplied. "Considering fresh lines and excitable moods, it's just head-scratching that Garnet didn't in turn tag his partner in this investigation. Then again, maybe he was a selfish bastard or thought his partner was a dickhead."

"Maybe. We'll see what Bix has to say about it."

"Looking forward to it. Well, shall we proceed?" Janburry said to his partner.

"See? Reads a lot."

Enjoying their rhythm, Eve split off to prepare for the interview.

In her office, she put together what she needed, then sent memos to Whitney and Webster, leaving it to them to inform their superiors of the interview she'd scheduled. She put in a request for Mira to observe, if possible.

Then she tagged Feeney.

"Progress?"

"Nobody likes a nag."

"Hey, it's been hours."

"Not in e-time. We're getting there. We're close." He crunched down on one of his habitual almonds. "It's not like replacing a motherboard, you know."

"Fine. You should be aware I've just come from pissing Renee off, adding some more pressure. She said she didn't like me."

"That must've hurt your feelings."

"They're bruised. I ratted her out to her old man re Garnet's temper tantrum last night, and if he didn't head down there and give her a spanking, I'll dress like McNab for a week. She called me a bitch, right to my face."

"I'm shocked by her use of harsh language."

"I could barely conceal my pain and embarrassment. I also tweaked her boy, Bix, and have him scheduled for Interview in a few minutes, regarding Garnet's possible use of Renee's weasel, the now deceased Keener, as Renee graciously opened that door."

"She's going to want to do more than use harsh language on you."

"You think? What's Peabody's status?"

"She's hunkered down in your office here. That's all I know."

"Roarke?"

"What am I? The freaking hall monitor?" The screen filled with his aggrieved face. "He's doing rich, important-guy shit. He's in and out."

"Okay. Keep me updated. Text only."

"When we've got it, you'll know. Otherwise, don't bother me."

"Jeez," she muttered when he clicked off. "Temperamental geek."

She started down to Interview, and spotted Baxter at Vending.

"Did you close up the wit?"

"Is that a rhetorical question?" He chose

a coconut cream bar, which made her stomach curdle. "You want?" he offered, obviously in a generous mood.

"Not if I were trapped under the rubble of a fallen building for five days and it was my only possible sustenance."

"I like 'em." To prove it, he ripped the wrapper, bit in. "Trueheart and I are working the suspect in Interview. We're taking a break so he can sulk and reflect on the error of his ways. Funny thing, when I came out I saw an Illegals detective going into B. Bix."

"Do you know Bix?"

"No, I haven't had that pleasure. So how did I know it was Bix, you may ask."

"I may."

"I call it cop curiosity." He took another bite, chewed. "My LT is butting heads with Illegals LT Oberman, I just have to find out a little more about the opposition and her crew. Hence, my recognition of Bix."

"Hence," she repeated. "You must read a lot."

"I've been known to crack a book. Now my cop curiosity extends to Bix in Interview, perhaps sulking."

"Perhaps." She hooked a thumb in her pocket. "I can't tell you, Baxter."

"Well." He bit, chewed. "If and when, I'd like in."

"Why?"

"Is that yet another rhetorical question?"

She had to laugh, but shook her head. "A storm's coming."

"As a trained observer with considerable cop curiosity, I already figured that. If you need another umbrella, just let me know."

"So noted."

"Meanwhile, it may or may not be of interest to you but there are mutters that you're after Oberman because she's on the fast track to captain, or because she has bigger tits. Or because she spurned your sexual advances."

"You made that last one up."

"Actually I didn't, but I wish I had. Those mutters aren't getting far as they're overpowered by louder mutters that Garnet was an asshole and Oberman didn't rein him in. Or that you spurned her sexual advances. Mostly the other mutters haven't gotten a foothold because people are more scared of you than Oberman."

"I like fear. It's versatile."

"In the right hands."

She left him contemplating his choices

for washing down the coconut cream and walked into Interview, where she'd kept Bix waiting.

"Record on. Dallas, Lieutenant Eve, entering Interview with Bix, Detective Carl. Detective, I'm formalizing this as our discussion will involve another police officer whose death has been deemed a homicide and is being investigated by other detectives. Do you understand and agree?"

"Yes."

"I'm going to Mirandize you to keep this interview formal, and to adhere to the letter of procedure." She read him the Revised Miranda. "Do you understand your rights and obligations in this matter?"

His jaw twitched, just a little. "I'm a cop. I know what being Mirandized means."

"Excellent. Detective, your direct superior is Lieutenant Renee Oberman, Illegals, correct?"

"Yes."

"Under Lieutenant Oberman you have often partnered with Detective Bill Garnet, of the same squad."

"Yes."

"Most recently, you and Detective Garnet were assigned as lead investigators on the Giraldi case. According to my information, Detective Garnet believed that case was about to break."

"We were pursuing several lines of investigation."

Eve opened a file, skimmed it as if looking for specific data. "Were any of those lines of investigation pursued due to information received from your lieutenant's CI, Rickie Keener, now deceased?"

"Not to my knowledge."

She cocked up her eyebrows. "You had not solicited information from that source?"

"No."

"Had Garnet?"

"Not to my knowledge."

"It runs a very high probability, Detective, that as both Keener and Garnet were killed at the same location, their murders are connected, either by perpetrator or purpose, or both."

"I don't believe Keener was murdered. I think he overdosed, as his kind often do."

"That determination isn't yours to make, Detective. It falls to the ME, to me, to the evidence, which all weigh in on homicide."

She closed a file, opened another, exposing Keener's crime scene photos, then slid out one of Garnet's and set them side-by-side.

"It would be a very strange coincidence if Detective Garnet was murdered in the same location and his death had no connection to Keener's. Adding to that, you and Garnet entered Keener's residence, after his death, and performed an illegal search."

"We believed we had cause, and did not—at that time—know Keener was dead."

"The cause being a possible connection to your investigation."

"That's right."

"But you had not solicited Keener prior."

"I didn't. I said I had no knowledge whether Garnet did. He said he had a hunch, that we needed to give Keener a shake."

"What was the hunch? What was the purpose of the shake?"

"I don't know."

She leaned back. "You and Garnet were working what you consider a major case, one you believed would shortly break. He has a hunch, and you both go to the flop of your lieutenant's CI. But you don't ask why, or what you're looking for when you conduct the illegal search, you don't ask how Keener might be connected to your investigation."

Bix shrugged, the first move he'd made since she'd come in to the room. "Garnet wanted to give him a shake. I backed him up."

"You don't have much cop curiosity, do you, Bix?"

"I do the job."

"You follow orders. Did you consider Garnet a partner or a senior detective?"

"He was both. Now he's neither."

"Did you get along with him?"

"I didn't have any problem with him."

"Friendly, were you?"

"I didn't have a problem with him," Bix repeated.

"You had no problem with the fact that your partner and squad mate used illegal substances? The same substances you are assigned to get off the streets."

"I don't know anything about that."

"Don't know anything about that," Eve repeated. "You're either lying or stupid. I'm going for lying as nobody stupid enough not to recognize when their partner's riding up would make it to detective, and sure as hell wouldn't make it in Illegals."

"Think what you want."

"Oh, I do. I think Garnet had been screwing up lately. I think he pushed at Keener." She nudged the photos across the table. Bix barely gave them a glance. "Had to be a reason for Keener to move out of his flop and go into a hole. Had to be a reason for somebody to dig him out long enough to kill him. It's a screwup, losing a weasel that way, especially the boss's weasel. Then he screws up and illegally enters Keener's flop, conducts—with you—an illegal search. When he's called on it, he goes off on a superior—embarrassing his own and earning a rip. But he's not done screwing up yet. He then gets high and goes after me to the point of drawing his weapon.

"Must know he's cooked then," Eve added. "So he finds a drinking buddy—another squad mate, but not his partner. Then he goes back to my crime scene, breaks my seal, enters, and ends up with his throat slit."

Bix said nothing.

"I think when somebody screws up that large in that short amount of time, the man who works with him knows something about it. I think when a cop's partner develops an illegals habit, the partner—who one assumes is trained to recognize this—knows something about it.

"What did your partner know about Keener's murder, Bix?"

"You could ask him." The tiniest hint of a smirk moved his lips. "But he's dead."

"Conveniently. You were military, right, Bix?" she said, opening another file.

"I served."

"Weapons trained, combat trained. You know how to use a knife. Quick, silent kills—it's an important skill." She looked up. "Your parents were military also, and your older brother still is. It's your heritage, so you understand the importance of following orders. When your LT gives you an order, do you follow it, Detective?"

"Yes."

"Without exception? Without question?"

"Yes."

"You respect your lieutenant?"

"Yes."

"And you're loyal to her?"

"Yes."

"Garnet's behavior, his actions, his lack of discipline, lack of respect reflect poorly on Lieutenant Oberman."

"Garnet was responsible for himself."

"You know how the chain of command works, Bix. You've lived your life in it. Garnet was a screwup, and that makes Lieutenant Oberman a screwup."

That lit the first fire in his eyes. "She's twice what you'll ever be."

"I admire loyalty, even misplaced. Garnet's actions and behavior made your lieutenant look inept, made her look like a fool, showed her to be lacking the power of command to control her man or discipline him. Her own father is disappointed in her lack of leadership."

"Commander Oberman's time has passed. Lieutenant Oberman runs a tight and efficient unit."

"Garnet makes her third man down since she took command. That's not real tight in my book."

"Homicide comes in after it's done. Illegals works the street."

"Oberman rides a desk," Eve corrected, then shrugged. "Did Garnet ever brag about how he used to bang the boss?"

His eyes stayed cold, nearly blank, but his hands fisted on the table between them. "You deserve more than the couple slaps Garnet gave you."

"Want to try your hand at it? He embarrassed her, he demeaned her, he ignored her directives and put her in the position of defending herself, her command. He jeopardized your squad, Bix. What do you do when your unit's in jeopardy?" She bit off the words, spat them out. "What do you do when your lieutenant is under fire? What do you do?"

"What needs to be done."

"Where were you at oh one hundred, when Garnet went down?"

"Home."

"Where were you the night Keener was murdered?"

"Home."

"What is your response when and if your lieutenant orders you to eliminate a threat?"

"Yes, ma'am." His voice snapped like a salute. "When and how?"

"And if that order includes murder, do you question it? Do you hesitate?"

"I do not."

"What did Keener have, what did he know, what had he done to make him a liability? Why did he have to be eliminated?"

Bix opened his mouth, closed it again. He squared his shoulders. "I have nothing more to say to you. If you want to question me further, it'll be in the presence of my department rep."

"That's your right. Let it be noted that not once during this interview did Detective Bix address me as sir or by my rank. This disrespect will be included in his file. Just a little icing on the cake I'm baking," she told Bix, then rose. "Interview end."

20 Her Lieutenant and Bix had been gone about ten minutes when Lilah saw her window. Four of the squad were in the field, Brinker off on one of his many lengthy trips to Vending or the bathroom. Sloan and Asserton sat at their desks plugging away at paperwork. Freeman and Marcell had just gone into the break room.

Lilah picked up a report from her desk, walked briskly to Renee's door, shoved the master she'd palmed in and out of the slot. And walked inside. The minute she had the door closed, she stuck the report in her back pocket.

Five minutes, she told herself. Tops. Freeman and Marcell were bound to bullshit in the break room that long.

She hit the desk first, crouching down to the locked bottom drawer. And using the skill she'd learned from her doomed brother, picked the lock.

It shouldn't have surprised her to find so many personal items the rest of the squad was denied. High-end—way high-end—face enhancements, a top-of-the-line VR unit with a collection of relaxation and sex programs.

She'd already judged Renee as useless and vain.

She ran her fingers under drawers, along their sides, checked for false bottoms. She found a little cash, but nothing over the line.

She closed the drawer, secured it again. Careful not to disturb Renee's pristine organization, she riffled through others. Flipped through file discs, opened and scanned a memo book, an appointment book before moving on to the furniture, the counters, the windows.

She *knew* Renee had a hide in there. Knew it hid more than expensive lip dye and eye shadow, more than fancy imported perfume that sold for a paycheck an ounce.

Her gut told her she'd hit the time to bail—sweat had begun to trickle down the center of her back.

One minute more, she told herself, easing the seascape off the wall to check behind it, to examine its back, its frame.

The minute she replaced it, carefully adjusting it so it hung perfectly true, it struck her.

"You idiot," she muttered. "You wasted those psych courses."

She looked at the portrait of Commander Marcus Oberman, in full dress blues.

Too heavy to take off the wall on her own, she judged. Not unless she dragged the table under it out of the way to gain more leverage and a better angle.

She managed to get a hand behind the frame, ease it out an inch—and cursed herself for not thinking to bring in a penlight.

She braced the portrait with one hand, ran the other behind it while trying to angle her head to see. Eased it up another inch, praying she wouldn't cock it off its support.

Her searching hand bumped something, and the surprise had her pulling the bottom of the portrait up in a short little jerk. Her breath sucked in as it continued smoothly up, hinging at the top. And revealing the safe behind it.

She grabbed her 'link, used its camera to take several shots. Even if she'd had the time, was willing to risk the time, her thievery skills were limited to picking simple locks, not to breaking what looked to be a complex wall safe.

Taking it slow, she brought the portrait to rights. Stepped back, checked the alignment, the position. Wiped her damp palms on her thighs. At the door she tipped one of the blind slats a fraction.

Asserton and Sloan still at their desks. Brinker still wherever Brinker went a dozen times a day. Freeman and Marcell still in the break room. All clear.

Move, she ordered herself. Go now.

She pulled the file out of her pocket, stepped out, closed the door. A quick slide of the master re-engaged the lock. Hearing the quiet click, she walked briskly toward her desk. She was halfway there when the break room door opened. She sat down, aimed her eyes at her screen as if checking her data. And considered her options.

Business as usual, she reminded herself. Head down, ass in the chair. And when her shift was over, she'd use a public 'link on the way home to contact Dallas.

When Eve walked back into her office, Mira turned from the window.

"Oh, good. I didn't know if you'd been able to make it down to observe. Do you think—"

"What are you doing?" Mira interrupted.

Eve saw what she'd missed through the interview high. The doctor was pissed.

"About?"

"Why are you deliberately baiting a man you believe has already killed at least two people in a matter of days? A man with no sense of urgency, nerves, or regrets regarding those murders? A man who has every reason to see you as an obstacle and a threat, to himself, but more important, to the woman he follows with absolute loyalty, all while knowing that woman has every motive, and would have no compunction, to order him to eliminate you."

"Because it's my job."

"Don't use that on me. I know you. There are certainly other ways to build and close this case, ways I have no doubt you're pursuing. You enjoyed baiting him. You *want* him—through Renee Oberman—to try to kill you."

"Okay." Eve moved to the AutoChef, programmed some of the herbal tea Mira drank. "I think you could use this."

"Don't you dare try to brush me off."

"I'm not." Eve set the tea on her desk, programmed coffee for herself. "I'm not," she repeated. "You're not wrong. You're rarely wrong. I did enjoy it. Hell, I relished it. And I do want him to come at me. But I'm not wrong either. All of that *is* my job. Okay, maybe not the relish, but I'm entitled to some perks."

"This isn't a joke, Eve."

"You're damn fucking skippy it's not. They're cops, Doctor Mira, and cops don't roll so easy. Bix sure as hell isn't going to roll on Renee because I ask nice or the PA offers him a sweet deal. She's his direct superior—his commanding officer.

She's given him a mission, made him important to her—made him her right hand, and that's a powerful seduction. She's created an atmosphere where they're above the rest. Elite. Like . . . like Special Forces—which he applied for and couldn't get. They do what needs to be done—and his CO decides what that is. Following orders is part of his code, and his code is his god."

"You can't tell me the only way to stop them, all of them, is to make yourself an irresistible target."

"Not the only way, no, but it's a sure way, not only to stop them, but to carve them out of this department, to absolutely crush them. To make certain Renee, Bix, Freeman—every one of them—pays the heaviest price allowed by law. Every one of them, because believe me I will weed out and carve out every one of them."

Eve held up a hand before Mira could speak. "I'm under orders, too. Chief Tibble ordered me to take Renee Oberman and every cop in her network down hard. Bix isn't the only one who takes orders seriously. I will take them down, and I will do everything in my power to minimize the damage to this department when I do."

Eve picked up the tea again. Mira wasn't just pissed, she'd noted, she was tired and . . . sad.

"Here. Maybe you could sit down."

Mira took the tea, sat. "I'm so angry with you."

"So noted. She has strings to pull. She has to have a judge, probably a couple of politicians. She's got lines in the courts, in the department, maybe the lab, maybe the morgue. I'm stacking it up against her, and the rest of them, but I have to weigh that stack against her lines. She could wiggle out of this—evidence gets lost, lab results doctored, the wrong motion filed, wits vanish or recant."

"This entire investigation began because of a statement by what we'd agree is a sterling witness."

Struggling not to be annoyed—did she tell Mira how to do *her* job?—Eve ticked points off on her fingers.

"Peabody never saw her. Bix's name was never mentioned. Garnet's dead. And

if this isn't nailed shut by the time it becomes known what she did see and hear?"
Eve shook her head. "I'm her lieutenant.
I'm her partner. Do you think I'd leave her
ass hanging out with a target on it?"

"No." Mira finally sipped her tea. "No, I
know you wouldn't."

"Bix would stick his blaster in his ear
and fire before he'd turn on Renee. Am I
wrong?"

"No. I believe he would sacrifice himself, and consider it honor, to shield her.
Which means, if he does try to kill you—
and you survive—you only have him."

"I've got some geeks up my sleeve, but
even without that, collaring him puts a big
crack in her wall. She's disgraced, her career takes a hit it can't recover from. And
we open the floodgates to the money. Garnet's, Bix's, hers, the others. Explain that,
bitch. She'd be scrambling. More, I think I
worked Bix into casting a hard shadow on
her."

Calmer, Mira sipped again. "You showed
him, by his own words and demeanor, to
be a soldier—one who follows orders without question, one with intense loyalty to
Renee. Not a man who goes outside his

CO, who breaks ranks and acts on his own volition."

"So I also have a top shrink up my sleeve, because you'd testify to that, in really big, fancy words. Janburry and Delfino, the cops on Garnet's case, they'll draw in on Bix. If Bix makes a run at me, he's going to end up with his face on the sidewalk and a cop's boot on his neck. I hope it's mine, but I'll settle for any cop's boot."

"I know she observed as well. You wanted her to so you could let her know you're looking in her direction. You did that because it will unnerve her, anger her, and—you hope—push her into giving Bix his green light. But you also did it, Eve, because it's personal."

"It's absolutely fucking down to the bone personal." And a relief to say it. A goddamn thrill to say it. "She's spit on everything I value, on everything I am. On everything I made myself out of a nightmare she can't even conceive of. It matters."

"Yes," Mira murmured. "Yes, it does."

"When I take her down I'm doing it for me, for the badge, for the man who trained me, taught me, who helped make me someone who deserves to wear it. But that's only part of it. I'm doing it for you, goddamn it."

"Eve—"

"Be quiet," she ordered, and stunned them both. She had to get it out, she realized. Had to, here and now, let this vicious stew of emotion roiling in her guts spill over.

"I'm doing it for Whitney, for Peabody, for every man and woman in my bullpen. I'm doing it for every cop she killed and a dead junkie. I'm doing it for every cop who deserves to wear the badge. And though I'll do everything in my power to bring them all down, I'm doing it for every cop she turned into a disgrace."

She stopped herself, took a breath. "If you know me, I guess you should know that."

"I do. I know that very well. I let it be personal, too. You're personal to me."

Eve felt the little pinch under her heart. "Are we good?"

"I can't help but wish you hadn't made your case so well; then I could still be angry." Mira rose. "I'm not going to bother to tell you to be careful. I don't need to tell you to be smart. Do you have questions for me?"

"You've already answered one of them. Just one other. I figure I know the answer, but it never hurts. Does she know I'm daring her to sic her dog on me?"

"While she knows now you're looking at her, and looking hard, she'd never put her life at risk. I don't believe she can conceive of you doing so, not for something as unimportant to her as justice, as honor. If she sics her dog on you, she'll believe it's her idea. And it should be soon."

"Okay." The sooner, the better.

"Are you having nightmares, Eve? Flashbacks?"

"No. Not really. Not in awhile. It feels, mostly, done. It's never all the way done." Still down there, she thought, down in the deep, but . . . "It feels mostly done."

"All right." Mira took Eve's hand in hers for a squeeze. "Thanks for the tea."

Alone, Eve started to check in with Peabody, then Janburry tapped on her doorjamb.

"You clear, Lieutenant?"

"Yeah. Sorry, have you been waiting?"

"No problem. Might've had a little one if you'd managed to get a confession on our dead guy."

"That's going to take a little more work. I just set up the play, passed you the ball. Could you close the door, Detective Delfino?"

After she had, Delfino leaned back against it. "Renee Oberman," she said. "Commander Oberman's baby girl."

"Is that how you read it?"

"He's the reader." She jerked a thumb at her partner. "Me? I smell it, like shit and blood in the water."

"She's got a descriptive idiom," Janburry commented. "I'm wondering if we can borrow your homework, Lieutenant, seeing as we missed a couple days of school on this."

"I haven't been given full authorization, but I can tell you we're both looking in the same direction. I could give you this." She took a disc out of her pocket. "It would save you some time. But before I do, let's make a deal."

"We're listening," Janburry told her.

"You can have Bix when it's time to haul him out of the shit and blood in the water, but Renee's mine. Not because she's the bigger catch. You could just say it's personal. The rest, well, share and share alike."

"How much rest is there?"

"Still working on that. Do we have a deal?"

The partners exchanged a look. "Is there a secret handshake?" Janburry asked.

"We'll settle for regular." After they'd shaken on it, Eve offered the disc. "You'll find multiple false IDs, multiple secret accounts, and considerable real property tracked back to Renee, Bix, Garnet, and others we've nailed down."

"How involved is IAB?" Delfino wanted to know.

"Thoroughly. Lieutenant Webster is point man there, but his captain has been briefed, as have Commander Whitney and Chief Tibble. This is NTK. Nobody else needs to know until we take them down."

"Blood and shit in the water," Delfino repeated. "That's what dirty cops smell like. Cops who kill cops? They have a special stench over that."

"He's going to come after you." Janburry studied Eve. "You know that."

"I'm counting on that."

"You want cover?"

"I've got it, thanks. But I will contact you if and when. Whoever takes him down, he's your collar. That's the deal."

When her office emptied out again, Eve flipped the lock. She deserved a little reward, a little boost before she got back down to business.

She took a tool from her desk and hunkered down beside her recycler. But when she removed the panel, no sealed evidence bag of chocolate waited for her.

"Damn it! This blows. This seriously blows."

Sulking, mourning the loss, she stared at what she'd considered a brilliant hiding place. Her mistake, she admitted, had been leaving her stash in place while she'd gone on vacation.

She'd given the despicable Candy Thief too much time and opportunity to search and consume.

Now she not only wouldn't get her reward, her boost, but she had to find another hide.

She replaced the panel, tossed her tool back in her desk drawer. She gave herself another thirty seconds to sulk before contacting Peabody.

"Status?"

"I'm a little more than halfway through. Devin had one hell of a collection. Maybe this is a dead end. If she kept documentation or notes, one of Renee's crew probably found it and destroyed it."

"Keep at it. Follow it through. If they didn't find and destroy it, it's because she hid it well." Eve gave her recycler a dirty look. "I've got some things I need to finish up and tie up here, then I'll be in. How about the e-team? Are they— Hold on," she ordered when she heard the faint click at her door.

Rising, she drew her weapon.

Roarke opened the door, cocked his head. "Well now, that isn't the greeting I'd hoped for."

She let out a breath, holstered her weapon. "Keep at it, Peabody," she said. "Tag me if you find anything. Otherwise I'll see you when I get there." She broke transmission.

"That door was locked."

"And your point is?" He stepped over, kissed her thoroughly. "I didn't knock as I thought you might be taking one of your sprawled-on-the-floor-unconscious naps."

"Maybe I need a better lock. Maybe I need to start locking it more often." She dropped into her chair. "Not that it would stop the Candy Thief. My stash is gone."

"You were going to stun your Candy Thief?"

"I might, come the day. But no, I thought Renee might have snapped and sent Bix down to try to throw me out of my own office window. I gave her plenty of incentive when I had Bix in Interview, and I wanted a reward. I want candy."

"I haven't any on me. Get something from Vending."

"I want *my* candy."

He smothered a laugh. "There, there."

"Bite me." But she shook it off. "Why are you here? Why is everyone in my office today?"

"I'm here as I also deserve a reward. As do Feeney and McNab."

"You pulled it off."

"We did. For the most part they did, but I managed a few flourishes."

"We need to set it up, need to get IAB tapped in."

"Feeney's dealing with it. It's his baby, after all. Or more McNab's. Ian flashed some brilliance today. And what have you been up to, Lieutenant?"

"Too many meetings. I'd go psycho if I

had to face days stuffed with meetings. There are all these people in them."

"Typically, yes."

She filled him in quickly, but paused when she'd moved onto the interview with Bix—and when Roarke walked to her window, looked out.

As Mira had done.

"I went around about my strategy, purposes, reasonings with Mira, who wasn't thrilled with me after. Until I laid it out. Do I have to lay it out for you?"

"No. I understand your strategy, purposes, reasonings. I imagine Mira did as well. But it takes a bit to push through and accept them."

"Roarke, I'm so covered I'm practically wearing a blast-proof body glove."

"I know it." He turned back to her. "But it takes a bit. You know, you're a lean one, darling, but it would take some doing for anyone to throw you out of a window this size."

She smiled, and because she understood he needed it, leaned into him when he stepped over to brush a hand through her hair.

"But since you're my lean one, I'll stick close for the time being. I've some things to see to. I'm going to find a place to see to them."

"I've got to write a couple reports, update my board and book. You can use the visitor's area."

He looked at the pathetic chair. "Do you actually call this an area?"

"No."

"I'll find a space."

Lilah continued to keep her head down and her ass in the chair when Renee and Bix came back in—and when Renee, her face thunderous, closed herself in her office with him.

Nearly end of shift, she thought. Not much longer now. She considered requesting some personal time and ducking out early. But her lieutenant frowned on such requests, and in her current mood might make an issue of it.

Better just to ride the road.

She said nothing when Manford and Tulis came back from the field, and Tulis dropped files on her desk.

It was, she knew, expected she write up

the fives, clean up the report, file it. The lieutenant considered her field men too valuable to sweat over paperwork.

She started in on it, telling herself it would keep her busy, distract her from watching the time. She'd eaten up that time when Renee came out and walked straight to Lilah's desk.

Though her heart took a tumble, Lilah looked up placidly. "Yes, ma'am?"

"You're with Bix," Renee said briskly.

"With Bix, Lieutenant?"

"As I said. We're short a man, if you've forgotten one of your squad went down. Do you have a problem with field work, Detective? I was under the impression you were eager to break away from your desk."

"Yes, ma'am!" She infused her voice with enthusiasm. "Thank you, Lieutenant."

"Bix will give you the details en route. You're cleared for OT, should it be necessary."

Bix stood, looking at Lilah with his flat-eyed stare. "Let's get it done."

This is bullshit, bullshit, Lilah thought as she forced herself up to fall into step with him. She'd left some sort of tell, or one of

the others had seen her go in, come out,
had given the alert. Or . . .

Didn't matter how, she thought. She was
made.

"Where are we going?"

"One-man cook shop on Avenue D.
We're going to pick up the chef, put some
pressure on him, see where it goes."

Bullshit, bullshit, Lilah thought again.

"Something you and Garnet were working on? Look, I'm sorry about Garnet. I
know the two of you worked pretty close."

"He knew the score." Bix stepped into
the elevator, and since it was crowded with
cops, Lilah got on with him.

She'd be damned if she'd be led like a
lamb to the slaughter, and every instinct
told her she'd been slated to be put down.

Quickly she replayed every minute she'd
spent in Renee's office, every move made.
She'd left everything exactly as it had been.
Besides, if there had been something out
of order, Renee couldn't know who . . .

Unless she *did* monitor the squad room,
and not just when she was in her office.
And if she monitored the squad room, she
could have her office on monitor. She
could've seen everything.

Stupid. Stupid. Stupid.

"Have you dealt with the chef before?" As she asked Lilah tugged at the neck of her top as if plagued by the heat. It wasn't much of a stretch.

"Yeah. I'll handle him. You're along for ballast." He cut his gaze down to her when she began to hyperventilate. "What's wrong with you?"

"Sorry. Claustrophobic. I . . ." She popped off the elevator, shoving cops aside when the doors opened. She'd have run then, but Bix was right beside her. Instead she lowered her head between her knees. "Couldn't breathe."

"How the hell did you get on the force?"

She let his disgust roll off her back. All the better if he thought her weak and useless. "Look, I'm a good cop. I just have some trouble with tight spaces. I'll take the glide down, meet you in the garage."

"We'll take the glides." He curled a hand around her arm, steered her toward a down glide.

Duck into a bathroom, she thought, call for backup. And if he followed her in, he'd have her trapped. She jerked her arm, but his grip only tightened. "Hands off, Bix. I can stand on my own."

"Probably faint at the sight of blood."

"Up yours." Lilah elbowed her way down the glide, trying to put space between them. Bix stuck with her like Velcro.

They'd have to switch to one of the garage elevators soon, she calculated. Or the stairs. Where did he plan to do it? Not in Central. But once he got her out . . .

So she wouldn't let him get her out.

"Hey." She whirled on him. "Keep your hands off my ass."

"I never—"

She slapped him, hard enough the crack of flesh on flesh drew as much attention as her shouted protest. "Goddamn asshole!" There were plenty of smirks as she shoved down the glide.

He made a grab for her, might have yanked her back, but a couple of cops— one a female uniform who looked like she could bench-press a maxibus—blocked his way.

She heard the shouts, the curses behind her, glanced back. His eyes were absolutely calm as he bulled his way through and closed the distance she'd gained.

She went with instinct and ran.

She leaped on the next glide, slithering and coiling through other passengers like a snake. Lose him, lose him, find a hole, call for help. Sprint straight out on the next level, she told herself. She'd always been fast.

When another check behind told her so was he, she shifted to push through. She broke clear, took one quick heartbeat to gauge the best direction. The roar behind her came an instant before someone plowed into her, propelled by Bix's violent forward progress. Lilah threw a hand out to catch herself, but her legs shot from under her.

For one breathless second she watched the dull silver steel of the glide rushing toward her. Her arms came up, an instinctive attempt to shield her face, but her shoulder took the first vicious hit. For an instant the world revolved—ceiling to floor—then it exploded when her head struck the ridged steel.

She went tumbling, tumbling, bonelessly to the unforgiving floor below.

Nearly ready to close it down at Central, Eve snatched at her signaling 'link. She'd hoped Peabody, struggled against annoyance when she saw Webster on the display.

"Dallas."

"Detective Strong just took a header off a down glide between three and four."

Eve shoved to her feet. "How?"

"Not yet determined, but Bix is being held."

"He fucking pushed her—in Central?"

"Not yet determined. Conflicting accounts."

"Is she alive?"

"Unconscious, beat up from the fall. On her way to Angel's. IAB gets a shot at Bix. Renee's already running interference. We'll review the security discs, keep him under wraps for now."

"Is Strong covered?"

"She was in the bus and away before I got word."

"I'll cover her." Eve slammed out of the office, zeroed in on Baxter. "I want you and Trueheart at Angel's ten minutes ago. You cover a Detective Lilah Strong who's being transported there with injuries from a fall. You cover her like skin on bone. No medicals alone with her, no other cops near her. This is a direct order, and I don't care if God Himself countermands it, you will follow it."

"Yes, sir."

"Go now. I'll be right behind you."

As she moved—back into her office to grab the jacket she'd shed while she worked—she tagged Roarke. "Garage. Hurry." She clicked off, then called in a friend.

"Dallas." Dr. Louise Dimatto beamed at her. "How—"

Struggling into the jacket, Eve switched her 'link from hand to hand. "I need you at Angel's Hospital asap. Incoming patient, transported from Central, Detective Lilah Strong. Injuries from a fall."

"How—"

"I don't know her condition. I need you to get there, Louise, and to take her. Her life's on the line. I need you to report as her doctor, and I need you to fix her. I don't want anyone near her you don't know and trust with your life. Not another doctor, nurse, orderly, not a bedpan near her you don't trust. Baxter and Trueheart are on their way there now. No other cops get near her without my clearance. None."

"I'm on my way. I'll call ahead, set it up."

"Thanks."

She sprinted from floor to glide, from glide to elevator, and across the garage where Roarke waited.

"How fast can you get us to Angel's Hospital?"

"Very. Strap in."

21 Sirens blasting, Roarke went airborne the instant they shot out of the garage. He touched down, punched it to plow through a field of traffic, two-wheeled it at the corner. He skimmed by a couple coats of paint between a cab and a sedate town car, then tore into a hard-line vertical to rocket over the heads of pedestrians clipping across the crosswalk in spite of the screaming sirens and flashing lights.

"Strong's down," Eve told him. "I don't know how bad."

He simply nodded and ripped a line

through the city canyons. When he swerved onto the ER ramp, he said, "Go."

She was already slapping the release on her safety harness, shoving open the door. She slammed through the ER doors, caught sight of the medicals whisking a gurney around the corner of Admitting with Baxter and Trueheart flanking them like guard dogs.

"Status! What's her status?"

Blood from the head wounds, the face lacerations soaked Lilah's clothes. Eve saw the splint support on her right arm, another caging her leg, the brace collaring her neck.

The MTs were spewing out a string of medical terms to a man in scrubs who barely looked old enough to order a brew. He in turn reeled out orders as they shoved the gurney through another set of doors.

He shot another order at Eve. "You have to stay back."

"Her doctor's on the way. Louise Dimatto. She's in charge."

"Right now I'm in charge." He counted off to three, and they lifted Lilah's bloody, broken body, strapped to a stabilizer, from gurney to table.

At the movement, Lilah moaned. Her eyelids flickered. The doctor peeled an eyelid up to examine her pupil while another medical cut away her pants to reveal a nasty break beneath the splint cage.

Eve managed to slip through, grab and grip Lilah's hand as the team worked around her. "Report, Detective. Give me a report."

Lilah's eyes, blind with shock and pain, rolled open. "What?"

"Detective Strong!" Eve watched the eyes widen, very slightly. "I need your report."

"Killed me."

"No, they didn't. Why did they try?"

"Oberman. Behind Oberman." The words garbled as Lilah's fingers moved weakly in Eve's. "My mother. Tic."

"I'll get your mother. I'll get Tic."

"Scared."

Fresh pain jerked her body, shuddered in her eyes. Eve made herself stare straight into them. "I've got you covered. I've got you, Detective."

"Oberman." Eve could feel Lilah fight for the words. "Safe. Bix. Blew it."

"No, you didn't. I've got it."

"Mom. Tic."

"I'll get them."

Eve leaned in as Lilah's eyes rolled closed again, as machines beeped, as the young doctor snapped at her to back off, threatened to call Security.

"You don't die on me, Detective. That's a goddamn order."

Behind her Eve heard Louise's voice—calm, brisk, full of authority. She stepped back, watched her friend shove her arms into a protective cloak.

"Trueheart, stay with her. Baxter, with me."

Eve shoved through the doors. "Did she say anything else before I got here?" Eve demanded.

"You were about thirty seconds behind us. She came around for a few seconds when they were off-loading her, but she didn't say anything I could make out."

"One or both of you sticks with her, all the way. Nobody gets to her. Nobody touches her unless Louise clears them."

"Did somebody help her fall down that glide, Dallas?"

"Undetermined, but probable. If there was reason for that, there's reason to go at her again."

"They won't get through us." His gaze ticked to the door, back to Eve. "She's one of Oberman's?"

"Not anymore. She's one of mine."

Louise pushed out while Eve paced the hallway.

"We're taking her up, prepping her for surgery. She needs an orthopedic surgeon, a plastic man, a neuro. They have good ones here," Louise said before Eve could respond. "I know them. She's got internal injuries, and I'll take those. If she makes it through, and her chances are decent with this team, she'll need more work. And she'll have a hell of a road back."

"She'll make it. One of my men has to be with her, every second. I need you to handpick every doctor, nurse, orderly who comes near her, give their data to Baxter."

"OR Five," Louise said. "I've got to go scrub in. You can fill me in on this later."

"Louise . . ." Eve strode to the elevator with her. "How decent?"

"How tough is she?"

"Pretty tough, I think."

"That helps. Trust us to do the rest."

With no choice, Eve stood back, watched them roll Lilah toward an elevator, watched

Baxter and Trueheart fall, once again, into flank position.

"We'll watch out for her, Lieutenant." Trueheart put a hand on the side guard of the gurney, and Eve nodded as the doors closed.

"How is she?" Roarke asked.

She closed her eyes a moment as her mind replayed all the chaos of the exam room.

"Broken arm, including a shattered elbow. Compound fracture of the leg, cracked skull, damaged spleen and kidney, severe facial lacerations. Those are the highlights."

She looked down at the hand that had held Lilah's, and the blood smeared on it. "I have to wash up. I'm going to wash up, then I'm going to take Renee apart."

She needed to bank her anger. Anger could wait.

On the more sedate ride back to Central, Eve contacted Feeney. "Can you run your new toy from a conference room in my division?"

"We can set that up."

"I need you to do it now, and on the extreme QT. Since her boy's back in the basket, she'll have to start wrangling. And I have something else."

"How impossible this time?"

"You tell me. She's got to have eyes, maybe ears, too, on her squad room, on her own office. She's got to be monitoring or spot checking. Possibly she's got some sort of alert set up in her office to let her know if anyone goes in when she's not around. Can you tap into that, give us the feed?"

"Well, for Christ's sake. Without knowing the system, the placement, the keys, or the alert specs?" He gave her a long, sad look. "Hell, why not? What's another freaking miracle today?"

"Can you do it really fast?"

"Not as fast as I'd boot your ass if you get within range."

"I'm bringing my geek in to give you a hand."

"Send him. You stay away."

Eve scowled when he cut her off, then turned to Roarke. "Can you do it really fast?"

"Tap in and redirect an unknown and at this point theoretical system with potential and unidentified keys and fail-safes? I wouldn't mind booting your ass myself. Yes," he said before she could speak. "Because you're going to get her out of her office and clear her squad room long enough for me to get in, run and scan, locate and identify, and get out again."

"How am I supposed to clear her squad room?"

"That, Lieutenant, would come under the heading of your problem. I'll need five minutes."

"If I can get you fifteen, there's something else I want you to do while you're in there."

"And what would that be?"

"It involves stealing."

His face brightened. "I like it already."

"Just let me pull Peabody in, then I'll lay it out for you." Before she could order the code, the 'link signaled in her hand.

"Dallas, I got it!" Peabody all but sang it. "I got it! Over three months of notes, times, locations, overheard snips of conversation. Names—she'd been digging in hard and she listed names she believed to be involved in Renee's network—and she backed it up with a lot of documentation."

"Bring it in."

"You're not coming here?"

"Change of plans there. Copy it, bring it in."

"I'm on my way. Jeez, Dallas, I almost missed it. She had it shielded with a layer of jock-shock music. The disc analysis barely gave me a blip—and then it looks like a standard override—before I—"

"Explain later. We're taking this down tonight. I want you in."

"Tonight? I'm even more on my way."

"That's good work," Roarke commented to Eve. "If the disc was layered and disguised as an override, it was good work on Devin's part, and on Peabody's."

"I'll pat her on the back later." She glanced at the time, calculated. "Here's what I need you to do once I clear it—and clear the squad room."

"I take it you've figured out how to do that."

"One cop on the slab, another in surgery, and a third being grilled by IAB? That's a quarter of her squad right there.

I'd say Renee and her men have earned a good talking-to."

She started setting it up while Roarke finished the drive to Central.

"The commander and Mira," Roarke commented. "What you'd call a command performance. Concern, a bit of stern disapproval, with a touch of group therapy thrown in."

"She can't say no. I'll signal you as soon as I get the word they're in the conference room. If you need more time or just can't pull it off, let me know asap."

"You've just earned another boot in the ass for insulting me."

They rode the elevator out of the garage, then got off to take the glides, as was her habit. Deliberately she crossed over between three and four to the sector where Lilah had fallen.

They'd blocked off the down glide, and would keep it blocked until IAB made its determination. She imagined Webster would draw that out even if the discs showed no culpability by Bix.

"She kept Strong chained to that desk, but today she sends her out in the field? And with Bix. He had orders of execution.

If he'd gotten her out of here, she'd be dead instead of in surgery. Strong suspected the squad room was monitored, but she went in anyway."

"She took a risk. All of you take them every day."

"I *knew* it was monitored after my last trip there. I *knew* Brinker was dirty. But I didn't get word to her. Not in time. I saw an opportunity to have an inside man, so I took it, pulled her into this."

"And, it seems, she saw an opportunity and took it. Risk and opportunity, Eve. It's all part of it."

"Louise will fix her. Goddamn it, she'll fix her, because that bitch isn't taking down another cop." She strode over, got on the up glide.

Her com signaled, three short. She checked it, scanned the code. "Whitney's called the meeting."

"I believe I'll mosey over, take a closer position while they file out."

"Your face is pretty familiar around here. Don't let any of them see you."

"Insult after insult." With a shake of his head, he moseyed.

Eve veered off to meet Webster, as she'd arranged.

"I've got five," he told her when she slipped into his office. "We've got Bix on simmer. His lieutenant just broke off a heated exchange with my captain. Orders to report from the commander." Webster tapped his temple in salute. "Slick timing, Dallas."

"What's on the discs?"

"He didn't push her, but was unquestionably in pursuit. They were both shoving, running, knocking people aside. Somebody went down between them, and they fell like dominoes. We're lucky she's the only one who took the hard fall. She was off-balance, running flat out, and couldn't catch herself."

"How's he answer it? Why was he pursuing a fellow officer?"

"He says she started shouting and clocked him, then began to run on the glides, endangering others. He pursued out of instinct, and because he feared she would harm herself or others. It's close enough to what happened, we'd have a hard time pinning it on him without her statement. He doesn't deviate from the story, not by a single word."

"I want to see the run."

"Figured." He took a disc from his pocket. "If you're looking to fry him, yeah, you could interpret it as he shoved through the right spot at the right time, calculated the angles, and caused her fall. But it wouldn't hold up on its own. Renee's playing the outraged boss, but we get that a lot around here. How can we question her man when it was obviously a terrible accident, and seems to have been precipitated by the injured officer who had been displaying some unstable behavior? As is noted in her evals."

"Then she has to explain why she was sending an officer she deemed unstable into the field."

"She's shorthanded. She lost a man last night. She's got an answer for everything. They're shaky if you pick them apart, and you know what we know, but they're answers."

"She's about to run out of answers." Eve shoved the disc in her pocket. "Don't let him out of here, Webster. Not for another thirty. I'm going to contact Janburry and Delfino, put them on alert. They may want to take him for a round soon."

"Oh, we can keep him busy for a while yet. What's Strong's status?"

"She'll hold her own." Eve checked the time. "I've got to move. I've got my own dominoes to flick."

She went straight to the conference room where Feeney and McNab were set up. Feeney sent her a reproachful look. "Do you know how much easier this would be if we could run it from EDD? And nothing about this is easy."

"EDD's everywhere, but if I'm hanging around EDD somebody we don't want wondering might wonder. We're boxing her, Feeney. I want this side of the box solid. Roarke's had about five minutes since we emptied out the squad room. If he has any luck, the rest of the job should be easier."

She plugged the disc into the room comp, watched the sequence. She toughened her mind when she watched Lilah's fall, then landing.

"She knew she was in trouble," Eve murmured. "She's tracking, looking for a way out. He's keeping her close, even grabs onto her. She played it pretty damn well, up to the end. She nearly made it."

"He pushed her. He didn't lay a hand on her," McNab said when Eve glanced around. "But he pushed her. Look at him. Doesn't even break a sweat. Mowing through people, dodging, weaving—and he never takes his eyes off her. Like the hound to the rabbit."

"You'd be right. He had his orders. If he could've gotten to her after the fall, he'd have finished her—if he could've found the way, he'd have killed her right in Central."

She turned, wanting coffee, turned back when she heard the door open.

"Couldn't you get in?" she began.

"Really, it's a bloody litany of insults." Roarke tossed a small duffle on the conference table. "I borrowed the bag from one of your supply rooms. I hope I won't be arrested."

"You're in, done, and out and back here in ten?"

"Well, I did have to stop to get the bag. And to scan her security system." He tossed a disc to McNab. "That should quicken things up."

"Yeah, baby!"

"Care to see what's in the bag, Lieutenant?" Roarke asked. "What was safe behind Oberman?"

Eve pulled the bag open. "Her running kit—the ID, credit, cash—about two hundred K?"

"Oh, two-fifty, then there's another hundred large in euros."

"Clean 'link, clean weapon, PPC—and discs."

"Her books," Roarke supplied. "Her payroll, operating expenses, income—all very tidy. I had a bit of time so I took a quick glance."

"Say hallelujah," Eve breathed.

"If you like. I didn't look through them all—just enough to verify. They're encoded, of course, but fairly simply. I'd say she was confident no one was going to have a peek. Her security is more complex. If she'd set the alarm before leaving her office, it would have tripped the minute Strong went in. A silent alarm that would engage the cameras. Renee would have seen it when she went in herself and shut the alarm off."

"But she doesn't clear out the safe. Not yet anyway. No real time to do it," Eve concluded. "She has to eliminate Strong. If she can't get to Strong, she's going to have to answer a lot of embarrassing questions. She can clear out the safe, put something not incriminating inside."

"Strong took a severe blow to the head—is and was obviously confused." Roarke nodded. "Many ways to circle it, but eliminating Strong is sure and it's tidy."

"She likes tidy, and she doesn't know I have two men on Strong. She couldn't know yet. Crap, I forgot about Whitney and Mira." She took out her com, signaled Whitney the all-clear.

"Give my boy a hand, will you?" Feeney asked Roarke, then jerked his head so Eve followed him to the other side of the room.

"You've got her in that box, Dallas. With everything we've put together, with what the boy says Peabody's bringing in. Top that with the little heist Roarke just pulled off, she's done."

"Maybe. Maybe if we look through her discs and find she's written out chapter and verse on her operation, on her orders to kill cops, Keener, whoever else she might've done."

"She's going to have to explain the ID, the money."

"Graft, corruption, falsifying docs aren't murder."

"You and I know that while Bix might stand like a rock, others'll roll. It only takes one to start an avalanche. You make a deal with one of her men, the avalanche is going to crush her to dust."

"Is that how you'd handle it?"

"I'm saying you could walk right out of here and put her in cuffs."

She turned, took a couple paces away to try to settle her temper. Turned and stepped back when she decided she didn't want it settled.

"Make a deal with a dirty cop or two to snap off the head? Fuck that. Fuck that, Feeney. No deals. No deals if I have to sit on the PA until he cries for his mommy. I don't want to deal to take her down. I'm going to take her down my way. I'm going to play her like a goddamn piano."

He started to grin at the first *fuck that*, and then let out a snort. "You can't play the piano."

"But I can break one to splinters with a sledgehammer."

"It's a good choice. I was just checking."

She puffed out a breath, felt the temper die. "You'd go sledgehammer?"

"Maybe a chain saw. I've got to think of my back."

She glanced toward Roarke and McNab. "You get me the feed. I'll get the hammer and saw."

She paced while they worked. She wondered why things always took longer than you wanted them to take, unless you wanted them to take a lot longer—then they didn't take nearly long enough.

Time sucked.

Peabody walked in.

"Put the data up," Eve ordered. "I need to see it."

"Yes, sir."

"Good work, Peabody. You did good work today."

"I needed to." Peabody glanced over as she installed the disc. "I want to be able to go back to her mom and tell her Detective Gail Devin helped bring this down. Dallas, can you get her a commendation? From the top? Could you put her in for one from the commander?"

"I can. I will. But I believe the commander will issue one without my request."

Eve stood, studying the data. "God, she was thorough. Look at this. Times, dates, length of time, participants of closed-door meets in Renee's office. Coordinating them with busts or ops gone sour—or where the take from the bust came in well below expectations and information. In-voice changes—she logged them down whenever she caught one. Logged once-a-week meets between Renee and Den-nis Dyson in Accounting. Here's another who shows up regularly, every couple weeks, and routinely after a sizable bust. From Records.

"Notations on inconsistencies in files, in reports. Here's a cop who dug into her re-search."

"She was building a pretty good case," Peabody added. "She's got records of street contacts she'd started to develop on her own. She went through court docs checking wits, did follow-ups. She went to see dealers in their cages. She was start-ing to push hard, then . . ."

"Pushed the wrong way, and Renee caught the scent." Eve ordered the data to share the screen with Renee's. Cued them up.

"We got names matching here. A lot of her names match what's looking like Renee's payroll."

"You got the payroll?"

"I'll fill you in. Feeney! I'm getting tired of holding this hammer."

"Then set it down a damn minute."

"Look at all this money." Peabody gaped at the open duffle. "And . . . a passport, ID. You found her hole? You found her hole without me?"

"You were busy doing a good job."

"Now you can say hallelujah." Roarke turned to her. "You're tapped in, Lieutenant."

"She's not back in her office yet." Eve watched the screen image of Renee's office with narrowed eyes. "Went back to IAB to try to squeeze her boy out. Okay." Eve rolled her shoulders. "Time to play."

22

In her office, Renee gathered her forces.

"We're going to clean up this mess tonight."

She stood behind her desk, met the eyes of each man under her command—something she'd learned from her father. She spoke in clipped, confident tones.

"There will be no loose ends. There will be no mistakes. Freeman, get to the hospital. If Strong makes it out of surgery, she'll need to be dealt with. You're on hold until I contact you. Do what you do—blend."

"You got it, LT."

"Go now. And Freeman? If and when? Don't leave any marks."

"You know me. I'm a ghost."

"Marcell," she continued when the door closed behind Freeman, "you and Palmer are going to deal with Dallas. She's over."

"How do you want it done?" Marcell asked.

"I've been giving it some thought. We take it back to Keener." A full circle, she calculated. Closed and locked. "She's so in love with the little bastard, it seems appropriate. You'll take her in the garage when she's leaving. Armand, you'll need to give us a security glitch."

"Can do."

"It'll have to be fast and clean. Wait until she's at her vehicle. I don't want you to give her room to maneuver. Stun her. Then take her and her vehicle to Keener's hide. Once you've got her in and secured, do it however you want, but make damn sure she's dead. Take anything on her a chemi-head would pawn for scratch. We'll be planting some of it later to give Homicide our fall guy. When you're done, contact Manford. He'll pick you up."

"What if she's not alone in the garage?" Palmer asked.

"If she's with her partner or one of her men, you take them both. Tulis will keep an eye on her, contact Armand when she heads down."

She looked at Tulis, got his nod.

"Armand will handle the cams and elevators. He'll give you the window, you'd better damn sight go through it. Until then stay clear of her. No contact, no connection."

"Consider it done."

"When it is, go to Samuels at Five-O. He'll cover you. He's closed the place so you could hold vigil for Strong, wake Garnet." She checked her wrist unit. "My sources say Dallas rarely if ever leaves end of shift, which makes it easier to grab her alone. You've got some time, and I'll toss her something to hang her up here to make sure of that."

"What about Bix?" Marcell asked her.

"Armand's going to hack her comp, plug in some data that takes the heat off Bix, makes it clear the bitch was on some sort of vendetta against me and mine."

Destroying her sterling rep as well as her

life would almost, Renee thought, make up for the trouble she'd caused.

"Meanwhile, IAB's got Bix so he'll be in the clear when Strong and Dallas go down. With her and Strong out of the way, everything goes back to normal. We have a moment of silence for our fallen comrades. In a week, we clear the Giraldi case and have a nice payday.

"Now." She paused, smiled. "I'll get Dallas busy being supercop, then pay another visit to IAB to express outrage over this business with Bix before heading out to check on Strong and express my deep concern there. Everybody does their job, this ends tonight, and we move on."

They worked on refining details, coordinating timing. After, alone at her desk, Renee sat, stared at her father's portrait, blinked until her eyes watered. Then used her 'link.

"Dad." She pressed her lips together as if struggling to control herself. "I know you're disappointed in me."

"Renee—"

"No, I know I've let you down. Let myself down. I should never have let things with Garnet get out of hand. I should've been stronger. And I'm going to be. I need to talk to you, Dad, to ask your advice. I have to go by the hospital and check on one of my people. She had an accident today. After that, can I come by and see you?"

"Of course."

"Thanks, Dad. I know I let my personal feelings get in the way of my job, of my responsibilities. My feelings about Garnet, and about Dallas, too. I see that now. She's so much more the kind of daughter you wanted. I resented her for that."

"She's not my daughter, Renee. You are."

"I know. I know, Dad. I'll see you soon."

She clicked off, stared with icy eyes at the portrait. "I'm your daughter? Too bad for us both you wanted a son, isn't it? Too damn bad I could never measure up to your lofty standards. Would you be proud of me, you fucker, if you knew just how much I command?"

"Daddy issues," Eve commented as she watched the monitor. "Definite daddy issues."

"That's one cold, fucked-up woman." Feeney shook his head. "A cop briefing other cops on how to kill cops."

"I was starting to worry she wouldn't go for me. I'd have hated to miss that opportunity."

"She plans to eliminate you because you're a threat." Mira had come in to observe, and now looked at Eve. "But only partly. What she said to her father was truth, as she sees it. You're more what he would've wanted in a daughter than she. And that's just as much a motivation to eliminate you."

"We'll worry about her motivations later. I'll need the e-team to handle the glitch she plans. They'll need to think it worked. Peabody, check on Strong. I need to talk to Louise the minute she's clear. I don't want Louise or any of the docs to talk to anyone else, even Strong's mother, the boyfriend. Nobody."

"I'll take care of it."

"What are you doing?" Roarke asked as Eve took out her own 'link.

"Setting up my counter op. I'm texting Jacobson, then I've got to go be seen by her man. We want her plan to move right along."

"You're building a bigger box," Feeney said with some pride.

"Jumbo size. And when we're done, it's still going to be crowded in there. Oh look. I believe I'm getting an anonymous tip from an unregistered 'link. *Check records and reports for Garnet, initialed by Strong, incl all expenses. Proof Garnet & Strong did Keener.*

"Set them up for Keener." Feeney pursed his lips. "Being dead they can't argue about it."

"She'll take a hit on Garnet, but she's got her notes and evals on Strong. It's not bad for seat-of-the-pants," Eve decided. "And it's enough to keep me busy here through end of shift. Can you redirect this hack they're going to pull on my comp?"

"Redirect," Roarke told her, "track to the source and deal with this busywork of records and report searches so the source confirms you took the bait."

"All that?" Eve smiled at him. "Handy. Gives me time to tag Janburry and Delfino, put them on Bix so they can wrap him up. They'll need to time it."

"He won't betray her," Mira put in.

"He won't have to. She'll betray him. They'll get their collar, and Garnet will get more justice than he deserves. I've got to go be visible. I'll keep in contact via 'link. Peabody, give me two minutes, then head to the bullpen. I want you at your desk until end of shift."

"We're moving close to that now."

"Two minutes," Eve repeated, but when she got to the door, Roarke put a hand on her arm. "I've really got to get going on this. Timing's crucial."

"They don't need me here. I'd prefer to be in the garage."

"I need you here because whatever they can do you can do faster." Now she put a hand on his. "I'm going to be covered in the garage. I trust my men, every one of them."

"Yours against hers." Oh yes, he understood his wife, his cop. "Another form of you against her."

"Maybe. It makes a point. It makes the kind of point that will resonate in the department, in the media. That's a matter of politics and morale, and those things matter. But it matters, too, that we show, without a shadow, not only that she gave the orders, but the ones under her had no compunction following them."

"You're very cool for someone who just heard her own death warrant."

"Because my men are better than hers. In every possible way. If you trust me, you trust them."

He touched her cheek. "The drinks are on me, for the house, when this is over and done."

"Free drinks? That guarantees no-fail. I'll keep in touch."

She walked out, picked up her pace. Cop in a hurry, she thought. Records to check. When she stepped into the bullpen, Jacobson hailed her.

"Lieutenant, can I have a minute?"

"Do I look like I've got a minute?" Then she cursed, shrugged. "My office." She strode in, waited for him to follow, then shut the door.

"Okay, I interrupted you. Why am I interrupting you?"

"Long story, full details to follow," Eve told him. "For now . . ." She turned to her computer, called up pictures and data on Marcell, Palmer. "These two men are planning to ambush me in the garage in a couple hours. Their orders are to stun me, toss me in my own vehicle, take me to my crime scene and kill me very dead."

As Jacobson studied the images, his

eyes went hard as stone. "Is that fucking so?"

"It is."

"They're soon going to be having a really bad day."

"Yes, they are. Lieutenant Renee Oberman gave them that order, and has ordered this man—Tulis—to keep an eye on me, and this one, Armand," she added as she brought the next image up, "to hack my comp, to provide their cover re garage security."

He looked at her then. She could still see that stone, but with it a kind of grief. "How many are in it, Dallas?"

"One's too many, and there are a lot more than one. Your focus will be on Palmer and Marcell, and not to alert Tulis. The e-boys will take care of Armand. Others are being or will be dealt with."

"How do you want it done?"

His words to her echoed Marcell's to Renee, she realized. And what a world of difference in meaning.

She told him how she wanted it done.

When he went out, she texted Peabody, updated the e-team. When her 'link signaled, she saw Louise on the readout.

"Is she alive?"

"She is," Louise told her, and those pretty hazel eyes drooped with fatigue. "And her chances of staying that way are good. They're finishing up the ortho work—that was the most extensive damage—then we'll move her to recovery and onto ICU. Her recovery will depend, to a large extent on—well—how strong is Strong. The PT is going to be extensive, long, and painful.

"Now tell me why Peabody's asked nobody tell her family."

"I'll get to that, but I need you to inform someone else, but with a few variations. You kept her alive through this part, Louise. Help me keep her alive through the next."

Over the next hour, Eve learned she didn't much care for running an op via 'link. She preferred looking into the eyes of the men she coordinated, seeing in their faces their determination, their humor, their willingness to put it all on the line.

When the end of shift came and went, she started counting down the clock.

Step One, she thought. Louise.

* * *

Renee, her face covered with weariness and worry, hurried toward the surgical desk. "I'm Lieutenant Oberman," she told the nurse in charge. "I'm here to check on one of my people, Lilah Strong."

"Lieutenant?" Louise, still in her scrubs, stepped over. "I'm Doctor Dimatto, one of the surgical team. Why don't you come with me?"

"Is she out of surgery?"

"Yes." Louise kept walking. "Why don't we go in here and sit down?"

"Oh God. She didn't make it? I was told she was very badly injured, but I'd hoped."

"She came through very well." Louise gestured Renee into a small office, shut the door. "Her age and physical condition were on her side. There's no reason she shouldn't make a full recovery."

"Thank God." Renee closed her eyes, sat. "We've all been so concerned. I'd hoped to get here sooner, but . . . doesn't matter. Can I see her?"

"I'm sorry. She can't have any visitors at this time. Not even family. There's a serious risk of infection, so we've had to quarantine her. In any case, she's in an induced coma. She did suffer very severe trauma, and we want to give her body time to heal. We have her in the East Wing, on the eighth floor. It's quiet and closed off from the rest of the wing. Infection is her enemy at this point."

"I understand. But is someone with her? If she wakes up—"

"We hope to try to bring her out of the coma in about twenty-four hours. Meanwhile an ICU nurse will check her vitals and progress every thirty minutes. Rest, quiet are what she needs most now. She should be able to have visitors by this time tomorrow, or the following morning."

"Her room number? I want to tell her squad mates. And send flowers when she can have them."

"Of course. She's in Eight-C. I'd be happy to contact you when she's cleared for visitors."

"I'd appreciate that very much." Renee rose. "Thank you for all you've done. Believe me, Detective Strong's recovery is of deep concern to me."

"I understand. I'll walk you to the elevator."

Louise walked her out, waited until the elevator door closed, then took out her 'link. "All right," she told Eve, "I've finished my mix of lies and truth to this Lieutenant Oberman. If you're done with me, I'd like to go check on my patient."

"Thanks, Louise." Eve clicked off, updated her team. And thought: Step Two. Renee to Freeman.

With a cat-smile of satisfaction, Renee slid into her car. When she was a block away from the hospital, she engaged her unregistered 'link. "She's in Eight-C, East Wing. Quarantined, checked every thirty by an ICU nurse. Critical condition, induced coma, outlook optimistic."

"Not for long."

"Finish what Bix started, and take her out quick and quiet, Freeman. I want it to look like complications from her injuries."

"I've got something with me. I've already scoped out the locker room. I can get in as a medical, add this juice to her IV. She'll just go under. Like putting a sick dog to sleep."

"Get it done, then get over to Five-O. I want everybody alibied, just in case."

"Just need to set up a distraction so I

can ghost in there. If I can work it fast enough, I could come back, help out with Dallas."

"No, do what I'm telling you to do. Nothing more, nothing less. Marcell and Palmer have Dallas. They should move on her soon. Contact me when it's done. Text only. I don't want to take a 'link call when I'm with my father."

"Whatever you say, Lieutenant."

Whatever you say, Eve thought, following the conversation through her feed. *Add another count of conspiracy to murder on your plate, Renee.*

"You copy that, Dallas?" Feeney asked in her ear.

"Every word. I'm going to shut down here, start the next phase."

"Keep your ass covered, Lieutenant." Roarke's voice sounded in her ear now. "I'm fond of it."

"So am I."

She shut down her comp, rolled her shoulders. Now, she got to play. Step Three, Dallas to garage.

"On the move," she said into her mic.

She walked out of her office, through the bullpen, where Carmichael and two uniforms glanced up.

"Good night, LT."

"Good night, Detective. Officers."

She took the glides, giving Carmichael and the uniforms time to move into position, time for her shadow to report she was on the way.

She switched to an elevator for the ride underground, listened to Feeney.

"They tweaked the other cars, so they'll stop two floors above your level. Anybody planning on coming down to yours will have to wait or take the stairs. We got the source. Roarke's redirecting the glitch. Armand's going to expect to be blind, to hold until Marcell or Palmer gives him the clear. But we'll have you here."

She nodded, and she walked into the garage when the doors opened.

They couldn't move on her until she'd reached her vehicle, uncoded the locks. Then they'd hit her from behind. If she was wrong about any of it, she'd take a hit.

Hell, she'd probably take one anyway.

Her bootsteps echoed as she strode to her car, entered the code.

From behind, she thought again when she heard the faint, faint sound. Window going down, vehicle behind and just to the right.

It happened fast. It happened smooth, and exactly as she'd hoped.

Her men poured out from everywhere, weapons drawn. Now voices as well as bootsteps echoed. She took the hit— probably as much reflex as intent on the shooter's part—and felt the spread of heat, the faint but annoying sting through the protective vest under her jacket.

Her own weapon was out as she pivoted and saw Jacobson stick his right in Marcell's ear.

"Drop the fucking weapon, you fucking motherfucker or I'll fucking scramble your fucking brains. Hands up! Hands where I can fucking see them, you fucking cocksucker. You fucking breathe wrong, you fucking blink wrong, and I will fuck you up."

While Reineke and Peabody dragged Palmer out the other side, Eve stepped back, let Jacobson deal with Marcell.

"That was some very creative and varied use of the word *fuck*, Detective."

"Fucker." Jacobson snarled it as he shoved Marcell to the ground. "On your fucking face, you fucking shit coward. Stream my lieutenant in the fucking back? Fuck you."

There was a distinctive snap followed by a scream.

"I seem to have misjudged my step, Lieutenant, and stepped on one of this motherfucker's fingers. I believe it's broken."

"Could've happened to anyone." She crouched down as Jacobson yanked Marcell's hands behind his back and restrained them. "Your own partner. Detective Jacobson has already eloquently expressed my feelings. I can't think of anything else to say to a cop who would take part in murdering his own partner."

"I want a deal." Sweat poured down Marcell's face as she stripped him of his badge, his com, his 'link—and the disposable.

"I bet you do." *I'll see you in hell first,* Eve thought. "You'll roll on Renee for me, Marcell? Roll like a good dog? Get him out of my sight. Both of them, separate cages, no contact. Read them their rights. Get a medical to treat this asshole's finger." She rose, made herself take a calming breath, then looked at her men, made eye contact with each and every one.

"Thank you. Good work." She leaned back against her car as her men hauled Marcell and Palmer away, and Peabody joined her.

"Are you okay?" Peabody asked her. "I hear a stun stream can hurt through a vest."

"He had it on high. That'll add a punch—through a vest and right into the charges against him. Feeney, get your team to take Armand. We're clear here."

"They're moving in now."

"Copy that. Time for Marcell to give his boss an update."

"We'll do that here," Roarke told her.

"We'll be heading up then. Let's put the rest in play."

Step Four, she thought. Freeman.

In the scrubs and ID he'd lifted from a locker, Freeman slipped up the stairs to the eighth floor. He prided himself on his ability to blend in, considered himself a human chameleon.

He eased the door open, scanned right and left, then slid into the corridor and into the room across it.

Machines beeped and hummed, monitoring whatever poor bastard lay in the bed. Staying out of the range of the camera, he slithered against the wall until he could aim the jammer he carried.

Even as the alarm sounded he was out and into the next room before the ICU team came running. He repeated the process, grinning as the medicals ran by. He hit a third for good measure, then made the dash to 8-C.

By the time they determined it was an electronic glitch, rebooted, did whatever they did for the poor bastards in beds, he'd have done what he'd come to do and be gone.

He moved into 8-C. They kept the lights dim, he noted. Rest and quiet was the order of the day. Well, she'd get plenty of both where he was sending her. He moved to the bed, pulled out the vial in his pocket.

"Should've kept your nose out of our business, stupid bitch."

Baxter stepped out of the shadows, put his weapon to Freeman's head.

"Who's the bitch now?" Baxter said as Trueheart stepped between Freeman and Strong. "Who's the bitch now?"

Freeman's secured," Eve reported.

"They've got Runch," Peabody told her. "And the accountant, Tulis, Addams. They're rounding up her people like ducks in a pond."

"With Janburry and Delfino spending some quality time with Bix, I'd say it's time for the finale."

Renee sat in her father's study, loving him with every inhale. Hating him with every exhale.

"You don't know what it's like working Illegals today," she insisted, but kept her tone, her face respectful. "I can't afford to throw a man to the rats because of a slip. And at first, that's what I thought was happening with Bill Garnet."

"Renee, when one of your men uses the very thing you're fighting against, you have to take action. You're responsible for the code of your squad."

Go ahead, she thought, *give me the lecture on Marcus Oberman's standards. I've heard it all before.*

"I know that perfectly well. Loyalty is vital, you know that, too. I spoke with Garnet, kept it out of his file, but I ordered him to get into a program. It wasn't until a few days ago that I began to suspect him and one of my other detectives . . . Dad, I have reason to believe two of my people were using my CI to obtain product—for use and profit. I have reason to believe they killed my CI before he could contact me."

"Bix."

"No, not Bix. Garnet was using Bix for cover. I think he might have tried to set Bix up for the fall. Lilah Strong." She rose to pace. "She must have realized I was getting close. It must be why she tried to run today. Two of my people, Dad, betraying their squad, the department, me. Their badges."

She willed tears to sparkle in her eyes. "It's my fault."

"Fault and responsibility aren't always the same. Renee, if you believed this, if you had any evidence, why didn't you so inform Lieutenant Dallas?"

"I did." She spun around. "Just today. She brushed me off, just brushed me off. She's so focused on Bix—and me. She's so damn self-righteous."

"She's a good cop, Renee."

She's a dead cop now, Renee thought. "Better than me, I suppose."

"That's not what I said, or meant. You need to take this information to your commander. You should already have done so. You need to contact him and request a meeting, with Dallas included, and give them everything you know, everything you have on this."

"I wanted to be sure before I . . . I've been working it on my own. My responsibility," she reminded him, since it was one of his favorite words.

"Dad, I think they got in deeper than Keener. He was just a weasel. I think they moved up, and it got Garnet killed. I have a line on that. I wanted to follow it through. I know it's Dallas's case, but for God's sake, Dad—Garnet, Strong, even Keener, they're mine, and I wanted to handle it."

"I understand that. Command can be lonely, Renee, and it can be hard. But you're part of a whole, part of a system.

You can't step outside that whole, that system, for your own needs. You owe it to your men to show them true leadership. Two of your people went bad. Now show the rest there's no tolerance, no half measures."

"You're right. Of course, you're right. I'll contact the commander, request the meeting."

"Do you want me to be there?"

She shook her head. "I need to do this on my own. I shouldn't have brought you into it. I need to go, need to put my thoughts together. Thank you for hearing me out. I'll make this right."

"I trust you will."

"I trust you will," she muttered as she slammed her car door. It was just like him to lecture and pontificate, to give her that disapproving look because she hadn't followed straight down the Saint Oberman path.

He'd never know just how far she'd strayed, or how wide she'd beaten her own path. But now he was, again, a useful tool.

When they found Dallas's body, when Strong expired from her injuries, and she told Whitney what she wanted him to believe, dear Dad would confirm she'd told him all of it. That she had pointed Dallas toward Strong and been rebuffed.

It was all falling neatly into place.

She took out her 'link, pleased to see a trans from Freeman. Within seconds, though, she'd jerked her vehicle to the side of the road to read the text again.

Can't get to her. Can't get near her. Surrounded by medicals. Bringing her out of coma tonight. Orders?

"Goddamn incompetence. Do I have to do everything myself?" She beat her fists on the wheel until she could think.

Abort, she ordered.

Didn't matter if Strong lived, she told herself. She would be discredited. Who'd believe a third-grade detective—and with evidence and doubt planted—against her lieutenant? Against Saint Oberman's daughter?

No one.

They'd have to look at the safe, of course, when the traitorous bitch told them about it. Renee pulled back onto the road. They'd have to verify what the nosy bitch told them. So she'd clear out the safe, put in copies of the reports she'd put together with her suspicions and evidence linking Garnet, Strong, and Keener.

She'd just tidy up the rest of this mess herself, and then, she thought, in a couple of weeks she'd be taking a well-deserved vacation.

23

Renee walked through central to take care of business. She wanted a long, hot bath—with the oils she'd bought on her last trip to Italy. And one of her bottles of wine from the vineyard she'd invested in.

She could soak while she toasted Strong's disgrace and probable imprisonment—and most important, most gratifyingly, the demise of Lieutenant Eve Dallas.

Sentimental bitch wore a wedding ring, she recalled. Interesting piece, unique design. That would be a perfect item to pass to the scapegoat she had in mind—a particularly violent chemi-head who would pawn it at the first opportunity.

It would be easy to pin Dallas's murder on him, and Garnet's.

Loose ends snipped, she thought as she got off the elevator on her floor. Better, she'd find a way to be the arrow that pointed the investigators to the goat. That would erase any lingering tinge from the Garnet/Strong problem, and very likely give her a little boost toward those captain bars.

Really, things were working out even better than she planned.

She breezed through the night-security glow of the squad room, unlocked her office. She called for lights and went straight to the portrait.

"Screw you and everything you stand for."

She lifted the frame, then spun around at the sound behind her.

Eve swiveled the chair around, smiled. "That's not a nice way to talk to your father, Renee. Gosh, you look like you've seen a ghost."

"What are you doing in my office? My locked office? You have no right—"

"You're fast on your feet. I'll give you that. Faster than the dogs you sicced on me."

"I don't know what you're talking about."

"Please, Renee, they rolled all over you. Marcell was crying for a deal before we had the cuffs on him, and Palmer wasn't far behind. And even without that?" Eve reached out, tapped her recorder.

Renee's voice filled the room, arranging for Eve's death, for Lilah's.

"Detective Strong's fine, by the way. Freeman? Not really. He's pondering his options from a cage right now, like the pitiful pair you ordered to kill me. So're Armand, Bix, Manford, and at last count five more of your motley crew. You are so completely fucked."

"You're bluffing, or you wouldn't be here alone. So I believe I'll just contact—"

Eve drew her weapon, aimed it at the middle button of Renee's power suit jacket. "You're going to want to pull that piece out very slowly, then set it on the desk and step away. I know you've never terminated anyone. Never so much as fired that weapon in your bag or any other—at least not on record. I have, and trust me when I say I wouldn't hesitate to put you on the ground."

Renee threw the purse on the desk. "You think you've won this? You think I can't fix this?"

"That's right. I think I've won this. I think you can't fix this."

"You haven't; and I will. It's your head that'll roll."

Not panicked, Eve noted. Pissed. Hoping to give the temper another boost, Eve put a laugh on her face.

"Really? You tried for Strong twice, once with Bix, then with Freeman. Didn't do so well, did you? Now you think you can take me?"

"She got lucky with Bix. He never misses."

"He killed Keener—but Keener was a weak junkie. And Garnet. But Garnet was his partner and trusted him. I'd say that makes Bix lucky. They all trusted you, didn't they, Renee? As far as any of their type can trust. Are you so sure Bix will do what you tell him when he's looking at life in a concrete cage?"

"He'll do exactly what I tell him, and say

exactly what I tell him. That's how you command men."

"Yeah, it takes a lot of balls to tell a man like Bix to slit his own partner's throat, to stick poison in a junkie's arm."

"It takes foresight, vision, brains to develop someone like Bix so he'll do just that on command. None of your people would do for you what Bix has done, and will do, for me."

"You're right about that."

"That makes you weak. Holding that weapon on me, that makes you weak, too."

"Does it?"

"Have *you* got the balls, Dallas?" Renee slipped out of her heels. "Let's really see who's in charge here."

"Are you serious?" Of all the responses, this was the last Eve expected. A shiny bubble of sheer joy rose up in her. "You want to dance with me?"

"Weak. And a coward."

"Ow, insults. Sting. What the hell. I really want this, too." Eve set her weapon down, shrugged off her jacket.

As she circled the desk, Renee lowered into a fighting stance.

"Hey." Eve cocked her head, pointed. "Did you take lessons?"

"Since I was five. You're going to bleed."

"Wouldn't be the first time."

She took her stance, and they circled each other. She let Renee come at her, blocked the kick, the follow-up, the backhand.

There was power there, she judged, and style, and skill. Renee wouldn't go down easy; she wouldn't go down quickly.

So much the better.

She kicked Renee's fist aside, came in with a hard jab, had it repelled. And took a mid-body blow that burned her belly. The next kick caught her shoulder, zipped pain down her arm. She went with it, used the momentum in her spin, slammed her boot into Renee's chest with a force that knocked her opponent back into a chair and down.

Fists ready, Eve leaped forward, but Renee jumped up, slammed a kick into Eve's knee that shot her feet out from under her. She tasted blood now, told herself it woke her up, and when Renee poised to stomp her injured knee, Eve swept out her leg.

This time when her opponent fell there

was a satisfying crunch as the table under her collapsed.

They both sprang to their feet, and at each other.

Now it was something like jubilation that shot up Eve's arm as her fist rammed Renee's face, and her blood drummed to the cry of pain and rage. She took a blow to her own face, one that had stars exploding in front of her eyes. Flying on them, she twisted, came in low to ram her elbow into Renee's belly, jerked up her forearm to plant a backfist on Renee's chin.

"You're bleeding, bitch," Eve told her, and caught Renee's foot on the kick, shoved back.

Renee dropped, rolled, scissored her legs up, beat a double kick to Eve's hip before gaining her feet.

Bloodlust. Eve felt it pulsing and pumping through her, all primal fury that was somehow a kind of twisted pleasure. Circling, spinning, a blow landed, another taken. Sweat stung her eyes, dripped down her back—and she saw it mixing with the blood smeared on Renee's face.

Eve knew they were in the same place now, a place where winning was all and the taste of blood lay sweet on the tongue. A place, she knew, where that taste stirred a craving for more.

She told herself to end it, to step back over the line.

"You're done," she said. "This is done."

"I say when it's done!" Renee launched at her; Eve pivoted to meet the attack. They hit the door like a cannonball and spilled into the squad room in an intimate tangle of violence. They rolled, jabbing fists, hit the side of a desk with a crack like thunder.

Eve stopped the thumb aiming for her eye by gripping Renee's wrist, twisting it. On a cry of pain, Renee grabbed Eve's hair, nails gouging scalp, and yanked viciously.

More stars exploded in a field red as blood.

"Fuck me! Hair pulling? That's *it*!" She wrenched Renee's wrist back, reveled in the screech—and with her scalp screaming flipped Renee onto her back. "Pussy." She balled her fist, drove it once, twice into Renee's face, reared back for a third, but pulled up short when the grip on her hair dissolved, when the eyes staring into hers went glassy.

"*I* say when it's done." Eve swiped blood from her mouth. "And it's done. Jesus Christ, it's done." She rolled off, sat on the floor, tried to slow the air wheezing into her burning lungs. "Peabody!"

"Sir!" Peabody stepped forward from the crowd of cops—and a particular civilian—who'd already moved into the squad room.

This time Eve swiped under her nose, then pressed it gingerly. Not broken, she determined, just bloody. "She's yours."

"Huh?"

"I'm the one whose ears are ringing, for God's sake. I said she's yours. Your collar. Take her."

"But, Dallas, you—"

Though it hurt pretty much everywhere, she discovered, Eve pushed to her feet. She wondered if her injured knee had puffed to the size of a basketball, or just felt that way.

"Detective, I just gave you a directive. I expect you to follow it without any backtalk and arrest this individual who is a disgrace to her badge, her lineage, and her goddamn gender. Hair-puller," Eve said in disgust, and nursed a hand over her tender scalp.

"Yes, sir."

"One minute." Eve crouched down, painfully, bent close to Renee's face, and spoke for only the two of them. "You see that cop, Renee? The one who's about to take you? She's the reason. She's the reason you're down and you're out. She's more of a cop, more of a woman, more of a human being than you ever were. And she's my partner."

Eve straightened, with effort and with considerable discomfort. "Get her gone," she told Peabody.

"With pleasure, Lieutenant. Renee Oberman," she began as she bent to cuff the prisoner, "you're under arrest."

Peabody listed the charges as she dragged Renee to her feet. At Eve's head jerk, McNab moved in, took Renee's other arm. Peabody recited the Revised Miranda as they perp-walked her out.

"Lieutenant."

Eve struggled not to wince as she came to attention. "Yes, sir, Commander."

"It was unnecessary to engage in physical contact with the suspect, to break procedure and set aside your weapon, and do so when you clearly had the suspect under control."

"Yes, sir."

"Unnecessary," he repeated, "but just. And I believe it was as satisfying to experience as it was to observe. I suggest you visit the infirmary and get cleaned up and treated. It will be my unfortunate duty to inform Commander Oberman of his daughter's arrest."

"Sir, as head of the investigative team, and partner to the arresting officer, I feel that should be my duty."

"You know command better than that, Dallas. It's mine to lift. You did well." He turned, scanned the cops in the room. "You all did well."

And shouldering his command, he walked out.

Roarke walked over, handed her her weapon and a towel. She didn't know where the hell he'd come up with the towel, but it looked clean. She wiped some of the blood off her face.

"I'd kick your ass for putting your weapon down," he murmured, "except as I said before, I'm fond of it. And because at the core, I agree with Whitney. Besides"—he took the towel, dabbed at her face himself—"I took fifty off the new guy."

"What? Santiago?"

"I wagered him you'd bait her into a fight so you could pummel her a bit. He was the only taker." He leaned down, softly, softly kissed her swollen mouth. "But he doesn't know you as well as the rest. Yet."

She might've smiled, but knew it would hurt. "Well, he's the new guy. I've got to . . ." She trailed off, noting the room was still full of cops. Thinking of the kiss she would've scowled, but that would hurt, too.

"What're you all still doing here? Don't you have homes? Dismissed."

To her utter shock Baxter shifted to attention, snapped a salute, held it. "Lieutenant," he said, and every cop in the room followed suit.

She forgot every ache, every pain, every bruise and cut. There wasn't room with the pride.

"Good work. All of you. Good work." She returned the salute. "Dismissed."

As they filed out, Feeney walked to her. He laid a hand on her shoulder, and he nodded. "Not bad," he said. "Not bad at all."

When he walked off, it was with a strut in his step.

Eve let out a breath. "I have to sit down a minute." She did, then lowered her head into her hands. "God. Oh, God."

Hearing the tears in her voice, Roarke knelt. "You're in pain. Baby, let me get you to the hospital."

"It's not that. Or yeah, it's a little that. But it's mostly . . ." She dropped her head on his shoulder, smearing blood on his beautifully cut jacket. "What they did. All of them. How they stood up. All of them. Knowing what I have in them. I can't . . . I don't know how to say it."

"You don't have to. I think I know."

"They're everything she's not. Everything she abused, raped, killed, exploited. They're the reason I . . . not the reason I do it, but the reason I can." She lifted her head, swiped at tears and blood. "You'll buy that drink for the house?"

"I will, yes. Darling Eve." He laid his lips on her cheek. "My cop."

"Roarke." Tears pressed and burned again. She let some go, just let them fall. She could let them fall with him. She gripped his lapel, transferred more blood as she looked in his eyes.

"I want to go home, okay? I just need to go home now. You can fix me up there. It's not so bad. You can take me home and fix me up. Because at the end of the day you're what does. You're what fixes me up."

"Eve." He pressed his lips to her brow, held there a moment. Just held. "All right then. I'll take you home, and I'll fix you up."

"Thanks." When he helped her to her feet, she leaned against him. "You're the reason, too. Why I can do it."

"Then I'll fix you up so you can do it another day."

As they started out of the room, she hissed. "Shit! It is pretty bad. Still go-home-and-fix-me-up territory, but, Jesus, she could fight. At least until the hair-pulling incident."

"You were holding back a little."

She frowned. "Who says?"

"Who knows you?"

So she sighed, leaned on him again. "Maybe I held back a little, until—"

"The hair-pulling incident."

"It was insulting, and really demeaned the moment."

He laughed, and he took her weight. She hobbled to the elevator so he could take her home, fix her up. So she could do it all another day.